The
Angel of Wessex

The
Angel of Wessex

MICHAEL J. H. TAYLOR

Best wishes
Michael Taylor
2011

F4M
FICTION

Published in 2003 by F4M
P O Box 72, Langport, TA10 9XJ

Copyright © Michael J H Taylor, 2003

Michael J H Taylor asserts his moral rights to be identified as
the author of this work

reprinted in 2005, 2008

A CIP catalogue record for this book
is available from the British Library

ISBN 1 874337 08 X

Main cover photograph: copyright
The Francis Frith Collection, SP35QP
Portrait of Michael Taylor by
Elaine Boles Photography Ltd, 2003

Copy editor G Jill Todd Cert Ed, DipPRE
Cover design Annabel Trodd
Pages designed by M Rules, London, England
Printed by BOOKMARQUE, Croydon, Surrey, England

F4M is the fiction imprint division of The Fun4Men Company
Limited

DEDICATED TO

The life and memory of my father and writing mentor,
my wonderful mother,
my long-suffering and lovely wife,
my darling and delightful daughters,
and my many friends who encouraged me to continue
through years of research, writing and redrafts.

CHAPTER I

The year 1877

The untamed expanses of Dartmoor, gripped in an icy haze of snow and chilling winds until their very bleakness merged trees into the surrounding hills, and streams lay as frozen paths, was a place of salvation for Jacob Stone. For forty years he had seen the moor through its many moods from the garden of his tiny cottage in Hoxbury Wold, but, although he had lived through as many winters without straying from the district, it was today as if he was seeing it for the first time.

Feeling beads of ice on his flowing red whiskers, he threw a scarf once more around his pockmarked neck, but otherwise remained completely still. His mind was captivated by the scene to a point of hypnosis, his brain feasting for more than his eyes could provide. He craved every detail. All that he was ever to remember of the moors had to be stored this day.

"Come in, Father!"

He acknowledged the caller with a wave, but stopped after a pace and turned back. Putting a shawl about her shoulders she joined him, slipping her arm around his waist.

"It's no good fretting. What's done is done."

He sighed with the depth of a sob.

"Tell me again, daughter, what it said."

"Oh, Father, I've read it to you three times already."

"Please?"

After a moment's hesitation she reached into his pocket for the envelope.

"I know what you want to hear, so I'll miss the first bit."

She unfolded the paper:

And so, friend — you see I still call you this — if you will not finally renounce your ridiculous notion to there being demon Wish Hounds hunting across the moors, then you leave me no choice but to have you sent away. Goodness, Jacob, I have given you opportunity enough to satisfy your accusers. Even now it is not too late. Do it man! Say you don't believe in these dreadful things from hell, even if quietly in your heart you hold other private opinions, and I will see to it that you keep your job and home. I beg you to show sense.

"Shall I read on?"

"No, child. That's quite enough."

"Oh, Father. Why are you being so stubborn? The master wishes you well, you can read that much into his letter, but you must see that he can't have his bailiff going around talking of demons over the moors. He brought you here as a young man to break village superstition, to put an end to unnatural folklore that tied these poor uneducated folk to the past, and drag them into the nineteenth century. You showed them what modern farming meant, and you did so well. Old conjuror Badcombe didn't stay long when you proved that it wasn't his onions that kept foot-and-mouth from the shire's cowsheds, and that tansy flowers couldn't cure infertility. It took a long time, but you finally won them around. Now, I ask you, what are they to think? Was it all for nothing, your efforts and their anxiety at leaving the past behind them? Can you expect their respect any longer?"

"You don't understand either, do you?"

"I have tried. God knows I have tried. No, father, I don't understand this, or why you would throw your life away? The village needs you here; we want you here. *I* want you here."

"Then you really mean to stay?"

"Yes, but with a heavy heart if you go. I love Charles and I intend to marry him. You know he'll be offered your job if you go, don't you? You taught him the trade well. I can't stand in his way or would I. With a home for us, we'll be married in the year."

His stare hardened. She squeezed his arm gently.

"I love you too, you know that, but you're making yourself go. I don't want your house. Charles will find a place for us sometime, but I'll not see a stranger move in. Father, my future lies here. I love the moors, the ruggedness and danger. It's in my blood. You taught me that. When I'm out there I'm in a different world; silent, possessing, romantic."

"Aye, daughter, the moors are that, but then a storm comes, dark on a moonless night, when the wind no longer whistles through the trees, but breathes low through the scrub and sends a chill piercing to the marrow. You look up for light and reassurance, but there is none. A noise breaks and you turn, hoping to see nothing but emptiness behind. Then a crack from the front and a rustle to the side and you feel watched."

Father and daughter held silent, but she detected the slightest tremble of his hands.

"What is it?"

"*Quiet* . . . Listen, Mary!"

They stood motionless, staring into the fading light. His hands began to shake violently.

"Oh, God, here it comes again. Get in Mary, get in!"

"There's nothing out there! Stop pushing me and listen, Father. I'm not afraid because there's nothing to be scared of."

"For mercy sake hurry and don't look back."

"Do it, Father. *Do it*! Break now that which haunts you. Face it and see the chill wind for what it is. I'll stand with you. God will protect us if there's a need. Trust him. You of all people must do that!"

"I can't. *I can't.* I'm scared. It comes. I have seen it, and the once more will kill me."

Taking his trembling shoulders, she turned him into the wind with a strength that was unnatural for her stature. The cold was intense. His red hair and scarf streamed back and her shawl flew away.

"Let it go, Father. Stand firm with me."

"There!" He pointed into the distance. "There. See it?"

"See what? There's nothing."

His heart began to beat irregularly and his face turned a misty blue.

"Listen, it's the Hounds baying at the hooves of the horse. I beg you, let us turn away before it's too late."

"*No!* Face your fear. A few more seconds and you will know the truth. Stand firm I say."

CHAPTER II

Consequences

A low mist and light drizzle silhouetted the cortège that carried a simple box up the narrow path to the tiny churchyard. None of the bearers needed to slow the pace as the incline steepened, although the ground had become saturated and sticky. Behind, the young and the old walked with their heads bowed, the rain piteously removing tears of real grief. The uppermost point was reached and the coffin disappeared into the depths of the earth.

A wave of faces turned to stare at Jacob Stone, who stood apart at the foot of the hole. He withered, but made no sound. He was mute, not through choice or permanently, but nonetheless mute since a few days before. Only a shepherd approached him, standing by his side until he felt that his silent presence had caused him maximum discomfort. The man bided the moment by stroking a shaggy black and white dog that had sheepishly walked around the back of his master to settle at heel.

"See what your meddling with old ways has done!" said the interloper, at last breaking the silence.

Stone looked up at the shepherd he had once called a friend, but could only produce a throaty sound in reply. Yet, whatever words failed to pass from his lips, he felt desperate and abandoned. The dog alone looked up with open expression, begging to be caressed. Stone lowered a hand.

"Don't you indulge my beast!"

The shepherd's fist lashed out at the dog's nose, causing a whimper that ended abruptly after a kick from the master's boot. Not wanting to be struck again, the faithful dog stretched out its paws and lay on the ground.

Sorrowfully, Stone returned to his cottage, which was no longer a home. He packed Mary's clothes for the orphanage and gathered his own few possessions.

On his last evening in the village the wind again rattled the loose-fitting shutters and sent a howling through the chimney. The pitch heightened and the door began to strain under immense pressure. Stone stopped eating and looked towards the window. The dark outside was total. His flesh began to creep.

"So you return," he screamed, throwing the plate down and grabbing a weapon. He released the catch and the door flew open, leaves and debris whirling inside. "Come on, you devils. This time I'll face you." He pushed his way out, glaring ferociously into the wilderness. The wind suddenly dropped, laughing low as it swept away across the moors.

"Come back, damn you!"

Dawn broke and he awoke on the cottage floor, his hand bloodied from the knotted stick he still grasped tightly. He felt a lump on his head. Stumbling to the pump, he let the cold water flow over his face.

"So, this is how it ends."

Although his voice had returned, there was nobody to hear. Not a single villager cared. After tugging at the bindings holding two small bags to the saddle of his horse of purest white, he trotted away from Hoxbury Wold for the last time, leaving no friends after forty years.

As he passed the last cottage he turned for one final look. A few ragged curtains twitched. The shepherd's dog that had run ahead of its master as they returned from the fields leapt innocently around Stone, tail wagging and barking furiously. Stone dismounted and caressed its jaw.

"Thank you, boy. There are things about our world that mere mortals can't understand, science and reasoning cannot explain, but perhaps you know something of them." His eyes glistened and a single tear rolled over his ruddy cheek. "I have a friend after all. You'll never forget my darling daughter, will you, boy. My wonderful, brave girl. How I miss her. She made me look at the Hounds that night when I was so very scared. I saw them far off, malevolent balls of ashy smoke with legs pacing inches above the ground. They came closer, as if drawn by my stare. I shut my eyes and said *The Lord's Prayer* out loud. The wind raged around my ears, harder and harder until I could hardly stand. Mary steadied me and offered courage when I had none. Then, when I thought we would be knocked to the ground, it ended. The wind dropped and my muffler fell long over my coat. I waited some moments before looking, but when I did, Mary was dead at my feet, her unseeing eyes wide with terror. I now know the meek really are blessed with the greatest conviction. My faith has returned, but at a cost too great to bear."

By now the shepherd had closed the gate and swaggered into the lane. He stopped abruptly on seeing Stone and shouted angrily for the dog to come to heel.

Stone gave it one last pat.

"God bless thee this day and for always, boy. Now, run along before you catch it from your master."

Taking up the slack, Stone flicked the reins and rode away.

CHAPTER III

Out of the Past

$\mathcal{J}$acob Stone was a broken man. He no longer wanted life. He had lost everything, including unknowingly his fear of the Hounds, for a man who has no fear of death can fear nothing less. He was also elderly, and in a few years he died, alone. But, while a man can walk the earth without care and uncared for, a soul freed becomes unburdened, and with his final breath Stone had vowed penance for his mistakes of the past.

It is impossible to explain matters outside the natural laws, and perhaps the feeling people get on occasions that someone is watching over them is merely a subconscious wish in anxious times. Nonetheless, a century later a journalist enjoying a few days vacation began thumbing through a book he had received by mail from a friend.

The accompanying note read:

7 May 2003

Dear Pete

Found this at a car boot sale last Saturday. Couldn't put it down. Cried all night. Thought you might make something of it. Strange, but pleasant looking old guy I got it off, with masses of hair and the longest sideburns. Looked a bit like good

old Georgie Best in the sixties, except much, much older with
carrot-coloured whiskers and his neck covered in the most
dreadful scars that he tried to hide with a long scarf. Wouldn't
take a penny piece for it, but was insistent that I took it, so I did
to get away from him. He was so grateful he blessed me this
day and for always. Imagine my embarrassment. Anyhow,
really pleased I did. See what you think.

Regards Jay

P.S. Don't forget who gave it to you if it turns to gold with your
creative genius.

The journal, as it turned out to be, was immense and being hand-written and old was at times difficult to decipher. However, page flowed into page, full of the words of a young man in love, the writer's feelings so deeply expressed that every feature of the woman he described became known to the reader. Over the coming days the journal became a constant companion, an obsession that hardly abated with his wife's return from an overseas assignment. She asked him about the lady described.

"Christabel, you mean? That was her name," he told her, folding the book shut. "I can't. I'm not sure that another woman would perceive her fragility as I do, but I know I can't let it end here." He looked up at her puzzled face. "Helen, darling, I know you've only just got back, and I feel really bad about asking, but would you mind if I say I have to find out more about her, and urgently? It would mean a couple of weeks away."

Her expression showed disappointment. She coyly reached for her travel bag and unzipped the top.

"See what I bought in Paris." She removed a small parcel. "I bought these for you to wear tonight, just for me."

He laid his hand gently on hers to prevent her removing the contents. She looked up and, after a few seconds silence, let the parcel slip back into the bag.

"Why the rush, for God's sake?"

"I don't know," he whispered coyly. "It's just a gut feeling.

Something's wrong, if that makes any sense at all." He kissed her forehead before taking her bags upstairs.

The moment his steps were heard on the landing, she grabbed the journal to read the first pages. Suddenly she felt strangely threatened and banged it shut. After a moment's thought she followed him upstairs, finding him on their bed, his head resting on his hands and her bags unopened at the foot. He had not pulled the curtains that morning and the room was subdued in a soft grey hue. He didn't notice as she unzipped her skirt, and looked across only as her weight disturbed the mattress. He smiled as she ran her slender fingers through his hair and down his face, where her thumbs teased the corners of his mouth. He sensed her warm breath and alluring perfume. She rubbed her foot on his leg, but he resisted as she tried to slip on top. She smiled wickedly as she fell back.

"Okay, you win. I've known you long enough to understand your funny little ways. Nothing I can say will stop you, so you'd better get on with it and get her out of your system so that we can have a sex life. Only, I can't see what you hope to gain!"

The funny thing was that he couldn't either. There was no obvious scoop in it, no story to sell to the highest bidder. He merely had a tingle in his spine when he thought of her. He just needed to know more about her than what happened after the writer first met her in 1881, when she was seventeen.

Helen kissed his cheek and arose, feeling the floor for her skirt.

"Pete, should I feel jealous of a woman who would now be knocking on 130 years old?"

His short laugh was almost inaudible.

"Come back to bed."

Again her skirt fell to the floor and she remounted, pulling gently at his trouser belt.

"Well, you sod, answer me. Should I?"

In truth he should have said, 'Yes'.

So it was that the next day he began his research, which one autumn afternoon finally led him to the village of Christabel's childhood.

It was so unfair. The bodies in the churchyard were being disinterred for removal, disturbed from their resting places and broken. That somewhere among the twisted and fleshless bones could be the remains of the lady he longed for was too much to bear. He tried to look away, but morbid curiosity wouldn't let him, although he feared above all else that he could lose his feelings for her among the horror of thin limbs, eyeless sockets and yawning jaws that fell limply from split and rotted boxes.

All at once songbirds scattered as enormously powerful bulldozers turned off the lane, intent on filling the empty graves and flattening the church to remove all marks of its existence from the landscape. Unaware of its imminent fate under Home Office approval, Pete had driven half the length of the country to be here, to feel the atmosphere of a village that belonged to another century.

The proud walls began to collapse and the spell of the past was broken. It was the true end to the story in the journal, the close that only he could now inscribe into the written account of that earlier time. He opened the journal at the final entry to read some profound words, their Victorian formality hiding none of their beauty:

> *That one person can ever be so brilliant a light upon a dismal earth that their very existence illuminates and entirely fulfils the lives of many is a belief I now hold dear. It is true that I was once of the opinion that the rules and standards by which we try to live serve to guard the good against evil, the just against injustice. My own life has been unremitting to this end, and I suppose for most people it is so. But, that a succession of circumstances can make this otherwise I have come to know, and here I lay a ghost that has tormented me ever since Christabel entered my life.*
>
> *How I have loved you Christabel.*
> *John*

From his signed name an ink line scratched down the rest of the page and fell off the edge, smudged in places by tear stains.

From John's Victorian words Pete too had fallen in love with Christabel; an irrational passion for a once living person that troubled him. No, more than that, she enveloped his every waking thought. Irresistibly driven, he had searched for, and discovered, the truth about her early years that harmonised well with that he had read. But wait . . . Two bodies had become entangled and stubbornly refused to part as workmen tried to separate them into new boxes for their final journey to an urban incinerator. Oh, God, he just knew it. He had to do something before they were torn apart.

"Leave them alone," he shouted. "Can't you understand?"

At last he knew he looked at her and was not afraid. Restrained from getting any closer, he watched as the bodies were now gently separated. Under Pete's watchful eyes, new boxes were loaded side by side into an awaiting vehicle. By fate he had done his part. He had been given the chance to help her even now, and he felt humbled.

"Take care, my love. Take care. I'll use all my skills to start a media campaign to have this land reconsecrated, however long it takes, and things will be as they were. In the meantime, I'll stop anything else happening while I buy a new plot for your reburial. Trust me. I'll not fail you."

"I know you won't," whispered an old man looking down from a nearby hill, his flowing red whiskers only partly covering dreadful scars, his long scarf blowing in the wind.

Although no noise reached Pete's ears, he instinctively turned to see the shadowy figure silhouetted against the light mist that hung low over the incline. Pete stared for several seconds before slowly lifting his hand in a slight wave.

"God bless thee this day and for always," came a soft voice that swirled in the breeze.

CHAPTER IV

Christabel's Story

It began with regret — The year 1864

It was March, and in the hamlet of Westkings little broke through the carpet of snow that now covered the rolling countryside. Only a week before, a calm in the winter weather had brought about a miraculous sweet air of spring, pretty wild flowers bursting into early colour along the myriad of hedgerows that criss-crossed fields. Even the harsh blackthorn rendered clusters of white petals to entice the first migrant chiff-chaffs, although this prickly shrub had its more earthy uses to field hands, who gathered its stems for hay rakes.

Now strong south-westerlies once again took hold of the hills and vales, the snow blowing almost horizontally into the faces of any travellers caught walking the winding lanes. Horizons were lost to a pallid sky that formed a dome over the earth, casting the illusion of there being no world outside the few discernible acres. Perhaps there was a beauty of sorts in the sterile whiteness, an almost incandescent quality, but it was lost among those who needed to work the soil for a livelihood. With only the lines of tall hedgerow to depict the boundary between firm path and field, few ventured out while the storm raged, better huddled by their fires during this dormant part of the agricultural year.

* * *

On the highest point overlooking the farm cottages and civic buildings that composed Westkings stood 'Samain', a manor house with high, bold chimneys now partially hidden behind a parapet of later addition. It was an embodiment of rural aristocracy, a magnificent display of opulence and family dignity with architectural straight lines, embellished terraces and manicured gardens radiating the self-confidence of the Victorian age.

'Samain' was home to James Elvington. He was a fine man to all appearances, not tall, but strong in limb and with raven hair that bestowed a striking aspect. Fripperies to embellish his pleasing features were never used, his clothes suiting a man skilled at running an estate by example and not ascendancy. He enjoyed the manor's substantial income with characteristic prudence; a generous income won by his ancestors from the Abbot of Darly at the time of the dissolution of the monasteries at King Henry's hand. In all Wessex no gentleman was so completely and deliberately detached from the vagaries of society.

The merest glance at James showed a generosity of spirit, a man not normally given to raising his voice beyond command or rebuke, although, like many men of great passions and responsibilities, he possessed a see-saw temperament that on few occasions rocked from thoughtfulness to sudden temper. Most who met James quickly understood and admired him, but this night a woodcutter trudging his way home laden with damp firewood was stopped in his tracks by shouting, for the chill outside in the wilderness was nothing compared to the bitterness within the manor's walls.

"I'll hear no more, and I say so at the top of my voice. I repeat. As soon as the bastard child is born, it goes out!"

Terror struck deep into Charlotte, a sweet and beautiful woman of twenty, and nineteen years James' junior, fresh in face and entirely loving in spirit, but now reduced to kneeling voluntarily at her accuser's feet in an almost reverential position. To her shame she was about to bear a child that was not his, as only just discovered by him.

The first outburst sent her cowering. She braced herself for more.

"Damn and blind you, madam. You have disgraced me and this good house. I shall not be laughed at."

Poor suffering James hurt, but chose to mask his grief behind the very dignity he so often ridiculed. Reality was different, for while bricks and mortar can endure any number of tragedies, and family reputations that are lost in a community can just as speedily be regained, human tragedy lasts a lifetime. There was no question that this man's heart was broken. His marriage, his happiness, his very world lay on a knife edge.

His stare fixed on her, his jaw clenched. With firmness he wrenched her head back to make her look up into his unyielding eyes.

"You faithless slut! Think you're too special for one man, is that it? Perhaps the greatest stranger to your bed has been me!"

"God willing, I can explain," she croaked.

"Don't you dare bring the Almighty to your defence," he screamed. "I care nothing for your opinions or excuses. We all face temptation at some time or another, and the rest of us resist it, but, oh no, not you. You couldn't be like the rest of us, fools as we are. Remembering that you have a husband was altogether too much to expect. So what do you do the first time I leave you alone? Well?" His grip tightened between shaking hands. "Nothing to say now, ah? Then I'll remind you. Sin . . . Sin against the laws of the church, sin against your vows to me and sin against the virtues of womanhood. Whatever you say, whatever you do, nothing can ever be the same again. Hear me, see my face and know that I mean it."

He fought to remain strong, half believing that if he hurt her sufficiently for the punishment to match the crime, then the crime itself would somehow become less real. Her scared face made no gesture of rebuff. He tossed her away with a jerk. She fell silently to the floor.

"As God is my witness, you have made me say things that should never pass between a man and his wife, and yet I boil with anger to say more." He willed himself to push her still further into the mire, to gauge the depth of her remorse by the strength of abuse she would take.

She picked herself up, and with eyes wide she nodded acceptance.

"To act like a beast in the fields, taking pleasure where it can be found, debases you lower than a grubbing snort pig, for that animal knows no better. Oh, you may look gracious in your curls and jewels, but they decorate a common strumpet!"

Spitting the last words, he lunged at her throat. She gave a loud scream. With a single tug, he snapped her jewelled necklace and threw it across the room. Only slowly did Charlotte recover from what she thought was to be a murderous attack. Panting, she rubbed the back of her neck.

"I ask you, what have I got for a wife? What have I done to deserve you? Am I really that awful to live with?"

He meant to go on, but he discerned the slightest movement of Charlotte's bowed head, so incongruous with its finely arranged hair, that gave away the secret of her confined weeping. He watched as she gently looked at her figuretips, making no fuss when seeing them blooded. He lurched forward automatically with concern, but stopped himself before she noticed. He turned away, but then, as quickly, looked back as his impulse snapped, for he loved this woman to distraction who was now the magnet to the iron of his wrath. In nature's bizarre contrivances, it was this very passion that made his grief and temper worse.

He felt like striking her where she knelt, not to injure, but to stir a backlash against which he could vent more fury, for this one-way traffic of abuse was giving him no satisfaction at all. But, he could no more hit than forgive her. In any case she would have taken any blow, however forceful, as deserved at the hands of a man she had vowed to honour only a year and a half before.

Without reaction beyond sobbing, he condemned the ploy as useless and lowered himself trance-like onto the grand seat, staring with steadfast gaze at the flames in the hearth that danced in torment on his pinched features. In these empty moments she dared to look up slightly at him through a mist of tears. His face bore the reflections of orange and red, but she noticed more his eyes, which glistened. In compassion for his manhood, she turned back to the floor.

Minutes hung silently except for the crackling of burning wood, until through the heavy atmosphere came an unnatural monotone that was alien to her.

"Char, what *have* you done? I believed you good and chastened. It seems that we have lost everything."

In this repression, where the devil himself would have found no sport, such utterances were worse than his temper, for she knew that these words were considered and not merely the outpourings of rage.

The situation unresolved, the wound open and festering, she fumbled silently for an excuse, but she had none beyond the meagre facts of the case. In her head she contrived a hundred ways to avoid a reply, although none seemed sincere. Yet in this turnabout situation she had misread the signs, for her husband no longer wanted excuses. He already knew the facts, as wilfully told to him only minutes before by a thin-lipped old gossip who swept the floors of his sawmill. Charlotte didn't know how much better advised she would have been to remain silent.

Her heart at last opened up with the freedom of the condemned.

"James, as I'm lost to you, I've nothing to lose by offering my account of the circumstances that have brought me to this pitiful state. You can think no less of me. All that spiteful woman's words are true in essence, although knowing her evil tongue I expect she did me no favours in the telling. Pray listen now with a little compassion.

As you will remember, last summer was hot and long and, although quite newly wed, you went away on business to Glastonbury for much of the season. The distance between us was small, but for the little I saw of you it might as well have been London."

She gathered her thoughts and continued, sometimes looking at him and then away in shame.

"As the days grew into weeks I began to long for company, the servants being too cast with obedience to offer friendship in my solitude. Still I remained alone as a dutiful wife should, taking pleasure in walking the grounds. It was while strolling through Kingsden Wood one day that I saw a number of labourers and maids setting up a high pole on a tumulus. Wondering what they were doing, I rested there and bit by bit they built a great pyre around it, laughing and jollying as they worked. They had such fun. I could only watch. Presently, with their work completed, I foolishly approached the woodcutter, Jack Mere, and asked the meaning of their efforts. He explained that the morrow was Midsummer's Day and that every eve they lit up and celebrated through the night, sometimes carrying burning reed-sheaves around the hamlet and placing burnt sods from the fire in the cowsheds for good luck. This I had never seen before, being new to the district.

That evening I returned to the festivities. I stood by Jack Mere and gradually my joining them seemed to make no difference to the enjoyment of the occasion. No disrespect was meant, and before the others left for their beds I asked Mere to escort me to the manor. I don't think he wanted to and his young lady was none too pleased, yet he did it with perfect propriety, but, to my own weakness, as I approached the cold starkness of the portico after the warmth of the fun I felt my youth tug for young company. By idle contrivances I stopped Mere from returning. At first I think he wanted to go, but I was persuasive that he should not. It grew cold where we sat outside on the wall, for I couldn't ask him to enter the house. We shared his jacket and talked into the early morning. By and by our laughing brought a bond of genuine friendship that transcended our social differences. Once my long hair blew across his face. He swept it away and with a feather-like touch brushed it behind my ears as I held the jacket tightly around us both. I could feel the warmth of his fingers against my cold neck. It was extraordinary. Not sensual, but sensuous. He too felt the moment, for he laid his other hand on mine. None of it was real, nor that which followed in reckless passion. It was a tingling second as false as the ritual on the hill.

Of course, I now see it was all too real, not at all a stolen moment as brief as the twinkling of a star, that I confess, but not once from that day to this have I so strayed from the good morals I truly believe in. That I swear solemnly. For the new life growing in me I can't, in truth, feel disinterest. It is a child of innocence to my wrongdoing whose life now seems certain to begin in tragedy. For what I've done I have no right to beg forgiveness. I cannot hope for your love and protection any longer. That is plain from my actions and your words, but I would die if you took another woman in my place."

There. Charlotte's tone throughout the ordeal had remained calm, his mood unchanged. James' concentration had been unwavering, but now big fingers beat a thoughtful rhythm on oak.

"My dearest husband," she added as if a codicil to the earlier, "I'll not question your will. If you don't love me any longer it would be far better not to pretend that you do."

Her honesty had effect. He threw back his head and stared at the ceiling.

"Am I to believe that you still see any kind of satisfactory future for us?"

Humbled, she leaned forward and rested her dainty head on his lap, clinging tightly around his legs.

"I've been praying that I might be punished for my sin before you found out. It hurts me to see the pain I've caused you. I'm no child, yet I haven't the courage to leave this house of my own accord, even though I expect I shall be made to go."

"Stop saying such things, damn you! Perhaps you should have married a younger man, someone to give you the fun you so obviously seek."

"No, James. Our marriage has been good, very good, up to now at least."

James was tired from thought. Whatever the outrage, it remained true that she could have a hundred suitors and yet she only wanted him. He had wanted only her. Whatever conclusion was reached, he realised in these moments of reflection that he had to decide which was the greater ill, to see her leave and eventually take up with somebody else, or grab whatever happiness could be salvaged while burdened forever with an uneasy mind?

He crossed to the window from where he could see the familiar landscape covered by the purest white. What, he thought in numbness, had materially changed since yesterday when he had believed the child was his? The fields and lanes were unmoved by the new circumstances. The great house remained solid on its foundations. Was he to let his sense of outrage outweigh any future happiness that might still be possible if he allowed time to heal the wounds? Charlotte's single moment of ecstasy with another man was now only a memory to her and the same flesh would never touch again. He had the power to ensure that, even if her will was weak. What was more, she seemed to understand her crime and regret it fervently. It was undeniable that he had left her alone far too long, not least as many impromptu social engagements with acquaintances in Glastonbury had added several days to his trip. He, too, had enjoyed other company. Perhaps he should have thought more about his young wife then, but, still, a man had a right to expect chastity whatever the provocation. The alternative was to make her a captive within the estate and burn with jealousy if she even talked to another man. This would not be living.

Charlotte remained where she had released him moments before and when he returned she took hold again. James was almost relieved at the change these last seconds had brought over him, the wide view outside somehow dissipating the greatness of his troubles. Whatever grief he felt, he knew deep down that he could not completely despise the person he had reduced to a timid and wilting thing. He took her shoulders firmly, but kindly, in his hands and lifted her from the floor.

"Why didn't you tell me all this before? Hearing it through gossip only made it worse."

The question hardly begged an answer. How many women would have been forthright while there was even the merest chance of secrecy? Charlotte said nothing for a few moments, but what came out presently was as ill-considered as entirely honest.

"James," she began in a tone much closer to her normal. "I've been fooling myself that I could deceive you into thinking that the child was yours." A pause to moisten her lips and wait for a reaction. There was none, so she dared to continue. "Having committed the greater sin, I could see no reason not to commit the lesser. I knew I had to stay quiet about it and I was sure the workers would. Silence was all that stood between my salvation and damnation at your hands. I took salvation."

Charlotte's last words, although from the heart, tipped the fine balance between great love and agonising torment that had been struck which, had it been nurtured, might have brought about some measure of understanding. Widening the hurt to include others was too much.

"What he doesn't know won't hurt him, you mean? Good God, does *everyone* on the estate know? Is this farce representative of what our marriage has meant to you? Let the bloody workers titter behind my back, but leave me in darkness as to why I'm their fool! What did you do, hand them a few shillings for their co-operation and silence?"

"I thought it best."

"What! You really did that?" He let out a great cry.

Why, oh why, had she not denied the old woman's accusations in the first instance, Charlotte thought to herself as she looked at James with new horror. He would have believed her. What sense of morality had compelled this honesty? She clung tighter to his legs, seeking comfort from the very instrument of her torture, her eyes firmly shut.

"Have mercy, Sir. Your sorrow kills me as surely as any knife to my body. Do with me as you wish, but do it quickly!"

The die was cast.

"Then you are out of control of your senses. Get away from me, woman!" He prised her loose. "Your actions express love, your words piety, yet your belly conceals a bastard child. I see you, I feel your tears on my leg and I even regret hurting you, but you are not fit to remain by my side and I do not want you there."

She pleaded forgiveness.

"I know how much worse it is that my mistake was with a common fieldworker but —"

He leapt in new anger, his face needing no fire to show red.

"Pox to your opinions! Your sin is one of unfaithfulness and that alone. I don't care whether it was with a labourer or the Prince of Wales. It's not the lowly issue of the child that is the problem, but that it's not *mine!*"

Desperation tore through her.

"Is there anything I can say that you won't jump on? Can't you see that I only meant to appease? A woman is won by reason, not shouting."

"By reason? Don't you mean sex? Don't all women flaunt their bodies and in this vanity expose as much flesh to others as society reasonably allows, then to wonder at the reactions of unwelcomed men? It's all a game to women, but I can assure you not such a game to their husbands or boyfriends who are expected to remain placid. Do you really think any man believes that his woman dresses for him? It's an unspoken truth that women flaunt to attract attention, any attention, even if they intend to remain faithful. I tell you in all honesty, there are times when men hate the women they love, if that makes any sense to you. If only women understood that some husbands seek company outside marriage not because their wives are too gentle or boring or ordinary, but because they are seen as decorated egotists that displease them and have to be tolerated, not liked. Perhaps it's high time men turned the tables and did the same, that's for sure. See how women would like that. After all, many men are the better look-ing halves of their partnerships, and the male torso in good shape is the most wonderful thing in nature. What's more, men control the greatest incomes to buy the apparel, and our ancestors certainly knew how to show off the male form, even if it is presently a forgotten art."

"Please, James, I didn't —"

"No more!" he bawled. "I need to be free of you and by God I will be."

The door slammed, leaving Charlotte wide-eyed and alone. Soon he was out and making footprints in the snow, but he had not reached the two crowned pillars that marked the end of the drive when Charlotte's face appeared at the window.

His long strides soon took him beyond the boundary of the formal lawns and along the lane by the fields, on one side ploughed and the other forested with a timber mill in a clearing, all under the rich layer of snow. Within a quarter of a mile he had reached the schoolhouse where occasionally Charlotte taught. Set high on a bank, the school's tall clock tower and nine pillared arches gave it a grandeur that was out of place in a hamlet. Close by was a quadrangle of almshouses — modest dwellings in contrast. James pressed on.

Half a mile later he stopped, looking left at the church from a low boundary wall. James entered the churchyard, picking his way up the path that was now invisible, but well known to him. The tower with its battlements loomed high. He diverted right and came to the centuries-old railings that marked out a select area of the churchyard kept solely for Elvingtons. He turned the heavy key, having first cleared an arc of snow with his boot. The gate groaned as he pulled it open. Here the graves were marked by magnificent stonework, but he noticed the elaborate arches, piers and mouldings only in passing. At the farthest corner, partially hidden and disgraced by its plainness, was a perpendicular niche cheaply carved into poor stone. After taking several deep breaths to calm his beating heart, he brushed it down and read the words as he had a thousand times before when troubled, drawing inspiration from its uninspiring epitaph:

HERE LYETH THE BODYES OF OLIVER ELVINGTON OF
WESTKYNGS AND STALBRIDG ESQVIER WHO DECEASED
THE FIRST OF FEBRUARY 1638 AND ANN HIS WIFE,
DAUGHTER TO WILLIAM LORD HUBERT VINCENT
WHO DECEASED TENTH OF NOVEMBER 1638.
REMEMBER ALL WHOM SEE THY STONE,
THE BODYES NO MATTER WHEN
THE SOULS HATH FLOWN.

Back at the manor Charlotte was uncertain of what to do. With each chime of the clock she became more restless until she could stand the suspense no longer. Grabbing a shawl, she took off after him. Though suffering the cold, she followed his footprints, half running and half walking, but never daring to call out. Anyway, she knew where he had gone.

His recognition of her as she crunched her way through the soft snow was so indifferent that he was again looking at the epitaph when she arrived at his side. She waited a few moments before saying:

"I too am moved in spirit by Oliver and Ann. Hers must have been a rare love, as she could live only a short time after he died . . . I know you think little of me now, but I too am Ann."

With these words parted from her shivering blue lips, she visibly shuddered and collapsed in a faint. He had no idea that she was so cold; he hadn't looked at her long enough to see that she wasn't wearing a thick cloak. As if the ancient Elvingtons were drawing their newest convert to their bosom, Charlotte laid full square across the grave of Robert Elvington, the youngest of the family entombed. Above her head he could read:

NINE MONTHS WROUGHT ME IN YE WOMBE
EIGHTEEN MORE BROUGHT ME TO THIS TOMBE
SINCE THIS TYME ON EARTH IS BUT A SPAN
VSE IT SO THAT THOV MAIFT BE
HAPPY IN YE NEXT WITH ME. 1604

There he stood, shaking. Was it accident or omen? They had been married only eighteen months; she had borne her child for nearly nine. He quickly placed his jacket around her, then, lifting her with the delicacy afforded a broken flower, he carried her back to the manor and their bedroom.

Despite the events that had led to this tragic scene, he stayed by her side, teasing her hair from its gathered formal style to lie spread over the pillow, until interrupted by the housemaid who carried a warming pan into the dim room. He dismissed himself and, armed with a bottle and glass, once more slumped into his seat in the drawing room.

CHAPTER V

A woman's guile

*T*he night was a cruel intrusion. As Charlotte slept, James sat below with his thoughts and the bottle. He had thrown the last two logs onto the fire soon after midnight, and as the cold gradually enveloped the room so his perceptions grew darker. By cockcrow the final flickers of compassion had flown away.

Alone, James felt the equilibrium of his life twisting out of shape. Charlotte had brought a rare sparkle to the place, and even in the present grey sombre of the drawing room her 'touches' somehow pervaded the atmosphere of gloom. He closed his mind to them, turning to bury his head in the winged arm of the chair. As the candle wick flickered its last in a pool of liquid wax, his eyelids closed and he finally fell asleep.

Daybreak grew strength from a willing sun whose beams were sufficient to erode the evidence of secretive night animals that had scurried across the white, crusty snow. Row by row, pane by coloured pane, the huge drawing room window brightened from blackness to white, green, purple and red, shedding a languid glow to the interior.

James stirred to the light of a new day that could only be an improvement over the previous, aware of cramped muscles and a noise in his ears like the grinding of wheels and hissing of great power. No new snow had fallen overnight and the old was now melting fast. Rubbing his eyes, he walked blankly to the window. A gossamer mist hung suspended above the tall hedgerow some distance down the lane. Slowly, the mist crept around the bend.

Moving in the direction of the forty-acre field was a great convoy, led by a single man carrying a red flag. Some thirty yards to his rear trundled the origin of most of the noise, a ten-horse-power steam traction engine with smoke pouring from its tall stack. Ahead of the boiler sat the driver grasping a huge wheel, tasked with steering the tons of metal and steam as it navigated the country roads. The huge flywheel to one side of the engine remained completely still while all motive power went to the rear treaded wheels, which crushed everything in their path. In charge of the machine was an older man standing on a plate at the back, with a face and clothes as black and greasy as can be imagined. In tow was a threshing machine, followed by a straw elevator. Next came a horse with its head bowed, pulling a low-loading two-wheeled cart with only the driver standing behind a hurdle, followed by a two-horse wagon on which were seated chattering women on their way to feed the winter quartered dairy cows before release into the fresh spring pastures. In marked contrast, the remainder of the ensemble walked drudgingly behind, anticipating a day of sweat on the last remaining corn ricks or piling timber cut in the mill.

An elderly hedger wearing a sack for a smock and thick heavy mittens stopped work as the procession passed by the manor, waving his curved cutting knife to acknowledge the engine driver's throw-off remark that he probably didn't hear:

"'Tis burning just sixteen pounds-o-coal a mile, 'tis *Hero* this day, Henry."

Only as the wagon cleared did James notice two stragglers, laughing and fooling about as they walked uncaringly up the centre of the lane. The man's arm was around the shoulders of the woman who, attired in an ankle-length, coarse dress, white working apron and flapping bonnet, might well have been more suited to better weather had it not been for the meek provision of a shawl, and rags that bound her legs. Still, she seemed warmed by her companion's company.

James couldn't help staring at the woman's peasant beauty, made none the less favourable by an unfashionable ruddy complexion. The man's face was hidden until he passed the manor gates, where he turned and pointed jokingly. It was Jack Mere.

Weary and cold from the uncomfortable night, James had not gathered his thoughts since waking, but upon recognising Mere, the earlier trouble paraded itself once again. He stared at them until they turned the corner and disappeared fully from view.

In a flash, the bright new day became perverse. Difficulty seemed the only certainty. Still transfixed on the now vacant scene outside, James sensed a presence. He turned. Just inside the door stood Charlotte, white faced and drawn, but expelling an aura of cultured feminism that could not be matched in these parts.

Charlotte had decided to wear a sombre dress that might reflect piety to her husband, although the roughest rags would have looked well on her. Since the coming of the train to outlying districts, Glastonbury, Winchester and even London had become accessible to the wives of the ruling class, some might say at the expense of the traditional values of housekeeping. Charlotte, although young, did not favour country women bolting to London for the season. She would say such women were, "hens leaving the coop" or speak of them as, "the wives of wealthy merchants living in the country only for effect".

How she so often judged them correctly yet, while loving the countryside for its own sake, she spared no effort in dressing well and thereby exuded an elegance the 'bolters' could not better. Her beautiful, straight hair was once again plaited, falling gently on one shoulder. In essence she had managed to execute exactly what she had intended – grace and piety that concealed all yet revealed most of what she wanted seen.

There are moments when such exacting displays of female science can build confidence, when admiration can raise hope, but this was not such a time. Her appearance belied her true resolution. She felt no security, but merely awaited her fate. She knew her very happiness lay in the events of the next few minutes, whichever way the balance tilted, and knowing this could do no more than she had managed with mirror and comb. Whatever else, she felt a strange air of calm that was new since her husband had discovered her secret, a feeling of finality becoming someone whose fate was no longer theirs to determine.

Charlotte was ready to be commanded in fullness, to be a servant to his wishes. If he wanted her stripped of position, cast out into the wilderness, tormented and scorned, she was ready. The only thing she couldn't stand was indifference. Reality was the child that grew inside her. The old woman's words had placed an executioner's sword above her head.

James looked hard at her and then turned away. He felt unusually awkward. It was his habit to plant a kiss whenever they met, when she would call him 'darling' and he would counter with 'sweetheart'. Now it seemed inappropriate, and yet not to do so was almost petty, but he could not and she was too nervous to proffer a cheek. Whatever became of her, Charlotte had not lost sight of the unquestionable truth that James was also a loser, perhaps the greater, for he had done nothing.

"Am I still not the woman I was in your eyes?" she said presently, to break the silence.

James looked up in amazement.

"You are the same person as yesterday."

"Then I take it I'm finished as your wife?"

He writhed under the gentle inquisition.

"I don't know yet," he murmured in pitiless reality.

"Only, I thought you no longer find me respectable."

"Respect for you and *your respectability* are two different matters, Charlotte."

She allowed her glance to drop, wondering how that could be. Wasn't one the same as the other? What did he mean? Did he still respect her slightly, but think her unrespectable as a woman, or had she retained some measure of outward womanly respectability, but that he no longer held any regard for her as a wife? She had lost something, but if it was his respect for her as a wife the situation was beyond repair and hopeless.

"Then since I'm fallen I can have no opinion opposed to yours. I took the precaution of packing some clothes first thing. I'll make arrangements to return to Portchester."

With this said she gathered her train and graciously turned for the door. James could see his happiness slipping away.

"Hold, Charlotte. We mustn't act in haste. Once you leave I feel we'll never see each other again."

"You want to?" she asked with the same gentleness.

"In truth, I don't know. It's all too much to deal with quickly. What's happened is beyond my forgiveness. On the other hand . . ."

"Yes?"

He withdrew defensively, surprised at his own words.

"It changes nothing, but with shame I admit that this has happened to our family before." He closed the window, drowning the last sounds of the steam convoy. "It was to unhappy Oliver Elvington that Ann confessed to being pregnant when they married. She had been wronged by a drunkard just weeks before their wedding. Yet, despite the bodily afflictions she suffered in her struggles to keep herself undefiled, she knew proud Oliver would no longer consider her pure and virtuous. So, secretly, she left for her sister's house and sent word to Oliver that she had decided to stay with dear friends that she would miss seeing after moving from her native district. The weeks of absence healed her wounds, but confirmed a worse fear. As fate had it the child was premature and came too early in their marriage for any doubt as to its lack of kinship."

Charlotte was moved by the sincerity of his telling.

"Oliver tried to put a brave face on it, always calling the child 'son', but slowly his great piquancy for life ebbed and he died young from an illness he didn't fight. Ann followed him to the grave soon after, although no physician could find anything wrong. The child was reared by his grandparents as an Elvington, but they never forgave Oliver and Ann for their duplicity and were denied burial in the family plot. Only a rude stone marks their existence as Elvingtons, erected by Ann's son after his grandfather's death." His face flushed. "See, Charlotte, how truly you spoke in your ignorance yesterday when you said that you too were Ann!"

She turned to him with a mellow look. How sad, how beautiful was the story and how gently it was told. James' heart had not turned to rock after all.

He continued:

"Plainly speaking, at present I can't look on you as a wife, but we may be companions if you agree. You must understand that I will not want to come to your bed and you must deny any other. To fail in this is to fail in everything. Can you make such an undertaking with sincerity as God is your witness?"

She turned and nodded.

"Good. I doubt that I'm any stronger than Oliver of that previous age, but I trust I'm no weaker." His glancing attentions to her were now replaced by a full glare of authority. "Yes, my mind is made up. I now realise that my decision of yesterday must remain if we are to escape Oliver and Anns' fate. The child must go as soon as it's born!"

Charlotte shrank visibly, but could not withstand the reasoning. She almost feared her acquiescence as inevitable.

"To think that I have been the cause of so much sadness."

"To think," replied James, his thoughts racing elsewhere. "Ah, and one more thing while we are about it. The child shall be given a plain name to fit its circumstances for later life. I will have nothing fancy. I see Tom fitting for a boy and Polly for a girl. What say you?"

"I say no, Sir. Thomas is a fine, strong name for a boy. A girl will be Christabel, a child born to the faith under the sound of the church."

"So be it. I have no further opinion."

Charlotte stood her ground, watching James busy himself until he realised and looked up.

"You have something to add?" he asked in an abrupt voice while sifting through papers in his bureau.

"Yes, and it's important."

He laid the papers flat and closed the lid.

"With one breath you hint that someday you might again find it in your heart to love me and in the next you make me feel abandoned. I can wait if there is hope, but you make me choose between my happiness and the happiness of my child. God help me, but if I must choose I'll put myself first and suffer for that choice the rest of my life. I beg you, must my unborn child of innocence suffer too? Can't you find courage from Oliver Elvington?"

His fixed expression was answer enough. Charlotte could hardly believe his determination to see her offspring gone, and in that moment they finally parted in all but presence.

"Very well, but let it be your doing, not mine!"

No sooner had Charlotte finished speaking than the clouds separated and James was suddenly bathed in rays of coloured light that poured from the heralded window to surround him in an unnatural brilliance. She was shocked by the occurrence, but he knew nothing of it.

"I think it best until the child is born that we remain under the same roof, but much apart. This room, if you agree, will be mine. I will only be your provider until then. After the birth, I shall review what must be done."

"You will keep me," she reflected in a soft tone.

"Just so."

"You play hard, Sir."

"I haven't the will to be philanthropic."

"And I can't take your persecuted looks."

"Then go, Madam, as I have asked!"

They lived through the next helpless days under a common roof, but far apart in spirit. James knew he could end the strange separation at a stroke – in a single word – but his resolution remained strong. An unusual air took hold of the house, husband and wife going about their business in a restrained way that no longer filled the rooms with intimacies and made the presence of the housemaid, two other indoor servants and the cook almost overwhelming.

"You noticed how pale Madam looks nowadays?" said one maid to another. "Hope she's not sickening, what with the baby due and everything."

"Haven't seen her smile in days."

"That's right. Usually she laughs at anything, just like her grin was attached to her heart."

"Well, it's ruled by her head now!"

Charlotte, who like most women of similar social standing had taken no great interest in the detailed running of the household beyond a daily interview with the cook, now found active participation a way of overcoming the emptiness of her existence. She knew little beyond the cursory duties of housekeeping and so it was with some irritation that the day-to-day routines had to be explained by servants whose own schedules left little time for such matters.

"Fine young ladies should not concern themselves with below stairs keeping," was typical of the sentiments expressed by the servants as they met for snacks and meals, but Charlotte was determined to resist the snubbing that she felt, but never heard.

One day in particular was a trial, and on his return from the sawmill James found Charlotte sobbing in the hallway. Asking the reason for such melancholy, she explained how the first six days of their strange relationship had passed well enough, given the unusual circumstances, but the seventh had brought her around to when the monthly allowance was paid to the cook for food and other kitchen consumables. For the first time she questioned how cook would spend the £30, given that there were only six in the house and that she and the master were not fancy eaters. Not satisfied with the reply, she had instructed cook to write down in full the food allowances given to each of the staff and make an inventory of what appeared on the kitchen shelves and in the larder and scullery.

The inventory was a revelation. The cook allowed each of the servants a weekly quota of two pounds of cheese and sugar, together with half that quantity of tea and fruit preserves, a dozen-and-a-half eggs, two four-pound loaves, and one shilling and four pence beer money. On top of this, she ordered fresh meat and fish for her own table, with little regard to the amount of food remaining after the preparation of the master's meals.

"What happened next?" asked James.

"I had words with her," Charlotte muttered through her tears. "I told her she was to give each of the staff only one-and-a-half pounds of meat a week and that no new orders should be placed with the butchers until I had seen what remained from the previous day. I suggested that more pies should be baked using leftovers. Then I instructed that only three-quarters of a pound of cheese, a dozen eggs and a quarter of tea was to be given to each servant, and that rich cake and preserves were for Sundays only. I said that I had no objection to the quantity of potatoes eaten and that the amount of bread could be increased as it was taken both at breakfast and supper, and likewise milk was not rationed as it comes from our own dairy, but that one quart of beer a day was more than sufficient for each maid."

"And?" enquired James, expecting more.

"That's it!"

"Come on, Char. That's not enough to upset you so much."

"Well, there was something else. Cook flew at me and made me look a fool in front of the other servants. She said . . ."

"Go on."

Charlotte knotted and twisted her fingers.

"She said, I suppose I want them to go back to having flour, butter and water for breakfast, and that anyway it wasn't six to feed, but seven when including Jack Mere's bastard!"

Charlotte broke down. James was red with fury.

"Where's that damn woman? I'll wring her bloody neck. Call her now while I'm boiling. I'll deal with the matter myself. If she leaves here without being struck she can consider herself very lucky."

Charlotte grabbed his hand as he took hold of the bell rope.

"There's no need. She's gone."

"Gone?"

"Yes. I bumped into her carrying her bags out. She said she wouldn't work for a loose woman."

James flung his fist at the wall.

"Blight the woman. I'll not give her a reference."

"I gave her one!"

"You did what? What in heaven's name possessed you to do that?"

"She seemed to have the better of me. I shook as she stood firm. She was so moody I probably would have done anything she asked just to get rid of her."

"Then why, dear Char, do you still feel upset?"

It was hard to explain and she unknowingly tightened her grip on his hand as she spoke. It was a moment of unconscious tenderness and neither pulled away.

"Because I have failed you for the second time. It's my duty to oversee the running of the household and I've been lax in that too."

James begged her to enter the drawing room and they sat together. The aloofness had gone and Charlotte was at once transfigured from the diffident young wife to the complex woman of his desires. He drew her head to his chest. She acquiesced immediately, the throbbing of her young heart drowning the wind that whistled past the window. Warmth radiated from the fire and played on the couple.

The evening drew in and presently candles were lit. Both felt the extra light was an intrusion, but it turned the windows into sheets of blackness through which nothing more could be seen of the outside. Their island was secured. With the remains of their supper left for the morning, James and Charlotte slowly climbed the stairs to the bedchamber.

CHAPTER VI

The end of the beginning

The almost religious silence of many winter dawns seemed this day to have ended. Work folk were already walking the now clear lanes with purpose, although patches of cloud and mist gave the early morning a coldness that would only slowly clear to vent full glory to the fluttering of butterflies and other insects emerging from their retreats. The 'tsee tsee' of blue tits combined in song with thrushes and other birds, while toads made for breeding grounds along familiar routes.

The first daisies had popped their heads, and more wild primroses and violets appeared along the hedgerows, offering heady perfumes to attract bees. Osiers of green and purple were budding along the watery edges of fields, soon to be cut back to promote clumps of new growth for harvesting during the summer, when they would be boiled or stripped of their bark for basketry. Cattle had been turned out to pasture, joining the spring-footed lambs on the rich grasses.

Charlotte awoke to the chattering chorus, but found James gone. It was likely to be the final day of threshing and he couldn't stay away. Still, given the depth of their troubles and the warmth of their reunion, he might have overslept this once, she thought.

She no longer minded the loneliness of mornings, believing that they had begun a course of reconciliation. No, it was more than that. She felt considerable triumph, not that she deceived herself into thinking that her difficulties were over, but she believed that she had used her talents well. She felt changed, finished with the last vestiges of girlish servitude. A bubble of anticipation tickled her spine as she dressed, making breakfast a chore she would happily forego.

Pulling on buttoned, kid walking boots, she set out for Potti Bottom where the threshing was underway. The air outside was crisp and carried the distant peal of church bells. Her pace was steady and joyful, but once off the lane and through the gates her long skirt became a handicap as she picked her way cautiously towards the ricks.

The scene ahead was both repressive and exhilarating, as ordinary in the lives of the labourers as new to Charlotte. From a distance nothing could be heard above the 'chut-chut' of the great steam engine, the large flywheel turning so rapidly that its iron cross spokes had become invisible to the eye. From it passed a circumambient belt that traversed the thirty feet to a small wheel on one side of the red thresher, which in turn caused other wheels and belts to revolve and the machine to pulsate in rhythm.

On top of a huge corn rick, built after the previous year's harvest from hundreds of dried stooks, worked eight men and women. Each carried a hand fork and was either topping off the remaining section of the thatched roof or formed a link in the human chain to pass sheaves to the women on the thresher who spread the load and pushed it into a guzzling hole in the top of the machine. Great care was taken not to put their gloved hands into the jaws of the whirling cylinder that beat the corn from the straw. Winnowing and dressing saw the removal of chaff and any weed seed, leaving the corn and straw to spew separately from the rear.

While two men moved full sacks of corn to a horse cart, another raked the falling straw from the thresher and deposited it onto the steam elevator, where it was carried up to the slowly growing straw rick, forming on a platform suspended over staddle stones that prevented the rats and mice that infested the corn rick from re-entering. Only the black and greasy mechanic shovelling coal into the traction engine's furnace sweated more than the labourers.

Charlotte continued across the muddy ridges, unable to discern individual voices from the general mêlée until she came quite close. It was then that she noticed James for the first time, sitting astride his horse and pointing his riding crop in the direction of the falling straw.

"This is no good at all. Look how much grain is still in with the straw. Good heavens, you're wasting half my crop."

The elderly gaffer wearing home-made knee pads as protection against the hardness of the ladder rungs, looked on with a puzzled expression.

"'Tis all very queer, Sir. I've been working this here thresher for years, but I'll be hanged if I can make the blessed drum work right today."

James ordered the engine stopped and the long umbilical belt to the thresher gradually slowed to a standstill. The day had hardly started and yet already the workforce looked done for. Those on the top of the corn rick flopped in a huddle and began chattering, while the straw rick was still low enough for both men to jump clear with ease. It was a different story for the three on the thresher. For some moments they clung to the machine to regain their equilibrium now the pulsating had stopped. Bottles came out and a light air descended over the lack of proceedings. Comments were shouted across the field to the sawmill, where men had no time to rest from feeding the steam-driven cutter.

"Beg your pardon, Sir," said one of the women stepping from the thresher as she wiped chaff from her neck. "Do you think that's Madam coming?"

James hurried across to where Charlotte had stopped, her boot having sunk past the ankle and stuck solid. She was already quite red from her exertions to get free and willingly took her husband's shoulder while he pulled the boot clear. She laughed as James grovelled in the mud, and beamed with joy as he arose with dirt on his face.

"Charlotte, you goose, you should know better than to come here in your condition. You're quite exhausted. If you intend staying you must sit over there and recover."

James led Charlotte to a spot at the rear of the engine where a young lad piled three corn sacks as a makeshift seat. It was away from the plume of smoke that flowed from the engine's tall stack and under an alder tree heavy with hanging catkins.

"Just look at the fuss they make over her, Flo," said one woman to her neighbour, as she sat below the straw rick and pulled on a bottle of ale. "I reckon life's so unfair to the likes of us. I know the scriptures say there's righteousness in being poor, but I can't see it."

"That's blasphemy."

"What if it is? Looking at the mistress I truly think I would risk damnation in the next world for the chance to give my children a full belly in this." She paused as she watched Charlotte take a pure lace handkerchief from her purse. "Earn a bit, spend it all and still our families go short. What will she be eating when me and mine sit down to thin soup and bread? It takes all of us to keep them rich."

Flo, who shared in poverty, was more irritated at seeing her own husband fuss around Charlotte, although his reasons were purely selfish and he thanked her for a sixpence.

"Why are we like we are? I don't know. It seems that even our menfolk can't recognise *her* as part of our trouble. We've been picked for the muck and her for the silk and no mistaking." She shook her head in resignation. "It will never change. You've only got to look over there to know the rightness of my words."

They both stared across the field in the direction of a heap of rotted timber and rusted metal that had been dumped long ago and now formed part of the hedgerow.

"'Twas my grandfather and his friends who did that, oh, must be thirty years past by now. That pile of mechanical bones is all that remains of the first threshing machine brought to these parts, and many say it was a wondrous eater. My grandfather, used to the hand flail, believed it would put an end to much of the winter work and was afraid for his job. One night he and some others smashed the monster to bits and much pleased they were with their efforts. I think the same happened all over the countryside." Her expression changed. "But no good did it do them. Master's father went off to buy another and laid off helpers until it arrived. It was then that my grandmother joined the struggle, making quite a name for herself. She carried on stirring things up and was packed off to Newgate prison for six months. She said the filth there was terrible, with nothing to do but sit on the floor watching other womens' kids running about uncontrollably. She was never the same after that. You know, looking here, now, it's hard to picture a time when muscle and mobs terrified ordinary folk, when neighbour set on friend if they worked the thresher for the reward of a few pennies. God knows there must have been frustration among the men who held firm against it, but had to go back begging weeks later."

"Empty bellies and the pleading faces of hungry children force folk to do things they don't want to. We would do the same, Flo, heed my words, although God prevent ever the need. But they were right, weren't they. The machines did take much of the work away. You can't stop so-called progress, even when ordinary folk get hurt."

"And what about gleanings? I remember as a girl standing with my mother at the edge of the fields after the harvest had been gathered, waiting for the bell to ring. It was a grand free-for-all collecting up the leftover corn. For sixpence or a favour the miller would put the gleanings in his grinder for us. My father often joked that my little brother looked a lot like the miller. I don't reckon my mother had to buy flour all winter long to feed us. Of course the mechanical reaper ended that too, leaving so little corn behind that it wasn't worth the effort of bagging. I sometimes wonder whether any of us will be needed by the time baby Arthur grows up."

"My old man says only a war will get the land back on its feet as it was in old times, but I don't know. Seems to me only the landowners would benefit. My Tom would as like get himself volunteered while drunk and have his legs shot off. Mind you, girl, he's so useless in bed I doubt that I would notice the difference."

"Still, if *she* stays where she is long enough she'll get a shock when the rats come running out of the rick. I wager she'll not stay to collect the penny a tail. I wonder what the bitch is thinking. She can't have worries like us."

James returned to adjust the thresher, leaving Charlotte to wander along a narrow path to the sawmill. Steam pressure for the engine was kept high. The mechanic and his driver appeared separated from the other labourers by more than distance. They seemed to belong to another age, shovelling coal into the furnace in strong aesthetic contrast to the farm folk in their traditional rags and carrying simple tools.

The noise and dust of the mill were too much, and soon Charlotte returned to the ricks. With nothing much happening, she began to take in the wider views, the now clear day and the low roll of the fields making it possible to see over long distances. Only a short walk ahead was Muncome Hill, the nearest rise in Cople Wood, where the dense canopy of trees gave irregularity to the otherwise smooth horizon. Slightly south the scene was similar, although an outcrop of evergreens on the lower reaches gave a splash of colour to the general ground sepia, and a little farther to the left a windmill stood isolated, its sails locked rigid.

Charlotte turned her attention westwards. There lay Kingsden Wood and the tumulus that had been the place of her error. She shuddered at the thought and looked away, although she knew it would always be there to remind her. She felt rather surprised at her own prejudiced reaction. Perhaps some day soon she ought to walk the wood to allay any unnatural fears, "but not yet awhile," she said out loud.

To the east, in the general direction of Glastonbury, was Bramgate St Mark, but this sleepy village nestled in a valley and was invisible beyond the merest glimpse of the church tower. Much farther on she fancied she could just make out what could be Glastonbury Tor, rising majestically like a subjugated tower from a greater building. On top of its hill, ringed by lychets forged by Anglo-Saxon ploughmen, it still commanded dignity over the ancient Isle of Avalon, as if to remind newcomer churches that *it* held the first English Christian altar. Its presence was poetic, its majesty over the nation's religious beliefs recognised by strong, unfailing buttresses and a battlement crown.

James had disappeared head first up to his waist inside the thresher's feed hole, his legs waving about in mid-air as he stretched to reach awkwardly placed parts. She admired how he got stuck into any work that needed strong leadership.

"It's straight now – don't let it slip. Tighten that bolt. No, the next one down, damn it! Blast, it's gone again."

James knew how to handle the men, to exact obedience without aggression. She, on the other hand, had melted in the face of an angry cook who had given nothing for her position, shuddered at the mere thought of a walk through Kingsden Wood, and had felt it necessary to see James to confirm that their reconciliation continued. His composure was truly a gift and one Charlotte now became determined to adopt for herself. To be devoid of ambition, however small, meant never to fail, but to succeed in the face of possible disappointment was to gain new heights of achievement. The starting point for her could be here and now and in a trice Charlotte made up her mind to be strong willed, to be the kind of woman any man would be proud to call a partner as well as a wife.

In setting about this new image, Charlotte had not given enough thought to the right time and circumstances for its display. For, as surely as it could have benefits, its misuse would be guaranteed to antagonise. Unseen, the greatest trap lay in an arbitrary stiffening of resolve rather than carefully chosen demonstrations of authority. James never thought about it, it just came naturally. He listened to others, nodded his head whilst hearing them out uninterrupted, and did things his way.

Uneventful time passed slowly and still James and the gaffer worked on the thresher, the low hissing of the engine under steam now and again giving way to a spasmodic 'chut-chut' as the belt drive was ordered 'engaged' for testing. The labourers had now begun stretching out, surprised at the length of the delay and concerned at the growing likelihood of having to work on into the night to finish the job.

On top of the corn rick, Jack Mere joined a huddle of men playing cards, but his attention constantly wandered as, from the vantage point, he had a clear view of Charlotte. His eyes were drawn irresistibly to her, although his feelings were mixed. Apologising more than once for his lack of concentration, he was soon left out of the game.

Charlotte too was finding the lack of action a little boring. Anyway, the novelty of her new resolution made her listless to put it into practice in some small way. Rising from the sacks and shaking the bits from her skirt, she crossed to James, but was unable to draw his attention as he worked inside the feed hole. Finding no stick to poke him, she climbed the four-step ladder running up to the standing board. Clinging to it with one hand and her skirt with the other, she lifted herself onto the board. She was now close enough to tell him that she intended to return to the manor, but at that moment he lifted himself out from the opposite side of the machine and signalled for the drive to be engaged. Instantly the 'chut-chut' started and the thresher pulsated. In panic, Charlotte grabbed for something to hold on to, but missed and fell backwards from the thresher, thumping to the ground.

The scream of her fall drowned even the engine and instinctively the mechanic shut down the drive, believing someone had lost fingers in the threshing drum. In an instant James jumped down and knelt beside Charlotte, raising her head and shoulders to see whether she was conscious.

"Oh, James, my back!"

He looked along her prostrate body to see if there were any twisted limbs. Everything looked normal, she having taken the full force on her back. He suddenly wondered if he had done right to move her at all.

"Can you move your head, Char?"

She moved it with discomfort.

"Your arms, hands, fingers?"

Again she responded.

"How about your feet?"

Yes, they twitched too.

"Thank God," he sighed. "We'd better get you home and fetch the doctor. I'm afraid it's the corn cart for you, young lady!"

His attempt at frivolity was received with a pained, but responsive smile. Carefully she was lifted onto the cart once the sacks had been thrown off.

"I'll come with you, Char." He turned to the nearest workman. "Dobbs, take my horse and ride like hell for the doctor."

The fine mount with its rustic rider galloped off across the mud. James squatted beside Charlotte on the cart.

"Dear, Char, you really should have known better. You might have hurt yourself badly."

"And the baby!"

"You must take more care of yourself."

"*And the baby!*"

James showed no willingness to bend.

"Hang it all, you won't make me say it!"

"Then it is not like old times at all."

The reply was unquestionable, her expectations answered.

"No, it's quite different. I'm not the man I was and you're not the woman."

"But I thought after last night . . ."

"Charlotte, last night was last night. It is now that counts. I saw Mere looking at you from the rick, even if you didn't. I ask you sincerely, what in essence has changed?"

The heavens opened, thunderbolts fell from the sky, the seas swelled into tidal waves and earthquakes and volcanoes erupted, but only in Charlotte's angry thoughts. She remembered her new image, now born from hurt.

"You deceiver. You false lover. You, you . . ." She burst into sobbing to the great dismay of all around. Red faced, she pushed him away. "Get off this cart. I don't want you near me."

James stepped off and a labourer took up the reins. Slowly she moved across the field, staring a rearward look at James who stood lost in astonishment until she was out of the gates.

The old woman who had been instrumental in opening the chasm that now separated James and Charlotte walked across to Jack Mere and crouched close to his ear.

"It's her time, Jack lad. I wager she'll be having your bastard this very day."

CHAPTER VII

Dispossessed

*J*ames returned to the thresher, passing faces seemingly para-lysed by their audience to the private scene, their stares too conspicuous to escape his heightened senses. Never before had Charlotte or anyone spoken to him in such a manner, or rebuked him so publicly. His gaze jumped from one pair of eyes to the next.

"What in damnation are you lot looking at? Get about your work."

He leapt back onto the machine and flung a cover plate to one side, causing it to shudder with the ferocity. The labourers obeyed instantly, but without the machine running there was little real work that could be done.

There were times when James hated the closeness of the people he employed, but that was the penalty of leading from the front. He had the undeniable power to take from them their livelihoods and homes, giving him almost the dominion over life and death. Yet, he knew this transgressed a moral duty not to inflict harm and desti-tution because of personal anger.

"Things are changing around here," said one of the older men. "You can feel it. If the master doesn't get his private life sorted, I reckon we'll all be in for troubled times."

"Can't see why, Vic. How can it affect us?"

"That little bugger, Mere may have dropped his trousers once too often. There's no saying where it might end."

"Oh, come on. You can't believe that rumour? Mere may be a free spirit, but he wouldn't get past the kitchen maids at the manor. Mind, the thought of Charlotte Elvington fair curls me whiskers."

"Don't upset yourself. *You'll* never get a chance."

"But wouldn't you love to know if Mere really had done the job?"

"I'm staying out of it. Mere's only got one thing I envy, and that's his freedom. No family, no ties, no commitments. He'd be a fool to give that up."

The old woman stepped from the rick ladder and straightened painfully.

"God preserve me joints."

"Feeling your age, Mary?"

"I'm good for a year or two yet if left to sweep floors. Going up ladders is too much at my time of life. Can't think what the master is playing at making me do this work."

"Maybe none of us will have jobs after today," said Vic. "Jack Mere may have queered things for everyone."

"If it hadn't been him it would have been someone else," grinned Mary scornfully. "Why else would '*the Madam*' come to see the threshing, all dolled up and smelling like a tart's closet? Now she's had rough she'll want more, mark my words."

"For a frail old woman you're mighty keen to bite the hand that feeds you. Take care your tongue doesn't tie a noose around your neck."

"I still have my uses," she said, looking towards James.

"I wish you wouldn't speak like that, Mary, and don't let Verity hear you either. She loves that no-good Jack Mere and would throw you off the rick if she heard you now."

The hag looked across to where Verity Bates happily talked young things with her friends.

"Hussy!"

* * *

It was no use. James couldn't concentrate and was irritated by the triviality of adjusting the worn out drum. He threw back the cover plate and left on foot.

Although desperate for news of Charlotte, he walked slowly, sure that there would be nothing to learn until the doctor had completed a thorough examination and he had to come from Batsborough, some four miles north. In any case, he thought to himself, she hadn't appeared too badly hurt from the fall. Probably more shock than anything."

The cheerless walk from Potti Bottom to 'Samain' took James far longer than it had taken Charlotte in her happiness that short time before. It was full of turns and twists, the tall hedgerows on both sides punctuated at one point by closely growing trees that hid muddy paths and a meandering brook. Here, nature paced his steps rhythmically, sending throbs of dull March sunlight through niches in the roadside curtain. James climbed through and wandered some way by the water's edge.

As he finally approached the manor he saw an unfamiliar black gig and pony. The doctor had made excellent time, the better roads leading north from Westkings to the market town of Batsborough making his journey quick. New urgency entered James' step.

It is one of the inconsistencies of human nature that a person often has to search long and hard for a simple truth, whereas a complicated thought may flash to mind in a subconscious moment. So it was that James now stood at the head of the driveway and all the complications and troubles of the past days focused on what the doctor might now say. A single sentence could change his life irrevocably. The loss of the baby might help him re-establish a relationship with Charlotte, while the baby born would be a permanent trophy of her unfaithfulness. He made briskly for the house.

It was now more than two hours since Charlotte's fall. On entering the manor James could feel a coldness that was heightened by the emptiness of the downstairs rooms. Nobody bustled about. Fire grates were still heavy with the previous night's ash, and supper plates and glasses remained untouched in the drawing room.

That room in particular had a strangely vacant air, a blandness that only activity would dispel.

Creaking floorboards above suddenly announced where the household was concentrated, and once heard, other movements became more discernible. The quick footsteps of a maid on the stairs were followed some while later by a slower, lighter tread as she ascended carrying a bowl of scalding water. Only rarely did a voice break through the long silences, the words spoken in such low tones as to be inaudible below.

As time passed the noises intensified as maids fetched and carried, performing without comment every command given by the doctor. James, who had taken a book from the shelves and had begun reading, suddenly dropped it and stood motionless as the low panting moan built up into a crescendo of pain. He could stand no more and rushed up the stairs, throwing the door open.

"Get out, James. We're in trouble here."

Wide-eyed, he gently closed the door, but sat on the floor outside, listening helplessly.

"Who's done this before?" asked the doctor. "Come on, one of you must have?"

The girls shook their heads.

"Good God, I can't manage by myself. We've got a large baby in breech. Is there anyone you know who could help me? Someone very close by?"

"There's the schoolteacher, Miss Ayres. She used to be a nanny," replied Meg.

"Then for God's sake fetch her. Whatever she's doing, drag her away."

"No!" cried Charlotte. "Don't leave me, Meg. Please don't go."

The doctor took Charlotte's hand.

"Now, now. She'll only be away a minute." He looked back at Meg, who was white with indecision. "Hop it!"

Meg flew out of the manor and across the lane to the school, bursting into a classroom.

"Madam's in labour. The doctor can't cope. Can you come urgently?"

With a pupil hurriedly sent to fetch the headmaster, the schoolteacher grabbed her jacket and left immediately.

"I only hope we're not too late," grunted Meg as they ran over the lawn. "That's her screaming now."

Charlotte spasmed.

"I can't hold back."

Heavy footsteps pounded the stairs. James quickly stood up to let the women pass.

"Don't try to. When you feel the need, push."

"What can I do?" asked Miss Ayres as she washed her hands.

"It's coming!" shouted Charlotte.

Part of the baby appeared, but the effort was short lived.

"I've seen it, Charlotte. Come on, do it again."

"I can't. I can't!"

"I don't like this one little bit," whispered the doctor to Miss Ayres. "I could make an incision through the abdominal and uterine walls, but I haven't got anything to kill the pain. Anyway, I think the baby might be very distressed or dead. Fetch a towel."

Again Charlotte spasmed.

"Let's have another go. I'll try the clamp."

She pushed, her face red and tight.

"More, Charlotte, I have the legs."

"It won't come. Help me! For pity's sake, get it out."

"Miss Ayres, quick. Inside my bag you'll find a knife. Pour some of that clear liquid over the blade and bring it here, fast."

She shook with panic and dropped the knife on the floor.

"Calm down, woman. You're no good to me in that state. Take a deep breath. Now, pick it up, wash it and pour that liquid as I asked. That's right. Give it here. Now, when I say, I'll enlarge the tear, and don't let go of these legs. Meg, you fold a handkerchief and put it between Charlotte's teeth, then sponge her face. When I count to three, hold her down. Ready? One, two, three."

Miss Ayres lifted the baby's legs and the doctor cut a deep, straight slit beneath. The cry of agony was terrible and Charlotte fell back in a faint.

"That's done it for better or worse. Here it comes. Nearly . . . It's a boy! Hold her down. Hold her."

He pulled the baby free, cut the umbilical cord that wound around his neck and thrust him into Miss Ayres' arms, leaving himself free to see to Charlotte's needs while Miss Ayres forced a finger down the baby's little throat to clear an air passage. There was no movement.

"He's dead," screamed Meg at the doctor.

"Don't give up. Not yet."

Quickly grabbing the baby, he lifted him over his shoulder and slapped hard, then again and more, but it was useless and he gently lowered the little blue body into his arms, sure that there was no life to revive. Meg ran to the basin to be sick. The tiny limp body was carefully wrapped in a towel.

"You, Meg! Take the baby from the room. Now."

"I can't touch it!"

"I said, now! I've got the afterbirth to see to."

She meekly held out her apron and the little bundle was dropped in. Outside James buried his head in his hands.

"Doctor!" shouted Miss Ayres, wide-eyed. "She's having contractions again."

"What! My God, there's a twin."

Charlotte revived and lifted her sweat-soaked head.

"What's happening to me?"

"Lie back, dear and take deep breaths. It's not over."

"Where's my baby?"

The doctor looked at the others uncompromisingly.

"You haven't given birth yet. Try to control your pushing."

"Help me. I can't do any more."

"Yes you can. Just take it steadily. When you feel the need, push gently, but long."

She fell back panting.

"Ah, I can feel it coming."

"That's my girl. Here it comes. I can see it. Come on, a bit more. One more push. Yes!"

James heard the shrill cry of an infant.

"Is it a boy?" asked Charlotte wearily.

"You have a fine daughter," replied the doctor.

Charlotte smiled contentedly.

The deed was done, the die cast. No longer could James discuss Charlotte's child as an inanimate intrusion. From that moment Charlotte was not just his wife, but a mother too with new loyalties. All had changed, allegiances redrawn, and outside James felt more isolated than ever. He walked away, head bowed.

Work started on making the room presentable. Clean bedding was brought in and a subdued carnival air took hold of the proceedings.

"Listen all of you," said the doctor in a muffled tone. "Charlotte mustn't be told about the first child. Do you understand? She's too weak and it serves no purpose. Just thank heaven she's got the other, a strong, healthy girl. I'll see to the boy."

"Begging your pardon, Ma'am," said one of the maids as the baby was placed in her cot, "but shall I fetch salt and a piece of iron for the little one?"

Charlotte, still in shock, looked unsure.

"Why, ma'am, in these parts we do it for keeping the demon spirits out."

Drying his hands, the doctor sat on the corner of the bed.

"It's just folklore, my dear, and not to be taken seriously. Superstitions are like prejudices, they take generations to fade away among countryfolk. I have often come across this one. You see, salt signifies health, and who wouldn't wish that on a baby!"

Charlotte's thoughts suddenly wandered to James, but it was too horrible to contemplate further.

". . . bowl of primroses of all things as a talisman against witches. I dare say these old ideas will be with us for some considerable time yet, and I'll have to continue removing hard lumps and evil smelling brews from baby's cots until better education for the poor ends such ignorances."

"I'll go now," smiled Miss Ayres, touching the baby softly under the chin.

Charlotte held out her hand.

"Thank you. You have been very kind. Please stop for some refreshment."

"And that's from both of us," added the doctor. "When Meg said you were a former nanny, I hadn't expected one so young and, may I say, so beautiful."

Checking once more on Charlotte and the baby, and having stuffed his instruments into his bag, the doctor also left the room. He made his way to the drawing room where he greeted James with a warm handshake.

"You have every right to be a proud man, James my boy. You have a sturdy little girl."

The spurious father put on a brave face and offered a drink.

"I'll toast your offspring with pleasure, but not with one of those, I hope," he said, pointing to the half-empty glasses of flat wine from the night before. Five minutes later he had gone, finding James sullen company.

Meg returned to the kitchen and made tea for Charlotte and James, also asking Miss Ayres to take a cup. She accepted. As usual Meg looked after Charlotte first, but on leaving the bedroom she saw Miss Ayres about to carry the second tray into the drawing room, having knocked lightly on the door.

"Not in there," Meg called from halfway down the stairs. "I meant in the kitchen."

Miss Ayres stopped as James' surprised look met her.

"Ah!"

Smiling at her embarrassment, he held the door fully open and begged her to enter. She looked back at Meg, shrugged and stepped inside.

"I feel like a censured schoolgirl. Only I misunderstood."

"Feeling naughty for coming in unannounced?"

"Yes, something like that. I'm so sorry. I really didn't know."

He pressed a finger to her lips.

"I have to thank you, not spank you!"

"All in a day's work, as they say, and, please, my name is Sally if you wish to use it. Sally Ayres."

"Mrs or Miss?"

"Miss."

"Sally. Yes, that name suits you well. Tell me, how long have you been working for Ben Gurston."

"Who's he?" she enquired with open expression.

"Why, the doctor of course."

She shook her head.

"No, you've got it all wrong. I've never met him before today. I'm a schoolteacher from over the road. I was sent for."

"Then what you did for my wife was hardly part a normal day's work."

"No, I guess not, thank goodness," she replied.

"Funny, but I can't remember ever seeing you around the village?"

"I only came to Westkings a few weeks ago. When I'm not working, I prepare lessons for the next day, so I hardly get out. Unfortunately I'll be returning home soon."

"Don't you like the work?"

"It's not that. Far from it. No, you see, my mother is ill and someone has to look after the family."

"You didn't mind me asking, I trust?"

"Of course not. It's open knowledge. I always thought I would like teaching. I thought I had something to give."

"You don't anymore? A minute ago you said you were going for personal reasons."

"I am. It's just that it would have been much harder to give up teaching here if things had gone better. To be frank, the headmaster is a bit old fashioned when it comes to girls' education. He's unmarried and treats them like porcelain dolls. You know, all fragile, to be guarded from any knowledge of life. A school like ours needs new ideas. I've been frustrated at every turn."

"For example?"

"Well, I thought of staging a play, something classical like *Romeo and Juliet*, but he wouldn't let the boys kiss the girls. When I offered to use only girls, he wouldn't let any put on trousers to act the part of the men. Same for the boys, with dresses I mean, although in this case I think the boys were heartedly relieved."

"I see your problem. Are there no plays for girls alone?"

"Do you know of any? I don't. Oh, please don't misunderstand. Percy Brillings is not a bad sort and I must admit I thought I'd get around him given time, but now that won't be possible."

"Sounds to me as though you like teaching far more than you admit."

"Maybe. I certainly like it more than being paid a pittance as a nanny for looking after the children of just one family, excluding my own brothers and sisters of course. Now that's really boring. As for teaching, a bigger school might be different. In a way it's lucky I'm going. I would die a crumbly spinster if I couldn't do more things. I suppose I'm a bit of a maverick, a romantic, but girls need to see a wide aspect of life, just as much as boys. I dream of taking pupils to those places you see only in books, where the heat plays on the sands of Arabia, the wild beasts fight over the parched earth of Africa, to see the sun over the jungles, the moon over Paris. That's why I teach literature and geography. I know it's all fantasy, but I think everyone needs a bit of ambition."

"Perhaps you were setting your ideals a little too high."

"I suppose so. Teaching about these places is probably as close as I or they will ever get. I know that deep down, and finally realising it was half the battle in making up my mind to go home. Only, the thought of mental stagnation appals me, but enough of such gloom. Today is for merrymaking."

When Sally Ayres left, James was stirred with emotion. He had not been prepared for her lightness when all about him seemed to have collapsed. For, the only advantage a woman has that a man will readily accept on making a new acquaintance is one of soft tone, where in truth a superior intellect may sometimes lurk unseen. This woman exuded both beauty and a manner that guaranteed that any man would quickly acknowledge intelligence without feeling threatened by it. On first seeing her, James had been entirely distracted by the former, which split into charm and a full figure; two attributes that vied for supremacy. Within his private thoughts he freely acquiesced that he liked her – a lot – and in the cause of truth, she too had seen something in his dark good looks that was beyond her experiences of men, perhaps a glint of refinement that showed through his working clothes. Whatever the appeal, they warmed to each other from that first meeting.

If fate had decided to play a game with his feelings at this low ebb in his life, and those of Miss Ayres, the ill-conceived plan had not taken into account the imminent departure of one player. It was all to the good, and the briefest of attachments was quickly forgotten as James heard the cry of the baby above.

For several days after the event that brought so much joy to all the women of the manor, James reflected below, eating from a tray to avoid company. He retired late and rose early, giving the mistaken impression that he spent the nights huddled on the drawing room chair, for the maids were forbidden to enter his bedroom. The maids found his mood inexplicable. Stranger still, they began to wonder why he hadn't visited Charlotte and the baby.

On the ninth day of Charlotte's confinement the matter came to a head. Doctor Gurston had called by and was walking back down the stairs when he stopped a maid who was carrying a tray into the drawing room.

"Ivy, dear, may I have a quiet word?"

"Yes, Sir."

There was awkwardness in his voice.

"I'm not entirely happy with your mistress's recovery. She seems a bit melancholic. Has she said anything to you that I ought to know, as her physician you understand?"

"Why, no Sir," came the reply.

"Just so." He pondered and decided on a more direct approach. "Has your master appeared to be in good spirits, over the baby I mean?"

"I hardly see him at all, Sir."

"Has he been upstairs?"

"To his bed?"

"No dear, silly girl, to visit the child."

"I can't rightly say, Sir. I mean . . . I haven't seen him, but that doesn't —"

He cut her short.

"How many times has he been in to see Charlotte?"

"Including the first?"

"Most certainly, and no exaggerating mind."

"Once!"

"Only once! Hasn't your mistress asked after him?"

"Oh, no Sir, never. She knows where he is."

"Then he's avoiding her?"

She became agitated.

"I really don't know anything. It's not my place to say. Now, if you will forgive me, Sir, I'll get this food to the master while it's still warm."

"But it's a plate of cold meat!"

She hurried off.

The good doctor was deeply troubled. He knew Charlotte's full recovery and peace of mind was bound inextricably to James' feelings, but there lay the problem. Was he to confront James as an old friend and risk an ugly incident or should he return to Charlotte and chance making her unhappy by his suspicions? Both options were unpleasant. Just then, however, fate took a hand. A knock at the servants' door brought visitors, who were shown into the drawing room; a young man fresh from the fields accompanied by a younger woman. The doctor returned upstairs as the only remaining option.

Charlotte now bore the inconsistency of two moods, whichever she portrayed being entirely dependant upon whether she had company. She smiled when the doctor knocked and re-entered the bedroom, but this quickly fell away once his purpose was revealed, when the other vulnerable mood took hold. For the first time since the child was born she laid bare her worst fears.

". . . so you see, his only visit was full of hate. Not for us, of course — he wouldn't harm us — but for the situation. He won't budge an inch."

"And you can face me now, Charlotte, and tell me you accept *his* terms?"

"Stop it! Stop it, for God's sake. I am the one at fault."

"I see that. However, events have passed recriminations. I'll wring common sense out of him if you can't."

She looked out from the window to avoid his scowl.

"It can be no other way. Can't you see? He is my husband and he has moral law on his side."

"Moral law, be damned! What morality would see a mother and daughter separated? If he can't accept the child, then you and she must leave him. You make that choice and I personally will see to it that you are well looked after until long-term arrangements can be made with your parents or anyone else of your choosing."

"I know you mean well, and I'm grateful. I just can't," she said softly.

"Charlotte," he begged, lifting Christabel from her cot and holding her close, "it just can't be true. How could you say goodbye to this beautiful child. She's utterly perfect. Look at her little hands and nails. I helped to bring her into the world and I love her dearly. Say, sweet Charlotte, that it isn't going to happen."

"It is as it must be. The truth is, I've grown weary of my life. I mean to live it out with the man who offers me no love, but a comfortable existence. I am entitled to no more and will accept no less."

With sadness, he rose from the edge of the bed and tucked the baby back into her cot. In silence he grabbed his coat, but added as he opened the door to leave:

"I thought I knew you, but I can detect an inner courage that takes my breath away. I'll not come back to this miserable house unless you change your mind or need me as a doctor on a different matter. I shall never enter again in friendship." He took a last look at the little sleeping head resting between tiny hands. "God protect you, little one, and God help you, Charlotte."

James' shout of "Goodbye" to an old friend leaving went unanswered and the gig pulled away from the house, soon passing the young farming couple seen entering the drawing room. They wore a serious look on their weather-beaten faces. The doctor stopped the horse and waited for them to draw alongside.

"Could you by chance be Jack Mere?"

"What of it?"

"Then you, my pretty wild thing, are Verity Bates."

"I am, Sir," she replied in a pleasant tone.

"Leave her be. We give you no cause to stop us, you being a gentleman like. We've had trouble enough for one day."

"I look down on no man or woman who does an honest day's work, my lad. I meant no offence. Here, take this." He handed Verity a calling card. "Can you read, my dear?"

"I can, Sir, but not Jack, but why should I want a doctor? I'm not ill."

Gurston took up the reins and signalled the horse to prepare to walk on.

"If you should ever need my help, wherever you are, whatever the circumstances, that's where I can be found. Keep it safe."

They stood bewildered as he drove away.

Too soon for poor broken Charlotte, the day came for her to fulfil the promise. March had slipped furtively into April:

The first of April, some do say – Is set apart for All Fools' Day

Outside the manor at first light stood a hay wagon laden with well-worn pieces of furniture taken from two unoccupied estate cottages. Jammed alongside were wooden crates filled with working and Sunday best clothes, consumables, personal belongings and a selection of hand tools. Several unmatched pots had been roped to one side of the vehicle, which 'clanked' with every slight movement. The whole was crowned by a cotterel, its kettle lost somewhere at the bottom of the pile.

A small area had been left clear in the back of the wagon and from the manor maids brought out a trunk of good quality and the fine cot, which were placed carefully in the space. A tarpaulin was then stretched over and secured, although the sun was bright and it looked to be a good day for travelling.

Away from the wagon James was in conversation with Jack Mere, a man he detested and after today would never have to suffer again.

"Then you understand, Mere, and I have fulfilled my side of the bargain. The rent is settled on the cottage and a few acres of good valley land in Shalhurn. That makes you the livier. Make fair use of it and you will be content, that I can assure you. Keep the purse safe and be prudent with the coins. Next, and this is most important, you understand you are to bring the child up in good Christian ways and have her baptised. Oh, and get yourself married. I'm told Verity Bates is a worthy maiden and will make you a good wife. Treat her right. I mean that! Now, you get on your way and out of my life forever."

James walked briskly back to the manor, passing Verity in the hallway carrying the child in her arms. Sobbing maids followed her out, fussing around and adjusting the blankets.

Watching the scene from above was Charlotte, who had promised faithfully not to interfere in the proceedings, but whose heart was in tatters. Her desperation at seeing the child in Verity's arms was total, her grief unchecked. She pressed her face hard against the glass, her arms upstretched, tears rolling down the panes in a waterfall of hopelessness.

Verity climbed on board and Jack took up the reins. At once there was a terrible scream:

"*No, no, no!*"

Mere had been told to pay no attention to any last minute outbursts and he guided the team around. At that moment Charlotte came running full flight from the house, her clothes flowing and her face a ghostly pale. She grabbed Mere's hand, releasing three small objects onto his palm.

"The snuff box holds salt and the key is iron. These talismans will protect my child. The gold ring is my heart, which you take from me. Keep the ring safe and use its value if the need is dire for the child's sake."

Like an explosion, two great hounds leapt from the manor's door, followed by James who grabbed Charlotte around the waist and carried her off kicking.

"Be off, damn you!" he shouted to Mere.

The wheels of the wagon turned, the precious cargo firmly held in the caring arms of the surrogate mother. Charlotte tried to break free, but the hold was total. A crack of the whip and Charlotte's child was lost to her.

Charlotte couldn't believe it had actually happened – no amount of talk had truly prepared her for the moment. The nightmare had played every card and the game was over. She collapsed onto her knees and looked up to the open sky, her tortured expression speaking volumes.

"Have mercy on my child, my dear own Christabel. My child, *my* child!"

The great passion moved all assembled.

"Oh, merciful Jesus, protect my poor baby and guide her through life's perils. I don't care for myself. Do with me as I deserve, but have pity on the innocent one."

At once a great wind caught Charlotte where she knelt, streaming her long hair and blowing away the tears from her cheeks.

"She is saved," she said.

CHAPTER VIII

A new life

*C*ruel fate had intruded upon the infant life of Christabel, leaving behind her proud home for very different new circumstances, with the only parents she was to know. From this point forward she was the daughter of an impoverished smallholder. Such a monumental alteration to what might have been at her young age should have banished any inbred vestige of propriety. Yet, as time would reveal, within the little child lay dormant the ways of her natural mother.

Jack Mere, who had never owned anything much, and up to this moment had seen few prospects for advancement, viewed the pending new life with genuine enthusiasm. True he had been put upon to accept a ready-made family during the wildest fling of his youth, but then, what the hell! Only one other person in Westkings cared what happened to him, that being Charlotte. There was nothing dreary or foreboding about the long journey ahead to Shalhurn, when its fulfilment promised so much. His cheer blossomed into song.

Verity too was in good spirits, tapping her foot in time to the merry tune and the clanging of loosely strung pots. She also had no regrets, for her status as a married woman – or soon to be – had lifted her from a cramped dormitory to a home of her own with the man she loved. She had already forgiven Jack for his brief affair with Charlotte, understanding well enough how passions of the moment can rule the head, and she left Westkings carrying her own unborn. Very soon, the child in her arms began to feel familiar.

Once the wagon was out of sight and the rumbling of heavy wheels had passed into the distance, Charlotte ended her public grieving and returned to her room in an attempt to recover composure, or in other words to dwell unsympathetically and alone on the cause of her distress. James, who had been unflinching throughout the ordeal, had taken an earlier opportunity to place a letter against Charlotte's mirror. This she picked up and read:

> *My dearest Char,*
>
> *I judge myself called upon by our sad circumstances and my position as your husband and dare say once companion, to put pen to paper and tell you of certain matters about which you have the right to be assured. Please forgive that I do not have the courage to tell you face to face. Your unhappiness, which I understand must be of the bitterest kind, will pass with the passage of time. I shall not be seen wanting in my duty to ease this severe misfortune in any way that is correct.*
>
> *To the subject of the child, your child of late, be rested that I have made fitting provision with her new parents and no harm will come to her. I am inclined to believe that her life will be simple and perhaps that is no bad thing, for that way no person will ever enquire of us. It is the realisation of this that I hope will enable you to see that I acted in the interest of all. If you cannot find it possible to understand now, I truly believe you will at a future time when the hurt of Christabel has faded.*
>
> *In honesty to myself and any happiness we might still find together, I feel compelled to reiterate that you must not intrude upon your daughter's life or try to discover her whereabouts.*

Again I say, her future is assured by the provision of the wherewithal for Mere to provide for his family. I believe him to be a feckless fellow, but this change may be his making. The prosperity from the tenanted acres will be supplemented by occasional work expected of Verity Bates by the landowner, who made this a proviso for renting, but affirmed to my questioning that this right would only be called upon during harvest and other such laborious times and that her payment would be generous.

I hope I have done right, for I have made arrangements for you to spend some weeks with your parents in Portchester. They know nothing of the circumstances and, I am ashamed, I have led them to believe that your child was stillborn. I beg you to consider the reason for this half-deception and not to think too ill of me. The wretched state of our marriage can only benefit from this temporary parting and there is a powerful case for secrecy even as to why you are making the visit. Forgive me, Char, but I am intending to occupy this time in business away from Westkings. I need space to myself and to get away from 'Samain' for a while. I have used this as another reason for your journey.

How unfortunate it is that one person puts such faith in another and thereupon gambles his or her happiness. I am sick at heart for the old times. If you feel at all, one little bit, as you used to before our troubles, then you will grant me the wisdom of knowing what is best now. If you can regard the child as a past thing, at least in constant thought if not occasional memory, then there is hope.

James

The letter read, Charlotte pondered the words *half-deception* as she began collecting her bits together. The next day she left.

James also prepared to leave the cold grey of the manor, but was surprised when a knock at the door brought Miss Ayres into the hall. He took her into the drawing room, having shifted a pair of large leather cases that blocked the entrance. She shuddered.

"Please forgive the chill. I'm locking the house up for a while and no fires have been lit since last evening."

His words were polite, perhaps too polite considering the ease of their earlier conversation, but time and events had made their previous flirting seem almost silly.

"Don't concern yourself on my account. I'll keep my coat on."

She was asked to sit. James took a tobacco pouch from his jacket pocket and began filling the bowl of his pipe.

"I have come on a personal matter. In all honesty I'm unable to think where else to turn."

James was intrigued.

"Old Brilling given up trying to bring you round to his way of thinking?"

"He never stood a chance."

"No, I don't suppose he did." James smiled at her discomfort. "Come on, we know each other well enough to be frank."

"I was hoping so." She raised an eyebrow, just enough to be a subtle arousal to a responsive partner. Their eyes met in a prolonged stare.

"Well?" enquired James, snapping from the stare and keeping a lid on his feelings.

"This is so hard for me. I'm not used to begging for help."

James placed the pipe on the mantelpiece.

"Begging, by gad? Look here Sally, we are friends, aren't we? Friends don't beg for help, they ask. Look how you helped my wife, for heaven's sake. No more talk of begging. If it's in my power to assist, you can be assured that I will do it without wanting anything in return. So, please, out with it."

"My goodness, I love you," she said softly.

James was startled.

". . . as a dear friend" she added quickly.

She offered her hand and James almost unconsciously felt himself lifting her, so slightly that she could have ignored it, but she didn't. She needed no persuasion. He stroked the back of her hands with his thumbs, leaving a sweet itching sensation on her flesh. Her eyes closed.

At that very moment of tenderness the door swung open with a loud crash. They moved apart embarrassingly as Meg entered pushing a trolley, its rattle destroying the atmosphere.

"Good God!" exclaimed James, striding over to lift the wheels free from the edge of the carpet.

"Begging your pardon, Sir, but knowing how cold it is I took the liberty of making hot tea." She placed a silver tray on the side table and laboriously set out the cups and saucers and a plate of buttered toast. "With Madam away for just a few days, Sir, I was wondering if I should stay here after all to keep the fires going? This place tends to be damp if not properly heated. It's really no bother, or I could pop in now and again, unscheduled like?"

Her intonation was all too obvious.

"We'll leave the arrangements as they stand, thank you, Meg." There was no response. "I said that's all, thank you!"

She looked harshly at Miss Ayres. James caught the glance, but chose to be kind.

"I don't know how long my wife will be away. No doubt she will inform you of her intention to return in plenty of time to get the house ready. Meanwhile, have no fear, I will not be popping back to use it without your knowledge, so no maintenance will be necessary. I hope that satisfies you?"

Meg curtsied and left, closing the door behind her. Sally giggled, but James put distance between them and her smile dropped. She leaned across to the teapot.

"Shall I be mother?" she asked, hiding a blush and more than a little frustration. "She's pretty," she added, pouring the milk.

"Can't say I've ever really noticed. I gave up looking at very young girls years ago. Charlotte . . ."

She stopped pouring at the mention of Charlotte's name.

"Charlotte . . . seems to like her, and that in turn makes Meg very loyal. Hence the unscheduled tea. I think she sees you as a threat." He smiled and sat by her. "Anyway, that's enough small talk. Tell me why you've come?"

She took a sip and lowered the cup to her lap.

"I hadn't realised that your wife was away. This must seem very improper."

"I dare say the maid thinks so, but I find it most agreeable, so hang the girl."

"I'm leaving! My family has a cottage in Midford."

"Midford" said James with interest.

"You know it?"

"No."

"Oh! Only I thought you were about to say . . . Well, no matter. Father is the manager of a flour mill and is paid from profits. At the moment the mill is only making enough to pay its running costs, with very little over. So, for my family life isn't easy. Poor father. He once had his own business, but it went broke when the price of wheat fell. Low prices now once again mean he works just as hard as before for almost nothing. The point is, I had a letter this morning telling me that my mother has died. She had been ill for some time. They say it was weakness brought on by constant childbearing; something to do with the sweetness of her blood. As I'm the eldest, I'm expected to go home at once and take her place, only I haven't got enough money for the journey."

"You return to be mother and housekeeper?"

"Pitiful, isn't it?"

"Frankly, yes! Aren't there relations who can help?"

"None that I can call on. We originally came from the Midlands. My aunts and uncles still live there, but they're poorer than we are. In the old days we used to help them with gifts of food and clothes, but not anymore. The present difficulty is that I haven't worked long enough to save the fare to Evercreech, although I have enough to buy a railway ticket home from there."

"They must pay teachers very badly?"

"Not really. What I've said isn't strictly true. The governors make us work a month in advance of pay. So, although I've worked seven weeks, I've only had a month's wages. That, I confess, I spent on romantic books for the girls – the ones Mr Brilling wouldn't buy with school funds."

"Well, good for you! Those children need a bit of enlightenment from what you've told me. I tell you, I've often thought they're too regimented. Politeness has its place, but it's gone far too far under Brilling's stewardship."

"It's nice to find someone of a like mind. The other teachers disapproved of my purchases."

"And now you haven't any of your wages left?"

"None at all. I only have the money I came with. I thought under the circumstances that they might pay me a week early, seeing how I've almost completed the second month, but they said they couldn't. The best they offered was to post it on when it's due, with reductions for the week I won't be completing."

"I'm not surprised. Compassion rarely interferes with business."

"Teaching isn't a business, it's a vocation."

"Ah, but governors deal with other people's money and so hold to established principles."

"Well they shouldn't."

"Perhaps not. We won't debate that point. Please, go on."

"That's it really. My father hasn't any spare cash to send me, and I wouldn't put him under strain by asking. So I couldn't think who else to approach and then I thought of you. Goodness knows why you should help me, but I'm desperate."

"You want my help with a cash advance?"

"Mercy, *no*! By talking the governors around into paying me now."

"Changing their penny-pinching minds?"

"If you could."

"Not a chance."

She looked distressed.

"How far is it from Evercreech to your home?" asked James with more than simple interest.

"Some twenty miles – an hour's ride. I don't think I can manage the walk to Evercreech with my pack. The books are so heavy, and I wouldn't leave them to stoke the school's boiler."

"Then I shall take you to Evercreech!"

"Oh, no! That's too much generosity."

"It's less trouble than seeing the governors, and will prove far more profitable to you."

"I really can't accept."

"Nonsense. It's the obvious answer. You won't be taking me far out of my way. My business in Glastonbury can be postponed for a few hours. However, if you would prefer, I will get my coachman to take you to the station and return for me later."

Sally could hardly refuse.

"Admit it," said James to rest any further anxiety, "your destination is remarkably close to mine, so accept my first offer. I would welcome the company and you will owe me nothing."

She nodded in acceptance.

"There, then. That's settled. Let's have a glass of Madeira wine for the road, and then another," offered James cheerfully, pushing the tea trolley to one side and reaching for the decanter. He poured out two large measures.

"Steady! I've a long way to go today. You're not a hard drinker, are you Sir?"

"No," turned James with glasses in hand, "I find it dead easy! I raise a glass to myself, a knight in your hour of need. Good men are the foundation of great English houses, you know."

"So is dry rot!" she added with a smile, suspicious of his motives.

The carriage pulled away after lunch, intending to meet the 4.28 p.m. stopping train at Evercreech.

Quite different circumstances now saw three vehicles radiating away from Westkings; Charlotte, James and Sally Ayres in carriages and the Meres on a wagon, the loose wheels of which forced an overnight halt at the smithy in Hornford-on-Brue.

For those on the wagon, setting out by the half light of the next dawn, the pace was sluggish, but the level roads on the haul southwards allowed Market Magna to be reached by one o'clock that afternoon. As James had provided twenty pounds, Jack decided that they could afford a hot meal at a commercial inn. The new experience of money in no way fired Jack's usual reckless nature, and having removed a single sovereign from the many intended for seed and livestock, he pulled the drawstring tight. Verity nodded approvingly.

The Waterloo inn was among the last of several buildings that edged the cobbled main street. A thick smell of cooking, and in particular boiling, pervaded the pipes and ugly steam-choked windows around the back of the building where the wagon was tied up, away from the roadside facade that greeted other paying customers. That smell provided the lasting memory of the village after the wagon eventually set off once more. Sherborne Castle was skirted by three o'clock.

Since before Sherborne, the terrain had altered markedly and now each mile seemed like three at the start. To their left was the mysterious Wiltcombe Valley, remaining in clear view until the party entered Duke's Wood on the final leg southwards. At a chalk ridge Jack stopped, looking across at the expanses of wilderness on which only coarse vegetation grew. Scattered bands of sheep nibbled systematically at the thin grass, but on the more difficult reaches harebell and squinancywort grew unabated, dotted with the occasional orchid. He couldn't see its beauty, judging it only for its potential as money-making agricultural land.

Verity watched for the first glimpses of Shalhurn as they drove along the final narrow and winding lanes, and when at last they were told of its close proximity their hopes soared, only to be crushed as quickly. Seen from above, their holding was indeed somewhere in a valley at the heart of Shalhurn, but the village itself was no more than a dozen assorted cottages with outbuildings in various stages of decay. There was no shop or inn, although it had a church of unnecessary grandeur at its southern edge.

Obviously Shalhurn had once been a larger and more prosperous village.

A steep slope led down to the cottages, causing Jack to rein back and brake hard for the whole descent. At the bottom, dug fields and open pastures stretched out on each side, bordered on the horizon by gorse and wooded hills. Shalhurn was, after all, beautiful if not large, with little formality.

The first building passed was the Gothic church they had seen from above, of typical grey stone and sitting on an island patch within a field that could only be reached via a short slab path with a wire fence that led from the lane. Neglected gravestones slumped in all directions. A drystone wall marked the edges of the plot. Strangely, the square tower had its circular staircase running up the outside in a separate hexagonal extrusion, while the nave and chancel faced away from worshippers approaching from the lane. The lancet windows of the tower were blocked on all sides. In comparison, the nave and chancel boasted ornate glass. In total, the church was mysterious, but something else bothered Verity. High on the corners of the tower perched four short spires, one of which leaned at a most curious angle. Yet, except for this imperfection, the valley church sat well against its hilly backcloth.

From the church the gentle sweep of the muddy lane brought into view the first farm cottages, which transcended the vernacular tradition of small stone construction and were built of large blocks, topped by thatch, some needing repair. They were set at all angles to the lane, as if rolled like dice.

Jack had been told that his cottage was the last in the row. Driving on, his heart sank at seeing the ramshackle structure with half of its roof gone. He was speechless, his head sinking deep into his chest. Verity tried to keep a brave face, suggesting that they looked around the back before condemning it. She handed Christabel to Jack and jumped down, soon disappearing from sight. She too was almost in tears, but was determined not to let him see. Her depression was short-lived.

"Quick, Jack. Come quickly."

Grabbing his arm, she pulled him beyond a row of trees at a bend in the lane, where one more cottage stood hidden from the rest, indeed the last in the row. He brightened immediately. It was nothing short of wonderful. Fairly wide, but shallow, it was built from a curious mixture of small stone and block. The central door had small windows on either side, and two upper windows peeped from under the thatch. To the rear was a more traditional out-building with a tiled roof and another that was in a poor state due to its cob construction. The huddled group lay bordered on three sides by a simple drystone wall. The fields all about were its garden. Only a single larch tree stood within the plot, permanently bowed by strong wind.

"My God, Verity. If someone had told me James Elvington would arrange this little lot I'd have called him a fool. I wonder if he knew what he was renting for us. Today being such a fine day, I'm inclined to think he did. God bless the man and all who sail in him! Why have we been so lucky?" He took Verity in his arms and kissed her forehead. "You want to stay, then?"

"Yes. Oh, yes, yes!"

"Very well then," he added playfully, "I'll tell him that after consideration of his offer, we have decided to stay."

They had been told to wait for the key, and used these moments to stable the horses and unload the furniture that had fallen into tangled disarray during the journey. Eventually the bed and the remainder of the load rested invidiously against the cottage walls.

Verity struggled to pull the tarpaulin over, carefully burying the cot deep into the middle.

"What now, Jack?"

"I'm going to look around my fields. *My fields*. I like the sound of that, but first come here."

He led her to the door and pushed her hands against it.

"What are you doing, Jack?"

"Bide with me a moment."

He took a handful of earth, washed his hands in it and rested them on top of hers.

"This is our first home, my girl, and most likely our last too. What we make of it depends on us. We're not married yet so now, right at the beginning of our life together, I make this pledge to you. Although the law says that I'm the livier of the cottage and all we have is rightly mine while I live, I hereby swear half of everything I own to you on making three promises."

"Stop being silly, Jack! For a start you don't own anything."

"The horses, wagon and furniture are mine, not to mention my bulging purse, and there will be more as I work hard. So, three promises I say."

She gave in.

"Go on then. What three?"

"Do you swear to be true to me?"

"Of course. You know that!"

"Just say yes or no. Do you swear to be true?"

"Yes."

"And do you swear to work as hard as me for equal shares?"

"Yes, but I'm a woman."

"I know that right enough, don't I?"

"Oh, Jack, you dirty minded old scrod."

"And third, do you swear to keep your hands cleaner than they are now?"

He broke off laughing. She hit him.

"No, seriously Verity, I know I joked with the third, but do you swear the first two?"

"I do that."

"Then that's agreed. Sealed with a kiss, married or not. Now if you don't mind, partner, I'm off for a little look-see. Do as you like, but stay close in case someone brings the key."

Verity lifted Christabel into her arms and walked casually towards the church. Close up it was even more ornate than she had at first thought, with the well-worn carved image of a king or disciple on each side of the heavily studded doors. She gently pushed at the doors and entered. The exterior had been interesting, but sombre, but the inside was of an entirely different character. Despite the restricted seating in the nave, the area above and that of the chancel were criss-crossed with cable ribs. At each juncture where the ribs met the walls a life-sized figure of painted wood projected out horizontally, menacingly hovering with a fixed gaze on any would-be sinners below. She guessed that they were the twelve disciples and found some comfort in that. Overall, it wasn't a place she liked and so quickly left, wandering slowly back towards the cottage, fully occupied with the baby and unaware of a lone rider approaching.

"Hey. You woman!"

She turned in surprise. The dark rider wearing a tall, black hat drew alongside, almost squeezing the baby between Verity and the saddle. She stepped back into nettles.

"Me, Sir?"

"I don't recognise you, so you must be the one I want."

He looked her up and down, his legs jabbing the horse's hind quarters to keep her squashed. Verity swung the baby to her side, offering her own body as protection from the horse.

"Sir, must you do that? My husband is a little way down the lane, within calling distance."

His crop fell hard behind his boot as the horse veered at Verity's one-armed push.

"Allow me to know my own mind, damn you! And take your grubby hand off my animal. Are you Mere?"

"I suppose I am."

"Then I suppose this is yours."

He tossed a key towards her, which she tried to catch, but dropped. As she bent to pick it up, he whipped the horse, causing it to kick and jump. He leered at her struggles to grab it.

"Lose that and you'll pay for another! That's all." He pulled the horse's head around. "Oh, except that I expect you up at the top field by six o'clock tomorrow. Six sharp, damn you!"

CHAPTER IX

To the earth, a victim

*V*erity hurried to the cottage, thrashing her arms about and shouting wildly, but Jack had his own problems and she could hardly be heard above the quarrelling.

"I don't give a hang how long you've used that stable as a meeting place, it's mine now and I won't be party to poaching," argued Jack.

Villagers, gathered by the commotion, mumbled in agreement. Nailor, the leader of the three outsiders stepped forward, his mastiff pulling fiercely, eager to bite flesh.

"How could we know this place was taken? It's been empty for months. Me ferrets have the taste for blood and I'll not be leaving without a couple of rabbits for the pot. Nor will the others when they come."

"Others?" exclaimed Jack. "Are more coming?"

"Aye. At least six."

"Not here, they're bloody well not. We'll see about that."

Nailor shortened the leash, then stepped towards Jack with a raised and threatening finger. The dog jumped up on its hind legs, snarling with exposed teeth.

"You're not the man to stop us. Step aside before I set me dog on you."

Another of the outsiders got between them.

"Hold on. We can settle this a better way." He turned to Jack. "Get your own dog, friend, and join us. There's plenty for all. These parts are rich pickings. Here, I'll even lend you me own best ferret."

He pulled a ferret from deep in his pocket, dangling it by its neck. It snapped to bite. Jack pushed it away.

"In God's name, man, where's its teeth?"

"I broke them off with me pliers. The rascal has a habit of chasing rabbits into deadends. Before I can dig 'em out he bloats himself on 'em. Now he can only suck 'em to death."

Other men arrived, empty bags strung across their shoulders.

"Tom, this young whippersnapper has taken the cottage. Won't let us in."

"Which one?"

Nailor pushed Jack forward.

"So you want to spoil our sport, neighbour?"

"It's not sport, it's poaching."

"Who says so?"

"You don't own the land."

"It's part of country life, stranger. No man robs me of my pleasure and gets away with it."

"And our families like it," added another. "Nothing like rabbit to fill bellies on a Sunday."

"That's as may be," quarrelled Jack, "but it's still against the law. Apart from the trouble you may bring on yourself and me if I help you, each one of you ought to be ashamed at the suffering you cause. There's better ways of catching rabbits than using mutilated ferrets and dogs. They should be snared or shot, clean and quick."

"Oh, yeah! We're bound to bring attention on ourselves by banging off guns around the woods. Anyway, rabbits are vermin. Don't you even know that?"

"It changes nothing," forced Jack.

"We didn't come all this way to hear preaching," added Nailor impatiently. "Let's get on with it or it'll be dark before we set the nets."

"No! Don't take a single step on my property. I won't be involved in it!" said Jack.

Several villagers bravely moved in support to block the way behind him. Tom looked at them, unsure of what to do. He had the muscle, but it was going to be ugly.

"Look, friend. Who's asking you to be involved? Not I, for one. Just walk away as if you'd never seen us and give us a few minutes to clear our stuff from the stable. None of us has ever been caught, and I would think very unkindly on anyone who squealed. DeByers owes every man here something for the trouble he causes."

"Who's DeByers?" enquired Jack.

They laughed.

"The man's a simpleton. I thought you had this cottage?"

"I do."

"Then you have it from DeByers."

Verity pushed through.

"Jack, that's what I've been trying to say. I've just met this horrible man and he gave me this." She handed him the key. "He says I have to work in his field tomorrow. Jack, is it true? I don't want to."

"Oh dear, missy," offered a neighbour. "You've met Sir Kenneth DeByers from the big house right enough. Was he a rough sort of gentleman with a face of iron and a tall hat?"

"That's him. Jack, what can I do?"

Jack looked at his neighbours in disbelief as Tom stepped forward and put his hand on his shoulder. Jack flinched.

"As to that, the only advice I can give is to keep away from him as much as you can. He's an unnatural curd and I'm glad he has no hold over me or mine."

"But what can we do about it?" pleaded Jack.

Tom took out a battered clay pipe with a half broken stem, and began filling it thoughtfully.

"You must have known he only rents to those with womenfolk he can use as cheap labour. Dare say he doesn't pay more than nine pence a day for working dawn to dusk. Oh, dear me, you have got a problem, no mistake."

"For heaven's sake, Jack," pleaded Verity, "our life here has only just started and already we're in trouble."

"Look, young fellow," said Nailor having cooled off. "We'll not add to your problems. I'm not saying we ain't going to ferret, 'cos we are, but we won't bother you no more. Give us a chance to get our nets and ferret spades from the stable where we've been hiding them and we'll be on our way and not return."

Jack nodded. The villagers made a space for the outsiders to pass. Verity waited until they had gone.

"The old master said only *occasional* work to me."

"Right, and I think James Elvington's been good and straight with us. This can't be with his knowledge."

"It's no use you thinking DeByers would stick to any agreements made by others far away," added a neighbour. "Face it. At least for the time being she'll have to do his bidding. Be mindful of his temper, though, and keep your head down, missy. In the meantime get a letter off to this master of yours to sort it out."

"I suppose you're right. Look Verity, we have a good parcel of land here and the rent is settled. The only other choice we have is to leave. We don't want that, do we? Where could we go? Let's see it through together. It won't be for too long."

"That's it, friend. Take it as it comes until you hear otherwise." He looked at Verity. "You're a strong woman, if you don't mind me saying. I don't think you'll suffer too much from the work they're doing right now."

Verity wasn't persuaded.

"Do it. Do it! For God's sake do it! Is that all you two can say to me? It's not you he wants. Can't you see that he frightens me?"

"I'll be off now," said the neighbour, embarrassed. "Oh, and many here will want to thank you for stopping those men. We needed someone to stand up to them. You'll be well liked for it. By the way, you weren't ever in any danger of being caught by the police as one of the poachers is the magistrate from Haddlebridge!"

"Blimey. It's a funny old world. Yes, goodbye and thanks," shouted Jack.

Verity misunderstood the courtesy for condescension.

"Why don't you go with him? Find an inn somewhere in this forsaken dump and laugh at me through the bottom of a quart pot."

"Verity. Verity. Calm yourself. I feel betrayed as much as you. Tell me what you want me to do?"

She grabbed his waist.

"Just hold me tight for the moment, you rotten sod."

"If it wasn't for the work we've got to do, I almost feel like joining in with the ferreting. Strike at that DeByers while me blood boils."

"Then I'm glad we're busy. We must do this right."

"We'll fight the bugger. Justice is on our side."

"And James Elvington when he hears."

"That's more like it! Cheer up now. We haven't even looked inside the cottage yet."

The ups and downs of the day hadn't yet ended. They stood stunned as they absorbed the gloom, the cold, the damp and the darkness of the inside, as foreboding as DeByers himself. Even the few sticks of furniture hadn't weathered the rigours of time.

The main room doubled as the kitchen and living area, kept dull by the tiny size of the windows, and floating in a thick odour of nastiness. The floor was bare brick and moist. A heavy black range nestled at one end in an inglenook, its kettle draped in cobwebs hanging above the central fire section that separated the two side ovens. A copper perched precariously on one side of the range, a pot on the other. A mangle stood beside. It was clear that without the door and windows open, the room would become extremely unpleasant once the cottage was in proper use, with heat from the fire and the steamy smell from the copper mixing with the general fug of cooking and sweaty damp bodies back from the fields.

The only remarkable feature of the room was a slatted tread-wheel, redundant from the days of dog spits, used once to turn meat roasting over the fire. There was no water supply to the interior, although a cast iron pump stood close to the back door, and a water butt with dipper captured rain from the roof. A potato sack doubled as a rug, its rough and grimy surface suiting its surroundings admirably. There was nothing, not a picture or colour of any sort, to lift the general aspect of depression.

Jack sniffed lazily. He suddenly felt very weary and beaten into submission, the wonderment of his first impression of the cottage now forgotten.

"Firewood. That's all this stuff's fit for."

Verity ran her hand into his, at once becoming the stronger partner for, curiously, she felt almost at peace with the place, and not because both were at a low ebb. Forcing a stiff door, they looked inside the only other downstairs room; the best parlour in better days. It was even dirtier than the first and a great deal less attractive, for at least the kitchen breathed stale life from former occupation, whereas it was clear that this room had been totally neglected. A window-pane was broken and through it a starling had entered and nested.

"Oh, look Jack."

The bird pricked up and twitched. Verity held out her arm, but in a hop and three flaps it had gone. Jack returned with the sack and poked it into the hole.

With enough seen of the downstairs, their attention turned to the upper floor. They looked at each other in trepidation before climbing the dangerous staircase. Space under the thatch was at a premium and ceilings were low and angled, allowing only three tiny bedrooms. The air was bitterly cold, with no means of heating. Jack opened the window in the largest room.

"This has to be ours. I can't stand up in the others." He took stock of its dimensions. "I will have to make a bed in here. We'll never get ours up that staircase."

It was this room that convinced Verity that she liked the cottage.

Jack's body tensed as she nuzzled into his back, her hands on his thighs, but he was too down-hearted to respond, and arousal hadn't been her intention anyway. Almost by reaction he slipped his hands backwards and onto her firm buttocks, lifting her skirt and feeling the fullness of the shape beneath.

"Big enough for three?"

She screamed at his cold hands.

"For three?"

He drew her stare to the window, where the starling perched and then jumped inside.

"Well, the bird was here first, you know."

"It's in a terrible mess," said Verity, stating the obvious as they finally descended, adding to her criticism by rubbing her finger along the table top.

"Horrible," was Jack's short reply.

"I like the cottage, but I can't think where to start the cleaning. It's all so bad."

Jack sighed, showing little enthusiasm. While he would have stood pondering his bad luck, Verity took the initiative and flung her hat out of the door to begin wiping.

"Has it been a false move after all?" enquired Jack with honest concern, remembering that by now she would have finished her day's work at Westkings. He watched her kneel to empty the grate.

"Hum?"

"Well, woman, won't you give me an honest answer?"

She straightened.

"No, Jack, it hasn't and I'll tell you why!" She pushed back a lock of hair with her wrist, leaving a grey smudge across her forehead. "Because this is our own home. Yours and mine, and we're together."

"Yes, but . . ."

Verity glared at Jack, implying the futility of argument.

"That's enough, me lad. I've given you the reason and I'm content with my lot. If I do one thing in this life, it'll be to make this a good home for you, Christabel and the new baby when it comes. Oh, and our feathered friend of course."

She spoke so earnestly that he knew she would. There was no pathos in her voice, only sincerity.

The evening was drawing in and together they made the best start they could, knowing that Christabel had her own needs and the next day Verity had to be up early.

As the dust from sweeping subsided and some order returned out of chaos, a picture emerged of how the cottage could look. It was exciting. Their scant furniture looked well and a fire crackled in the range to add warmth and comfort. A pot of tea brewed alongside a pan of meat soup. The night seemed darker here than in Westkings, the silence deeper. They missed the noise of friends, but they were together and little else mattered.

The little shutters at the windows began swinging as the night air gathered pace across the fields. Jack rose to close them, plunging the room into further blackness, and for a second everything went absolutely quiet as they got used to the change.

Then, suddenly and furiously, the door burst open. A heavy chill and swirling leaves poured in. The fire splattered as hundreds of glowing embers took flight. Frozen by the suddenness, Jack and Verity strained to make out the dark shape that filled the opening against a moonlit night.

Hardly able to stand, DeByers held tightly to the frame, his large head weaving. His hat blew away. A bottle dropped from his hand and smashed to the ground. His stomach spasmed and watery vomit gushed onto the clean floor. Wiping his arm across his face, he lifted himself back up, pointing to Verity.

"I'm the master hereabouts! You'll do my bidding tomorrow."

The wind caught him and he buckled. Jack rushed over and pushed him bodily out into the night, slamming the door shut.

"I think I'll get that dog after all," said Jack.

CHAPTER X

Reality

$\mathcal{F}$or Verity, the next morning came too quickly. Despite exhaustion, she had been unable to empty her mind sufficiently to manage settled sleep, but she was less scared now than last night. The rising sun had seen to that.

On the other hand, Jack was almost dropping. He had left her to sleep while he lit the range and fed Christabel, which was kind, and had placed a wedge of skimmer-cake, an apple and a jar of ale in a wicker basket, together with milk and a change of clothing for the baby. What Verity didn't know was that he had been up on several occasions during the night, awakened by strange noises.

They decided that Jack would accompany Verity to the top field, to make his manly presence felt to DeByers in case of trouble. He waited by the door, pulling on a jacket.

"You look a picture, what with the babe and all."

She agreed wistfully.

"You know, Jack, I'm not a proper wife. What will the other women think when they find out we're not married?"

"Bide any wagging tongues while arrangements are made. You'll be wed soon enough, my girl."

* * *

Verity soon outpaced Jack as the lane steepened. He stopped, doubled up and panting, his hands on his knees.

"You'll have to go on without me," he shouted between gasps, "I'll not see the top."

She nodded in acceptance.

"I'll make a start on the land after a quick nap." He turned back, if I ever get off this blasted hill, he thought to himself.

She watched him descend.

"Don't forget to send that letter I wrote. It's very important."

He acknowledged with a backwards wave, but stopped after a few paces.

"Now what, Jack?"

"It's no good. I can't leave you. Hold on, I'm coming back up."

She smiled as he struggled back up the hill.

"What's up with you, Jack?"

"Not much. I'm so damned tired. I had a rotten night. After you dropped off I heard noises outside. I couldn't see anything from the window. All was still. It could have been a fox, I suppose, but as soon as I got comfortable in bed, it happened again. This time I thought I caught a glimpse of someone scuffling around the stable. I put my boots on and looked outside, but there was nothing. After that I lay awake for an hour or so listening. Darn me if it didn't happen again the minute I fell asleep. This time the horses were disturbed and there was the clatter of tools being knocked over. I can't tell you how angry I was, as I needed my sleep. I almost ripped the door off the hinges in my haste to get out. I became a fearsome beast not to be trifled with. I threw tools and boxes around. Goodness only knows how you slept through that, especially as you tossed and turned so much."

"And?"

"I'm coming to that. The stable was empty, except for the horses, and they were content enough. As I was leaving I trod on a blasted rake. Darn me if the handle didn't fly up and hit me full square in the face. That made me bloody furious. It bloody hurt."

"I bet it bloody did," she chuckled.

"Glad you think it's funny. Anyway, I grabbed a spade and searched everywhere, running about in the pitch black and shouting like a banshee to scare the living daylights out of whoever it was. I could almost taste that someone else was about. There was only one thing for it. Cunningly I pretended to go, but instead I stalked around the back and climbed in through a window. I listened for the slightest movement, the slightest sound."

"And?"

"And nothing. Not a thing, except for my heart beating. So I torched the cob."

"You did what!" she exclaimed in disbelief. "You didn't?"

He nodded.

"You daft fool. How could you?"

"I don't regret it."

"No? Was it ours to burn?"

"Blimey, I confess I hadn't considered that."

"You idiot, Jack. You might have lost us our home after one day. What possessed you?"

"I'm an *idiot*?"

"We agree on that, at least. All we can do now is keep our heads and hope that nobody saw it happen. Come to think of it, why didn't I see any smoke?"

"It burned ever so quickly. Even I was surprised by it. By the time I looked this morning, it had burnt to the ground. That bit of rain we had damped down the ashes. Anyway, it was no use to us. I'll dig up the patch for carrots."

"What if you've killed someone? How can you be sure it was empty? What about those poachers?"

"I didn't care at the time. My mind was in a haze. I've looked since and it's okay. It's all clear."

"And that's why you're fit for nothing now?"

"S'pose so. I've hurt my big toe too."

"Chasing burglars! My big, daft, unthinking hero."

"Actually, I stubbed it on the cupboard getting back into bed."

"Oh, you."

She punched him on the shoulder.

"That's nice. More injuries," he protested.

Her smile faded.

"You don't think it was DeByers, do you, Jack? Maybe he won't leave us alone."

"I wondered that at first, but it could have been anyone. We don't know anything of what goes on around here. Still, we're learning fast."

In the semi-light of this early hour they walked arm in arm the rest of the way up the steep lane, Verity almost dragging Jack while balancing Christabel and the basket. From the top a clear view of the green valley below lay behind them. Other womenfolk were gathering in their drab grey dresses and bonnets. Their greetings were polite, but subdued. Babies and small children were huddled into a corner of the field, put under the charge of the eldest boy of six. Upturned crates acted as makeshift cots.

Jack toyed with the idea of leaving, but Verity insisted that he waited until the work began. They sat on the grass.

"God, it's bleak up here. All this quiet makes you realise how busy Westkings was."

Christabel cried. Verity took milk from the basket. The glass bottle was cold and she warmed it between her thighs. Jack poured a small measure of ale into a beaker and sipped. It ran down his chin and onto his lap.

"See that? I'm so ruddy tired I can't even find my mouth."

From the north gate two riders appeared. One was DeByers and the other his gaffer, but DeByers remained in the saddle.

Taking up hackers, the women spread themselves across the newly-turned field, plucking out witch grass and beginning waste piles to be burned later. Jack left.

There was something almost picturesque in the scene; a timeless study of agricultural life that begged the artist, but the romance was for the viewer, not the hunchbacked workers. A few pretty faces stood out amongst the older stumpy women resolved to the harshness of their lean existence. To the elderly it was subsistence living, ever nearing the time when weak muscles and frail bones would place them at the mercy of the parish. To them life was to be endured, not enjoyed, something the young girls knew, but hadn't the experience to take as absolute.

Verity took an hour to complete her first furrow. Rubbing her aching back, she could see Jack far below guiding a team of horses along the lane. She stood watching for some time, mopping her brow with the broad curtain-like flap of her bonnet. She so wanted to be down there too, digging her land and not scratching over another's. Surrounded by hillside, Jack looked like a tiny insect crawling along the bottom of a giant bowl, but between Jack and Verity lay more than distance. There was the impenetrable barrier of her commitment to DeByers, an ocean of laws and social privileges that subdued the wretched, swallowed the dissatisfied and forced her to work against her will.

"Is that all you've done?"

Verity jumped. Behind stood Breaker, the gaffer.

"I was just looking at my man."

She grabbed her hacker and tried to pass.

"When you're up here you work until you're told to stop. No resting unless I say so. You even piss where you stand." He held up a handful of couch. "Just one row done and these left standing. The others have finished two."

"It's new labour to me. It makes my back ache."

"What you don't finish the others will have to do for you. Explain that to them when they want to go home."

Verity bit her tongue, unsure of his temper.

"Sir Kenneth only pays those women I tell him have earned a day's wages."

"I'll do my bit."

"You'd better. My bonus goes if the whole field isn't cleared by tomorrow."

"Then I suggest you roll up your sleeves and get stuck in too."

"Why, you little trollop."

He raised his hand. She held firm, defying his nerve.

"There's worse than me, as you'll find out. Cut along, the master wants to see you."

Verity deliberately brushed shoulders as she passed, resisting his authority. Immediately, his hand fell hard on her leg. Red hot, she turned violently and struck him across the face. With difficulty he held himself back, following her stare to Jack below.

"Never mind me. Compared with some I'm mild mannered. You'll see. You're about to get yours," he said mockingly.

Never had she felt so threatened. This was indeed a strange and horrible place. Slowly, she crossed towards the dark figure of DeByers.

"Come closer," he sneered in a deep tone.

His sunken eyes warned her not to. His horse took a stride.

"I'm told you're a slacker."

"I do my best, since I don't want to be here and have no heart for it."

"Yet you'll take my money."

"Of course. It's little enough."

He lifted her chin with the end of his horsewhip.

"Damnation to your insolence!"

"And damn your methods of cheap labour." She pulled the whip aside, holding tightly to the end. "I'll work hard for as long as I'm needed. That, you say, is the agreement, but as soon as I'm free of you I'll go with a smile and a whistle."

He pulled the whip free of her grasp.

"You speak wildly for someone I could crush as easily as an egg."

"I can bide my time."

"But you'll always be needed! That's how I get my fields clear of weeds when others can't. I'd love to employ children, they're even cheaper, but the law won't let me, and I'm certainly not paying for men."

"I'll not be here long. One way or another."

"You think that? You have a lot to learn." He pointed to the other women still bent in work. "They too thought like you. Now look at them. Timid little peasants grateful to take the few coins I give them. I know what it is, you despise me for what I have."

She shook her head.

"Not for what you have, but for what you *are*. I've no use for wealth. Just enough to get by is sufficient for me. I could never make people work against their will. It's inhuman."

"Fine words that cut no ice when I sit up here and you stand in the mud. Around here people do what I want. Be warned. I keep a special watch out for troublemakers. Nip them in the bud, so to speak."

"Inflict hurt, you mean."

"It's amazing what a bit of gentle persuasion can do. Makes folk see things as they really are. Shows them the light, so to speak. Points out a few home truths. If necessary, I get my men to smash a few things and that seems to clear the fug."

"Arms, legs? That kind of persuasion?"

He grinned, assured of his power.

"Why would I do that? Put myself on the wrong side of the law? For what? You forget, I own everything around these parts. You women are nothing without me, and have nothing. No cottages, no money, no food and no hope. What do I need with violence? There's no law against me damaging my own property. A roof or maybe a water pump. I could burn Shalhurn to the ground and spit on the embers and nobody could do anything about it. I own it all and that's a fact. Where would you go if I demolished your cottage for its land? Ah? Weep in the ashes I expect whilst I rode back for lunch from a silver plate, without a care in the world."

"We're all free people."

"Only in your mind. Nobody's really free who looks to someone else for a living. The only way to be free if you don't own land is to be dead."

"We're getting a dog."

"Good. You might need something to eat if you cross me again."

"You're evil!"

He laughed.

"You still don't understand. I forgive you for that. Look, the mortification of wenches in my fields, and all over England's countryside for that matter, is the natural order of things. There have to be the poor to make the rich, because without the rich there's no investment in the land. Then the country would go back to the Middle Ages. It's as right as . . . the sheep we fatten and slaughter. Not too nice for the sheep, but the city diner doesn't care. You infer that you have ill luck to be here, when you really mean ill fortune. It all comes back to wealth and position in the end. It's not luck you need, but money and marriage, and from what I hear you have neither."

"Marriage, Sir, I can make, but you hold the balance of my happiness at this time and from what you say I have no influence over that. Time will tell how it will be resolved. I will work for you until then, but without respect."

Angered, he slashed a path across her shoulder with his whip. She winced with new pain.

"Don't need violence, ha?" she cried.

"You *still* think I can be beaten?"

"More than ever."

She turned, still holding her shoulder.

"I haven't finished with you yet!"

She ignored him. He called again, but she continued to walk away, not daring to look back, but listening in case he followed. Her steps quickened as she passed the other women.

Where Verity had left the hacker a starling perched on the handle, maybe the same bird that lived at the cottage. She tried to suppress her tears, but her shoulder hurt so much. The little bird hopped towards her. It was a friend in the darkness of this bad place. Once again she raised her arm, but the movement scared it off. She watched as it flew two huge circles, coming down only paces away. This time she remained motionless. Its head twitched as it looked about for danger. She took a step and stopped. Quite suddenly it made several sprightly hops forwards, then, losing its nerve, flew off and down into the valley. She watched it swoop, landing on the coulter of Jack's stationary plough. So it was the same little bird, she thought to herself.

Midday passed without further incident. DeByers had gone and Breaker used a handcart to carry the small piles of weeds to a large fire that was raging in a corner. A light drizzle began to fall, and as mothers left the furrows to put their children under cover, Breaker decided to call a halt for lunch.

"Oh no, he's back," said a woman, nudging Verity with her elbow.

DeByers stood at the far end of the field, tying his horse to the fence.

"What should I do if he comes over?" she asked, her lips tight and dry.

"Keep your nerve. If we stay together you should be okay."

"He's coming! Oh God!"

As he approached the friend got up.

"Don't go," Verity begged. "You said you would stay."

She shrugged and left.

"I just called on Jack Mere," said DeByers. "We had a good chat. Apologised for disturbing you last night, not that I remember much of it. Gave him a shilling. He seemed ready to let bygones be bygones."

"Did he?" she answered with indifference.

"Didn't mention our little argument this morning. Best put it behind us. What do you say?"

"Maybe, if I'm now left in peace."

He leaned back against a post, removing his hat and drinking from a hip flask.

"It's best if we all understand each other and our respective positions around here. Let's say we got off to a bad start."

Verity packed her cake into the basket and pulled the cover over Christabel.

"Ignoring me?"

"No, Sir."

"But not willing to talk?"

"I would rather not."

He looked away, pretending indifference.

"Of course, there's the serious matter of the cob."

Verity looked up, horrified.

"What about it?" she asked meekly, controlling her racing thoughts.

"It's gone! There yesterday, gone today. Like magic. Believe in magic Verity Bates?"

"No, Sir."

"Now, the question is, what should I do about it?"

A chill pierced through her.

"Have you decided?"

"Not yet. Of course, I didn't tell Jack that. No point in spoiling his day. He thinks it's all forgive and forget."

"But it isn't, I suppose?"

"You see, it's a question of the greater good. My cob versus Jack's freedom. Let's examine the facts. You and I don't see eye to eye over this work yet, do we?"

"I don't know," she mumbled, cornered for the first time by Jack's rash actions.

"Then we'll take it a step at a time . . . Yes? No?"

"Maybe."

"You still don't get it, do you? Look around at the other women. Do you really think they labour any harder than their kind in the cotton mills of the north or the match girls of London, or could clear more furrows a day if I paid an extra two pence? I would be the only loser in such an arrangement. They know their place, even if you don't yet, and make the best of what they get. You think having a cottage and land down in the valley sets you apart, as they have no land to fall back on, and yet even you have to dig my soil when I demand it. Where's the difference? Woman are such fools, but a hard season's work often helps to clear the mind."

Verity felt contempt. To him they were cattle, or worse, to be manipulated and used. A means to an end, without fear or feeling. On balance, she preferred the conflict of their first meeting to this exaggerated talk. How different he was to James Elvington, and so much coarser in finer clothes.

"*There is* a way out of the impasse."

"Is there?" she enquired suspiciously.

"You scratch my back and in return I'll let Jack off the hook. Everyone benefits that way and Jack need never know how you saved his neck."

"What do you want of me now?"

"I have feelings, you know, my own needs that money alone can't satisfy."

"Oh, here we go. I should have guessed. It always comes down to sex in the end, doesn't it? I'm poor so I must be available. Only, because of Jack, you want it for nothing. Or do you think I'm secretly gagging for you? Well, Sir, here's my answer. You have money, so buy yourself a whore."

"I'm trying to."

"How dare you."

"Don't deny it. I see a swelling under your dress, yet no ring is on your finger."

"You don't understand."

"Oh, but I do."

"Just go or *I will* tell Jack, and that's a promise."

"Then you like the stain of weeds on your hands and the smell of sweat on your body?"

"At least they're virtuous."

DeByers called for Breaker to bring over his horse. He mounted.

"You know you'll finish up like the rest of the hags out there. Is that really what you want? Or will you let me show you an escape?"

"Mount your horse, Sir, not me."

"I offer you a way out and you throw it back in my face."

"You say you do, and maybe it's true. If it's a cleaner job with less bending over, I'll gladly accept. If it's anything else, then I'll stay here."

"Bending! Oh yes, you'd bend all right." He laughed. "You ought to know the way of things, being a country girl. One day you'll beg me for it!"

"I don't think so." Her look gave him no hope. "You can do your worst. Nothing would be as bad as touching you."

"And what role have you for the arsonist in your plans?"

"Jack will understand, whatever comes of us."

"Then damn you. I want no more than any normal man. Try me for just one day, then decide. One day against the value of a cob building, it's a fair trade. Do it! Put yourself in my hands and for a while you can enjoy the fruits without labour. Any number of these women know what I can do for you. They lived better for a while and found me generous." He offered a hand. "Come with me now, this very minute, and I'll bring you back in plenty of time to leave with the others. Jack Mere won't know and your debt will be settled."

She backed away.

"Come on. You're not even married. I don't want commitment, and false affection as you say I can buy in town along any street corner. You don't like me? Okay, I can live with that. In fact, I find it exciting. Let me show you what I've learned from a thousand willing women while you kick back. I guarantee you'll get pleasure beyond anything you've known."

She feared the wrong answer, knowing he spoke one truth, that Jack's future lay in her hands. Slowly, deliberately, she turned away, taking each step as it came. He shouted after her angrily.

"Very well. Since I cannot convince you to see me as a benefactor, I'll have you crawl across my land. You'll need no reminding that I own your destiny."

The final working hours seemed to last an eternity, but presently the light faded and Jack reappeared at the gate. Verity was almost overcome to see him, to feel the security of his touch. She gathered Christabel and strolled back to the cottage. Jack seemed to have gained new strength.

"What's troubling you, sweetheart? You're very quiet."

In the distance she could see the burnt patch where the cob had stood.

"Oh. Nothing much. Take no notice."

"Women's things?"

"Something like that."

Jack, being less complicated in his thinking than Verity, immediately dropped the subject. He told her excitedly of his day and his plans for the coming weeks. She put her finger to his lips.

"Not now, darling."

They went indoors.

Jack had pushed all thoughts of yesterday's intruder to the back of his mind by the time his head hit the pillow that night. The room was black and his eyelids further compounded the darkness. He hadn't even kissed her. She wouldn't have noticed anyway, being completely wrapped up in her own thoughts. But return he, she or it did, with a bang!

Jack's subconscious heard a noise, but his body refused to believe it. He didn't care so long as he was left alone, but Verity sat up wide-eyed, poking him.

"Oh God, no!" he mumbled into his pillow.

"Jack. *Jack!* There's someone outside."

He turned over.

"*Jack*. Wake up will you."

"Leave me be woman."

"Jack!"

He didn't move. "Okay, I'll go then."

She had hit his weak spot.

"Don't bother," he whispered as his leg felt for the floor.

Lighting a lamp wasn't easy with shaky hands and tired eyes, but once the wick was glowing he took his jacket, unbolted the door and went out into the bleakness. It was cold, very cold. He shivered, wishing he had put on more clothes. There wasn't time to go back. A definite grunt and moan came from the stable. Holding the lantern high, he approached cautiously. A dim glow exuded from inside. Pressing his head against the slats, he listened. The noises stopped.

Carefully, he reached for the lift-catch. It was tied back. Taking a knife from his jacket, he put a shoulder to one door and gently pushed to force a gap. His fingers slipped through and the string was cut. At last he could see inside, where feet stuck out from the wooden cattle manger. Hugging the wall, he approached, taking slow, deliberate steps. At last he could make out the outline of a man, bathed in the soft glow of a shaded lamp. Stretching for a spade, he held it high and then in a mighty one-handed swipe crashed the flat metal down onto the man's leg.

"Oh, my God, don't kill me," screamed the man, springing up in a frenzy, but collapsing into a heap on the floor.

Jack knew the voice. He dropped the tool and took his shoulders. The man hobbled to a tub, moaning in agony.

"Bloody hell. You've broken my kneecap."

Jack sliced the man's trouser leg and brought the light closer, feeling the bone.

"Ow! What are you playing at, you bloody moron?"

"I don't think it's broken."

"Bloody feels like it."

"Best get you indoors. Put your arm around me."

The man stood painfully, limping to the cottage.

Behind the door Verity was waiting with a raised frying pan.

"Sir?" she said in amazement, just in time to stop the swing.

"Is *she* going to hit me now?" enquired James Elvington as he felt for a chair.

"What happened, Jack?" asked Verity in a panic.

"My fault," returned James, wincing as Jack pulled off his boot.

"Goodness, that's quite a wound. Let me bathe it," said Verity, taking a bowl. "The water's still warm on the range."

Jack poured two mugs of ale, heated by a poker pulled from the embers in the grate.

"What are you doing here, Sir, if you don't mind me asking?"

"I suppose I owe you an explanation. Ow! Go gently with the rubbing, Madam. The simple truth is, I'm in hiding."

"What?" returned Verity in shocked tone. Jack shushed her quiet.

"Maybe hiding's not the right word." He turned to face Jack. "I can't say I like you, Mere, but this is your home and you deserve some kind of proper explanation."

Verity dried his wound.

"Thank you, my dear. Now, where was I? Oh yes. You'll have to indulge me, but I can't easily explain if I don't recount what's happened over the last few days. Let's see. Where to start? Well, soon after you left Westkings I took an acquaintance to her home town."

"A lady, Sir?"

"Indeed so. It was for the most noble of reasons, you understand. I meant to take her part of the way, but the company was good and I offered her the whole journey. I meant to go on to Glastonbury that day, but my plans changed." He whispered to Jack. "I stayed overnight."

Jack acknowledged with a slight nod.

"You won't tell anyone, man?"

"Of course not! I know how much we owe you."

"I should jolly well think so. Anyhow, after that I couldn't be bothered to go on to Glastonbury at all. Business had lost its urgency, if you understand me. Yet if I returned to Westkings I could be contacted and awkward questions might be asked. Didn't want that either. Well, not yet. I need to be free of pressures and people for a while. There was also a little matter of revenge!"

"Against us?"

"Yes . . . no . . . well against you, Mere, not her. Anyway, I'll come to that. I needed to be anonymous, so I couldn't stay with friends, and inns were out."

"So you came here because nobody else knows of our little arrangement and you could attack me at the same time," added Jack defensively. "Kill two birds with one stone. Only my spade stopped you, didn't it? If that's the truth of the matter, you're not welcome."

"Calm yourself, man! There's more to it. I haven't been myself since you and Charlotte . . . Not going to Glastonbury gave me time to dwell on my problems, to which I now add my own unfaithfulness. You've got one hell of a lot to answer for, Mere. Taking Christabel from us served my purpose at the time but you've really messed up everything for me. Yet, if truth be told, *you've* only gained by it. I thought you ought to suffer a bit as well, and I was determined it should be so. To keep this place secret, even to the coachman, I was set down on the main road. I walked the rest of the way.

I hid from you, moving between the stable and that ramshackle building you burned down, waiting for the moment to strike. You nearly caught me once, but you scared me too much to make a move last night. Believe it or not, I hadn't a plan of what to do to you. Burning your cob crossed my mind too, knowing it would deprive you of a building and probably get you into very hot water with DeByers. It seemed a perfect crime for a while, but then you beat me to it. Today, when I saw you three together, I realised that I hadn't the right to spoil your lives. I was going to move on, but strangely the thought of roughing it for another night almost appealed. Total anonymity. For the first time in my life nobody can reach me or ask anything of me. Can you understand that? Nobody knows about this place, but us and my solicitor. I had intended to knock tonight for a bed, but I felt too ashamed to ask. Anyway, you needn't be frightened, I'm now going to leave you in peace."

"I'm grateful for that. Well, we both are, but what of your wife, Sir?"

"She's settled, although I don't like you asking after her. Let me tell you, it hasn't been easy this past while. So much has happened in as many days. I think she's taken to the habit of criticising me in front of other people. I've lost at least one good friend. She used to think the sun shone out of my . . . excuse me, Verity. Let's say it now glows dimly."

"What will you do?"

"First things first. A bed for the night?"

"Ah, yes, of course. You'll have to take ours. Verity and I can sleep down here. I'll stoke up the fire."

"Won't think of it. I'm fine on this chair. Just give me a blanket."

Verity had been looking forward to her first visitors, but this wasn't to plan. They huddled in bed, warming each other.

"It's a funny old world, isn't it, Jack? Just think, *we're* entertaining the old master."

"He don't like me."

"Can you blame him? He was pleasant enough under the circumstances. You can't expect miracles. Did you mention our trouble with DeByers?"

"Blimey, no!"

"You must do it first thing in the morning. First thing mind. What a stroke of luck. I think someone's looking after us."

"Seems so."

The next day was bright and sunny. Verity descended the stairs.

"Where's the master?"

"He's already gone."

"Oh, Jack!"

He held her.

"I know, I know. Life's a sod after all."

CHAPTER XI

Verity's homecoming

*T*he lamplight was gentle and the conversation soft as the Meres sat to an early breakfast. Jack had already been out rabbiting along the lane, away from the DeByers' estate, but had returned empty-handed with his gun broken under his arm. Verity was on edge. Her hands shook, though she still managed to force a smile. A ludicrous situation. Only three days had been spent in the cottage and already more unexpected things had happened than might have been reasonable for a dozen years.

Verity's cheerfulness was half-hearted, though, but enough to fool Jack. He was so enthusiastic for the coming hours and what might be achieved, that he couldn't contemplate Verity being any different. She wanted Jack to walk with her to the top field, but felt that she couldn't ask. He was champing at the bit to plough another acre. He was happy, so she let him go.

Only Breaker turned up to oversee the work, and when at midday they stopped for food she felt a good deal better. Christabel had cried for most of the morning, but now nestled warmly and contentedly in Verity's arms, sucking on a bottle.

"A pretty sight!"

She turned abruptly to see DeByers approaching. He had risen late.

"You have a handsome child."

His tones were new and unexplained.

"Thank you, Sir."

He sat beside her, leaving sufficient gap between them to prevent anxiety. Christabel's tiny fingers touched the ring on his outstretched hand.

"Perhaps she would wish you to have a ring like mine?"

"I'm sure it would be wasted on me," was her quiet reply.

"But every woman longs for beautiful things," he commented assuredly, "and how much better it would look on your dainty hand than mine."

He took it off and tried to slip it over Verity's finger.

"No, I don't want to try it, with respect, Sir."

"Oh, very well, silly girl. I didn't mean you to keep it."

DeByers, believing Verity's snubs had resulted from his naturally abrupt manner, had decided to try a new ploy and push brightness ahead of hostility. He would woo rather than frighten, disarming her by offering no threat. If that got her into his bed, then the result would be the same and the gesture worthwhile.

"She'll soon be dancing to his tune," offered a young girl, seeing them talking.

"Not that one," replied Beth, a woman a few years older. "She has a man. I think this time the master won't get his way."

"Then she's a fool to herself. Didn't do you no harm. I bet you enjoyed the life of a lady while it lasted."

Beth looked ashamed.

"I wish I'd never clapped eyes on him, or him me. I was fooled into thinking he thought special of me. He said I was . . ." She bowed her head. "Should have known different. I hope his body is burnt to ashes."

DeByers took out a hunter watch and sprang the silver cover.

"Breaker wanted to make an example of you, by letting you go without pay, but I stopped him."

"Thanks, for nothing!" said Verity sarcastically, putting Christabel on the ground.

"You know, it would be so much more pleasant for everyone if you accepted your commitment to me as inescapable. I couldn't believe the terms and conditions James what's-his-name wanted me to agree to when he negotiated for your cottage. Sent me a letter spelling it all out. Me, who was farming when he was sucking the breast. He even had the barefaced cheek to tell me to mechanise, and spouted all sorts of newfangled ideas on spreading chemicals. Where's the profit in it? I asked him. Couldn't answer that. Won't buy any more of his fencing timber, though. That'll teach him to interfere in my business. Now, as to us . . ."

His words had hardly left his lips when Verity suddenly flung out her hand and gripped his arm tightly. Her eyes screwed up as she held her stomach.

"What is it?" he asked, wide-eyed.

"Oh God. The pain!"

"The baby?"

She nodded.

"What can I do?"

"Get help. Hurry!"

She turned to Beth, moaning loudly, but as he jumped in panic, he caught Beth's returning wink.

"Nice try," he shouted, his jaw hollowed in a fit of temper. "What a dreadful thing to do, by anyone's standards. By God, the battle of willpower goes on?"

Without warning he lunged at Beth, grabbing her by the bonnet and pulling a knot of hair between clenched fingers. He pressed her cringing face close to Verity's, her eyes popping.

"See this pox-ridden excuse for a woman? I've had her!"

Slowly and bravely Verity rose and prised his fingers loose. Although he could have resisted, he let go. Beth dropped to the ground, holding her head and crying. Panting hard and furiously, he used the underside of his boot to push her over. She rolled submissively.

"For pity's sake, stop it!" shouted Verity, helping Beth up. "You're poisonous."

"Poisonous eh? Right, I'll show you."

His clenched fist, now white at the knuckles, readied to strike.

"No! Get away from her! I beg you."

"See, *you* made me do that" he shouted, waving a menacing finger at her. "It was all your fault. I came down here to be nice. I can be nice. You are responsible for what I did. I could have hit you both and feel no shame."

"You just did!"

"Well, for that I'm sorry. You shouldn't provoke me."

"You're nothing but a wild animal."

"I'm a man of responsibility," he returned in a trembling voice.

"You wouldn't do it if my Jack was here."

"Your Jack, your Jack! It's always your bloody Jack getting in the way. Well he ain't here. He's nothing to me. He'll never amount to anything."

"That's where you're wrong. He'll make a go of things. He's twice the man you are."

"So be it. I've tried with you. No more! You can rot in the decay of poverty. I'll rub your face in the muck so deep you'll eat worms. I'll have you dig when the ground's cold and hard, and stoke blazing fires when it's blistering hot. You'll crawl over my land like those other broken maggots and look like them in a year."

"To eat soil is preferable to chicken in your company."

He looked across at Beth, grabbing her by the arm.

"You coming?" he called firmly, looking all the time at Verity.

She nodded compliantly. Verity shook her head in disbelief.

"My belly aches from hard bread," said Beth timorously. "I want a moment of comfort. Tell Hilda to look after my baby."

He led her from the field. That night Beth conceived her second child.

From the end of a furrow Verity looked down into the valley. Jack was below as before, jauntily walking behind the plough.

"Oh, Jack," she prayed to the wind, "if only I was down there with you. I'm bursting to work by your side. Only now I wish you were here to protect me from something I can't tell you about for fear of your arrest."

DeByers didn't return the following day or the next, but on the fifth he was seen in an adjacent field silhouetted on horseback against the rising sun. The first field was still heavy with witch grass and Breaker was in a sour mood.

It was the ceaselessness of the hand-picking that Verity hated, every long row abutted by another wanting attention and with only the occasional trip to the tip piles relieving back pain. The only meagre consolation was that the nine pence was paid daily, helping to eke out the money put by.

Verity had made a good friend of Josie Pruett, a girl of similar age and intelligence, although Josie lived on a nervous knife-edge thanks to constant scolding from mindless parents. Whenever possible they worked together, with only a furrow between them.

Verity stepped up to Josie in self-sacrificing mood, removing her gloves and pulling at her friend's shoulder.

"He's back!"

"I know."

Josie, a good natured, but plain girl, became anxious that Verity shouldn't be left alone with DeByers when work stopped for lunch. She took Verity's arm and together they marched off to the far end of the field where they sat with their backs against a simple rain shelter.

"By the way, did you hear what Dorothy was saying?"

"What about?" enquired Verity.

"Why, Beth of course. It seems that Dorothy was taking some eggs to market when she saw DeByers and Beth passing in his cob. She waved to her, but Beth turned away and put up a new parasol, the tiniest thing the size of a plate."

"I hadn't heard that."

"Wait, there's more. A little later Dorothy was passing the iron-mongers when she saw the cob outside. She snooped through the window and spied Beth arguing with the shopkeeper. It seems that DeByers was buying her a mirror, but whichever one she was given she didn't like the reflection that came back and blamed imperfections in the glass. In the end DeByers got so cross he took down a carpet beater and gave her a thoroughly good thrashing in front of everybody."

"Blimey. What happened next?"

"Beth stormed out, bumped into Dorothy and ran off. DeByers went the opposite way. That was the day before yesterday, and now comes the best bit. DeByers apparently didn't know that Beth's father is Slimy Grimms the knacker. He's a great big, drunken mule of a chap."

"And?"

"Be patient and I'll tell you. Anyway, yesterday, after downing a few quarts of ale, Slimy staggered up to the big house, shouting for DeByers to come out and face him for abusing his daughter. Of course, DeByers wasn't going to do any such thing so, getting no answer, he busted the door in. On the way over he'd picked up a dead fox and, holding it by the tail, he started banging it about like a hammer on the furniture. Blood and guts went everywhere. DeByers should've stayed quiet, but instead he screamed for the servants to save the china. Only, he'd forgotten that he'd given most of them the night off on account of the woman he'd brought back, who was even then warming his bed. Those servants who were left in the house knew Slimy by reputation and weren't getting involved."

DeByers had been watching the destruction from the top of the stairs and, wanting to save the last of the china, locked the upper rooms, putting the keys in his pocket. Only, when he heard Slimy coming up he realised he'd been stupid because he had nowhere to hide and couldn't find the right key to fit any lock. In panic he hid behind the landing curtain. That would've been that, but when Slimy reached the top the effort went to his head and he tumbled down the stairs again, taking the curtain with him. According to

Collins the footman, who is Dorothy's boyfriend, in the confusion DeByers tripped over the curtain pole that had ripped from the wall. He too went headlong down the stairs after Slimy. When the rumpus was over and the dust settled, DeByers was out cold with his head on Slimy's chest, as would a couple of newly-weds, the curtain over them like a blanket and the fox's head poking out the top. Heaven knows what would have happened if Slimy had awakened first."

Verity broke open a loaf, which they shared with a wedge of strong cheese and cakes. She tried not to notice DeByers as he strolled over and stood in front with legs apart and arms crossed. She continued eating in his uncomfortable shadow.

"Here I am again."

"So I see," was her uninviting reply.

"What of my new suit? Does it not look well co-ordinated? A proper dandy, am I not?"

"The blue certainly matches the swelling around your eyes," she said with a sideways grin to Josie.

"Oh, that. Fell off me damned horse. How about the cut of the jacket?"

"Trimming your whiskers and changing your coat doesn't alter the inner man, but I suppose it suits you."

"There. I knew it." He smiled at her eating. "My aunt used to bake cakes like that when I was a boy. Hers had icing in two colours. They took patience to make, but she had plenty of time after my father and uncle copped it in the Crimea. I used to stuff cakes in my pockets and eat them up the nearest tree. Always tasted best twenty feet above ground. Funny that."

"Childish things."

"Yes, but memories are important to cling to. If I should ever have a son I would know not to mind if he ate them up a tree, even if he tore his trousers. No need to get upset. Shouldn't beat a lad for that." He became conscious of his own voice. ". . . You're right. Damn silly nonsense."

Verity studied his anguished look.

"That explains a thing or two."

"What?"

"I mean, you *have* a son."

"I most definitely do not!"

"Yes you do, Beth's."

"Oh him! No, he's a bastard."

"He's *your* bastard."

"Not so. Could be anyone's. Show me the proof."

"You want a son, you have one. Why not accept it?"

"That peasant boy became an outcast the moment he took a breath. His mother should have been more careful."

"Don't you feel anything for him? What if he died?"

"He's merely a drain on the capital growth of our country. I'll not part with a penny to support him. If his mother can't cope, it might be best if she expires with him."

"Do you care where Beth is now?"

"Which Beth? I know so many."

"The woman with the ginger hair you fancied yesterday."

"How should I know, and I care even less, and I'll not be upset by your tone either. She's had her moment. Twice, in fact. Room now for someone new. Changed your mind yet?"

She turned away.

"Come, walk with me. I've much to discuss."

Verity ignored his outstretched hand.

"I'm quite settled here."

"I'll not take no for an answer. If I trouble you it's because we never have a chance to talk properly."

"I wonder why? Perhaps it's because you've done nothing but threaten me ever since I first came to Shalhurn."

"I admit I've been a little hard, but now do me the courtesy of hearing me out in privacy. I promise I'll not lay a hand on you."

"No, Sir. I'll finish my lunch."

"What if I open up my heart to you and say I'm tortured in my desire?"

"I'd know it to be false."

"And if I swear to speak not as a worldly man, but as a person haunted by a spectre that cannot be reached? And if I added that my harshness is left dry, my willpower shattered, and that you brought on this reformation. What then?"

"I'd laugh in your face. I too can't make someone understand and that someone is you! I don't care for your games, favours or furrows. Get it into your head that I won't go with you now or ever, and nothing you can offer will make me change my mind. Look at my expression and know that I mean it, and end the playing once and for all. Your piety is as sincere as quicksand. I'm not flattered. I don't like you. Do us both a favour and pick on someone else."

"Don't deceive yourself. I may not be much to look at, but my money makes up for my appearance, or so I find. Around here you might be considered pretty, but go to the city and you'd be lost among the faces. To be thought pretty in Dorchester you have to be beautiful, to be noticed you have to be stunning. It's the way of the outside world."

"Then you belong in that world and me in this. Hate and despise me all you like, but go away."

He held his rising temper.

"As you see, I'm a sufficiently changed person not to go on arguing. One day you'll regret this, when you find Jack Mere backsliding. I'll be generous despite your wicked tongue and leave the door ajar for when you come."

"I will not, 'cos he'll not."

"That's as might be. I think differently." He began to walk away, but turned, giving a backward grey-toothed leer. "You may call on me this evening if you wish. I'll be ready."

"No!"

"Perhaps you won't at that." He took two more steps. "But not before eight o'clock, mind. I'll be dining until then."

Verity and Josie returned to their hackers, Josie with a million questions buzzing around in her head. On the far side of the field

DeByers ordered Breaker to have the land cleared of witch grass that day, however long it took. He made no exceptions to the rigours and all breaks were cancelled. To sustain the pace, a water bucket was brought to the workers every hour.

Verity instinctively looked towards the gate, not surprised to see DeByers perched on the uppermost bar, a hamper at his feet brought from the big house. He waved back, pointing to the food. She looked away. Each time she drank from the bucket his eyes met hers, raising a full glass of claret urbanely and blowing a kiss.

The afternoon passed and still many furrows remained untouched. The light dimmed into a pallid sunset, then to the incandescent moon, the dark soil becoming almost invisible. Extra fires were lit at intervals along the field, casting a copper glow that seemed to stick to the very sweat of their skin. All were pained and weary. The piles of weed for burning had grown large and Breaker struggled to keep pace.

Trips to the tip piles became more frequent as muscles ached from bending. Verity worked in a dream-like state, since darkness had blotted out all sight of DeByers.

Jack, who had come to meet Verity, offered to help her to finish, but Breaker refused to let him. Instead, he took Christabel back to the cottage, where she now lay safely tucked up in her cot. The other children still left in the field cried incessantly in the darkness, their young guardian himself in floods of tears.

The final hour hardened Verity's resolve. The last furrows around the edges were cosmetic to the overall farming needs, for here tramping horses would prevent anything worthwhile growing, and plucking witch grass was a pointless exercise. She also knew that it was her unwillingness towards DeByers that held them all in labour longer than was necessary. This was a hard burden to bear as she watched the old women suffer cramp in pained silence.

Jose had increased the speed of her digging as darkness fell, fearing the solitary walk back to Valbrook, which lay on the far side of the friary. She dug with experience and soon left Verity behind.

The evening turned bitter. Breaker decided to allot final furrows to each woman in the hope that a definite end to their work would act as a spur to greater effort. One by one the women removed the grey rags that bound their legs and left the field for the few comforts home could provide.

By nine o'clock only a handful of women remained. Verity had the most to do. Josie, exhausted but afraid for Verity, completed her own last row and then began working backwards along the straggler's furrow until DeByers called her off. Still Josie wouldn't abandon Verity, and she waited patiently by the hedgerow until her friend too had finished. By the white light of the half-moon they walked out arm in arm, taking separate directions at the road.

Going home after fifteen hours in the field was like waking from a seemingly endless nightmare. The feeling of relief was almost too good to be true. The only cloud was the thought of coming back the next day for new work.

The nightmare wasn't over. Within minutes of leaving Josie, Verity sensed DeByers walking a pace behind her in an unsettling manner. She stopped and turned.

"Please, Sir, leave me. Why do you follow?"

He laughed, pulling a hip flask from his jacket pocket. Not daring to look back again, she quickened her pace, her arms crossed to pin down the corners of her shawl. Every step brought her nearer home, but also into growing bleakness as the moonbeams became hidden by the increasing height of the hedgerow. She could easily detect his heavy steps behind.

"Please, you're frightening me," she said without slowing her walk.

He matched her stride for stride.

"Go away!"

They passed the church and he knew time was short. With determined step he overtook, grabbing her arm tightly and bringing her down with a twist of the wrist. She cowered below his stare, but then, just as suddenly, a familiar figure burst through the darkness. He snapped cold fingers around DeByers' neck with such violence that it rendered him paralysed. DeByers struggled, but Jack's hold was rock solid. Looking up into Jack's angry eyes, DeByers let go of Verity and fell to his knees. Only after Verity had hidden behind his back did Jack slowly release his hand.

"You're as good as dead," croaked DeByers. "You and her. Get out of my cottage by daybreak tomorrow or I'll have the police on you for burning my property."

Jack squashed DeByers back to the ground.

"We'll see about that. Verity, this came by hand."

Jack passed a letter that bore the Elvington seal. She quickly tore around the wax and scanned the contents. With a broad smile, she thrust it at DeByers.

"Read it yourself. It's from Westkings. You had no right making me work and now I have the proof. The letter says that you must relieve me at once or legal action will follow."

She waved it triumphantly in his face. He knocked it from her hand without reading it, treading on it as he got up and left.

"Talk about lucky! That came just in the nick of time," said Jack giving her a hug.

"Luck didn't come into it, but I'm glad he didn't bother to read it."

"Huh?"

"Because, Jack my old simpleton, it says nothing about work."

Jack stared in surprise. A grin formed across his face.

"Well? What does it say, then?"

She picked it up and flattened the creases.

"It's from the master, right enough. It says –"

"Hang on, Veri. I'm your master now."

She squeezed him.

"You're right, me lad. It says James Elvington has gone back to Midford, and he would be obliged if we don't say anything of his visit and are ignorant of his whereabouts should anyone ask."

"Midford. I wonder where that is."

"Remember, Jack. Nobody must know he came here."

"Which he didn't."

"That's me lad."

"And *you* don't have to worry about that rogue any more. He won't come near you like a dog to a bitch in season. He knows what he'll get if he does. Come on. Let's go home. Tomorrow you too can work our land."

The very thought warmed Verity. Hand in hand they entered the sparsely furnished cottage where Christabel waited. Verity was home.

"Life is just beginning for us, isn't it, Jack?"

So it was that the fields of April turned lush as the summer sun warmed the good earth, and on the once bare ploughed acres wheat turned from short, swaying green to tall stems of gold. Then summer faded into autumn and Verity blossomed as the child grew within her, but, although Jack worked from morning to night, his meagre prosperity was never fully realised. One field that backed on to the church remained dormant the seasons around, and try as he might he could do nothing to encourage growth.

Winter came and preparations were made for the new year's crop. Jack had not given up on the waste field and in this he spent many anxious hours reducing the soil to a fine tilth to give it every advantage.

Christmas month arrived and Verity readied the home for the new arrival. Jack had prepared another bedroom that was to become Christabel's, the girl now crawling freely and giving her parents joy beyond measure. It never once occurred to them that she wasn't of Verity's own body and, in turn, Christabel could want for no more caring guardians.

The day came for the birth. Jack had been sent out to the barren field while neighbours looked after the natural event taking place inside the cottage. Try as he may, however, he couldn't settle to anything much, so occupied were his thoughts on dearer matters. Having briefly looked over the soil for any signs of growth, he walked the boundary checking the drainage ditches before bad weather set in.

He was on the far side of the field when a woman ran towards him, drying her hands on a white pinafore. Jack dropped his ditch spade and rushed to meet her. She looked strained.

"Calm down, Jack lad. The news isn't good."

Jack glanced towards the cottage.

"In heaven's name what's happened?"

"It's Verity. Be brave, my boy. The good Lord has called her to his side."

Jack's eyes widened as the words sunk to the bottom of his consciousness.

"She's with her Maker now. All pain's gone. Take comfort in that."

The awfulness of her pronouncements were accepted without further explanation, for it was common for such tragedy at childbirth. Slowly his manly head lowered onto her shoulder and he sobbed uncontrollably.

"That's right. Let it all out."

She kept perfectly still, stroking his hair until he finally wiped his bloodshot eyes and walked purposefully towards his home and Verity. He climbed the steep stairs, down which he had slipped so many times, and entered the bedroom. The neighbours stood back, revealing Verity calm among the covers. Her face was pale, but full of the peasant beauty that had attracted him so very much.

"Oh no! Please, no."

He took her yielding body in his arms and brought her tightly to him, tears flowing down his cheeks. Only now that he felt the absolute limpness did he fully understand that she was gone forever.

"Oh Verity, Verity." He rocked her with a gentleness unfitting his stature. "I love you. I love you so much." His grip tightened. He looked at the closest woman, who was full of pity.

"She's mine forever. You know that, don't you?"

She nodded understandingly. Carefully he eased her back onto the mattress.

"I never even married her!"

"She knew what she meant to you despite that."

"Are you sure? Are you truly sure?"

"Aye, Jack, and we'll all help you to raise Christabel. You're not alone me lad. We are here."

Jack managed to force a half-smile in appreciation. He wiped his nose on his sleeve.

"What of the baby? Did . . ."

A tiny white bundle lay in the corner.

"The good Lord took him too."

Jack carefully unwrapped part of the shawl to look on the baby's face for the first and last time. Such innocence was revealed. In silence he covered it again.

"The child was as beautiful as his mother."

"Did Verity see him?"

"No, lad, I don't think she did. Be thankful in that, for he never took a breath."

Jack's eyes passed between the helpless bundle and his lifeless love. He took the child and put him into Verity's arms.

"Do you know what Verity once said to me when my crop failed in that bloody field?" He gulped. "She said, don't ask for the moon when you already have the stars." The thought overcame him. "But I want the moon and the stars. I want my family back!"

Fate had dealt a second cruel hand in the infant life of Christabel, who was now motherless, but the neighbours were as good as their word and over the years of her childhood they took care of her while Jack tended his land.

Jack became a model father, devoted to his child with an intensity that would have surprised anyone from his youthful days on the Elvington estate. He was often to be seen walking the short distance between the cottage and the church to tend the graves that lay together in the churchyard, taking flowers grown in a patch that Verity had cleared as a herb garden. In this way Jack watched over his beloved in death as he had in life, and Verity was down in the valley where she had longed to be forever.

CHAPTER XII

Doubts and discourse

*E*veryone has a sad story from their past that is remembered only when an event, word or happening triggers the memory. Christabel was no different. At seventeen years old, the memory of her mother could only be conjured up as an image formed from her father's descriptions. Jack had no photograph of Verity, but he often told her that by looking into the mirror she would indeed see the likeness of her mother, although secretly in his heart he meant her natural mother, Charlotte.

On one particular Monday morning a small congregation at Shalhurn church, comprising not only the usual women and girls, but a generous sprinkling of men, sank to their knees as Parson Trowsdale blessed farm ploughs that had been dragged before the altar. It was the Monday following Epiphany, Plough Monday, when man's dependence on the fruits of the earth was recognised in prayer.

The service over, the ploughs were manoeuvred back up the central passage under the fussing eye of the parson, whose "Oh!" rang out every time metal struck ornate wood. Onlookers remained seated until the aisle was cleared and the farmers gone, for it was still a working day and much had to be done within the few hours of winter light.

As the last plough cleared the door a well-dressed man rose furtively, each 'clip' from his leather boots on the bare grey stone punctuated by the 'click' of a steel-tipped cane. He had intended to leave unnoticed, but the parson was quick to reach the door, ready to accept any compliments from the congregation. The rich smile on Trowsdale's face dropped as he recognised the lined features of DeByers.

"Oh, sweet mercy!"

The perfect day ended, bittersweet before breakfast. Trowsdale swallowed nervously, but drove a hand forward.

"Welcome to this humble place of worship."

"Am I?" he asked sardonically.

"Are you what?"

"Welcome?"

"Indeed, yes. Moreso you than most."

"Ah! My reputation goes before me."

"You are known, Sir Kenneth."

"The intrigue is to know in what light, but I doubt you would want to tell me?"

Trowsdale blustered.

"It's enough that you're here. May I ask your purpose?"

"Do I need one?"

"No, of course not. It's God's open house. Only . . ."

DeByers looked up at the ceiling, scanning the elaborate carvings. The parson's eyes followed, but saw nothing unusual.

"Is there anything wrong with the structure?" asked Trowsdale gently.

DeByers remained deep in his own thoughts. The congregation pushed past until echoes faded into silence.

"Upon my word, Sir, I wonder if you might tell me what you look at?"

At last DeByers turned to face him, his weight bearing down on the sturdy cane. He was almost unsteady. His deep black eyes seemed less frightening, softened by the grey of his beard and hair.

"It's been a long time since I last came into the village. It holds associations best forgotten – I thought I had. Only, I can't explain why, but today I felt an irresistible urge to see it again. I thought I would find the answer here, but I haven't."

Trowsdale, still in his surplice, adopted his best clerical tone, feeling strangely superior on this occasion to the much feared DeByers.

"Then God has led you to my door. Come, follow me to the vestry where we can talk."

DeByers placed five pounds on the collecting tray.

"Pick up your money, Sir. You can't buy God's favours. If you want to give after we have spoken, it will then be welcomed. Firstly, you must believe the advice worth such a princely sum. Pay from the heart, not the pocket. Remember the parable of the rich man and the eye of the needle."

"And in remembering, I would have thought you would be saving my soul by helping me to part with my money."

"It doesn't work like that."

"It never does!"

DeByers stuffed the note uncaringly into his pocket and followed. The room was still and ageless. A window provided a view across the open fields to the trees beyond. The furniture was dark and heavy, well worn and scratched, but still of high lustre. Rows of ecclesiastical books lined the panelled walls. Trowsdale hung his surplice in a tall cupboard and they sat. The clock rattled off seven neat chimes.

"You know," began DeByers, "I'm not a religious man. I believe people make their own destiny. Maybe if I was religious I'd be a better person . . . Who can judge?"

"The Almighty judges us all by our deeds and by these alone may we enter the gates of heaven," replied Trowsdale in a well-worn monotone.

"Perhaps, but I doubt it."

Trowsdale walked over to a small table and poured two glasses of sweet wine from a nearly empty bottle, holding them up to the light and balancing the levels until both were exact measures. He handed one to DeByers.

"Tell me this," continued DeByers after a sip, "can you commit a sin by doing nothing? I mean to ease the suffering of another?"

"We're all the one body of Christ. You can sin against the lowest of the animals in such a way, even a flower if it is picked carelessly only to be crushed between your fingers, its beauty dishonoured. All living things are gifts from God. I believe it's the duty of those with much to help those with little. The wherewithal to give is something that only a few possess. In the religious and moral sense money is a hard burden, for those having it are under trial. I worry that in our time of industry and commerce simple compassion has been left walking while the world rushes ahead at full steam."

In normal circumstances DeByers would have thwarted such a suggestion, but not today. He was barely roused.

"Well, if you say so. I'll not argue."

"These are my views. What do you feel?"

"I feel, I suppose, like a shipwrecked sailor, cast adrift for the first time and yet strangely tempted to jump off the life raft."

"Go on."

"My mind keeps coming back to a vision from the past and I can't understand why. I thought it was long forgotten, but something has brought it back."

"It might have been the Lord's will that you should remember it again."

"Part of a larger plan?"

"Certainly."

"I can't believe that!"

"No! Then why come here? Listen, man, I beg you earnestly to take the wider view and trust in His wisdom, as I trust he'll guide me in what I might say."

He reached out a hand to comfort DeByers, but felt an unnatural coldness and withdrew it. He discreetly made the sign of the cross.

"You'd better tell all, before it's too late."

DeByers' humbled attitude confirmed his turmoil. He stood, shoulders bent, assuming the rigidity of the stones about.

"A man of my temperament stores up trouble. In a way it's bound to happen in my position. Believe me, you can't run an estate without incurring resentment. That's a burden that weighs heavy while young and impressionable, but with maturity one learns to laugh at the sneers of others. There's an art in getting the very last ounce of work from the poor without breaking their spirit to endure their ills. If I now care, I can only think that I'm entering my second childhood."

"Ah! So you do feel pity?"

"Not pity. Vulnerability!"

"Oh dear. Thinking of yourself again. I was rather hoping –"

"Stop . . . I know full well what you wanted, but it's not all self. I'll concede this much. I'll not bend to a living person, but I do worry about another."

"You present a riddle. You can't be telling me you worry over someone who is dead?"

"It was a long time ago. I forget quite how many years. I let a cottage and land to someone who came to the village to start a new life, but whose wife I treated badly."

"And now you feel remorse?"

DeByers ignored him.

"Only, you see, she died and I never made amends." He remembered her proud smile he had so often defeated. "I have to admit that I was rather taken by her, perhaps by the way she stood up to me even more than her natural beauty." He turned to face the inevitable scowl, but saw only compassion. "Oh, I know it was a sin as you see it, and no doubt you and your God reproach me, but, forgive me, she was someone I couldn't let go. Something special."

"Yes?"

"I wouldn't leave her be, even though I was rebuffed many times. I worked her hard despite her condition, and then, having been made to let her go, I found other small ways of making her life hard.

"How so?"

"Little ways, stupid ways, like having my men block their field drains. Nothing too serious, but very tiring to clear after other work. It was all so petty of me. So unnecessarily cruel."

"What are you telling me?"

"I think you know, and of whom I mean. She was pregnant. Oh, not by me, you understand, and her conception was quite new when she arrived. She must have done it behind my back, which, for reasons of anatomy, makes it impossible for me to have fathered the child." He tried a smile. It fell on stony ground. His cheeks dropped. "Only . . . Please forgive me . . . She died having that child and somehow I now see it was partly my doing."

"Remorse is to your credit, but I have to ask why you think her tragedy was your fault? Childbearing has its risks."

With pallid expression and eyes wide, but empty, he said sincerely:

"I don't actually know. I just feel that things might have been different. Truly I wish I could look into her eyes and beg her forgiveness, but it is too late . . . It's all too late."

"It is for her, I agree. So knowing that, what do you seek?"

"I've told you, I bloody well don't know."

The sudden terseness in his voice shocked Trowsdale.

"Forgive me. No, what I have just said isn't strictly true. I seek peace of mind . . . or something! A return to my harsher ways would be a kindness."

"For you, maybe. I doubt if others would view it as such. I can't absolve you of guilt and wouldn't if I could without more proof of contrition. You have built yourself a fearful reputation and in my judgement every curse on your head has been earned one hundred times over. Penance must come from inside your soul, but, if it's any comfort, I feel for your anguish. I will say this also, and I ask you to listen well. If you truly regret all that has passed, then the Almighty already knows it and you need nothing more from me.

What you seek is not within these walls and can't be seen or touched. You must feel for a change of heart, a rejection of bitterness, not look for absolution in the objects of man's own creation. These walls are stone and are no more than a rallying point for believers. Listen to yourself. Feel the warmth of brotherhood. Your heart has felt humility and you must let your soul know humanity. Can you admit that?"

Trowsdale was feeling the power of oration, even his own. He rose majestically and, with arms outstretched, shouted dramatically:

"Stand and say with me, I have sinned but I am from today reborn."

DeByers looked in amazement.

"I bloody well will not."

In a further flash of inspiration, Trowsdale grabbed him by the hand and began singing *Onward Christian Soldiers*. DeByers pushed him away, lunging for the door.

"Don't leave!" Trowsdale shouted, still in heavy inspiration. "Let's pray together."

DeByers drew out the five pound note and thumped it on the table.

"You've earned this."

"Then you repent?" he asked in musical voice.

"Then I go," DeByers said with contempt.

Trowsdale looked crushed and rather embarrassed.

"Look, Trowsdale. I understand you mean well, but I'm not ready for all that. It's not your fault. I may well be a hopeless case. I'm a sinner in your book and I suppose I'll die bad, as I have lived. Seek God's forgiveness, you say, well, maybe I will one day. You have given me much to think about. Only, why do I feel the memory today? That remains my mystery. What in heaven or earth has caused me to think of it at all?"

Trowsdale slumped on a seat, saying in soft tone:

"It isn't too late. Believe me. It was a colleague of mine who once said, 'the labouring class should see that for their employment and means of bountiful living they depend on the observance of the moral decencies, and thus should be left to experience the consequences of vice and of virtue'. Or words to that effect . . . Can't you see, my son, such observances apply equally to those who have been privileged with wealth? It's upon our moral and religious conduct that each of us stand or fall, and will be judged. I ask you sincerely, without peace of mind what is it all for?"

With a penitential shake of the head, DeByers left the room. He knew he had done wrong and didn't need telling, but why had he remembered that past incident?.

Trowsdale was left alone feeling inadequate. It hadn't been enough merely to say 'seek God and look to the inner man' to someone who had lived apart from his Maker and had found no inspiration from religion. The opportunity had been lost, probably for ever.

"But I tried," he murmured as he locked the vestry door, placing the money in his pocket. "I must buy some more sherry."

As DeByers left the church he turned once more in a final search of the pillars, walls and roof.

My life is haunted by bleakness, he thought to himself. Am I being prepared for death? Is this a final chance to absolve myself while there's still time? What should I do? A cold shudder pierced his spine.

A vole scampered timidly across the floor, taking angular dashes from pillar to post. It stopped in the shadow of DeByers, looked up, turned and ran for the darkest corner. DeByers raised his boot and crushed it until he heard the bones cracking.

"Such rubbish! Life goes on as before."

Outside, a small number of villagers huddled. Embarrassment at being seen in church quickened DeByers along the narrow path to the lane. Preoccupied, he didn't notice a stranger approaching on foot through the far gate, having tied his horse to a post. They collided before either could stand aside. The young man of about sixteen moved onto the grass verge, offering a one-sided apology. He looked wildly as DeByers pushed past.

Trowsdale gave a sigh of relief upon shaking hands with the jaunty young fellow, snapping him from his gloom.

". . . so you see, my mission is delicate and I trust you will treat it as such."

Trowsdale acquiesced happily.

"All I ask is that you point me in the right direction. No more."

He handed the parson a pound note for church funds, which was received with due deference. Although of transitional age between boy and man, the youth displayed all the bearing of someone well acquainted to position and responsibility, and found no difficulty addressing others on an equal basis who were many years his senior. He was, thereby, not at all put out by the chattering women and their giggling as he passed back down the path, and acknowledged them calmly with the slightest raising of his hat.

In an instant he was away and down the lane, riding as naturally as a cavalry officer. Beams of winter light caught the shine of his boots, and the metal of the harness was bejewelled. After a short trot he pulled up outside the last cottage. Christabel answered the door.

"Is this the Mere household?"

"Yes, Sir."

"Then may I speak privately? It's a matter of some importance."

She bade him enter. The youth knew nothing of Christabel and was interested only in Jack. He complimented her on how well the inside looked and that he had never seen cleaner, but their pleasant exchanges were broken by violent coughing from upstairs.

"I can't say whether he can see you, Sir", she said as she lowered her stare from the ceiling. "As you hear, he's very ill at present. Please take a seat while I go up."

She climbed the breakneck stairs and was gone for several minutes, taking the opportunity to plump up the pillows so that Jack could talk in comfort. She called the visitor up.

It was an unhappy sight that greeted him. Jack was pale and drawn, clutching a bloodstained cloth. The stranger smiled understandingly and stood by the bed. He turned to Christabel and asked in a whispering tone if she would leave them alone.

She looked to her father. Jack nodded and she closed the door behind her. Jack's voice was weak, but clear.

"She's a good girl. No man has better . . ."

A tickle in his throat caused more blood. He grabbed for a clean square of sacking, but the youth produced his own white handkerchief, which he gave with genuine concern.

"I'll be as brief as I can." He sat gently on the corner of the bed. "I'm Edmond Elvington."

Jack was clearly shocked.

"Oh, I see you recognise the name."

He drew an awkward breath.

"I know the *Elvington* name," he spluttered.

"I thought as much. As you might gather, James Elvington is my father, although sometimes I find it difficult to admit it."

Jack's face pinched with anguish.

"You regret being his son? I beg you not to say such things to me. I've cause to thank him as a fine gentleman."

The youth calmed Jack.

"I'm constantly hearing this from the older workers on the estate. Yet, and please pardon the contradiction, I'm saddened to say that I know him very differently. The fact is, whatever he was in the past, my father is now a waster."

Jack flung up his hands in horror, gesturing for him to stop. The youth smiled.

"I stand down. I mean no disrespect to your opinion. I only remember my father this way."

"Is he dead?" enquired Jack weakly.

"Bless you, no. Forgive my poor choice of words. As long as I can remember he's been indifferent to the estate and its economics. I don't know why, but that's the fact. He may have been different once, long ago. You indicate that he was and I accept that as the opinion of an honest man. Yet, over recent years our land has run down and much has been sold to pay long-standing debts. Oh, we live well enough, but I fear that the time has come when stock must be taken or we will become an unseated family."

Jack took a sip of water from a jar by his bedhead.

"So what business brings you here?"

"It's to solve a mystery. You see, my mother . . ."

"Charlotte! Is she well?"

The youth was surprised to hear this poor man call his mother by her first name, but made no more of it.

"Thank you, yes. That is, she has health!"

His words left other questions, but not for now.

"She's very concerned for our affairs and asked if I would take over some of my father's duties. Of course I agreed. It's in my interest that the estate remains solvent. Anyway, I digress and I must take as little of your time as possible."

Jack bade him continue.

"I decided that my first task was to see what kind of mess the finances are in, total the assets and debts and hope that we are solvent. I almost wish I hadn't. Believe me, they are bad beyond even my worst expectations. However, I think with prudent management we shall survive. Now I come to the nub. I'm forced to cut expenses to the bone while attempting to recoup old debts. That's where you come in. I came across documentation hidden deep among my father's private papers relating to rented land in Shalhurn, but without explanation of its use. My father isn't fit to tell me and for some reason my mother pleads ignorance. So, here I am to find out for myself. Can you enlighten me? Knowing if it is my expense or your debt would be a start?"

It was clear that the confidence of seventeen years remained intact, when not even the heir to the estate knew of the circumstances that had brought the cottage into rent. As his parents had kept the truth from him, Jack knew that he was bound not to tell more than was necessary to satisfy the immediate questions.

Therefore, cautiously, he explained how James had bought the lease in exchange for a favour.

"Thank you, but with respect, that much I already know. I told you, I have seen a copy of the agreement between my father and a certain Sir Kenneth DeByers. What I really want to know is why my father was so generous, and does the estate have a duty to continue?"

Jack eyed the youngster. He felt sorry for him yet he had to protect his daughter's interests.

"Yes, you do. For as long as I live. As to why, I really can't tell you."

"But you must if I'm to agree to carry on paying. Surely I have the right. What hold do you have over him?"

Jack shook his head.

"I have no hold. It's a matter of honour."

"But I insist upon knowing!"

Again Jack refused.

"I say no more. However, this much is true. Your father was a good and honourable man and it was he who offered me this land. I asked for nothing. That you must believe without proof. Whatever he's become in your eyes, he remains worthy in mine and I cannot, and will not, betray an old trust."

The youth stood.

"I thought as much. Oh well! I can't understand why my father holds such respect, but in a funny sort of way I'm pleased." He smiled kindly at the middle-aged man. "Rest, and I will leave you in peace. You are indeed a friend to my father. Your cottage is safe with me. I'll not turn you out. Good day, Sir, and keep the 'kerchief." He stopped by the door. "Is there anything you need to ease your suffering?"

Jack shook his head.

"I have all I need in my daughter."

He shut the door quietly and descended the stairs to where Christabel waited holding his hat and whip.

"I don't understand his generation, but then perhaps they don't understand us."

She smiled sweetly, unaware of the conversation in the bed-room.

"Are you his daughter or housekeeper?"

"Daughter, Sir."

"You've made him a proud man."

"He's a darling."

"I believe he probably is. Tell me, have you brothers or sisters?"

"None. There is just me and him."

"Then the Mere name dies with him if you marry." He suddenly realised how tactlessly he had spoken. "Oh, I'm so very sorry. I didn't mean . . ."

She looked at him with all the honesty of her young soul. He understood at once that he had not offended. Indeed, that moment he saw much in her that was beyond a pretty face and blossomed figure, a veritable stream of virtues that flowed; purity, a pleasant nature, honesty, compassion and sensitivity, but which mingled freely with the awakening of womanhood. He left with Christabel in his thoughts.

Small communities, such as Shalhurn, survived only by the willingness of neighbour to help neighbour in difficult times. Many villages had lost this tradition, broken by the advance of industrialisation and the migration from the increasingly mechanised countryside to the sprawling new towns with their abundance of factory work. The prospect of regular money enticed many folk from the open hills and valleys to cramped little houses with small yards that backed row on row, often built within soot and grime distance of the factory buildings.

Shalhurn and the surrounding villages being especially small had escaped such complete transformations of character, although their populations had declined. The remaining households stayed true to the old ways. So it was that neighbours now helped Christabel to prepare the land for the coming harvest.

After losing several weeks of good weather to Jack's illness, it was decided that there was no longer time to turn the fields in the

time-honoured way. Instead, they would hire the services of a
steam engine and mole plough.

As the sun rose on this first Tuesday after Epiphany, the steam
engine was fired up in one corner of Jack's largest field. Christabel
and several others set out the crossing pulleys. A wire rope was
passed under the engine's boiler, to join the dragging drum with the
pulleys and pass through a self-propelled, wheeled anchor appara-
tus positioned far across the field opposite the engine. From this the
wire rope returned to the engine to complete the loop. To the
slowly revolving wire band was attached the plough, on which two
men sat. Once work began, the plough was dragged one way across
the soil and then the other, with both the steam engine and self-propelled anchor gradually moving up the field as furrows were
completed. The rich soil turned to the coulters like so many pages
of a book.

It was a strange time in the country, a twilight zone between old
England with its rustic unsophistication and the new age of steam
mechanics and immense power. Christabel looked skywards, feeling the gentle breeze on her face that carried the taint of burning
coal. In the distance drifted a hydrogen balloon, moving noise-
lessly southwards beneath the cloud cover. It was wonderful,
exciting yet menacing. With so much change, where did her future
lie, she wondered?

In the lane a farmer drove his cows to be milked, wielding a stick
over the stragglers. Elsewhere horses galloped freely, and outside
the church Peter Trowsdale pinned notices to the board.

A voice called out for Christabel to move the pulley to the next
position, breaking her reflections. It was while she pulled at the
anchor peg that a message came for her to hurry back to the cottage.

She was shocked to see how weak her father had become in the
few hours since they had taken a small breakfast together. His
breathing was hard and irregular, and dried blood stained his
fingers where they grasped sodden rags. His head lay deep in the
pillow, his skin limp and falling in hollows and folds, lips a

purple-blue. She lowered herself onto the bed and took his hand. His eyes searched to focus.

"Christabel . . ."

"Shush, Father".

She wiped his forehead with a damp cloth.

"I must speak with you. Dear girl, I worry about your devout nature and whether I leave you prepared."

"How so, Father?"

"There's a time for goodness . . . But also a time to be young." He gulped, squeezing Christabel's hand for support. "I worry that you've not had a childhood. There have been so few young people in your life."

"I'm content, Father."

He smiled as much as he could.

"Have you thought what you'll do when I'm taken?"

"Don't talk that way. I love you too much to let you go."

"Love won't save me."

She began to cry.

"Don't fret, child. I've come to terms and I'm not afraid of what's coming. My body hurts and death will be a welcomed release. My fear is for you. I've nothing to leave you."

She kissed him, her tears left on his cheeks.

"Not so, Father. My heart overflows with all you have given me. I'm what you've made me."

"Evening's drawing in."

Christabel looked out at the midday sun.

"Soon the days will get longer, Father."

He became agitated.

"Listen, daughter. I must tell you while I can. It will save you." Urgency showed on his face. "Whatever I've failed to be, I've tried to be a good father."

"I know that." She dropped to the pillow and rested her head by his. "Nobody ever had better. You're the dearest of men."

His breath became suddenly short. She shot upright. He was fading and she panicked.

"Father, Father, don't leave me. I can't live without you. I don't want to be alone."

Tears filled his eyes with the helplessness of her plea.

"Listen. List-en." His trembling hand pointed to a small chest at the end of the bed. "There! Op-en it!"

Christabel rushed to take the key from a drawer and sprang the lock. On top of a small pile of Verity's clothes was a folded piece of sacking. His hand indicated that she should remove it.

"This?" she asked, with surprise.

He nodded. She unfolded it. Inside nestled a discoloured business card with faded writing, a key and a ring.

"Your mother. Be warned, she might not wa-nt . . ."

"What? I didn't hear, Father."

"Had snuff box, but sold it. Remember, she might not . . ."

His arm dropped and life passed away.

"Father. *Father!*"

She let go of the trifling ornaments that fell uncaringly onto the floor. Her arms embraced him, rocking him just as he had rocked Verity before. Tears streamed in unabated affection. She had been expecting the end of his life, but was still unprepared when it came. Nothing eased the pain. An old woman entered the room and removed the bloodstained rags and blankets that tainted the tranquillity of the man who no longer needed them. Christabel kissed her father's forehead in a lingering manner. She was saying goodbye to the greatest love of her young life.

"Look, Christabel. It's a miracle," said the woman, pointing towards the bed.

She turned, looking at the slight smile on Jack's face.

"He's finally at peace."

It was not until after Jack was buried that Christabel thought again of the ring and key. The ring had some worth, but they held no sentimental value. She knew Verity had nothing rich, yet the ring was a woman's. How so? she pondered.

It is probably true that Christabel would have happily swept them away had it not then occurred to her that her father had been particularly anxious that she should have them. Now, suddenly, they became treasured. She ran up to the bedroom.

It was an awful moment. She stared from the doorway into a neat little room with its bed empty and stripped. The air was cold and sterile. Fortunately the old woman had found the key and ring and placed them on the mantel. She slipped the ring onto her finger, but it was far too large. Pulling a ribbon from her hair, she threaded the ring and tied it around her neck, along with the key.

Despite his prophetic experience, DeByers received the news of Jack Mere's death in complete calmness. He was almost disinterested, other than as influenced by his intention to claim back the cottage and land. Jack had only been the livier, and the tenancy agreement had now terminated. To this end he wasted little time in relaying his plans to Christabel, who always knew that she would be made homeless on her father's death. Anyway, she actually doubted whether she could ever really be comfortable again in Shalhurn, where all her family had died early.

Unexpectedly, DeByers offered to let Christabel stay on free of cost at the cottage until arrangements had been made for new accommodation, although the land was taken over for immediate cultivation by new liviers. While not wanting to prolong this void period in her life, it provided Christabel with a breathing space that she used to her advantage. Spring arrived before she finally left for good, when signs of germination were abundant in the countryside.

To her relief, Christabel had received two letters from well-wishers. One was strange, offering her protection, but with no contact address. It said that her father had been kind to a wandering soul, offering his meagre lunch and the last two pennies in his pocket to a complete stranger who had been down on his luck, hungry and alone. He had been saddened to hear of Jack's death, and was concerned for Christabel's welfare as he too had had a daughter of seventeen when she died. It was signed simply, Jacob. The other letter was from someone living on the outskirts of Cerne

Abbas, a young gentleman whose widowed mother had been a close friend to Jack. He offered a room in exchange for light duties and companionship to his parent. This offer suited Christabel, although secretly she would have chosen to be farther than the ten or so miles from Shalhurn, wanting to make a completely new start as an independent woman.

At last the day came to leave and one by one she said her goodbyes to the good neighbours and friends who had played such an important part in her life. She felt exhilarated at the prospect of a fresh challenge, the first she had faced without the support of her father.

The heavy luggage had already been sent ahead, along with those items of furniture that were worth saving and would fit into her new room. The intention now was to walk the ten miles, carrying only a single bag of essentials. She had raised some money from the sale of the horses and wagon, although less than might have been realised on the open market, having been pleased to sell them to neighbours for whatever they could afford.

At midday she set off. As she climbed the steep lane – down which Jack had braked so hard on arriving at Shalhurn a lifetime before – she felt anxious for the first time. Ahead lay an unknown future. At the top of the rise she stopped and looked back on the village, the church with its precious graves, the irregular arrangement of cottages and her own little cottage with its fences and walls. It was all of the past, and if she needed reminding of this it came with the sight of a stranger working her father's fields. It was funny to think that she cherished her neighbours, and they her, yet in months or even weeks their separate lives would begin to dull fond memories, and bit by bit the Mere family's mark on the Shalhurn landscape would be erased like a healing flesh wound. Sooner or later the mention of Jack Mere and his daughter would be greeted by blank faces and the remark, "Who?".

As Christabel walked over the crest towards her new beginning, she had been watched away by the last kindly women waving their farewells.

"Take a final look at the poor little thing," said the first. "I am right sorrowed to see her go."

"It's a sad story that girl can tell. She hasn't much more than two farthings to rub together," said another.

"That wasn't Jack's fault. He worked hard enough. No, how could he make ends meet when that big field of his wouldn't grow anything proper?" She pointed to the land that bordered the church. "Some say that's because of long-dead Conjurer Peppergul's legacy. You know, the one who's buried half in and half out of the church. It was that very same parcel of land my parents used to call Pitching Plot. The story goes that Peppergul was galloping away one day when he realised that he'd left his book of spells open at home. Riding back to stop anyone from seeing it and hurting themselves, he jumped his horse right over the village, knocking crooked one pinnacle of the church tower, as you see it now. Where he landed they called Pitching Plot and it's said that the land has never worked right since that ancient time, whether ploughed for harvest or left for cows."

"Ah, that's just reckless superstition. Don't believe that, do you?"

"Well, that's as maybe, but I did hear say the same occurred in Winterborne Whitcombe. Be strange to happen twice if it's not true, wouldn't it!"

CHAPTER XIII

Call to women — The year 1881

*C*hristabel had become a changed woman. As she struggled with her bag to the first main road on the journey by foot to Cerne Abbas, her simple, almost childlike ways were left behind. Her face now depicted the analogous qualities of an adult, her arrestingly clear eyes reflecting a measure of the pain and tragedy that transcends youthful innocence. She was not demoralised, only bruised by the realities of recent experiences. Perhaps her harsh education in the ways of life and death had made her stronger, more resolute, with little time for vacillation.

As the daughter of a poor smallholder, Christabel had enjoyed few opportunities for real choice, but now, alone, she could relinquish the routine that had so dominated her earlier hard, yet happy, existence. To leave Shalhurn was not to obliterate its memories, but cast as false any feeling of subservience to poverty without escape. She was now her own woman, tithed only by the small number of coins in her purse and the generosity of friends.

The willow hedge that had been her companion up the steep climb came to an abrupt end at the main road. Ahead lay vast open spaces, less rich in colour than the valley, but with their own delicacy of airiness and scents. The quick way to Cerne was along the undulating track leading from the opposite side of the road, a narrow scar that cut a swathe into the first deep ravine with its occasional conifers of green and purple hues. To her left and right were the DeByers' fields, ploughed and showing evidence of an emerging root crop. Far in the distance lay areas of higher land where cattle grazed.

Although her journey would be long, she felt compelled to make a short detour. Only a few hundred yards to the left along the road that crossed the hill was an elaborate, stone seat nestling half-hidden in the undergrowth, known locally as the Shalhurn relic. Now rough and pitted, it nonetheless was said to give unnatural strength to travellers. Its importance to Christabel was mystical, and as she approached reverently her steps became more deliberate.

The seat seemed to expel a subtle aura that could perhaps only be detected by those acknowledging its ethereal presence. The spring air was chilled close by and a light mist that hung on the horizon appeared to be creeping in.

Unsure of her resolution, yet unwilling to be dispossessed of her mission through unreasonable fear, Christabel drew in bit by bit, half expecting to see something frightening. At last she stood in front and her doubts went. She touched its cold surface. Probably by inclination rather than reality, she convinced herself she could feel the scratch marks said in legend to have been made by the claws of pilgrimaging animals.

For such a small experience, Christabel had been overwhelmingly hesitant. She remembered how the seat marked the place where a shaft of fire had reputedly pointed to a lost holy relic, found centuries before by a priest. Christabel sat, bathing in the ambience of a miracle. With eyes closed, she was lost in thought when footsteps cut the silence. She jumped in alarm and, barely daring to peep, she turned.

"Flesh and blood," she said with relief.

"My apologies, girl. I saw you meditating and thought I could pass without disturbance."

"I was only resting, Sir, after climbing the lane."

"Ah! What price young legs. I find any journey tiresome, but you look lost?"

"Not at all. Please, sit by me if you wish."

"Better not. Wouldn't ever get up if I did. I'm bound for the friary, down the road apiece. Do you know it?"

"I know *of* it. I've never been there. They say it's a marvellous big place. I'll be passing that way myself."

"I suppose it is. You must forgive my doubts, but it's not through choice that I go there. Why not join me? The road is long and company will help to pass the time."

"Kindly, Sir, I cannot. I'm expected in Cerne and the quickest way is across the fields."

"Ah! That route is certainly beyond my old legs and my horse cannot be ridden while carrying such a load. Anyway, I'm in no hurry."

"Another reluctant wanderer."

"You too, child?"

"I'm going to live with friends."

"Ah! Faithful friends. They're a joy indeed."

"Forgive me, but you talk as though you have none."

"Sadly, that's so. I had one until recently, but he too has gone."

She reached into her bag for the bottle, offering him a drink to revive his spirits. He refused politely.

"Sorry, child, I'm stone. Beyond comfort, although your warmth reaches me."

He took up the reins of his packhorse and walked on.

She called after him.

"Who are you, Sir?"

There was hesitation in his voice.

"I told you. I am stone."

"What do you mean? What's the matter? Why not talk awhile?"

"Good day, maid."

"Wait!"

"You don't need me," said the man. "You have all you need about you. Use it to advantage. Hear me? Use it to your advantage and put your trust only in true friends."

Once again she called after him.

"I don't understand what you mean. Please, turn back."

He began to fade into the creeping mist, through which Christabel wouldn't follow.

"I'm unhappy too. Stay so that we might comfort each other."

He turned and with a last wave shouted;

"God bless thee this day and for always."

Christabel sat perplexed, watching him fade away while fumbling for the ring and key that dangled from the ribbon around her neck. Soon he had gone completely. In the stillness she heard rustling in the undergrowth. It moved in twitches, first one side and then the other, but hardly causing a ripple among the long stems. Then more on all sides. That was enough. She grabbed her bag and ran. Out of the undergrowth crawled several small creatures — those common among the fields — that gathered around the seat to scratch its surfaces.

Hurriedly, Christabel made her way back to the scar path to renew the journey to Cerne Abbas. She had wasted enough time. Every pace away from the seat seemed to brighten the atmosphere until all conceptions of mist, coldness and mystery had passed. She stepped lightly off the road and down the path itself, following the twisting scar as it rose and fell in quick succession. At first the path worked its way around the rim of the ravine, over red soil and heavy flint deposits broken fine by centuries of farming. Gorse in shades of brown and green ran down all untended banks in irregular patches until, at the bottom, its progress was held back by rich agricultural pastures.

Her course avoided the valley bottom, but transcended many an uphill climb and downward trot, occasional puddles of orange water forcing her to lift her dress and tread through prickly gorse.

After a mile or two the remnants of a hilltop farmhouse appeared. It seemed a good place to rest. Leaning against the barred gate, she carefully unlaced her tall leather boots, letting her throbbing feet melt into lightness. Probably for the first time in her life she became fully aware of the country perfumes that had a languid effect on all living creatures.

Fresh sweeping winds now confronted her as she forced the pace down yet another hill, areas of wilderness and tended land separated by naturally growing hedgerow hugging the dips and slopes. Way down, the path became much firmer, wider and dry, passing through a criss-cross of fields of lush green, tainted with patches of chalky white. She was leaving the bleakness of the upper reaches for more prosperous farmland, where managed hedges of recent cultivation edged the way. Buildings became more common, but none surpassed the splendour of the friary that came into view, the very antithesis of its inner austerity, where fancy brickwork and half-empty bellies went hand in hand.

The journey so far, with its highs and lows, had given Christabel a thirst that she was unable to satisfy. At the friary she could drink and refill her bottle, and with this in mind she turned off the path and passed through an arch formed from topiaried evergreens. A bell pull hung on a wicket and she rang and entered. The grey stone building seen from the road was, however, only the gatehouse. In front now was an entirely different building, its awe-inspiring, red brick walls and elaborate carvings paling the gatehouse into insignificance. To simple Christabel Mere, now standing alone at the head of a great driveway, this was another world, one in which she had no place. Scared of being noticed, she took to her heels, stopping at nothing until she was left panting back on the path.

A little further along was a modest cottage, unimposing and friendly. Its non-conforming attic room and lean-to gave it the irregularity of a working home, where function took priority over style. Christabel knocked. There was no answer. A flagstone path led to the rear, where she knocked again, standing between scrubbed milking pails. This time the door opened, and in the ways of the country she was invited to eat and drink with the family. Although the food on the table was cold, the black range crackled and glowed with burning fuel. In this congenial atmosphere Christabel had no inhibitions, laughing and joking naturally and helping herself to bread, cheese and fruit.

All through the meal Christabel heard the continuous drip of whey falling into shallow pails from cheese bags suspended on racks in the lean-to. Once the last piece of bread had been taken, the farmer's wife left the kitchen for the dairy, from where slurping noises began and the singing of, 'Come butter come, Peter stands at the gate, waiting for a buttered cake'. It was two o'clock and the revelry ended abruptly.

Refreshed, Christabel set off on the next leg of her journey. Not far from the cottage the pathway crossed a ford. A narrow bridge was provided for pedestrians, under which the water bubbled over cobblestones before disappearing through a gully in the field beyond. From there the walk became less adventurous and plain to the eye, the hard-surfaced road taking a straight course along the upper reaches of Cawlow Downs.

Soon the hills on each side appeared to rise as she made an almost imperceptible descent, taking her through flooded meadows that stretched away into the distance. This part of the walk was long, but without exertion, then, just as gradually, the lane rose once more as it transcended a ridge that hooked across from the right to mark the abrupt slopes of Rickley Hill.

Six hours had passed and with a heave of her bag Christabel began the last descent to Cerne Abbas. The light was now fading and the hills and valleys behind slowly began to merge until they married into a single murky darkness. It was only now that the full majesty of the hills could be understood, when the atmosphere had to be felt rather than the views seen. It could be said that the hills became one with the sky at such times, like huge black clouds rising above the nearby towns in sympathy with the heavens, when even stars were intruders, casting emphatic brightness onto a scene, the severity of which was its triumph. Few townspeople stayed high to experience this transformation, yet those who did were among the privileged who knew nature's fulfilment, when areas of cultivation returned to ageless sombre wilderness.

Arrangements had been made for Christabel to be met at Saint Mary's Church in the centre of Cerne Abbas, and it was to this end that she hurried whilst there was still some light to make safe passage past the neat rows of cottages, the forge, three inns and other buildings. Unknown to Christabel, minutes before a gig had entered the high street from the opposite direction, pulling up close to the stocks that stood outside the church. As Christabel approached, the driver jumped down and took her bag.

"She is in the church, Missy, bending their ears something terrible I shouldn't wonder, judging by the rumpus. You might as well go in as wait outside with me."

Inside, a row of diehard hecklers struggled with police to be heard, but they were no match for the blue uniforms and were made to sit. Christabel sat on the first available seat, behind a hundred or more women straining to see Isobel Madden in the pulpit through a sea of large hats.

"I shall carry on, just as our great crusade will never give in to abuse. It's not just a gentleman's right to be heard, but the right of all. I give no promise of silence."

The ladies clapped and cheered. The hecklers booed. One young man jumped up and shouted:

"Madam. I've seen your booklet and it is no great literature. I have written four long theses and know what I'm talking about."

"Then, Sir, you should know that it takes four ordinary wheels to make one fine carriage. I suggest you read it again, if you can!"

The women laughed.

"Contrary, Madam. You write about something you haven't experienced. I made a point of going to Plymouth when the first brothel opened." He wiped his moustache. "In truth, I found the reception warmer than here and the women much more to my taste."

He turned to his friends with a wry smile.

"Then you may be damned by it!"

He grinned.

"I'm not as sure as you that I've fulfilled the requirements for damnation, but if Plymouth is hell, please call me a coach!"

The men erupted into joyous amusement.

"Do you know what it is to be damned?"

"Certainly I do. To listen to you drawling on!"

The hecklers' applause grew louder.

"I *will* be heard. Women have their rights," answered Isobel.

Another young man jumped up onto the pew. "So do men. Get your bloomers off!"

A truncheon blow took his legs away and stunned and silent, he was dragged out by a policeman,.

"Come, come, gentlemen," said the sergeant. "If you don't want to listen, I would ask you to leave quietly, and no more smut in front of the ladies."

He waved to the speaker to continue.

"We can take it, can't we ladies?"

A tremendous 'Yes' rose up. Furtively, a third heckler unfastened his trouser belt and fly buttons. He leapt up, leaving his trousers around his ankles.

"If you can take it, I'm your man."

His friends fell about laughing as he gyrated suggestively. A policeman grabbed for him, but he dodged out of reach and tried to scramble into the next row. He might have made it, but for a fearsome woman who knocked him back like a tennis ball with a mighty swing of her bag. The police had seen enough and all the hecklers were hauled outside and bundled into a police cart, where their colleague already sat nursing his bruises.

The church fell into low whispers as order was restored.

"We'll be off now, ma'am. You won't need us anymore."

"Thank you, sergeant. Ladies, let us give a hand to our proud policemen."

Polite clapping echoed around the walls.

"Most kind, ma'am. Most kind and most appreciated."

"One matter, sergeant. Will you be charging those young men?"

He turned back.

"Not unless you press for indecency."

"No. I think not this time. What will happen to them?"

"I'll bang them up in a cell for the night. Let them cool off. In the morning they can go back to college."

"Perhaps a word with their principal?"

"No point, ma'am. It was probably him who incited them to come here in the first place."

The doors closed. Isobel's expression turned serious.

"And so, dear ladies of the National Association, let the politicians so gravely forget human dignity in the mistaken cause of progressive liberty and we, the women of England, will be made to suffer the consequences. We must not allow the grey men of Westminster to claim ignorance of the diabolical Act they have helped to pass merely because it came at the tail end of a parliamentary session, for the Association has provided each with such a weight of literature as should have dealt a fatal wound to that Act. Oh yes, it has been said by many eminent persons that the State Regulation of Vice protects respectable women against the poor moral standards of our fighting soldiers and sailors. It has also been said by these same men that by threatening prostitutes with imprisonment, and even enforced medical treatment should they solicit, many fallen women have been reclaimed and venereal disease contained – but is that true?

In other advocate countries such laws have only made the problem much worse, for a new black market of flesh arises and thrives alongside the brothels licensed by the state. For, if the law acknowledges that moral restraint is unnecessary and provides the means for unfaithfulness, then it follows that the government assumes vice to be venial. Women alone are punished by the Act, for no man has to contain his lust or disease under its charter. I know that Mr Gladstone received a letter from the ladies of the Geneva International Association advising of these very points, yet, even in the face of proof from abroad, where similar detestable systems have operated for decades, nothing is done. Moreover, even with the facts put before it, the Royal Commission set up by Parliament still produced a majority report favouring the Act and opposing our view. To its shame, the Commission hadn't a single woman among its twenty-four members, but upon the judgement of MPs, the ecclesiastic, medical practitioners, members of the House of Lords and a vice admiral, women have to live.

I'm not saying, dear friends, that these are uncaring or corrupt men, but I am saying in the strongest terms that some of their number were all too ready to follow the view of so-called experts who favour regulation rather than listen to their own hearts or the opinions of the majority of ordinary people. Indeed, our good, Mrs Butler, has since received letters from Commission members regretting the conclusion of the Commission in the face of mounting doubt about the system.

Surely as the whole question is aimed at containing disease in military towns and cities, it must equally be seen that the government thereby presupposes our gallant redcoats to be predestined fornicators. Does it mean that our brothers and fathers that protect the empire and tame the savage in far-flung continents must be treated as animals because their trade is cruel? If so, isn't the surgeon who plunges the knife deep into the flesh of his patient equally as brutal, or, as I suspect, are both defenders of good?

I have here a letter from a women in Plymouth, one of the respectable ladies that the Act is supposed to protect. She knows the truth of the matter. Copies of her letter are available at the door. She tells of a city no longer safe to walk in alone, for the legal safeguards that have in the past protected all women at all times, in common with the male gender, can no longer be applied, leaving the sacred freedom and inviolate security of English womanhood to the discretion of the police.

Ladies, the causes of the protest by which our great struggle will be remembered were published a few years ago in the national press, and yet the conspiracy of silence by our opponents that followed has meant that hardly a word has been printed in the newspapers since that time. That memorable day, the first of January 1870, shocked Parliament, for those law makers had no idea how to handle a revolt by women. Time has passed, but the struggle goes on. Why? Because it must for the general good. Be heartened, ladies, for remember that among our thousands of supporters may be counted such a person as Florence Nightingale. Who, then, in the public eye can argue against us?

So, that must be our future course. We must seek out the MPs and any other would-be social reformers who've forced the issue upon us, and publish their individual views. Not one, I would suspect, would then voice publicly a view opposed to our position. Indeed, in some cases we may have to visit the very brothels to seek their views at all! Oh, I know it's hard. I daily risk abuse. It's harder still to suffer when insult occasionally comes from other women, for I shock many of our own sex by talking of such matters in public and opposing their husbands. I'm further abused when our struggle is seen as part of the fight for suffrage, but we also have our supporters, both in Parliament and out. We draw great strength from the working masses, who seem to be clear in their opinions of right and wrong. It's our sacred duty to fight on until we win. I ask you this. Will it be the humiliation of innocent women or the purification of our sick community? Will it be justice for all women at any cost?"

With the church finally emptied, Isobel was overjoyed to see the daughter of her old friend. Her smile seemed capable of splitting to her ears as they walked arm in arm to the gig. Although the chat began lightly, Christabel knew little of the Act and was interested to hear more during the short journey to the Madden home at Nether Bow.

"I didn't know such places existed, and you say they are protected by law?"

"More than that, dear. The House of Commons voted over £3,600 last year from army estimates to pay for their upkeep."

"Those men tonight were so rude."

"The subject seems to invite that kind of behaviour. It's a symptom."

"Still, your quick replies squashed them. I don't know how you do it."

"It's simple. A lot of my speech was based on quotes by the Association's founder members. I just jiggle them around a bit, and I always take the trouble of reading up a few clever phrases by people like Samuel Johnson. That way I'm fully prepared."

"I'd like to become one of your apostles."

"Maybe, one day. We'll see. It isn't the kind of thing an impressionable girl should be involved in without fully understanding the subject. What I know isn't pleasant, but I've had to learn to be cold to it."

"I bet I'm already older than a lot of the girls working in the brothels."

"You're right, my dear. I see you have your father's good sense. Anyhow, let's return to nice things. Let's talk about you."

Christabel had never travelled in such comfort, and for the first time she became aware of her own disparate social standing. Isobel, by contrast, believed she thought nothing of class. Perhaps it really was easier to give than to receive, even when nothing greater than courtesy changed hands.

Wheat Sheaf farm, the Madden home, was a modest farm estate at the boundary of the village, its owners more upper middle class than rich. It lay in the beautiful Cerne Valley, nestling by the river. The name was strange, for as long as anyone could remember cereals had only been grown in one field, as feed for the prominent cattle and sheep.

Christabel leapt from the gig as it turned off the road onto the descending drive, pulling open two white gates. A few yards farther and the horse stopped outside the porticoed entrance. Already Isobel and Christabel were firm friends. The door opened and John stepped out. He took her bag, which held the girl's worldly possessions except for the little furniture that had been sent ahead and which now gave her new bedroom a measure of familiarity.

"Oh, while I think of it Christabel, you won't find your mirror put out. Unlike my son, I don't hold with vanity and you'll find no mirrors displayed anywhere in the house, except for his room. He needs it for shaving, although he spends much time admiring himself. Womanly virtues come from deeds, and vanity only attracts the base feelings in men."

She acknowledged gracefully.

"You know," she added in softer tone, "I've really missed your father's occasional visits. To the world at large he was a poor man of little education, but he had a strength of common sense that made him easy to listen to. We had many a good-natured debate, and often after he had left I realised that he had been right all along. Of course, I never told him so! Few people with strong views have the ability to be persuaded by reasoned argument, yet he could give and take in equal measure. I particularly remember . . ."

Not since Jack's death had Isobel talked of him openly. Even John was surprised at the apparent depth of her emotion. For the daughter, the raising of every intimate detail of her father's last few months was painful, leaving her with the uncanny feeling that he hadn't died, but rather was temporarily out of touch, and this just when she had begun to accept the loneliness.

"He had his dreams, you know, Christabel."

"My father?" she asked, with a melancholy shake.

"Don't sound so surprised."

"But I am."

"You didn't know? You didn't talk about them?"

"No, never."

"Well, there's a thing. Oh yes, he wasn't the simple figure you think. He always wanted more for you, and Verity when she was alive, God bless her soul. As the years went by his dreams never changed, his hopes for the future never faded, only the nagging reality that they might not be achieved. He never let go of them, for there was never such an optimist as your father. That's what drove him to work so hard. When your mother died it knocked him for six, but he picked himself up and started rebuilding again. I suppose it was all for you in the end."

"He didn't leave much."

"Stubborn old fool. No, I don't suppose he did, except that which came from the heart. Wouldn't let me help him either, except by accepting the odd extra loaf or wedge of cheese left over from a visit. In truth, I always provided too much food when he came and the old fool never realised, but that was his virtue. Never took a penny piece that wasn't earned. That's how we met as a matter of fact, when he did odd jobs to make a little extra money. He was proud, and I can say with easy conscience that I looked forward to our little soirées when he joined me on the terrace for tea."

An hour passed and still Isobel talked on. It needed only half a dozen words from Christabel for another long story to be recounted. John had been watching Christabel's tired expression.

"It's a fine evening now. I think I'll go for a short drive. Shame to waste it. Would you like to join me, Chrissie?"

"Chrissie!"

"Surely others have called you that? But if it gives offence?"

"No. I like it. Oh, yes please!"

"I don't think she . . ." interrupted Isobel.

"I'd like to get to know the area as quickly as possible, and it *is* a lovely evening. If you don't think me rude, I will go." She turned to John. "Wait while I get my coat."

She hurried off before Isobel could raise further objections.

John was a genial type, prone to exaggeration and popular with the ladies. He believed himself to be a bit of a philosopher, with a relish for living a bohemian lifestyle so long as it caused no discomfort to himself.

"Hope you don't mind if we use this cart. It was already rigged and we don't want to be long, do we?"

"It's what I'm used to."

"Ha! That's behind you now."

"I'm in no hurry to forget my past."

"You know, it's strange that we've never met before."

"Hardly, Sir, since father never brought me with him."

The horse trotted on.

"I suppose we'll see a good deal of one another now?"

"I'll have my work to do."

"Oh, fiddlesticks. You won't be asked to do much more than would a lady's companion. You might say that's your duty."

"Isn't what I do a matter for your mother to decide?"

"No, Chrissie, we shall see much of each other. I have decided."

A gusty wind blew raw, but the night sky bejewelled the little streets of Cerne. Couples were walking the paths towards the warm inns and coffee houses, from where rough singing and much merriment rang out. A company of cavalry officers rode by, their head-plumes streaming. A lamplighter pulled at a chain and ignited the gas, and from a large Georgian house a party emerged in ball gowns and black jackets, their carriage bathed in a translucent glow from brass coachlights.

"Stockbrokers and moneylenders" said John following her stare. "Got their noses hooked into everyone's business."

"What a wonderful place this is. You must be so happy here."

"It's like all familiar things. One has to be separated from them to appreciate what is taken for granted. Why are you wriggling?"

"There seem to be a lot of midges. I'm being eaten alive!"

"It's the spilt milk in the back of the cart. The blighters can smell it a mile off. I usually put a rug over the back when I drive this wreck, which I'm pleased to say isn't too often."

"Don't you ever help with the chores?"

"No fear! We employ people to do that stuff. Why keep dogs and bark yourself."

"Is that what you think of them?"

"Oh, Chrissie. Stop jumping on everything I say. I didn't mean that at all, and I think you know it. Here, take this."

He handed her a newspaper to beat off the flies. She looked agog.

"I see you're interested in the parish news. Good. It's the quickest way of getting to know things around here. Mind you, not much of importance ever happens. It's usually pretty dull reading. Still, that bit about the old boy is quite juicy. Everyone likes a scandal now and then, so long as it's at someone else's expense."

"Shush! I'm reading it now . . . Listen to this, John:

Blah, blah, blah . . . I also regret to report the unfortunate passing of my once friend, Jacob Stone, late of Dartmoor. His body was discovered near the friary, alongside his heavily laden albino mare. The circumstances of his death are not suspicious, according to official reports. It is not likely that many parishioners will remember him as a boy, the son of the late Reverend William Stone of Cerne. We must add his name to our prayers, not least as he had forsaken his father's calling to become a worldly man who became entangled in mystics and mysticism. We must remember him, therefore, with compassion and for his esteemed work with the rural poor. For all you antiquarians, I mention in passing that legend has it that it was one of his forefathers who caused the Shalhurn seat to be raised.

On other parish matters, blah, blah . . ."

"I know. I've read it."

"For goodness sake, John. This paper's dated 22nd April. It's a week old."

"Well? There hasn't been another."

"No. You don't understand. Stop the cart!"

He pulled over.

"In the first place, I think I'm going mad."

"What?"

"You're not going to believe me, because I can't understand it myself, but I think I met this man."

"That's entirely possible. I expect he'd been around."

"I don't mean weeks or months ago. It was today! He stopped and talked to me . . . Well, sort of talked."

"Give me that paper. There has to be a mistake."

"I know what happened!"

"This was printed ten days ago, so you *must* be mistaken. I expect you were distressed at leaving your old home, or perhaps the two men were of similar appearance. That would account for it."

"How would I know what this Jacob Stone looked like to make a comparison? Anyway, he called himself 'stone', although strangely not as a name as I recall, and he had a horse of the purest white. It was while I sat on the Shalhurn seat. John, I know what I saw!"

"This is a devilish conundrum. Look, I've an idea. Let's go to the parson's home. He wrote this, so he should be able to verify the facts. You can describe whom you saw and he'll put your mind at rest."

She nodded.

At the vicarage Christabel declined to knock, feeling foolish. John had no such reservations and presently could be seen through the window talking in an articulated manner. He returned.

"I have a question. What was unusual about your man's appearance ?"

"Not much except for deep scars on his neck. I suppose his red hair and big side whiskers were also a bit unusual, although not entirely uncommon," she said without pause.

"My God. That's exactly right. Apparently he was known for his wild hair. How did you know that?"

"I told you. I met him."

Unsure of what to believe, he signalled the horse on.

"I've been thinking," said John after some minutes. "I reckon you must have heard about this man before. After all, it seems that his family had lived in the district for ages. Perhaps the day tired you more than you think and you brought the old boy to mind in a sort of day dream."

"You can think that if it comforts you, but it's not the truth. I know full well what I saw."

"Then you misheard. Perhaps your fellow had a similar name, like Scone or Bone."

"Stop it! It's all nonsense. I can't explain it to myself, let alone to you. You asked me what he looked like and I gave you the correct answer. Can't you believe your own conclusions. There's no more I can say, so let's end it there."

"Well, thank me very much for trying!"

He whipped the horse and it flinched. He whipped it again. This time its head reared up and the cart shook and veered. A wheel dropped into a shallow ditch, throwing the occupants off balance. The horse pulled, but the cart was stuck, churning a rut in the softer sloping soil. John whipped again, driving the animal forward until, with a leap, the cart broke free under a lurch of sudden power, and the horse made off at a gallop. Only now from a blind corner and in the opposite direction came a heavily laden milk wagon taking the centre of the road, its rustic driver wide-eyed at the thunderbolt approaching.

"Get out of the way, damn you!", hollered John, more from fear than temper.

The wagoner pulled hard left, but his old nag didn't have the strength to quicken its plod. John pumped the brake, but his horse was beyond recall. With no option, he steered the cart for the narrow gap separating the hedgerow and the wagon, an inconceivably small space through which he managed to manoeuvre with the accuracy of a surgeon's knife. He slowed to a panting halt.

"My God. That was close. Are you okay?"

Christabel shivered, breathless, but calm.

"I think so. I'm obliged to you for not killing us."

He took a clean sack from the back and placed it over her knees. "Your hand. Look. It's bleeding!"

Christabel looked at her palm. It was badly raw and smeared red.

"I think I touched a wheel."

John was ashamed.

"Let me see more closely." He took her hand gently. "We'll drive home without delay. Mother will soon have that dressed. What can I say?"

Downcast, he prompted the horse forward without his whip, taking only a steady trot. She placed her arm through his and drew him close, the blooded hand upturned on her lap.

"Don't worry, John, I'll mend. Only," she added mischievously, "you might have waited till I've been with you a day before giving me the sack."

They laughed together.

"It pongs a bit too."

With John and Isobel in fussy attendance as the hand was cleaned and bandaged, and with more stories of Jack to bear as a hot drink was prepared, Christabel was nearing the end of her tether. She felt tired, wounded and very muddled. John took his drink to his room, but another half an hour passed before Isobel commented:

"I apologise for keeping you chatting at such a rate, and you inclined for your bed."

At last she was released and with a forced smile she left for the sanctity of her room. The upper passage was poorly lit, made narrow by occasional tables spaced along its walls and dimmed further by the matt brown of the wallpaper and woodwork.

"I still feel wretched about what happened," said John to Christabel's alarm as he appeared from nowhere holding a single candle. "I know I won't sleep a wink if you don't say you forgive me."

"Forget it. I have. Good night, John," she replied in sleepy tone, hoping to fall into bed.

"You know we might have broken our necks? If only I could turn the clock back."

"If I'm a judge, it won't happen again. So that's an end to it. Good night!"

"But —"

"John, I'm really worn out!"

He couldn't wait until morning to talk again, willing to risk the future for a minute more of her time.

"Chrissie, it's just —"

"Shush." She pressed her finger gently to his mouth. "We'll talk at breakfast."

To her surprise he kissed the tip. She withdrew it at once.

"I suppose that was another mistake?"

His face glowed and shadowed in the candlelight. Afraid of his determination and her vulnerability, her eyes half shut and legs frail, she pushed him back.

"I don't want to be kissed. At least not yet or at this time of night."

He shrank away.

"I'm sorry. Another misjudgement. What an idiot you're making me look. I wish in a way you hadn't come here."

"Then I'll leave in the morning."

"No! Please don't. I didn't mean that. Oh hell, what did I mean? Why do I say such things? I meant to say . . . Well, I think you know. Heaven knows I haven't endeared myself to you. I've managed to make an utter ass of myself in record time. I couldn't have done better if I'd tried, and, Chrissie, I only want to be assured in your thoughts. Damn!"

It took little to see that the anguish was genuine.

"John, calm yourself. I'm no great person to be worried over, nor am I frail and fickle. It's me, plain Christabel Mere from Shalhurn, the smallholder's daughter."

He smiled.

"Thanks for that, but I have to say it. I like you. That's why I've acted so ridiculously."

"I'm a new face, that's all, and a mighty tired one at that."

"Now you mock me. I'd better go, but first, tell me this. Despite all that has happened and my silly behaviour, do you think you might one day come to care for me?"

"Do you always offer your affection so quickly?"

"Of course not. It's just . . . I seem to have plunged in with both feet."

"And found the water cold?"

"Well, yes."

"Being cautious is *my* way."

"A lack of society has kept you ignorant of a greater existence, Chrissie. Preserving the status quo doesn't mean you can't enjoy yourself or express your feelings freely."

"It might pass among your friends, but I find it strange."

"You do mock me again. If you want to know, I think you're something pretty special. Others would have screeched murder at injuring their hand, but you were so calm, so kind and, well, feminine."

"I am grateful to you. To you and your mother."

"Grateful?" He stood back to relieve the closeness of their company. "We must be friends, good friends, always. That's all."

Christabel's rich lips acknowledged the sentiment with a slight touch to his cheek, not enough to be called a kiss.

"Maybe that's all. We'll see."

That done, she determinedly entered her room and closed the door. She sat at the dressing table without a mirror. The room was large and the ceiling high.

My things don't belong in a room like this, she thought, brushing her long hair. She heard John bolting his door. Surely such fast attentions aren't proper? I'm a cottage girl by circumstances, not by nature.

The next day, and the following, Christabel settled to a routine of light duties. She asked if she could also groom the horses and feed the ducks. 'I like to help out' was her reply to those who suggested that others should perform such menial tasks. Even with the extra work she still had time to read and explore the farm, its mill and forge, and wander about the little church that bordered the drive.

John on the other hand, who did everything well, but did little, made it his business to keep out of Christabel's way, which was no easy matter, but he considered the effort to be worthwhile if it would repair his esteem. He wasn't willing to add to his daily tasks, but if she considered work an attribute then he should at least give the impression of occupation.

Isobel soon realised the cause of her son's strange behaviour and contrived a way to end it.

"You know, my dear, you must let John show you our Cerne giant cut into the hillside. It's hundreds of years old and well worth a visit. Frankly, it might shock, but I know you to be sensible of such things."

Several more days passed without John at the breakfast table or indeed anywhere much to be seen. In truth he was beginning to find the game a bit tiresome, having run short of places to go and people to visit. It was then that he invited Christabel to a picnic on the giant's head:

". . . where, if we're lucky, we might see a courting couple dancing the maypole."

It was a perfect day for a picnic when John helped Christabel onto the gig. A delicious smell of baking wafted from food still warm in the basket.

"Can you sing?" enquired John.

"I'm no great singer, but I can hold a note."

"Then let's make a merry tune for the journey."

The simple jollity ended John's annexation. Christabel found the nude giant's oversized manhood quietly amusing, but pretended not to notice what form the white lines took on such a vast scale. The fact that others were able to make out the shape, judging by the giggles and muffled laughs, only made her denial more ridiculous.

In particular, one unhappy teenage girl suffered much scornful hooting and jeering from friends for refusing to tread on the lines, having been told of its mysterious fertility properties.

"Shut up, Cathy. Jump in or we'll give you something to cry about."

Through the lazy hours Christabel and John walked the hill and meadows, and from the vantage point of a tumulus looked down on the ruins of Cerne Abbey. They used stepping stones and a bridge to pass backwards and forwards over the meandering river, taking delight in every slight detail of nature. Boggy ground stained their feet a rich black. On the river bank timid water creatures emerged from their many hiding places, disturbed by dangling legs. The sun glinted jewels of wonderfully changing shapes on the water.

In the spiritual atmosphere of peace and happiness minds roamed into strange thoughts, and one occurred to Christabel as she lay chewing a long stem.

"Why is it that we can feel giddy from looking at the clouds passing by?"

John laughed.

"Dear, Chrissie. You're such a confounded simpleton. It's the ground that turns, not the clouds. I've never felt a bit giddy from looking up, except, of course, when I'm holding an empty gin bottle."

"Laugh at me would you!"

She took the stem from her mouth and waved it under his nose. Immediately and without forethought he turned over and took hold of her wrists, pressing them to the ground above her head. She looked piercingly into his eyes. He let go and sat up.

"You know, Chrissie, you're altogether too easily offended. Why can't you be a creature of moods like other women?"

"I may know very little of men, but then I wonder how much you really know of women? I don't mean the flirts you usually mix with, but *real* women who would remain constant at your side through the tragedies of life."

"I won't have you say such things. Life doesn't have to be tragic or serious. It can't be wrong for a man to show love to a woman he's only just met." He blushed as the words slipped unexpectedly from his lips. "Chrissie, I didn't mean . . ."

"Didn't you? I almost know you did."

Denial was pointless, but, yet, he couldn't appreciate the grounds of her coyness. She was bright in a rural sense, only lacking the general awareness that came with better society. So why was he going so wrong? Wasn't she prepared for the brief romantic encounters of the town, when the sexes played at love to build a reservoir of temporary knowledge. Perhaps she saw love only as a one-time experience, fulfilled or dashed and without tributaries from the main flow. There was one way of finding out.

"Actually, I did." He stared longingly at her. "Dear, Chrissie. Dear, darling Chrissie. I know I've trodden all over you like a clumsy oaf. God knows I hate myself at times, but I am what I am. I can't be changed and if I'm one thing now, I'm sincere."

His eyes searched her face for a clue to her feelings. Nothing came back.

"For God's sake, say something or give a reaction. I'm pouring my bloody heart out here!"

"It must be nice to be loved," she said in whispered tone, meaning nothing particular, but giving the wrong impression.

"Then you understand after all? Great!"

He slipped his arm around her waist and she didn't resist. Their hearts beat together, his upon gossamer wings and hers in turmoil. His fingers passed through her hair that fell long down her back, her bodily warmth radiating with his. She allowed her head to fall on his chest, her face in anguish, his in heaven. He held tighter, making the physical and mental capture complete. She began to tremble, her mind in a spin. She had to break free.

"We must go. Now!"

"Why, for heaven's sake?"

"It's all happening too quickly. I can't give a better reason."

"It's me, isn't it? I'm an open book to you."

"Hardly. In fact you puzzle me. Half the trouble is I don't know you at all."

"And the other half?"

"Your impatience."

"Then there's hope for me?"

She feared his lamentable expression.

"I'll say one thing, so there's no mistake. I'm not thinking of commitment yet to you or anyone else."

"You say no, then?"

"I didn't say that."

"Yes or no? It has to be one."

"Neither."

"If you don't say yes, you must mean no?"

"Okay, since you force me, I suppose I say no."

The outing was over, spoiled by the wrong words. Had John intended to pour out his heart he might have been prepared for refusal. As it was he had been thrown into chaos by the abruptness of his own impatience.

The journey home was pleasant, but not jolly, the two once more distanced by events. Uncharacteristically, he approached his mother on the matter, who was less than pleased that his liking for the girl had gone way beyond anything she had expected.

"You listen to me, John. This has to stop. It's one thing to be fond of a country girl, but quite another to consider her as part of a long-term future. When you marry you must think of your position and choose someone like Elizabeth Grant who called by this very afternoon."

For the first time, John became aware of the inconsistency of his class. His mother would have him marry Miss Grant, indeed a pretty little thing with social grace, but as shallow as her waist was thin, and all because she knew nothing of hard work and could raise the correct finger while sipping tea. Conversely, Christabel and her kind were rejected for the circumstances of their birth.

Willingness towards hard work counted for nothing. Given the income to employ, Isobel believed that there wasn't reason to marry a useful woman. An ornament was what a gentleman needed as a wife, but wasn't this contrary to a woman who allowed no mirrors for vanity's sake?

"You know Christabel, mother, and she has all the natural politeness of any lady. She can make cheese too!"

"Good grief! Do you really think a wife of yours will ever make cheese? We buy cheese from the wholesaler. Where's her knowledge of fashion, card games, handling servants? What could she add to a conversation at the dinner table, or is she to remain mute? I couldn't live in Cerne with everyone laughing at us. You would be making my life intolerable."

"Maybe there'd be difficulties at first, but equally I may prefer the company of those friends who wouldn't make fun of her upbringing. She's fine and good. That must count for something?"

"As a companion, yes, it counts for a great deal. I've no complaint of her. Remember, John, her father and I shared a close friendship over many years, but that's where it ended. I knew it and so did he. Christabel is a delight and I'm the first to admit it, but I repeat, a lady's companion isn't the same as a wife."

He wasn't put off by her argument.

"How can you, can we, talk of her in this way, like a ball bouncing between bats, as if her destiny isn't hers to determine? It's a damned bad business to brand her as a subspecies in the eyes of the world. I wish it was merely a question of standing still and letting her catch me to gain her favour. God, how I adore the soil under her craggy boots, the cut of her unfashionable clothes and that silly little bonnet she wears. My mind tells me to give her up because I see only a road of rejection ahead, but I think of her from dawn to dusk. She is everything to me."

"You only think you love her because she's uncommonly pretty, but that won't last for ever, mark my words. You're still a boy in so many ways. You ask my permission and I —"

"No," he interrupted, "I only sought your opinion, and she needs none. I shall marry whom I wish and be hanged with your prejudices. That's if she'll ever have me, which at the moment is unlikely."

"John! You see, already you act coarser."

"Perfectly right. If I'm unhappy without her, and she's below me, then what can I do, but sink to her level?"

"You're too ungrateful. I've given you everything and now you throw it back in my face. I'll be gone soon, then you can do as you like, but until then please consider me and my feelings."

"You're good for years yet and you know it. Hard as nails."

"I'm sixty-seven years old. Too old to have a juvenile to worry about."

"Mother, I've not been a boy for two decades. Stop treating me like one."

"Then stop acting like one. What if I send her away?"

"I'll follow."

"Oh, yes, that would start tongues wagging."

"Mother, you're being hysterical. I just want the woman of my choice."

"You young fool. There's more to life than love. Heaven knows love goes fast enough after marriage. A gentleman needs the right partner and plenty of money. You'll not get my fortune if you fail me."

"To whom else would you leave it?"

"The National Association always needs funds. I'd rather them have it than leave it to a fool."

"If you want to, do just that. Let your pride send future generations of Maddens to the poorhouse."

Isobel softened.

"You know I wouldn't really do it."

"Of course, or I wouldn't have agreed."

"Oh, John!"

"Don't 'oh John' me, mother. To anyone else you're a wonderful hostess. To Chrissie you show pleasure in her company, but spikes and thorns behind her back. Don't die of bitterness because she isn't wealthy."

"Show me a person whom I treat better! You know full well I like the girl."

"Ah, then I do detect a glimmer of hope?"

"Did I give that impression?"

"It was the first bit of common sense to come from your mouth."

"It's only that I don't want her as a daughter-in-law."

"Since when did you start choosing for me?"

"Since you showed no judgement."

"Can't you see yet? I don't just want to believe in love, I want to know it, and now I may have the chance."

"Youth finds its own way into trouble."

"And its own path back out!"

"Sometimes, my boy. I blame myself for the way you are. I've given you too much and let you do too little for your keep. You're naïve of the world and worldly matters."

"Hardly, Mother! I've just awakened to it and it feels great. Strangely, I said much the same to Chrissie."

John walked out as a final gesture of defiance, but some of Isobel's doubts now played on his mind and for the coming few days he looked at Christabel only from a distance, admiring her hard work.

By the end of the week he could stay a hermit no longer. One drizzly afternoon he found Christabel alone in the stables, guiltless in her hard endeavours. He waited until she emerged into the light rain before calling to her. She had no coat or shawl and would have dashed across the yard to the manor had he not summoned her. She walked to where he sheltered under a tarpaulin, but slipped and fell into the mire. At that moment no object could have looked less desirable. Her rain soaked face and bare arms became veined with running mud, while her hair and skirt were sodden and matted.

Even her cotton bonnet flapped limply. John could only laugh. She smiled.

"You seem to have this affect on me."

He took her under cover.

"I only wanted to ask if you've had a change of heart, not to see you drown."

Her expression changed to one of sobriety.

"I'm sorry, John."

The constancy of her opinion came cold from her lips, but he remained mellow.

"For a few glorious seconds then I thought you were going to say '*yes*'. I'd be an even greater fool to raise the subject again. The matter is now closed for good."

"I wish I could say something different, John. You deserve better."

His eyes were dark and moist.

"Honestly, it doesn't matter. I won't mention it again."

"You have a wonderful heart. Give it to someone deserving."

"Do you . . . Oh, nothing."

"Come on . . . Tell me!"

"I was only going to say, do you find my mother's opinions strange to understand on occasions?"

"I hardly know her well enough to answer, but I don't think so."

"We've had words. Did she mention it at all?"

"No. Does it concern me?"

"Not in the least."

Before leaving he asked whether she would care to visit Saint Mary's in Cerne Abbas that Sunday, where he had a meeting.

"No funny business. Just as friends, but you might be left alone for a while."

The man begged an answer that was cheery.

"Thank you, kind Sir. The lady accepts."

She took the corners of her wet skirt, curtsied and left.

Isobel guessed the outcome of John's talk with Christabel and was outwardly relieved. John too became lighter for knowing that there was no further reason for hope. He could now idle around the farm again. He even breakfasted with them, sometimes, for eating before nine was hard when he had been up into the early hours.

The Friday before the outing, Isobel had received a telegraph message from a trades union leader in Leeds. It told of his intention to speak at the next National Association meeting in Glastonbury and offered encouraging news of the latest working men's organisations opposed to the Regulation Act, the bulk of the membership comprising boiler fitters and steel workers from Liverpool and Sheffield.

"I hadn't intended to go to this meeting, but now I'm inclined to rethink."

"May I?"

Christabel took the telegram.

"Would you like to come, Christabel? You said you were interested. It'll mean leaving this afternoon and returning tomorrow. We could stay at The Bell. They're bound to have vacant rooms if we hurry."

"I'd like to, but are you sure we'll be back on Saturday?"

"Of course, but why the urgency?"

"John's taking me to town on Sunday. I really don't want to let him down."

Isobel looked suspicious.

"And you won't, dear."

When Christabel left, Isobel sent an anonymous message to the head of the medical college.

By one o'clock on Saturday large crowds were already gathering around the Corn Exchange. By half-past all seats on the floor and in the gallery had been taken and still hundreds more crammed in to stand around the edges and down the aisles. The speakers arrived with five minutes to spare, setting off a mob of medical students at the front of the gallery, who jeered and whistled.

For nearly an hour the mob prevented any debate, the crowd becoming increasingly hostile to the bullish behaviour of the students. A woman stood and, pointing to the youths, accused them of hypocrisy. Another stood, then more, until, as one, the massed hundreds chanted for their removal. The chairman asked for calm but the situation was on the verge of riot. The union leader from Leeds rose.

"Ladies! Gentlemen! Please! Take thee seats. Let us remember why —"

He was hit by an egg. The speakers left. Policemen burst in and to great applause lunged for the students, who were dragged away screaming. One, to his terror, was dropped from the edge of the gallery to awaiting custody below, landing in disarray, but unhurt until the crowd got to him, whereupon he was punched and kicked. Now, fearing the crowd more than the police, all the students except one gave up the fight and asked for protection to leave. The last student tried to chain himself to a guard rail, but was caught before he could snap the lock.

"Come, come, now Sir. That's no way to treat public property. I'll have to add the charge of criminal damage if we have to cut you free."

"Get your paws off me, Bluebottle."

"Now, Sir. I wouldn't kick out."

"What's the charge?" asked the red-faced youth, held by his collar and pants.

"Braying like a donkey, Sir."

At last the meeting went ahead, but the caretaker, being one of those opposed to the debate, insisted on closing the hall promptly at five o'clock as scheduled. No amount of protesting could prevent it.

"A rotten waste of a day, Isobel," said the union man.

"There'll be others. Are you staying over?"

"I wasn't planning to, but the police need someone to make a formal charge against those hooligans. It means that I can't leave until tomorrow at the earliest."

"Tell you what. I'll lay the complaints. I'm an official after all. Leave it to me and you can get on your way."

"You don't mind? That would be a great relief as I'd like to get home. Hasn't been very successful, has it?"

Isobel saw Christabel waiting patiently, clock watching.

"Oh, I don't know about that!"

Christabel was stunned at the news of the stayover.

"Listen, dear, you forget he's our guest. What right have we to make him stay away from his family so that you can go out joyriding? We must return to The Bell for another night."

Christabel knew that John would think she had stayed away deliberately, and the thought hurt. There was no way of contacting him.

All the way home on Sunday she worried, and finding the house empty she sat waiting for him. She missed dinner and tea, but when he still hadn't come in by ten o'clock that evening she gave up the vigil. That night she tossed and turned, half hoping to hear his heavy steps along the landing.

Breakfast began as usual with only the two women at the table. Then, as they cleared away, the door opened and John walked in. He was in his dressing gown, rubbing his eyes. Christabel stared at him guiltily. He yawned and sat down. The ladies stared, awaiting some sort of explanation. His eyes flicked between then.

"What's up?"

Isobel poured a cup of tea.

"Why, nothing is *up* as you put it. I'm surprised to see you out of bed. What time did you stagger in?"

"Not late. About two o'clock I suppose."

"Where *were* you?" asked Christabel in a soft enquiring tone.

"I spent the day with the Grants."

Isobel perked up.

"The Grants! Ah, excellent, and how is Elizabeth?"

John looked at Christabel's long face.

"Elizabeth? Oh, she wasn't there." He winked discreetly at the young girl. "I went shooting with Daniel and suppered with his parents."

Isobel looked daggers, but said gently to mask her annoyance:

"That must have been a disappointment. I know how you enjoy her company, and her yours."

"Not at all, Mother. I knew she wouldn't be there!"

Isobel left the room. As soon as the door shut John's expression changed.

"So, what happened?" he asked with unexpected composure.

"I tried to get home, I really did. There was a riot and we had to stay behind. I'll explain later. Now you tell me, did you really know Miss Grant wouldn't be there?"

"The truth?"

"Yes," replied Christabel with firmness.

"Actually, I didn't know. I was so put out when you left me flat that I went over to see her."

"Just as well she wasn't there, then, or I might have been jealous." She smiled in a way that indicated that she wasn't to be taken too seriously. "Anyway, I thought you had business?"

"Business can wait for another day, and, to be completely honest, Elizabeth joined us later. I spent an awful evening listening to interminable recitations. I can't tell you what hell it was."

"Poor boy."

"If I ever questioned Elizabeth Grant's empty head, I'm now in no doubt whatsoever."

"I'm not sorry I stayed away then."

"If it wasn't deliberate, there's always tomorrow?"

"Yes . . . Why not!"

By midday on Tuesday John had spent the morning preening, after rising late, while Christabel had cleaned out both duck houses, having thoroughly scrubbed the woodwork of droppings and infestation. She had allowed herself only thirty minutes to wash and change, but was still left waiting by the gig before John entered the courtyard.

Ever since the near accident she had become a nervous passenger, but was good at concealing it. John drove out, leaving her to climb on board after pulling the gates shut. Together they passed onto the road that led through the meadows of Cerne. It wasn't far to town and the pace was intentionally slow. John was happy to be close to Christabel; she, in turn, was content at the safe and steady progress. For much of the time only the clip-clop of the animal's hooves and the grinding of wheels broke the solitary country noises.

Every now and then John leaned from the gig to pick flowers from the hedgerows and banks, giving each scented bloom to Christabel until she held a large posy of fresh wild colours. Blue forget-me-nots, bright yellow kingcups and primroses, purple violets, white anemones, pink honesty and more filled her hand, crowded by catkins pulled from their pendulous anchors by John's acrobatics. She tied them loosely with the ribbon from her bonnet, leaving her hair to blow softly in the breeze.

After a ride of twenty minutes they pulled up opposite the church clock tower, beside a terrace of half-timbered houses built when the area had been one of the great forest districts of England. John explained how these houses were Elizabethan, the projecting timber joists of the upper floor remaining uncovered and the facing timbers set well apart because of a growing scarcity of wood at that ancient time.

John left Christabel to look around the church, pointing also to the Abbey ruin behind. On every wall of the church were scriptures and memorial tablets. At one stone she paused, struck by the prophetic inscription and saddened at the words that recalled the loss of a man's three children aged eight, nine and twelve in the course of two brief years. She moved on, examining in careful detail all of interest. The large east windows were less ornate than those of the south aisle, but brighter, catching the outside light. According to an inscription below, the windows had been taken from the ruins of the Benedictine abbey.

With nothing else left to look at, she turned and walked back to where John was now waiting.

"Did you see it?" he asked with intentional vagueness.

"What?"

"Then you didn't, and I thought you were so clever."

"What are you talking about, John."

"I'll give you a clue."

"John! Stop teasing. You can be very annoying."

"Do you want it or not?"

She nodded.

"Good, because it took me a while to think it up. It goes like this. Discoloured light marks the brother, a book in one hand and a clue in the other."

"That's it?"

"Yes."

"And you called *me* a simpleton! I can read your mind so easily."

"Okay, clever clogs, you solve it then."

The likely answer to the thinly veiled riddle came in a flash and she hurried to the east windows. Her eyes scanned the irregular panes until suddenly she stopped in complete amazement. Quickly pulling the ribbon that held the ring and key over her head, she thrust the key up to the window, glancing between one and the other. John joined her.

"I know this place like the back of my hand, yet when you showed me your key it took ages to remember where I'd seen the design before. I'm right, aren't I? The motif on the spine of the monk's Bible is the same as your key, isn't it?"

"Almost identical."

"Almost?"

"Well, okay, completely."

"That's why I brought you. You said you knew nothing about it. Now at least you know it has some historical significance."

"How can any key belonging to my father have value?"

"I didn't say value, I said, significance. I wouldn't put any value on the key. It's only iron and probably worthless. It's what it represents, or from where it originated, that matters."

"Why were the key and ring so important to my father, that's the question that needs an answer? Do you think he knew something that might benefit me?"

"Derangement I shouldn't wonder. He *was* dying. To be honest, I really don't think you should raise your hopes into believing that there is any great mystery to be uncovered."

"No, he knew what he was doing."

"So many questions and I can't answer them. You say you first saw the key the day he died?"

"He'd never shown it to me before then."

"Let me see it again."

She slipped it off the ribbon.

"It's plain iron, right enough, and nobody would pass it off as a great work of art. You see, the forging is quite crude. I should say it was made for a small cupboard drawer."

"But my father was so adamant that I should have it. So it must have some point."

"Or use."

"Use? That's a thought. Use, but what use?"

"Don't ask me. Was nothing written down?"

"No."

"Then it's either a worthless keepsake or the significance must be in the object itself. Can you remember the exact words he used when he gave it to you?"

Christabel searched her mind.

"He said the ring and key belonged to my mother, but she may not want . . . something or other. That's all. He never finished."

"*Want* is the present tense, but as I understand it your mother died when you were a toddler."

"Yes."

"I know this may seem a strange question, but is there any chance that she didn't die? Could she have run away and he decided to keep the ugly truth from you?"

"No, absolutely not. Her grave is in the village churchyard. We used to take flowers there on Sundays. Anyway, the neighbours spoke of her. I know she died just as he always said."

"Then we're no nearer."

"What now, John?"

"I suggest you forget about it and get on with the rest of your life."

"I suppose so. Yet, you know, he did mean to say more. What about that bit '*she may not want . . .*' . . . to see me, do you think? . . . to have them back?"

"Chrissie, take hold of yourself. Your mother is dead! You said so yourself not five seconds ago."

"We could look in the church records to see if they mention the names of the people in the window?"

The idea was good, but John returned within minutes.

"Silly of us. That window came from the Abbey, so there would be no details in the church records. It's a dead end. Give it up. I only showed you the damned thing for a bit of fun anyway."

Christabel became agitated, insisting that there must be something more to be done.

"You know, Chrissie, you're taking this far too seriously. I wish I hadn't showed you now. It occurs to me that your father must've wanted you to have the ring, which is worth something, but it was merely a coincidence that the key was with it. It's just a moulded lump of iron. I truly suggest you forget about it."

She slipped both back onto the ribbon.

"So be it, Christabel, but keep the blasted key only as a gift from your father. For heaven's sake leave it at that."

Silence was John's companion on the journey back to Wheat Sheaf. Christabel couldn't be shaken from her thoughts. The posy of wild flowers, so lovingly gathered that short time before, lay spread on the seat. One by one the blooms dropped off the edge and onto the road, leaving a trail of petals that stretched a good way back. John watched each fall, but saw little point in saving them. Towering clouds began an early dusk, draping the hills once more in sulky blackness.

John spread a rug over her legs.

"Chrissie, can't you snap out of your melancholy behaviour? What's wrong with you?"

She turned slowly to him.

"Oh, don't you worry. It's only about myself."

A little further and sharp-edged clouds gathered overhead, casting misery to the meadows. The temperature fell noticeably. Without warning a ferocious shower came rattling down, soaking the couple before they had time to cover their heads. The wind became violent and thunder followed.

John suggested that they moved closer to maximise the covering, Chrissie placing her arm around him to keep the rug from slipping off while he managed the horse. He felt no warmth in her hold.

"It won't keep us dry for long. I can already feel drips running down my back."

"We'll be home soon" said John more cheerily. "Do you mind if I hurry the horse?"

"How can you see ahead?" she asked, huge droplets cascading into her face.

"I can't, but the beast knows the way without my help."

A crack pierced the air from behind as a huge bough split from a tree, its tentacled branches fanning across the road and taking a large section of hedgerow with it. Yard by yard the gig pushed on, a weak light radiating from a lamp useful only as a beacon to other vehicles. An oncoming wagon met them at the turn-off. John acknowledged the driver as the same man he had scared that time before, who now refused to go until the gig had passed in front.

"Did you see how wet he was?" remarked Christabel. "His large brimmed hat was hanging down like an upturned bucket over his head."

"Come rain or shine the eggs and milk have to be taken to Pennystone. It's a bad journey on a day like this."

Once back in the kitchen they relaxed on stools by a warming fire. Steam rose from hot milk held in cupped hands, the heat soaking into their depths and burning delightfully. The air in the room tasted of soot brought down the chimney by the storm.

"One thing that puzzles me," said Christabel, holding out her cup for a refill. "I've been thinking of that poor man we saw. With Stratting so close and having its own station, why do you make him drive all the way to Pennystone? It must be twice as far."

"I should've thought that was obvious," he murmured into his cup, still staring into the fire. "Blame the railway barons. The Dorchester line from Stratting starts off northerly, but diverts eastwards to Frome, whereas the Pennystone line reaches Glastonbury. That's where we sell our produce."

"So why did they bother building the other line? Where does it go?"

The question was of no interest and his reply was barely audible.

"Nowhere much. It branches off at Castle Cary, going westwards to Taunton after picking up passengers from all manner of penny-farthing places like Loverton, Westkings and Sowerton."

That night the events of the day raced inside Christabel's fevered head, her thoughts jumping from one subject to another in quick succession and thereby making it necessary to return to each time and time again. Dawn broke, but still she had managed very little sleep despite much tossing and turning. Her temperature was high, her nightclothes damp. It was at the moment of realisation that she would have to face the new day tired out that she finally drifted off. Under closed lids her eyes darted from side to side, her face full of expression.

As a floating spectre in her own dream she looked down on her dying father, who sat up mute, hand outstretched. His face was huge and distorted, as if seen through the bottom of a glass. By his side sat the old man she had seen at the Shalhurn seat, with whiskers that flowed into infinite distance, beckoning her into a creeping mist with bent claw-like fingers. Her father pointed that she should go. She saw one more spectre through the cottage window, a young man mounting a horse with a strange mythical head. The beast stood on its hind legs. She called out and the rider turned, his face missing. With one mighty leap the horse jumped the church with its three straight and one crocked pinnacles and was gone.

She awoke in a heavy sweat, screaming. John crashed over the hallway, finding Christabel slumped against the wall, biting her nightdress and trembling. He called out frantically for his mother's help.

"What in God's name is it?"

"It's her. Just look at her. I think she's having a fit."

Isobel tried to wrap a shawl over the girl's shoulders, but she couldn't pull her away from the wall. She tried talking to her, but there was no response. John hurried away to fetch a bowl of water to cool her off.

"For goodness sake don't wake her up, John. If she's in a trance it could be dangerous."

"We can't leave her there!"

"Okay, I agree, we'll move her together, but for god's sake take it gently."

"She's soaking wet."

At last Christabel's eyes moved.

"Where's the chest? Where is the chest?" she shouted.

"What's she taking about?"

"Must be that old trunk she brought from the cottage. Where did you put it, John?"

"I shoved it in the scullery."

"Where's the chest?" repeated Christabel.

"We'll get it, dear!"

"I can't manage it by myself. It's huge."

"I can't help you unless we first get her onto the bed."

After a few minutes their manoeuvring paid off. By the time they returned with the chest Christabel was sleeping again. John heaved it back out and closed the door.

"God, what a waste of time."

* * *

At a little past ten o'clock Christabel awoke for the second time, the fever gone. Her mind was puzzled by the night. Her bed felt wet and the covers were in disarray, but she could remember little.

Isobel looked in with a cup of tea.

"Feeling better, dear?"

Christabel was unsure what to think, but bit by bit her memory of the dream returned. After a wash and clean clothes, she knocked gently on John's door. She had come to an important decision. Her future didn't lie here after all. The key and her father's dying words had made her a displaced person once again, every bit as much as when she had lost the cottage. She was ready to go, but to what and where?

A sleepy face looked around the crack.

"What ails you now, Chrissie? You look as dismal as a drowned cat."

"I'm leaving," she said.

CHAPTER XIV

The past was yesterday

"Edmond, Edmond", she shouted.

He reined in his horse. The woman, breathless, came hurrying to him. She dropped her bags and looked up. Edmond gazed uncertainly at her.

"Do I know you?"

She hardly knew how to answer.

"No," she replied after some little time, turning instead towards the manor to hide her lying.

"Is James Elvington at home?"

He jumped from the saddle with all the dash of youth, passing the reins over the animal's head and handing them to an attending boy.

"My father should be in the house. Follow me if you would."

He stepped forward, but she sprang to stop him. "*No!*" She let go, recovering her poise. "Is your mother at home?"

"I believe so."

"Kindly, I don't want to trouble *her*. It's only James I've come to see."

Edmond looked at her with curiosity.

"My mother usually greets callers. She wouldn't consider it any trouble I assure you, if Father knows you. He does know you?"

"Oh yes, they both know me."

"Very well then."

He put out an arm to beckon her forward. Still she didn't move.

"You really don't want to meet her, do you? Can I ask why?"

"I'd rather you didn't."

"And if I insist?"

"I'll turn around and leave the way I came."

"I see. Or rather, I don't. If I understand the situation correctly, it's not that you don't want to trouble her. More you don't want to chance seeing her at all. Am I right?"

"Yes," she replied with a shamed expression.

"You know my father is a little . . . How can I put it . . . strange?"

"I've had word."

"All right, have it your way. You'd better wait in the garden conservatory."

Charlotte, having heard an unfamiliar voice in the drive, asked Edmond who it was.

"Someone or other to see Father," he replied ambiguously.

"He's asleep and I'm not waking him. I'll make his excuses."

"No! She expressly asked to speak to him. Only him."

"Don't be foolish, Edmond. Who is she? Did she give a calling card? What's she like?"

"Don't know. No. Fine. In that order."

"What's got into you?"

"It's you. You're making something out of nothing. She just wants to see father, that's all."

"Then tell me what she's like."

"Oh, just an ordinary person. Not your type at all. Probably has no money, so you won't like her. She's very dusty, so she's probably been walking quite a way. I suppose she might want a job. In fact, she's so dishevelled I left her waiting in the conservatory rather than bring her into the house."

"You did right, but it changes nothing. I promised to let your father sleep in this morning and fifty times I say that's what he'll do."

"But it might be important."

"Oh, very well. Have it your way. Go and see if your father's awake, but for goodness sake don't rouse him if he isn't."

Edmond smiled and climbed the stairs. Charlotte watched until he disappeared from the landing and then hurried the opposite way.

The stranger in the conservatory stood with horror as she saw a familiar figure approaching across the lawn. Age had been kind to both women. There was only the one door and no escape, so confrontation was inevitable and imminent. The handle turned and Charlotte entered.

"My God, it's you! How dare you come back here."

"You recognise me after so long?"

"As I would the devil, Sally Ayres."

The visitor felt faint, grabbing the arm of the chair to stop herself from falling.

"May I sit again?"

"No, you may not!"

She became unsteady, her eyes glazed and wide.

"Please, let me rest a moment. I've walked many miles to be here and eaten nothing since yesterday."

"Then you're a fool."

"I'll go into the servants' hall if you wish. Keep out of your way. Only, for mercy sake, please allow me to rest awhile and take a little bread."

"Don't be so absurd. I don't want the servants witnessing my son greeting you as his mother? That's why you've come, isn't it? To tell Edmond you're his mother, and after all these years of silence. Or have you already done it? You have, haven't you? Outside, just now. You bloody little slut!"

Sally looked askance.

"He doesn't already know?"

"Not from me. Are you saying you didn't tell him either?"

"Of course not."

"Isn't that why you've come back? There can't be any other reason for this unwarranted intrusion into my life."

She shook her head wearily and sat without asking further permission.

"I admit I've often thought how wonderful it would be if he could acknowledge me. Just to feel his arm squeeze around my waist as he whispered 'Mother'. I envy you that."

Charlotte became panicked.

"So! I was right. You make no attempt to hide your plan. Nothing is plainer in your thoughts than the desire to be reacquainted."

"There's no need to be frantic on that score."

She glanced from a window that faced across to the great house, catching sight of Edmond unsaddling his horse.

"It never struck me that I could introduce myself as such to him. I couldn't. He wouldn't care for me if I did, so where's the point? He's become such a marvellous young man. I owe you much for that."

Charlotte remained tense, but with enough willpower not to be swayed by the overture.

"You owe me nothing, and for that matter, I owe you nothing. I hate the very sight of you and all that you represent."

Sally turned and smiled the best she could.

"Not just to oblige, but I can truly say I understand. I've kept the guilt of Edmond hidden for what seems an eternity. It's little consolation that the world outside is none the wiser for my silence."

"Ha! You should think well on what you say. There's vanity in your speech, for what else, but your deception of virtuosity, have you got left? And this, itself a woman's greatest treasure, you would throw away like a used hat."

The response was from the hip and unthinking.

"Am I now to learn chastity from you? You forget that it was your behaviour that drove James into my arms. I gratify myself that to sink in your esteem is not to be cast adrift by the world in general. We're so alike, if only you would see it."

Charlotte blushed and hurt. Sally noticed the change, so her tone softened.

"But, yes, in truth you're right. I'm perfectly indifferent to what others may think of me now. There comes a time, an age I suppose, when such things seem trifling when compared to all that has been lost. Come now, admit it yourself. Aren't I right?"

Charlotte secretly believed so.

"Certainly not. Your impertinence in thinking I would share your view is incredible. I correct myself. You're not merely vain, but thoroughly conceited too. No, more still, a simpleton. James didn't need you, he just used you. You were a convenient harbour, a rest-cure in difficult times."

Sally winced at Charlotte's scathing tongue.

"Must we speak like this? I fear we've already said more than was intended. I know I didn't come to cause you trouble or pain. You've been a good mother to –"

"Don't patronise me again. You've no way of knowing anything of the kind. I might have beaten him silly. You don't know and up until today you haven't cared. If I was the sort of woman who needed flattery, no doubt you'd be invaluable, but I'm not and I won't have it from you. Now, leave!"

The visitor stood weakly, taking a step towards the door before turning to Charlotte with head bowed.

"Of course I've cared. I've *always* cared." She looked up. "Can't I speak with James?"

"What? Only when hell freezes over!"

Charlotte marched to the door and held it open. Sally stepped out, only to jump back in and slam the door shut.

"Oh heavens, Edmond is coming. Please, I beg you, don't let him in. Not like this. I've seen him once today and that was unbearable. I can't face him again on these terms. I'll go. I promise."

The pleading provoked Charlotte to do the opposite, not thinking first whether it was in her own interest. All she knew was that the pain she could cause seemed a triumph. She pushed Sally to one side and welcomed Edmond with a wry smile. The flush on Sally's face betrayed a heated situation. Edmond looked at one and then the other, puzzled.

Charlotte took Edmond by the arm and led him to Sally, but was immediately shocked by their likeness. He put down a try of cold drinks and biscuits, waiting for an introduction.

"Well, Mother?"

Sally glanced at Charlotte entreatingly, not knowing what she might say and fearing the worst. Edmond grew impatient.

"Mother!"

Both women turned. Charlotte's lips became narrow and mean, and in a cold manner she introduced Miss Sally Ayres as a family acquaintance from the bad old days. The deliberate omission of 'friend' didn't go unnoticed. Edmond left feeling unwelcome.

"I thought for a horrible moment that you were going to tell him."

"I very nearly did."

"Thank goodness you thought better of it."

"Perhaps I should have. That would've ended your game. Driven you off."

"You know, I suddenly realise that I pity you. You nearly wrecked sixteen years of silence for a moment's vengeance. Can't you get it into your warped mind that his indifference to me is better than the hate he might feel if he found out. It's far too late to expect him to have any feelings for me."

"Hate?"

"Why not? I *did* give him up. Can a child forgive that, especially of someone who is now a stranger? I think not, but, then, what would he have thought of you, his proxy mother?"

"God, it's blackmail isn't it? I should've looked for the simple reason for your visit."

She became indignant at the cruel condemnation.

"Good gracious, no! Have I said or done anything to suggest that? I think not."

"Then, Madam, I can only see one other reason why you're here. It must be to reacquaint yourself with James. To wreck my marriage if you can. Yes, of course, that's why you only wanted to see him. I've hit the nail on the head, haven't I?"

"No, not that either."

"Then I don't understand."

Sally saw that the door had been left open, but her thoughts were read by Charlotte, who slammed it shut, standing with her back against the frame.

"It's been a terrible mistake coming. Best I go."

"And have you return another day when you feel stronger? I'm not moving. We'll face it out right now."

The unwelcome guest slumped down, now indifferent to her fate. Charlotte watched her for a moment. She had certainly won. Sally Ayres posed no threat. She poured a beaker of iced lemon and handed it over.

"Drink this. You'll feel better, but listen, any decent person would let bygones be bygones. Why bring back old memories?"

"You've misunderstood everything and so punish me too harshly. If only you knew how hard it was for me to come."

She trembled, unable to look into Charlotte's eyes. Charlotte offered a biscuit, which she gladly took.

"Yes, all right, it's true I came to see Edmond, but only for the one time and never to introduce myself. You've no idea what it's like to have your child taken away."

Charlotte winced, for she knew only too well. Was it possible James hadn't told even her of Christabel?

"Even if I accept what you say, you still tell me nothing. You continually leave me to draw my own conclusions. It's time for plain speech. Put down the biscuit and tell me why you're here!"

Instead of putting it down, Sally stuffed it quickly into her mouth, washing it down with juice. The dank humidity of the surrounding plants added a heaviness to the air, leaving a breathless atmosphere that was hard to suffer.

"I came, as I've said, principally to see Edmond once more as a man. Sixteen weeks to sixteen years. Everything in between is a mystery." She laughed. "My son. *My son!* I've never said that to another living person, only wept the words into my pillow. My only consolation has been that as the years passed I knew he wouldn't be anything like I remembered him. The Edmond I knew was a baby who no longer exists. Your Edmond is a stranger, that fine young man who didn't know me when I called out his name." She withdrew a lace handkerchief and dried the corners of her eyes. "The fact is I'm to be married, and after our honeymoon we're leaving for Africa to take over a Christain mission in Nyasaland. Imagine. I'm to be a missionary's wife. That's irony. I doubt if we'll ever return to England. Of course, he knows nothing of Edmond and it must stay that way. I reckon I've paid for past mistakes and I think God will forgive me for feigning sexual innocence if I throw myself into His work. It wouldn't cross Peter's mind that a middle-aged spinster has a hidden past."

Charlotte brightened visibly.

"Then you've fulfilled your plan. You're free to say goodbye to Westkings forever."

Sally looked into her lap.

"Not quite. My intention was also to see James. After all, we once meant something to each other . . . Ah, I see you disapprove even after knowing that I'll soon be gone from your life."

"Of course I disapprove. What else should I feel?"

"For God's sake, for once see it from my side. You might not believe me, and you can fight me over it if you want, but I'm going to tell you anyway. James pressed his attentions on me after I innocently accepted the use of his carriage, not the other way around, and in doing so he wrecked my life. I'll never forget that day, however long I live and wherever I am. He had offered to take me to the station. Instead he took me all the way home and to my bed! It all happened so fast. I would've hated him for what he did except that he came back and often stayed with me during the pregnancy. For years after I wondered if I'd done right by letting him take the baby away, but I now see that I was. With all my little brothers and sisters screaming around the small house, knee deep in dirty washing and boiling soil cloths, not to mention my father who was ready to throw me out, it was a favour. I remember James saying that by taking the child it would help you too. I didn't understand what he meant then, and I won't ask now. For my son's sake I see that he's benefited from his father's position and influence. It was good of you to accept Edmond when you had no children of your own!"

The story had a familiar ring. Sally reached for her purse.

"I thought of keeping this photograph of James, but now I can't."

Charlotte snatched it.

"You needn't have done that. I was going to leave it behind."

Charlotte had had enough. She wanted her gone.

"Is it money you need?"

"That's not why I came, but I did have to walk part of the way here. I thought James would give me my fare home. He owes me that."

She pressed five pounds into Sally's hand.

"Now go!"

Sally looked at the crisp white note.

"That's how it all began. My asking for help." She shuddered. Opening her fingers, she let the note drop to the floor. "Not again. Not ever again, even from you."

Sleep had not refreshed James' spirits, leaving an aching head and dry throat after his latest drunken bent. He hunted around his room for another bottle. Only one had anything left in it, which he drained in a mouthful and threw the empty aside.

On unsteady legs, he made his way down the stairs to the morning room, his collar studded only at the back and bouncing like a spring around his cheeks. Here Edmond sat eating and reading. Bread, cheese and ham were set out on the table. Edmond hardly looked up as his father entered. James took the knife and stabbed at the shoulder of meat. Edmond knew the signs.

"Here, Father, let me do it or you'll slip and cut your fingers off."

Ever since his visit to Jack Mere's cottage in Shalhurn, Edmond had viewed his father in a somewhat better light, even taking an interest in weaning him off strong liquor. These efforts had been rewarded by a small, but discernible improvement in the older man's temper, but there was still a long way to go. He poured the tea, passing it to James along with the plate of food. Through red eyes James stared with distaste at the swirling brew in the cup.

"I can't face that, boy. Get me a glass of Madeira to chase my headache away."

Gently, Edmond warned that alcohol would be useless at this stage of the malady and offered more tea when the first was spilled. Feeling too soporific to argue, James timidly complied.

"By and by, Father, you had a visitor."

James looked up from the rim of the cup.

"What?"

"Not what, Father, who? Someone called Sally Ayres."

He dropped the cup for the second time.

"Her!"

Edmond took a cloth to dry the floor.

"I came to tell you, but you were sleeping. She hardly spoke a word to me, but she and mother went at it hard when I wasn't around to see. I don't think they were friends at all.

James flashed back to the fresh-faced teacher of long ago.

"What was she like?"

"I tell you, she was a fair woman and no mistake for her age, with a soft-featured face. She's gone now, just before you came down. I think she was crying."

"Just gone?"

James threw his food onto the table and rushed to the window, the fog around his eyes magically clearing. He could make out a figure disappearing from the end of the lane.

"Quickly, Edmond, fetch my horse."

Edmond took his shoulders.

"Sit down before you fall down. You can't ride anywhere. Not in this state. Look, she's gone anyway."

He led his father back to the chair, where James cupped his head in shaking hands and began sobbing. He had imprisoned himself in the manor by the alcohol in his blood.

"For goodness sake, Father, what is it?"

Only two servants had remained loyal to the Elvington household. The others, and all those later employed, had left at one time or another, unable to put up with the abuse that normally accompanied James' tyrannical conduct while drunk. One had said on leaving:

"His dreadful ways are enough to make a devil from a saint." This was no exaggeration.

Much the same was true of Charlotte, who had stood by her husband during years of degradation only because of her memories of how things used to be before Christabel was born. She had ignored the loss of their friends, but social isolation had brought with it a change in her own disposition. The young and beautiful wife of yesteryear, so headstrong and full of laughter, had become a sharp matron with a ferocious tongue. The curate, a friend of long standing, had stopped calling some years back, and even for the doctor a mercy visit was a duty not to be welcomed. Indeed, the manor had taken on the atmosphere of a colossal mausoleum, its older incumbents living in sullen surroundings far removed from rich country life. Only Edmond breathed fresh happiness into its walls, although he was away so much that the general aspect didn't change.

The next morning began with much crashing as James descended the stairs half-dressed and brandishing his leather belt. The vociferation aimed at Charlotte were terrible. Having seen him in similar moods, she scurried to the pantry, afraid for her safety until he calmed down or fell down. In a rage he staggered from room to room, flinging open the doors and gripping the frame for support as he leaned in search of a victim.

From her hidey-hole Charlotte could hear his slow progress towards her. He reached the kitchen. She stayed perfectly quiet, but shaking, her face in blackness, but her eyes staring through a thin crack between the hinges of the poorly fitting door. She saw has dark shape pass back and forth.

"Come out, you bitch, you bloody little bitch."

He fell onto the table, scattering food already prepared for the day and sending some smashing to the floor. He trod through it without care. The cook backed away.

"Where is she?" he demanded.

Cook shook her head and ran out through the back door into the kitchen garden.

He lashed out one way and then the other, ransacking the cupboards until finally his face appeared fiendishly in front of Charlotte's. The smell of drink was suffocating. He peered into the blackness, but could see nothing, although he was clear to her. She made no sound, holding her breath until he pushed the door shut. With danger seemingly passed, she breathed out, but at once the door flew open again, catching her in the semi-light.

His hand tore in and, grabbing her hair, he dragged her out while thrashing his leather belt across her back. She screamed for him to stop. Panicked by the shouts, the cook peered in, but quickly slammed the door shut again.

"Bastard child, and now you stop me seeing Sally. How dare you!"

He struck her again, the full force falling on crossed arms that protected her head. Without warning he kicked her legs away. Her hands reached for the ground to break the fall, the belt cutting into her neck.

Several more blows followed, but it still wasn't enough to satisfy his temper. With sweat pouring from his face, he looked around the room and saw the stove in the corner. It glowed hot and red. Tightening his grip, he dragged her screaming to it. With his bare arm he swept aside the pan, shrieking with agony as some of the boiling water splashed onto his skin. Taking a folded cloth in one hand, he lifted the hot metal plate to expose the furnace beneath. In desperation Charlotte shrieked for mercy. His strength was immense. With one arm around her waist, he twisted her towards the fire. She pushed back, burning her hands on the surface. Her screams turned into mad cries for help, but they fell on deaf ears. With a final gathering of strength, he pushed her face down towards the hole of red searing heat, forcing her closer by the second. Suddenly the door burst open, the panting cook pushing Edmond through.

"What the hell . . .!"

Edmond, frantic, rushed over, shielding Charlotte's head with his hand and pulling her back, but James thrust his full weight onto Charlotte to counter the effort. His strength was terrifying. In the struggle Edmond could feel his arms weakening. In one final desperate move, he smashed his fist into James' face, at last breaking the hold. Charlotte fell to the floor, her face burning hot, but not flayed. She looked up at James with a piteous expression, her skin tight and red, but magically youthful, bearing none of the matriarchal harshness of recent years, as if cleansed. James slumped in the corner, gazing in disbelief.

"Heaven damn me," he cried, holding out an arm to her, but unable to move. "What have I done?"

She crawled back apace, afraid of any sudden moves towards her. Edmond restrained him as he stood.

"Charlotte, destroy me now while you have the chance and the reason. Take a knife. Do it! I don't want to live like this anymore."

Edmond stared at his mother, ready to stop her if she tried. Rows of carving knives lay ready and her eyes flicked towards them. She knew she could do it and be acquitted of guilt. She touched her cheek. It was still hot and very tender. Edmond braced himself. Her hand reached for the table, fingers wrapping themselves around the wooden handle of a meat knife. James stood rigid, eyes closed.

"No!" pleaded Edmond, putting himself between them, but still holding James.

The knife fell from her hand, the blade bouncing off the quarry tiled floor and striking James' leg. It drew a trickle of blood.

"I can't," she pleaded. "Not now, not ever. You're still my husband." She turned to Edmond. "Let him go."

"No! I mustn't."

"Edmond! Do as I say. Let him go!"

Reluctantly he released his hold by stages, ready to counter any aggressive move. Once freed, James slowly dropped to his knees. Instinctively he touched the cut on his leg, which was deeper than expected. His sock was already quite red. He looked up at Charlotte, feeling sick inside for what he had done. Softly he said:

"There's no return to my old ways. You have spared me and from this moment I too am changed. I curse the bottle and the devil that flows from its neck. You, Edmond, have proved yourself a better man than I ever was. No longer will I be master of this house. Take the title, Edmond, it's yours."

Although still in shock, Edmond could see good coming from the viciousness of his father's attack. There was some hope after all. With the slightest chance of restitution, he could not and would not take from his father the one thing that might give him a reason for living.

James turned to Charlotte, his expression resigned.

"You've both saved me, but still I must be punished. I'll do what is necessary to meet my own conditions." He lifted himself off the floor. "Charlotte, a mad dog has its teeth removed. I have madness that must be purged. I'll never have the capacity to strike you again."

With an alarming leap he plunged his arm deep into the stove, letting out a scream of terrible pain as his flesh burned and cooked. Again he fell to the ground, a charred, almost melted stump beside him. Almost in a trance from the horrific sight, Edmond grabbed a jug and threw water over the remains. James struggled to lift his head, to see for himself the raw mutilation of his actions.

"It's done!"

Edmond, now crying uncontrollably, took his weight and wiped sweat-stuck hair from his face. James convulsed.

"I'm back, Char. I love you again."

He fell back unconscious.

CHAPTER XV

Desperate measures

*C*harlotte entered the doors of Schofield and Fly – Solicitors of Law – a full twenty minutes before her appointment with Sir Arthur Schofield. She was normally so precise. Sir Arthur set his watch by her arrival every last day of the month, when outstanding estate business was discussed. She had thought of ending her personal visits, sending Edmond in her place, but he was still a legal 'minor', with no power to sign documents.

Ushered into the waiting room, she was given a glass of sherry and offered a seat by the open fire. Sir Arthur hurried out to greet her, shaking his watch and holding it to his ear. He disappeared again after a few words of apology, racing a reluctant client through the various, but too few, grounds for divorce. The man left with a long face, joining a woman who was not his wife in an awaiting cab. Back inside, Sir Arthur pushed the papers off the edge of his desk and into the bin. No more time would be wasted on that.

Nobody could call Sir Arthur an elegant man. He was red faced and dumpy, with a parting in his hair that stretched from one ear to the other. His clothes, although made by the finest tailors, were as tight as the skin of a sausage, rippling around his waist when he sat. His stiff winged collar was a bit too small, causing his neck to hang over in a neat circular fold, while his cuffs were a little too long, enveloping his hands to the knuckles. Despite his amusing appearance, he had the manners of the old times, as gracious and genuine as his honesty was sincere.

"My dear, Charlotte, do please forgive my timekeeping. My watch must be running slow. I trust you were looked after?"

She nodded and entered his well-worn office, heavy with fine, dark English oak that had matured over centuries. Mr Fly, the junior partner, knocked soon after and joined them.

"Good afternoon, Ma'am."

"You remember our Mr Fly, Charlotte?"

"Oh, yes. Hello again, Augustus. How are you?"

"Well. Very well thank you."

"And the family?"

"Good. Yes, indeed. My wife is expecting again."

"Again! How many will that make?"

"Eleven. I think we might make fourteen."

Charlotte looked askance. Sir Arthur tapped his pen on the desk, a silent instruction for Fly to leave.

"I have all the files on the estate here at hand. The bottom one has details of land and buildings held outside Westkings." He got up and shut the door. "This is indeed an unusual request you have made, Charlotte. I have to say I was quite surprised by your letter."

"You disapprove?"

He picked up his spectacles, swinging them by an arm. "As your solicitor I have two functions, to carry out your wishes and to advise on matters arising. As your friend I might also play the devil's advocate. The answer I give may depend upon the hat you want me to wear."

"I know I'm within my rights to ask you to carry out my instructions, so it must be that you disapprove?"

"I'm afraid so, dear lady."

"Why, may I ask?"

"With respect, Charlotte, I couldn't help questioning your motives, although I suppose they are legally none of my business other than how they affect the advice I proffer. My concern centres mainly on the matter of church missions in Africa. In all our conversations over the years I've never once heard you express the slightest interest. You're a good woman, and heaven alone knows James used to give a lot of money to charities, but I just couldn't understand this sudden philanthropy, especially with finances so tight at present. I might have to act on your behalf, but I also have my reputation to consider, let alone legal obligations and personal moralities. Not everything I'm asked to do, do I do. My advice would be worthless if I didn't make my own judgements on occasions. So when you offered to send all that equipment to Africa on board a specially chartered steamer, at very considerable personal cost to yourself, and financed through the sale of jewellery, and asked me to see that it was done according to your exact instructions, I felt obliged to check it out."

"You did what?"

"Calm yourself, Charlotte. I did it for your sake as much as mine. I had to make sure you were getting value."

"And?"

"I'll put my cards on the table. You offered the equipment for a particular mission, funded only if those taking charge accompany it to Africa and stay there for at least ten years. I suppose you had your reasons. I won't ask what they are, although they seem unusually specific conditions."

"I am helping a friend to fulfil an ambition, that's all." The words stuck in her throat.

"Ah! Yes, indeed. Quite admirable, very much so. Well done! I had pondered the likely reason, but I must admit I hadn't thought of that possibility. Yes, a very reasonable and generous act of kindness. Very laudable, but by heaven, then, it is even more important that my investigations bore fruit. You see, I found out through much searching that the ship you hired is a proper rust bucket. Probably would've sunk in mid-ocean. We couldn't have that."

"It wasn't any of your business."

"Charlotte! There'd be men and women on board, not forgetting your friend. No amount of charity is worth chancing lives

over, however well intentioned the gift. In a way I'd be as responsible for the safety of the passengers as the captain himself, having
found out what I now know. I tell you that ship isn't fit for the journey. It usually carries coal around the coast and hasn't made a deep
sea crossing for years. It would be a disaster in the making."

Charlotte flared.

"Cancel the lot, then."

"Everything? Don't you want to charter another vessel? I've
drawn up a list of suitable craft with available sailings, which I
have here somewhere."

"No, I'll not bother with anything. You've put a damper on the
whole idea. I'll save my money instead."

"Well, of course, that's your right, but I do think you're being a
bit hasty, having made the promise."

"You know how I stand financially. Can I easily afford it?"

"No, not really. Not easily, but if it's a question of additional
costs, I can assure you that the new vessels are much the same
price."

"No, my mind's made up. Cancel it and the devil help Africa."

"If that's what you want. The church commissioners will be
very sorry to lose it all. Would you consider a smaller gift perhaps? One more affordable. For your friend's sake?"

"No! Now let's get on with other matters, or am I going to
receive another lecture?"

Sir Arthur closed the file and opened the next. It was another
problem. He shuffled the papers, then looked up at Charlotte, wondering how best to keep the atmosphere calm.

"This business of Jack Mere. I'm afraid you're asking me to
breach a confidence with James. It puts me in a very difficult position, very difficult indeed. You see, Charlotte, when James set up
the lease for Mere it was on the strict understanding that nobody
else outside this room knew anything about it. It's been a four-way
secret ever since, between James, myself, Sir Kenneth DeByers
and, of course, Mere himself. Silence has remained sacrosanct over
all these years. Now you want me to destroy all records of the

arrangement and any other documents mentioning Mere's daughter, Christabel. To be straight with you, I'll need a very good reason for doing so if I'm not ordered. More to the immediate point, how on earth did you come by the information in the first place? I've never told you of the cottage and I feel sure James hasn't."

"No, you didn't and, if you want home truths, I've found it hard to forgive you for that. How many years have we known each other? Isn't it nearly twenty?"

"I was acting upon instructions."

"Yes, and that's the only reason I've let it go. Anyway, obviously I knew something of the general set-up between James and Jack Mere, but not where he lived. If you want to know, I came across a letter from Sir Kenneth written to James regarding the termination of the agreement after Mere's death."

"That explains much. Of course, I've formerly ended the contract and agreed to terminate payments forthwith. I've written for details as to when the cottage was vacated by Mere's child, in case he delayed telling me in order to collect a few extra rents."

"You might as well let it go. It's hardly worth the trouble."

"It's a goodly sum each month, I can assure you. Good land doesn't come cheap. Anyway, Edmond instructed me to press for details. Should I stop my enquiries?"

"Not if Edmond asked you to. He effectively runs the estate now. For goodness sake, however, don't involve us in heavy legal fees. It's not a matter of principle."

"I understand."

"As to the other business, you can't object to destroying the records now all that's over and done with?"

"We do like to keep these things on file, at least for a few years, but if you insist, I suppose there's no outright reason not to burn them. I will need James' approval though."

"Don't be a damned fool. You know he's not fit to approve the colour of his tie!"

"No, I suppose not, more's the pity."

"Good. Then you'll do it!"

"Yes, Charlotte."

He wrote a message on the cover of the top file and placed it to one side.

"Now we come to the next file, the one I keep on Christabel Mere herself."

"What! You have a file on her? Why in heaven's name? She's only a child."

"Not so much a child now, Charlotte."

"Tell me, and I want plain speaking, what do you know of her circumstances?"

"I think you'll find James has told us most things."

She blushed.

"Us?"

"Sorry, my dear, I mean me. 'Us' refers to the firm. This file is marked for my eyes only. See, look for yourself."

He passed it across.

"So I see. Thank you. Now, get rid of it!"

"Can I ask why this should be destroyed too?"

"Isn't it enough that I want it done?"

"Of course, at least it is in law. Now, please, watch me change my silly hat for the one labelled 'friend'."

"All right! Let's stop playing parlour games. Since James' accident you've relied more than ever on Edmond and I running the estate, with your guidance I might add."

"I do my best."

"I know that, and we're grateful. The point is, whilst it was once necessary to run things by committee because of James' ill health, the situation has changed since Edmond has become a man. What's more, James doesn't like being seen outside Westkings and will only journey if it's really important, which has the effect of drawing business to us at the manor. You know all that, so I won't bore you further with it. Not long ago I had a visit from a former acquaintance of James', who raked up old muck. I don't want it ever happening again. It's time to bury the past, all the past, and Christabel is part of that process."

"But she's your daughter."

"She's a stranger!"

"I see. Hum! If that's how you genuinely feel, it does make a difference. I should tell you, however, that in this file I have details of where Christabel now lives. I also have records of her schooling achievements, which aren't inconsiderable given the circumstances of her background, and a few other notes and bits and pieces."

Charlotte sat agog.

"You have all that? Did James ask you to keep an eye on her?"

"Quite the opposite. He instructed me to have nothing to do with her and to tell you nothing. The fact is, it was Jack Mere himself who wrote to me, or more likely someone writing on his behalf. The penhand had a distinctive feminine touch but the words were clumsy and undoubtedly his. Given that James has handed the reins to you and Edmond, so to speak, I could nip out to the lavatory for a few minutes and thoughtlessly leave the file open on the desk? Do I need the lavatory, Charlotte?"

"You must do as James originally wanted, to the letter," said Charlotte with forced determination. "Now I know that the records exist the only way of stopping me seeing them and run the risk of rekindling any feelings best forgotten, by fair means or foul, is to destroy them. More to the point, nobody else must see them, ever! What will you do?"

"As a friend?"

"Yes."

"Destroy them."

"And as my solicitor?"

"Destroy them."

A niggling doubt as to whether Sir Arthur would actually be as good as his word stayed with Charlotte for the remainder of the day. As it turned out, she had been right to be concerned.

Sir Arthur, having had much experience with matters relating to the emotions of the heart, believed sincerely that in hindsight Charlotte would come to regret her hasty decision to lose the file on her daughter. Therefore, instead of ordering the destruction of the file, he had bundled it away for long-term storage deep in the office vault. Charlotte would never be the wiser unless later she expressed regret.

The following day Charlotte, having entertained a visitor in the hotel lounge, relaxed in her carriage, content to watch the passing views as she returned to the manor.

That weekend's *Glastonbury Chronicle* headlined a burglary and fire at the offices of Schofield and Fly. Papers were missing.

That chapter of Charlotte's life had closed. A few days later Augustus Fly deposited one hundred pounds at Lloyds bank.

CHAPTER XVI

The Skimmity

"The poorest man," said William Pitt, "may in his cottage bid defiance to all the forces of the Crown. It may be frail, its roof may shake, the wind may blow through it, the storm may enter, the rain may enter, but the King of England cannot enter!"

Rarely is home so appealing than when, through one circumstance or another, it is taken away. Christabel Mere's experience of this loss was now twofold. The Queen of England may not have been able to enter her former home without invitation, but a lesser man had taken it from her, and now she had given up another.

Having told John of her intention to leave the farm at that moment of fever, Christabel had returned to her room to wait out the remaining time before breakfast, wondering whether she had been too hasty in making such an important decision. To leave was the right one, but to suggest going sooner rather than later was perhaps not well considered. She hadn't any idea why she felt that she needed to go, or where she should begin searching for the answer to a muddled dream. It had something to do with her father's trinkets, that she felt strongly, but was there any way of discovering why they meant so much to him? Any solution, if one was possible, might be trifling. What then? Would it have been worth leaving Cerne for? It was undeniable that the key and ring had done nothing to ease her father's life. So how could they change hers? She stretched out on the bed, staring up at the ceiling.

The more Christabel thought, the more likely it seemed that there would be nothing whatsoever to discover, but could she be sure? Of course not. The only way of knowing was to make the effort to find out, however futile. Anyway, if nothing came of it at least she could say at its end, 'I have fought the good fight, I have finished the course, I have kept faith and now I am happy once more!'.

Gradually the arboreous paths and lanes of the Cerne Valley came alive with movement, spring freshness crisp in the morning air. The sky seemed bluer than before, the flowers brighter, and long catkins on weeping branches kissed the cool, clean waters of the Cerne as it made its winding course past the lower reaches of Powerstock forest. Newborn lambs dotted the meads, leaping and jumping as if petals sprung open by the rays of warm sunshine. Cows idled through the lush pastures.

There was no denying that Christabel had been happy here, even more so since she had ended John's love-making. Isobel was kind beyond measure, appreciating Christabel's supererogation. Life was simple and ordered, just as it had been at Shalhurn, but without the poverty.

At breakfast Christabel was careful not to mention again her plans to leave, wanting more time to think around the angles. As the subject didn't come up, she left believing that John hadn't remembered her early morning visit. He had, his own silence hiding a genuine feeling of impending loss."

"Mother, has she told you she's going?"

"No! That can't be right. Where did you hear that?"

"From the horse's mouth, but, more to the point, don't you want to know why?" he cried with impatience.

"If you want to tell me, I've not the least objection to listening, although I expect it has something to do with you making a nuisance of yourself."

"Ha! You couldn't be more off the mark."

"Then it's that confounded key and you raising her hopes with daft ideas. I tell you, Jack was a fool muddling her mind. She'll regret going, and I'll regret losing her company, and you, John, what will you regret?"

He said nothing.

Christabel, having said nothing further to indicate that her departure would be within the next day or two, considered a week an acceptable compromise. Maybe even two. Thus decided, she settled back into her regular duties, a burden lifted. It was in the afternoon while rummaging in her bag for thread that John came excitedly into the house.

"What a laugh! What fun! I've come back especially for you, Chrissie. Grab your shawl. I'll explain on the way."

Leading her by the hand, John rushed through the kissing gate just beyond the church and out along the riverside bridleway that cut short the walk to Mangstone, reappearing in the village between the inn and the watermill. The noise was deafening. Far down the street stretched crowds of workfolk, shouting and laughing and some brandishing long poles from which dangled evil-looking animal skulls. The mad atmosphere to the stranger was frightening, but it gave John a good deal of pleasure. It was a carnival of riotous behaviour.

Christabel gripped John firmly as they wound their way to a vantage point. He began screaming with the rest. She peered through the waving bodies.

"What's going on?" she shouted over the din.

"It's a Skimmity. Look there. A married women has been caught having it away with a neighbour. Here they come now!"

From the other end of the village trotted a rider leading a donkey on which sat a man and woman tied back to back. Their heads were bowed in shame. She held a huge wooden spoon.

"Adulterer, hussy, whore!" blurted out the crowd as the donkey passed, the jeering onlookers jostling to keep up with the procession. The leader smiled and waved, inciting more fervency.

"It's terrible," said Christabel, turning her head away. "The poor things."

"Poor things, be hanged. It's good sport."

"How can you be so cruel?"

"They've had their moment. Now it's ours."

At the top of the street the donkey stopped. The ropes were cut and the shamed riders dismounted. The man joined his friends, linking arms and laughing as they left for the fields. The woman was in floods of tears, too distressed for comfort. She was spirited away by her daughter, unable to look at the faces of her neighbours.

The Skimmity over, the crowd dispersed, leaving only the old folk to discuss how it compared with those when they were young. Soon they too had gone home.

John led Christabel back along the lane to the inn, hoping to make amends by offering a pleasant tea. The inn was a tiny stone building, thatched and standing within its own small piece of land. Staddle stones that marked the boundaries stood only eleven feet apart. The inside was divided into two by a half-width wall that cast darkness over several corner tables.

"You know, my lovely," said the innkeeper, "this is the smallest hostelry in the whole of England. Five hundred years it's been standing on this very spot. It was a forge and foundry first. Quite a reputation it had for making fine castings when the blacksmith had the time to work his skills. People came from miles and the business passed from father to son over the centuries. There aren't many businesses that can claim to have stayed so long in the hands of one family. Of course, that all ended well before I took over the place, but knowing its history makes me take extra pride in it."

Christabel smiled slightly.

"Sorry," said John to the innkeeper when Christabel turned away. "She's not quite herself. Are you, my love?"

"If you want to know, I can't understand anyone enjoying the torment of others. You surprise me, John. I don't like that side of your character."

"It wasn't just me! The whole town was out."

"That poor woman."

"She got what she deserved! Anyway, I see you don't offer sympathy for the man."

"Why should I? He went off happy enough. His crime will be forgotten, but hers won't be."

"It's the way of things. People expect better of women."

The innkeeper gave up trying to interest Christabel in his story, presently returning with the tea and food. John had used the minutes to speak harshly to her.

"I'm so sorry," she offered to the innkeeper. "I forgot my manners. Please, go on with your tale."

"It's no tale. Every word is gospel truth. Look, you see this?" He pointed to a handwritten document in a style that was almost impossible to read. "That is the original licence to sell ale. Ought to be in a museum. Is signed by good King Charles II himself, who stopped on this very spot to have his horse shod. It was when the blacksmith couldn't sell him ale to help his thirst that Charlie granted a licence and made the forge an inn. The old place went back to being a forge when Napoleon went on the rampage, though. I suppose there was more money shoeing legs than getting legless at the time." He laughed, slapping John heavily on his shoulder. "My old man knew a bargain when he saw it and bought it for a song during the lean years back in the 1860s. He turned it back into an inn, the shrewd bugger. He left it to me a dozen years ago and proper grateful I am."

John nodded acceptance of the story to a sceptical Christabel.

"All these hangings around the walls are the original tools of the blacksmith, and I have boxes more of the stuff in the back. Would you like to see them?"

"Not just now," threw in John, but Christabel was keen not to offend further and two old wooden crates were brought to the table.

"Have a look through in your own time, me dear, but mind, they're a bit dirty. I think you'll find the casting tools and wooden plug moulds particularly interesting. The workmanship is very fine. I've brought this also to show you. It's a framed photograph of my old dad outside the forge with the last of the blacksmiths, the day he took over."

John wouldn't touch anything, but Christabel took each item out in turn, laying them onto the table. Soon the top was covered except for a tiny area that John had protested to keep for his food; a plate of bread already perched on top of the milk jug.

"Come on, Chrissie, put that rubbish away before the tea gets cold."

She began repacking, placing items back in neat rows to the approval of the innkeeper.

"My God! Hold it!" shouted John. That photograph. You see the carriage in the background?"

"Ah, I know about that," interrupted the innkeeper. "Had the last wheel to be repaired by the blacksmith. It was waiting to be driven away when the photograph was taken. Anyhow, I'll leave you to clean up."

"Look at it," whispered John once he had gone.

"Yes?" enquired Christabel.

"Don't be dense. Am I going mad or does the women in the carriage look very much like you?"

She stared at it.

"I don't think so. I find it hard to know."

"Well, she does. Spitting bloody image."

He called the innkeeper.

"Who's this person?"

"Can't rightly say. My old father would've known, but he's been dead many a long year. She was from a big house I reckon, judging by the carriage. Anything written on the back?"

"It says '51'."

"Ah! Well, that much I do know. Folk used to refer to a certain family in the old days as the '51s', because they were one card short of a pack."

"What do you mean?" enquired John.

"A screw loose. You know, not all there in the head."

"Mad?"

"Not mad exactly, but certainly very strange."

"I saw something else with '51' on it," added Christabel excitedly She rummaged among her neat piles of objects, throwing them back into disarray. "I knew it! Here, this wooden thing has the same '51' painted on it."

"Then it was made for them. Blacksmith obviously had a sense of humour."

John examined it carefully.

"Quick, give me your key, Chrissie."

"What for?"

"Just do it."

She untied the ribbon.

"Just as I thought, but it's almost too much of a coincidence to be true. Look, this mould was made to cast an object with the same motif on it as yours. What is this thing?"

The innkeeper picked up the mould.

"Gawd knows. For a door escutcheon? Could be to cast anything."

"But mine's a key."

"So bloody what! It proves that your key once had something to do with the old '51s'. Surely you see that?"

Hidden in a far corner behind the half wall Isobel was enjoying an early lunch in silence. She had at first thought of making herself known to John when they entered, having recognised his voice, but had then decided instead to let them argue about the Skimmity in private. Now she was glad that she hadn't intruded. She beckoned the innkeeper, whispering sternly in his ear. He returned straight-faced to Christabel.

"I'll put it all away now."

"Do you know anything else about this or the '51s'?" she enquired in an anxious tone.

"I told you, most of the stuff's been lying around for years."

"You haven't even looked at it!"

"Would do no good to. I don't know one from another. Sorry."

He scooped the remainder into the box with one brush of his arm and carried the first box out along with the photograph he snatched from John's hand. John shrugged and took another bite of his cake. The innkeeper returned for the rest.

"Is it all in the box?"

"There's something on the floor, Chrissie," mumbled John through a mouthful of crumbs. "Just by your foot."

Red faced, she reached down and passed it over, giving John a hard stare.

"For God's sake, Chrissie. Now he thinks you were going to steal it."

"Shut-up, John!"

They left the remaining food, paid the bill and walked home.

"What came over you to hide it like that?"

"I wasn't going to steal it!"

"That's not how it looked."

"This is why!"

She produced a ball of bread and butter that had been kneaded into a fine-textured dough and covertly squashed into the mould before giving it back.

"You crafty blighter. Let's have a look."

"Well?"

"All things considered, you've made quite a fair impression, but why bother?"

"Thought it might help. Thought there might be clues we missed. Has it helped?"

"No! A lot of detail doesn't show."

"It's worthless then."

"Afraid so. Do you want it?"

She answered by biting hard into the dough and throwing the rest over the hedgerow.

"There's nothing else for it, John. We've got to steal the original."

Recovering from the suggestion, John expressed in no uncertain terms his unwillingness to participate in the plan, but then she had her methods of persuasion. The deed was eventually set for the day after the next, to give the innkeeper time to forget Christabel's interest in the artefacts. Anyway, as long as they weren't caught, he would never realise that one small object of so many was missing. She said they could even return it later.

"A second break-in? Bloody hell!"

The lapse of a day gave John time to review the situation rationally. Surely there was no need for Chrissie's daring scheme? The innkeeper was bound to let them see it again. For the first time Christabel had displayed a dramatic side to her character.

The next morning, with an open mind, John rode to Mangstone to make his honest request, but the door was slammed in his face. The crime was on again!

That afternoon, while Christabel was mucking out the stables and John played cards with friends, Isobel received a caller. After twenty minutes the caller left with five shillings in his pocket. At dinner that same evening Isobel dropped a bombshell.

"What's this I hear about you trying to steal one of Taylor's casting moulds?"

Christabel glanced at John in amazement.

"Did you tell her?" she mouthed.

"Of course not." He rounded on his mother. "Where did you hear that?"

"From Taylor, of course. He was so angry that he came to see me. I can't believe you capable of it Christabel."

"It's a lie. It might've looked like that, but nothing then was further from my mind."

"John?"

"Don't drag me into it."

"That's not what he said. Mind telling me what's so interesting about the dusty old thing?"

"It was made in the image of my key. I thought –"

"It might help you to understand why Jack kept the key for you?"

"Did he?"

"Did he what?"

"Keep it for *me*? Especially, I mean?"

"That's enough! You're twisting my words. Aren't you happy here, child?"

"You know," interrupted Christabel, "it occurs to me that I've never asked much about your friendship with my father. I've listened to your side of the story lots of times, but never asked my own questions. I suppose if you knew why he had the key and ring you would tell me?"

"Everyone has secrets. No doubt your father had his, but don't you think he would've told you something about them before if they were of any importance?"

"I really don't know anymore. Depends on his reasons, I suppose."

"If that wretched mould is all that stands between you settling down and continually looking over your shoulder, I suppose we must do something about it. Got a plan?"

"I was going to . . . *borrow* it back."

"Without Taylor knowing?"

"Yes."

"How delicious. How can I help?"

Never, in her wildest thoughts, had Christabel imagined Isobel as an accomplice, but taking her along was now easier than explaining why she shouldn't go.

The next night, an hour after closing, the three huddled by the rear entrance of the inn. Somehow Isobel had taken charge.

"John, you stay here as lookout. Owl hoot if you see anything. Give me the lantern, dear."

"Owl hoot!" he replied with bewilderment on his face. "How the hell do I owl hoot?"

"Fart then, if that's all you're capable of, you silly boy. Just keep looking."

"How do we get in?" asked Christabel.

"I see you've not come prepared. A fine thief you'd make. Lucky I came, and luckier still that the door's so ill-fitting." She passed Christabel a folded sheet of newspaper. "Open it out and slip it under the door. Go on, right under, but leave enough this side to pull it back. That's right. Now, I'll use these hatpins to turn the door key and poke it through . . . There we are."

There was a dull thud on the other side of the door, but, unseen, the key had fallen clear of the newspaper. A shadowy hand on the inside picked it up and quietly placed it back on the sheet. Outside, the newspaper was pulled back, the key resting neatly on its side.

Isobel opened the door.

"Stay close. I'll keep the light low."

She stepped in.

Christabel grabbed her shoulder.

"Can't you turn the wick up a bit? I can't see a thing."

"We can't risk being caught. I can see enough. Follow me."

Isobel went straight for the cupboard storing the boxes.

"Here we are. Easy, wasn't it?"

Christabel dragged a box out.

"Not that one," mumbled Isobel.

"What! How do you know?"

"Oh! I don't, but isn't that a mould at the top of the other box, just where it should be?"

Christabel peered at it in the dim light.

"It might be."

"You said it was the last thing to go back into the box, so it has to be at the top. Come on, let's go."

Back at home Isobel prepared hot drinks while the other two examined the mould.

John sat back.

"It's a dead end. There are no clues here. Too much of the fine detail has worn away over the years."

"Doesn't get us far."

"It doesn't get us *anywhere*!"

"What now?"

"Put it back."

"What's that on your hand? Looks like black."

John sniffed it and then rubbed his hand on a cloth.

Isobel had waited outside the door and she now entered.

"Here we are my children. Get this down you." She sat, sipping her milk.

"Don't you want to know what we've found?" asked John.

Isobel stared across at him.

"Have you found anything?" she asked with false excitement.

"Well, no."

She continued drinking through a smile.

During the small hours John heard noises along the landing. He looked at his watch and it was 3.15 a.m. He turned over. Some time later the sound of creaking came back, only now from downstairs. Again he ignored it. At 5.10 a.m. the front door clicked shut. Furtively, he slipped his shoes on, grabbed a poker and tiptoed downstairs. A light shone in the kitchen. He squeezed an eye into the gap around the door before throwing it open with abandonment.

"What in God's name are you doing up, Chrissie?"

She held up a mould.

"So?"

"Sit down, John, by me."

He did as he was told, placing his arm around her shoulder.

"Stop that!"

He removed it quickly.

"Now, look at it."

"It's the stolen mould," he said with little enthusiasm.

"Well done! Now, look at this."

She produced another.

"Good grief! Where did that come from?"

She looked apprehensive.

"Don't take offence but I didn't trust your mother. So, after I went to bed I got undressed –"

"I know, and you look charming."

"Stop it!" She pulled her dressing gown across and tightened the belt. "I then sat in bed thinking everything through. Breaking in and stealing the mould had been too easy. Didn't it strike you that way?"

"Not really. Folk around here trust each other. I wouldn't have been at all surprised if the door had been totally unlocked."

"Maybe you're right, but I suddenly realised that we hadn't done the obvious thing."

"Which was?"

"To check that the mould your mother took was the right one, of course, and it wasn't! My key isn't anything like that one, and, look, I have black paint on me too."

"So, where did the other one come from, which I presume *is* the right one?"

"Think about it, John. Your mother got us into the inn. Once inside she kept the light so low that I could hardly see. Yet she went straight to the boxes. Can't you understand? She misled us."

"Oh, come on! Why on earth would she do that? Now you're being totally stupid. I'm sure she took what she thought was the right one. For goodness sake, she hadn't seen it before."

"All the more reason to let me examine it in a decent light before taking it. Then there is *this* mould, the correct one!"

"Yes, where *did* that spring from, then?"

"Her room."

"What? Was that you I heard along the landing a couple of hours ago?"

She nodded.

"Good God, but it's a bit of a liberty going into my mother's room."

"I know. I feel pretty wretched. However, she *was* hiding it, knowing how much it meant to me."

"Again I ask, why?"

"Why I looked in her room or why she hid it? Which do you want to know?"

"Both, if you have answers."

"One led to the other, so to speak. I tried to put the pieces together. It was curious the way Taylor first wanted to show us his artefacts, then, just as quickly, had a mood swing and grabbed them away. What caused that?"

"Perhaps he was busy."

"It was a rhetorical question."

"Sorry!"

"I reckon it had something to do with why he bothered to walk all the way here to tell Isobel of our interest in the mould. Get my drift?"

"Sort of . . . Actually, no!"

"Look, what's the big deal about a filthy old mould, discarded for years?"

"Absolutely nothing, as I keep telling you."

"Take me seriously, John, or go to bed."

"Sorry again. It matched your key."

"Exactly, but what finally convinced me that she was hiding something was remembering how indifferent she looked when she asked whether we had found anything out. I just had a burning feeling that she knew we had failed, so I waited until she was asleep and looked inside her bedside drawer, the one she keeps her jewels in. This was stuffed right at the back, and that's not all. I've been back to the inn."

"What! Tonight? In your dressing gown?"

"Yes, with a coat on top of course. It was scary in the dark by myself, but it was worth it. Anyway, I knew you would stop me if I asked you to come, so I didn't. I got in really easily. The door was unlocked, just as you said could happen. Think, locked earlier and unlocked now. What does that say about a set-up? Anyway, most importantly I took this."

"Taylor's photograph."

"Not quite. Don't you remember it was framed before? It isn't now because –"

"It's been cut in half. Don't tell me, the lady's been snipped off."

"Got it in one. Only Taylor didn't think it through. The names of the people in the photograph are written on the bottom. We didn't know that before because the frame covered the writing. From what's left, the woman was someone -vington."

"You're quite the detective."

"Thanks."

"So you're actually saying that my mother is in cohoots with Taylor to keep you in the dark?"

"I can't see any other explanation. She obviously knows there's a connection between my key, the mould and the photograph. Funny, I wouldn't have thought twice about the photograph if I hadn't found the frame in pieces on a table."

"But 'vington' won't get us far."

"Ah, but look at the correct mould. I've scraped some of the paint off. The letters D.E. were lightly inscribed under the '51'. This is *so* exciting."

"D.E.? That's no help, is it?"

"Oh, yes it is. Forget the D. That's a Christian name, past or present and, judging by the age of the mould, won't have any connection with the actual woman in the photograph. E has to be the family surname, which we know ends with vington."

"Eavington, Ebvington, Edvington, Egvington. Blimey, it could be one of many combinations."

"And that's if only one letter is missing."

"No hope then."

"Oh, John. You give up so easily. It's so simple, actually. I merely went through all the Es in *Peers of Dorset*. Your mother had a copy in the library and the good news is that only one name fitted. Elvington. There have been masses of Elvingtons in Wessex since the year dot. It doesn't mention places, but a drawing shows a ruin out Dynden way that once belonged to people of that name. It's a lead, isn't it?"

At that moment of discovery Isobel wandered into the room, awakened by the chattering. John squared up to her. He held up the two moulds.

"Well, Mother? An explanation would be nice!"

Isobel sat. She was bent and troubled.

"We're waiting?"

She looked up into the girl's eyes, the words soft and sincere.

"I didn't want you hurt, Christabel. There's no good to be had in knowing."

"That's not enough to excuse you. You answer one riddle with another," added John.

"Yes it is," cut in Christabel. She took the old lady's hand. "And I thank you for your concern."

"Will you go on with it?"

"I believe father meant me to. Can't you help me?"

"I'm sorry, child. You could be right. Maybe he did want you to know at the end, but, you see, I gave my word that I would never tell. I can't break that. I had too much respect for your sainted father in life to break that confidence in death. I'll tell you this, however. I promise not to stand in your way anymore."

For the first time, Christabel knew for certain that there was more to be discovered. John shared the excitement, but, Dynden being a considerable ride away, he decided to go alone on horseback at first light. Christabel wanted to accompany him, but she realised that the gig would be too slow to get there and back in a single day and any delay searching out clues was worse than being left behind.

During lunch the following day the women maintained a strained silence, talking only once of the animals on the farm. After the plates had been washed and put away, Christabel took out a half-completed antimacassar that she intended to give to Isobel as a leaving present. Time passed slowly.

Meanwhile, John had made good progress, but had been unable to find the ruins. He had been told by a local that only the gatehouse of the former mansion remained and that this was within walking distance to the north-west. Search as he may, however, he could find nothing. Twice more he accepted directions, until finally he knew that the structure had to be somewhere along a single stretch of road that he had already looked along several times. He found the farm buildings and knew that he was close, yet still, to his utter frustration, no gatehouse.

Soon evening drew in and he became desperate in his search. With total disregard for his clothing, he scrambled over hedges and through thickets, but nothing was obvious beyond bare fields. Exhausted and bewildered, he rejoined his horse. Although his face and hands were grazed, his boots caked in mud and his jacket pulled into a thousand loose threads, he still couldn't make himself give up. It was there. He knew it. With strong resolution, he decided to walk the road one last time, positively the very last time, from the farm at one end to the junction at the other. Yet, still each step only took him past familiar sights, with nothing left unexplored.

He reached the end once more. Having failed in his task, he wearily pulled himself onto the hard leather of the saddle. A light drizzle started falling, lowering his spirits still further. At that very spot where he had tied his horse to a gate guarding the entrance to a private house, he stared in amazement to see from the elevated position that the drive beyond forked. Only the left fork led to the house. Hurriedly, he jumped off again. Although a notice forbade anyone entering, he leapt the gate and scurried along the drive, careful to keep behind the cover of a tall hedge. Where the drive forked he gathered his strength and darted across the open space, keeping his head low. Suddenly, there in the dull light of dusk, was the old gatehouse.

Now out of sight from the owner's house, John threw caution to the wind. The gatehouse was buried in an overgrown patch of woodland, with no sign of the road it had once bordered. It was dominated by a central doorway, with smaller arched windows on either side that had become blocked by creeping ivy that encased the whole structure like a mystical castle from a fairy tale. Fallen stones had taken the symmetry from the ramparts. He drew closer.

Without any idea of what he was looking for, John searched the front with his eyes, then worked his way around the remaining sides through thickly grown bramble, cautiously crushing a path with his boots. It wasn't easy and by the time he returned to the front his hair was full of small leaves and tiny pieces of bark. By now the poor light left no time for half-measures. After a deep breath, he lunged for the ivy, pulling as much lose with each tug as his strength allowed. It clung tightly. Many of the stems were sturdy enough to take his full weight and he continued until his aching muscles could grasp no more. With a final effort, he jumped free of the wall, falling backwards as he landed, and cursing the whole business through clenched teeth.

Flat out on the ground, his heart pumping wildly, he could see that only one tiny patch of ivy had been successfully dislodged. The bull-at-a-gate approach had been a waste of time and energy. He needed a proper plan.

Returning to the wall, he tugged at the ivy only where it covered a window, for there it was thinner. Soon grey and brown glass began to show through, although much had cracked and pieces had fallen out. With a hand clasping the metal frame, he pulled himself up and smashed a hole to climb through.

The smell inside was rotten and the room empty. Yet, at last, the main doors were visible, although the exterior ivy prevented them from opening. With difficulty, he climbed back out through the window. Unknowingly, his efforts to open the doors from the inside had caused a lot of the crumbling exterior stonework to break free, taking ivy with it that now sank under its own weight to expose a plaque high on one side.

With no chance of reaching up, John crept back along the path to get his horse, leading it to the gatehouse while stroking its nose to keep it calm and quiet. By standing on the saddle he could touch the plaque with his fingertips. It was long, hanging slightly loose from the wall and disappeared into the ivy at each end. A figure 8 and the letters JUNII stood proud. He guessed that he had found something of importance. This was it, do or die.

Bracing himself against the fleshy movement of the saddle, he leaned once more for the wall, stretching on tiptoes and digging his fingers into the gap behind the plaque. The horse, now unbalanced, made a sudden side-step. To his horror, no amount of quiet coaxing brought it closer.

By now John's fingers were at crisis point and his muscles were nearing the numbness that comes immediately before release. He was going, so he might as well make something of it. With one last effort, he tightened his grasp over the lip of the plaque and made one huge effort. A rasping filled the air as the long hand-cut nails slipped from the stone, followed by a great cracking noise. John fell heavily to the ground, the two halves of the now broken plaque dropping alongside. Stunned by the experience, but not injured, he pulled the halves together, smiling at his cleverness.

OSTIUM ELVINGTON 8 JUNII 1740 – WESTKYNGS

Wet through, cut, bruised and very dirty, John burst into his home, the news hot on his lips, but everywhere was in silence. The thought that Christabel and his mother might not be waiting anxiously for his return had not occurred to him. In an instant of weariness came the suspicion that he had made a fool's errand, and the pleasure of the moment evaporated. His wounds began to hurt too. Dropping into a chair, he gazed angrily at the state of his clothes.

John was asleep over the edge of the kitchen table when the women finally came back, their coats dripping. Christabel looked at John in disbelief, his jacket a tattered heap thrown carelessly to the floor and his muddy boots lying on their sides. One hand that dangled limply grasped a nibbled crust of bread.

"Heavens, what a mess," said Isobel, removing her bonnet and kicking the jacket against the hearth. "You can wake him if you want."

"He did it for me, yet somehow it hardly seems important anymore. Will he hate me?"

"I don't think that's very likely." She gave him a prod. "We'll soon find out."

John awoke in a temper, taking several seconds to focus and gather his thoughts.

"Where in God's name have you been?" he asked in a pained tone.

"You might ask," replied Christabel in a softer voice. She pushed his hair away from his face. "Remember that poor woman at the Skimmington Ride? She hanged herself this afternoon and we've been comforting her daughter. You tell me what we should say to her? How can we explain why it happened?"

"Oh . . . I'm so sorry."

"I'll never rest again until women are treated the same as men. You should've seen her limp body, drained of colour and the purest white except for a rope burn around her neck. Why is adultery so much worse for women?"

"Don't take on so, Christabel," remarked Isobel. "It's not John's fault."

"It is his, and ours, and everyone's who laughed at her."

"It happens. It's not the first time."

"You of all people say that? Isn't it the sort of prejudice you fight against in the Association?"

"No, it's not. When you're older, and a little more worldly-wise, you'll see the difference between understanding a woman's role in life and the burdens of her sex. It's only by understanding what is expected of women that you may one day help us in our fight to keep womanhood pure. If you don't believe that a woman should keep herself chasten, whatever men do, then you have no basis upon which to claim that women should be given special parliamentary laws to protect them."

"You don't want special laws, Isobel, you only want to repeal an existing law."

Isobel had no answer, knowing that Christabel was right.

In the unhappiness of the moment John thought it inappropriate to tell his good news. Instead, he suggested that all three take a stiff drink. Christabel secretly looked at John as he poured. She was convinced that his shabby appearance and lack of conversation meant only one thing, that he had failed in his mission. Little did she realise that he was biding the moment and, when colour began to reappear in Christabel's cheeks, he could hold back no longer.

"You know, Miss Mere," he said with a leer, "a young lady who wishes to be pleasing to men should be lively and good humoured. Frankly I detect neither quality in you."

Isobel looked on disapprovingly.

"I don't feel very cheerful. That poor woman; I keep seeing her face as she rode the donkey past her friends. I'm sure she glanced at me for a second, begging with her eyes. I looked down, but I wish I hadn't. I can't now bury my thoughts in the sand and pretend that it didn't happen."

Isobel nodded in agreement.

"I beg your pardon, again, for I by no means want to suspend your misery. I hold here a full – nearly full – bottle of Madeira wine, but in your present mood you might only taste sour grapes. So before I pour again I wish to say . . . I found the gatehouse and the family of Elvington."

The gloom lifted irresistibly.

"Oh, my God. Did you, really? Really?"

"Yup!"

"What exactly did you find?"

"There was a plaque over the door, hidden behind thick ivy. It said 'Westkings'. Does that mean anything to you?"

Christabel beamed.

"Good Lord, yes! Where you told me the train passes through."

"Well, my beauty, Elvington is the name belonging to your key and perhaps Westkings might hold an answer. If I'm not mistaken, your destination! Admit it, I've been bloody clever."

Christabel flew at him, planting a long moist kiss on his cheek. He blushed for the first time. She turned to Isobel, who nodded slightly to her enquiring glance.

"Well now, I'll pour another generous Madeira wine," shouted Christabel. "This will raise our spirits."

John drained his glass and held it out for a refill.

"One more then, to raise my body too!"

CHAPTER XVII

Home and alone

"Good morning, sister," said a voice from behind the counter. "Good day, Sir."

The uniformed man of cheery disposition and happy features was an island in a dark and oppressive room which was strongly tainted by smoke that billowed from the platform every thirty minutes. A train was ready to leave. Porters scurried with bags and boxes, and the repeated slam of doors and hiss of steam added to the ordered confusion. Christabel clutched her bag tightly, her eyes closed as a shrill whistle blew and huge iron wheels scratched the rails for traction. More grey smoke blew into the ticket office, followed by a blast of cold air as the train pulled away. Then, just as suddenly, the noise faded and the air became still.

"I would like a ticket to Westkings, please."

"Can't help you with that. There's been a derailment at Sparkford. There won't be any trains passing west on this line for several days. Sorry."

Back in her bedroom at the farm Christabel wrote a tender letter to Isobel, although the older woman sat below in the drawing room, a spoken word away. She felt benevolently disposed to the woman, and poured out her heart in words of gratitude for taking her in at that moment of crisis when her father died. The recollections still burned deep.

John knocked gently on her door and she invited him in. He stood just inside, hoping that she would come over to him. He was saddened that she wanted to leave so quickly and that she had already worked out an alternative route, taking the Pennystone line to Glastonbury and then transferring to a coach and horses. She placed her pen in its holder and walked over, sliding her arms around his waist and burying her head deep into his chest. Outwardly, his composure held.

"Maybe, if circumstances had been different," she whispered.

He wrapped his arms around her, resting his cheek on her head.

"If only. Yes, I know those words."

She smiled at his self-degradation.

"Good old John. You're a good friend and one of the few people to whom I feel really close."

He mocked with a half-laugh that denied her words.

"But I'm the villain. My mother thinks I'm a waster and you've never wanted me."

"Don't be foolish." She squeezed harder to show genuine feelings.

He enjoyed it for a while before breaking free and holding her at arm's length.

"Now listen, Chrissie. Promise you'll let me know if I can help in any way? You know I care, which means I'll treat as a favour any job you ask of me."

"Don't be so serious, John."

His face held no smile.

"I mean it!"

She nodded and he drew her back to his chest.

"My dearest girl. Never, never, never, never feel alone again. Never feel in the slightest danger or in need of a friend. No distance, no difficulty, no danger can ever separate us. I'm here should you ever want me." He looked at the clock. "It's exactly 11:00 a.m. At that time every day I'll be closest."

His eyes shut, bathed in the warmth of the moment and she too felt – more than ever before – an overwhelming kindness that bordered on love itself. He meant to leave before he broke down, but she wouldn't let go. Once again he wrapped his arms around her, pretending for an exquisite moment that this was returned passion. Her hand rubbed his back as they embraced. Could it mean she wanted more of him after all? No, it was too much to hope. Yet, he couldn't break free. What to do? If he let her go and walked away, it could be his last and best opportunity gone. Should he chance it and override any sense of misadventure?

At the sight of her face in the pale light he was helpless to stop his emotions, deprived of self-possession. He was having to control his breathing to appear relaxed when really his heart thumped with exploding passion. Still she held him. Do or die, he gently slipped a hand beneath her arm and stroked her breast. Her eyes flew open in disbelief. Breath from his flushed face bore down on her neck. After a quick glance up he gave her the slightest push in the direction of the bed and he expected no resistance. To his disbelief, he found her an unyielding wall.

Thinking she had misunderstood the signal, he held the embrace, his hands now rough as he excitedly felt the shape of her body. Again he pushed her back, this time more obviously. Still she made no gesture of acquiescence or displeasure, ignoring or perhaps even unaware of his petting as she considered a way out through a mist of confusing thoughts. She had dreamt of a moment when a man would take her to womanhood, but such a moment would be sanctified and holy, not hot passion sneaked in a corner. Again he prompted her to the bed. Tears ran silently down her cheeks, her lip bleeding from her own teeth marks. At last John felt the change.

Instantly his face cooled. His heart no longer pumped with passion, but beat hard with fear. He quickly removed his hands and pulled back, hoping not to see pain on her face. He was deeply hurt.

"Oh God, no. Oh Chrissie, no!"

He went to step forward and comfort her, but checked himself. Now he couldn't even hold her. He had ruined everything, again. He was a fool, a bloody stupid, ignorant fool who couldn't tell the difference between an admirer's advance and friendly compassion. Ashamed, he left the room, leaving Christabel feeling friendless once more.

Only slowly did Christabel emerge from the experience, fussing about her few possessions until sufficiently composed to take up her letter. Every once in a while she stopped writing, reflecting on John and what might have been had they both acted differently.

Later that evening Isobel was called out on Association business, leaving Christabel and John alone, but in separate parts of the house. By the time she returned their positions had changed, with Christabel now in the drawing room and John in his bedroom.

"Where's the boy?" enquired Isobel, taking her favourite seat by the cold ash hearth.

"In bed, I think."

"So early? That's unlike him. Is he well?" She saw the empty bottle of Madeira on the table and needed no answer. "I see he's finished yesterday's work."

"It was three-quarters full at lunchtime. He downed the lot, a dozen glasses I shouldn't wonder. I found him slumped over the arm." Christabel lowered her voice in embarrassment. "I was obliged to undo his necktie and boots, and loosen his shirt and trousers. He was very scarlet about the face."

"Just like his father. The times I had to leave him in the chair with his tie and belt undone and a blanket tucked over his legs. Then, in the morning, he would sneak up and ruffle his pyjamas, and bring me a cup of tea. I would pretend that I didn't know where he had spent the night. No doubt John will sleep it off. Men are all the same."

"Surely not!" exclaimed Christabel with unexpected rebuff.

"Oh yes, my dear, all the same. Believe me, I know from experience. My first husband, dearest Thomas, was a fine man, but a confounded high-bred type who saw no good in anyone without a title unless through the bottom of a glass. Then even the lowest villager became a temporary friend after a drink or three. I don't think he ever put two and two together as to why everyone plied him with drink around rent day." She laughed in recollection. "We had such arguments about his drinking and high manner. I told him that if he died I would remarry at the first convenience a man of the lowest social order. That got him really cross."

Christabel took a glass of wine from a fresh bottle.

"And did you?"

"Yes, bless him. I was true to my word. When Thomas died I married a tradesman from Dorchester. He was so overcome by his sudden elevation in society that he died within a week of the ceremony, but not before I had conceived John." She chortled heartily. "So you see, that high strutting son of mine doesn't know it, but he's the heir of a fishmonger!" She began laughing uncontrollably, spilling wine as she tried helplessly to top their glasses. "Only, of course, I never had the stomach to tell him. Well, what I say is why spoil the lad's condescensions. As nobody could possibly tell who the father actually was of my two dead husbands, I took back my old name and put the same on the register of births."

"But you knew who the father was?"

"Not a doubt. Number one could raise a glass, but nothing else towards the end."

"Isobel!"

"Sorry, my dear. It's the wine talking. You see, John is a good example of something I've always believed. You tell a man he's important and he accepts it hook, line and sinker. The reality is you don't have to be born to a title to be worthy of one. John behaves like a gentleman because he believes he is one, although in truth he's a fishmonger's boy." She began clapping her feet and hands together. "Just think about it, a fishboy with a seal on his letters."

"I suppose that would make his intended a fishwife?"

"And his children would be sprats, not brats, if 'Cod' allowed it!"

Christabel crossed her arms over her stomach as she bobbed on the chair.

"Please, no more. It hurts to laugh so much."

"Oh well, I'm going to bed. Will you pass my kippers!"

"Was I herring you right?"

"They're not in the plaice I left them. Maybe they're perched by the window."

"Stop it! I hake so much."

Isobel stared at Christabel as she laughed.

"You know, child, I've grown to love you like a daughter. I'll miss your company so much. Nature never did fashion a finer young person for plain common sense. You must know you're a remarkable young lady. Any man of your choice and position who marries you is assured of a good worker and lifelong companion. You're a credit to my dearest old friend, Jack, God rest his soul."

"More fish," giggled Christabel, taking little notice of the praise.

The next morning was fine, clear and bright. A bag of clothes had been loaded onto the gig, along with a small hamper in Isobel's favourite basket for the journey ahead. In return, Christabel had left Isobel the antimacassar, lovingly completed by working long into the night and now waiting on the dining room table to be unwrapped.

They said their goodbyes. She looked for John, but he couldn't be found. The horse pulled away. Christabel turned and shouted to the standing figure in the courtyard:

"I'll never forget you. I'll return one day. You'll see."

A lump came to her throat. She dipped into her bag for a handkerchief and her purse felt strangely heavy. She lifted it out to look inside. A number of extra coins had been added, a note pinned to the lining reading '*Godspeed. John*'. She looked back for a second time, wishing she had seen him that morning. Her eyes lifted to his bedroom window and from behind the glass and the opaque mist of a lace curtain a man's lonely wave returned.

CHAPTER XVIII

The reunion

The gig pulled into Pennystone station just as the train from Bournemouth arrived. Christabel's mouth was dry from anticipation as she boarded a third-class carriage close to the engine.

The line, which had been opened in stages between 1862 and 1863, was fast and straight, and the first twenty-three miles were covered in just over an hour, at which point there was a delay. From Evercreech the line branched to Wells and Glastonbury, the train taking the second more westerly service for another eight miles.

Christabel had not been prepared for a town the size of Glastonbury, where it seemed that the whole of humanity lived shoulder to shoulder. Its long terraces, the bustle of traffic and the constant noise of heels on the hard pavements were unnatural to her. Even the shoppers walked with sulky expressions, dispossessed of pleasure in their surroundings.

Women who left little bow-fronted shops with courtesy, dropped their smiles the instant their dainty feet touched the stones outside. All was elegance, prosperity and sham. Christabel looked on distastefully and hurried to the outlying lanes, where she rested to eat the food in the basket before setting off to buy a coach ticket to Westkings from the Haslett and Bunker Carriage Transport depot.

Her travelling companions were a random selection from the many avenues of Victorian life. Immediately opposite sat a breathless, wistful salesman of herbal medicines, his thin features and shaking hands conveying a lifestyle dedicated to the art of natural cures. Next to him was a middle-aged woman in a coat several sizes too small. The sight of her straining buttons between mountainous rolls of uncontrollable flesh was all a man needed as an excuse to stay happily single. A mongrel nestled among the layers, its tongue incapable of remaining between its jaws for any length of time, frequently falling like a curling wet pancake onto the shy neighbour's leg.

To his right was a wiry gentleman of about thirty-five, his distinguished face half-hidden beneath a deerstalker held high on enormous ears. An abrupt hacking jacket matched the hat, while from under his gaiters stuck out the wraps of a bandaged leg, borne with all the subtlety of a yacht on launching day.

The wiry gentleman was, it emerged, an aeronaut. He delighted in the unusual nature of his occupation and was sure everyone else would be eager to hear of his many experiences while ballooning, and close escapes from tragedy. He professed to be lucky to be with them that day, a view that the others silently challenged after several long stories. The woman considered the whole matter of flying unjustifiable. The shy man was unable to decide whether he shared any interest or not, but nonetheless, was convinced of the beneficial effects of his angelica brew on all those attempting to leave the ground. Christabel listened with waning interest, having no knowledge of the subject but not wishing to offend, while the fourth traveller tried to show enthusiasm, but let his eyes slump and head droop with regularity until startled into awareness by a bump in the road or the sharp laugh from the story teller, at which time he nodded vigorously at whatever was being said without the slightest understanding. He was, in fact, a compatriot of the shy man, carrying a large leather bag on his knees on which was printed:

Charles Jordan, herbal hog, dog and cattle doctor — apply within.

The journey took in two villages before Westkings, the first at which the woman and the animal doctor alighted. Neither had spoken much since succeeding in frustrating the aeronaut's story telling. Christabel was sorry to see the woman leave, as the supine animal had annoyed the shy man for some miles by licking his trousers, and it had amused her to wonder quite how much he would take. His patience was indeed long.

The three who remained on board soon re-established themselves, the aeronaut and Christabel almost thrown together by the third man's shyness. Whatever path the conversation took, it always seemed to return to matters of the air.

"Oh, my dear," adding courage to his list of self-acclaimed virtues, "you completely misunderstand. It is the danger that makes the sport so exciting. Can't you let your mind go and imagine looking down on the earth from some great height, seeing below the people no bigger than ants and great oaks seemingly no larger than shrubs for the picking? And the silence, that has to be heard. The wind blows you one way and then the other, floating like gossamer upon the breeze and never knowing where you are to come down."

"It sounds ideal."

"No, it's not ideal, but it's as close as man will ever get to flying like the birds."

"Bunkum," retorted Herbal uncharacteristically.

Shaken, but not put off his stride, the aeronaut turned back to her. "Oh yes, once you have flown there's no other way of travelling. No thrill so great."

"Then why aren't you flying now, Sir, and offer us some peace from it?" snapped Herbal.

"Wind, Sir," was the reply.

"A lot of hot air," returned Herbal.

"There are times, Sir, when the wind does not blow in accordance with the direction of one's business!"

In justice to the truth it should be known that the aeronaut had flown, but only the once, and on that singular occasion he had indeed nearly died – of fright. The day in question had occurred some weeks previously when, at the invitation of a friend, and having arrived at the field on a bicycle and wearing what was considered in knowing circles to be the very best flying attire, he had risen a dozen feet before panic set in and he had jumped from the basket. The impact broke his ankle. Not since that day had he so much as looked at a balloon, although he continued wearing the clothes that, he fancied, suited him well. He continued:

"For anyone with the purse for flying, for it is a fearfully costly sport, there can be no other wish than when he or she can become airborne again."

On the outskirts of the second village several boys waited for the coach outside a private school catering for the young heirs of middle-class businessmen from Glastonbury and surrounding areas. The aeronaut sat back, squashed and muted between Herbal and a young schoolboy.

The boy had the look of a good family, but the manners of a bully. He had chosen his seat among the adults ahead of his friends, who sat in a group in the forward rows, but, as time showed, he didn't have to sit with them to assert his presence.

"He isn't good enough for the first cricket team," argued one boy to another.

"Just because you want his place, Bowyer Minor."

"It's not that. He's useless."

"I back Bowyer here," said a third. "He scored three ducks last season, while Bowyer clocked-up eleven runs."

"Okay, let's ask Pilk."

They turned to the back rows.

"Right, Tadlow's in," agreed the boys.

The horses trotted on, mile after slow mile.

"What are you doing, Bowyer?"

"I'm hungry. I'm for eating our lunch now."

"I will too," said another, reaching into his pocket.

"Put them away," remarked Pilk without turning his head.

The untouched sandwiches were returned to their blazer pockets.

Aeronaut began another flying tale, exciting the imaginations of the listening boys.

"My father says we'll be all right in the Sudan now the army's got balloons to spot the enemy."

"Your father! What does he know? My uncle works for the newspapers. He says it's a different kind of war that our old generals don't understand. Sort of hit and run he calls it. Only, they're doing all the hitting."

"Rubbish! I told you, we'll see 'em coming miles off, from our balloons."

"The army hasn't got any balloons."

"Yes it has. My father said some went out in 1885."

The doubter turned to Pilk.

"You'll know, Pilkington Major. The army hasn't any balloons, has it?"

"How the heck should I know?" replied Pilk with unusual honesty.

"Yes," said the first with the knowing father whom he now doubted. "Nobody knows. It's a military secret."

Herbal smiled at Christabel, leaning forward to meet her halfway.

"This lad's a natural for the diplomatic corps."

"Is he?" she answered. "Better ask Pilk!"

Mid-afternoon passed and the coach finally arrived at Westkings. Since Christabel had no idea where to get off, the driver drove through from one end to the other before returning to the only house of grandeur. She stepped down and peered through the gates with alarm, wondering if she had the courage to enter. Yet, the journey had been too long to falter now and her feet took her almost subconsciously to the entrance. She pulled the bell. A head appeared at an upstairs window.

"Who is it?" came a hidden voice.

"A chit of a girl, Ma'am. Just got off the van."

"What does she want?"

"How do I know? I've only seen the top of her head."

"Then answer the door, impertinent child."

Christabel whispered a message.

"Wait there."

The maid closed the door.

"She won't give her name."

"Why ever not? Do we know her?"

"Don't think so, Ma'am."

"What's she like?"

"Kind of ordinary. Yes, ordinary describes her, but she speaks well."

"Are we prepared to receive guests?"

"I don't think this one will expect much, Ma'am."

"In that case, let her in. Take her to the drawing room. I'll be down shortly."

"Shall I offer her tea while she waits?"

"I don't think that'll be necessary."

Christabel entered the room, its velvet curtains faded and wallpaper now curling at the seams, but it was still imposing. Unknowingly, she now stood in the very place of that earlier drama, in which she had played such an important, but innocent part.

Charlotte was unhurried in her preparations, but presently they received each other politely and Charlotte bade her sit. If ever there was an exhibition of the ridiculous, it was now. The moment was savage in its irony, laughable in its absurdity, although lamentable in its cause.

Charlotte had seen nothing in this grown girl to raise suspicion, for, although they bore a likeness visible to anyone looking for it, it would otherwise now go unnoticed.

Christabel sat hesitantly, not sure of how best to approach the matter in hand. She had thought it through a thousand times, the narratives, questions and replies, but somehow now they seemed to make little sense.

"Well, dear?"

Christabel looked embarrassed.

"Come. Let's start with your name."

She drew to the edge of her seat.

"My friends call me Chrissie. I've come from Cerne Abbas."

"To see me?"

"Yes . . . No . . . Well, sort of."

"Not getting very far, are we, dear?"

Christabel's eyes scanned the room. Her mind was blank and she felt out of her depth. There could be no connection between her father and this house. She wanted a let-out, fast.

"You must know Dorchester well. I found it breathtaking. It's so big and busy."

"It's very fine," answered Charlotte quietly.

"I was glad to see so many trees," added Christabel in a rush.

"Trees? That's a strange observation. As a matter of interest, many of the elms were planted by French prisoners during the Napoleonic wars. They say it was their way of thanking the townspeople for their kindness, but you haven't come all this way to talk about trees. May we return to the reason for your being here?"

"I'm here . . . to . . ." she just couldn't see any point in the truth. "To . . . ask . . . if you have ever heard of the Woman's National Association fighting the CD laws?"

Charlotte was aghast. The speed of the words from the girl's mouth, let alone the subject at her tender age, shocked her. She stared open-mouthed.

"Yes . . . I've heard of the Association."

Christabel fumbled with her bag.

"I . . . I was thinking that I might set up a branch here."

"And you need funds?"

"I don't know. I suppose I might."

"You are aware of what they're saying about the Association in the newspapers?"

"No?"

"That it's the worst display of feminine interference in law and order this century. How well do you know the organisers? Can you count on their backing if things get hot?"

"I'm not sure. I'm sort of acting on my own behalf."

"There'll be scuffles, even out here in the country."

"Yes, I know. I've see it first-hand. A friend is a member in Cerne. She preaches non-violence, but often as not the crowds are infiltrated by trouble-makers spoiling for a fight."

"Is what she says right and just?"

"Right, wrong, it doesn't seem to matter. The women listening don't need convincing and the others aren't there to debate anything."

"Well, my dear, knowing how the newspapers and parliament have demolished the characters of some Association leaders, sweet Mrs Butler being the best example, I wonder whether you can afford, at your young age, to be any kind of spokeswoman. Perhaps you would do best finding another reforming platform. Have you tried writing to the Association's newspaper? It's a coincidence that our house has the same name."

"Oh!"

"Of course, it's your life, unless you involve me in it! If you want meetings here, I can tell you now that there aren't enough women in the village to fill even a small hall. I can't, therefore, promise any real support. At best, it certainly wouldn't be much to shout about."

"I see. In that case —"

Christabel rose to leave, but Charlotte cut in.

"You seem easily persuaded? Lost your nerve already?"

"I'm sorry?"

"I thought as much. Sit down, dear, and tell me the real reason for your call."

"Real reason?" blustered Christabel.

"Real reason! You might be interested in the Association, but you don't know the first thing about it. You might as well be up front with me now. Any member worth her salt, and I count myself as one, would know instantly that *The Shield* is the name of the Association's newsletter, not 'Samain'. I admit to telling you a lie to catch you out. I also threw in Mrs Butler's name, which you hardly knew. When I think of the hardships she and her husband have had to endure."

"Ah!"

"Look, dear. Don't get involved in something you obviously know little about unless you're willing to be harangued, spat on, stoned and threatened."

"I've truly been to meetings."

"Then you know already. The Contagious Diseases Act states that prostitutes are in it for mercenary gain, but the men who hire them are only fulfilling a natural desire. See, even the law reinforces that biased attitude. So it's not just a fight for women and their rights, but a challenge to the very mother of parliament, that bastion of men!"

"I know that."

"Then you'll also be aware that any woman arrested anywhere and for anything by the police can be assumed to be a prostitute without trial or representation and may be required to undergo physical examination. The state gives police doctors the right to tie a woman's legs to posts and poke inside with all manner of shameful instruments to determine whether there is syphilis present. There's no redress, not even through the newspapers, as none backs the woman's cause, and if they decide that the poor person is a prostitute, rightly or wrongly, they make her carry a card and force regular check-ups against the penalty of imprisonment. Is that want you want to risk? Is your commitment so great?"

"I would give them no reason to arrest me, but, hypothetically speaking, even if I was arrested they would soon find out that I'm not."

"Think so? Tell me how any woman who has known a man in the love and decency of the church can prove that? How can a virgin prove that she is untouched once torn open by the probing jaws of the doctor's tools? It's blackmail to stay timid."

"My God!"

"Yes, you might well pray that it should never happen to you. So, I ask again, what is the real reason for your journey? You're obviously a country girl. Nobody else would talk about trees."

Game, set and match to Charlotte. Christabel shrank against the wilful use of shock tactics. She reached for her neck and untied the ribbon holding the key and ring.

"It's just these."

Placing them in Charlotte's outstretched hand, the effect was immediate. Charlotte's fingers snapped around them.

"Where in heaven's name did you get these? They belong to another."

Christabel went to take them back, but Charlotte withdrew her hand.

"I didn't find them. They are mine."

"No, that's a lie. I ask you again. How did you come by them?"

"They belonged to my father and he gave them to me."

Charlotte flushed.

"Your father?"

"Yes."

"What's your name, child?"

She watched trance-like as Christabel mouthed the answer, as if in slow motion.

"Christabel Mere. My father was Jack Mere!"

Charlotte fell faint, her eyes rolling in disbelief.

"Are you all right?" asked Christabel, taking her arm.

"I feel light-headed. Let me sit quietly for a moment."

"Shall I call someone?"

"Do nothing at all!"

The girl sat bewildered. Presently Charlotte asked:

"Tell me how old you are and where you have been living."

"I'm seventeen and my home is in Cerne Abbas. Of course, before then I lived in Shalhurn. You won't have heard of it. It's just a bit of a place."

Charlotte shook her head

"Is it far from here?"

"Not too far. A half-day's travel."

She nodded slightly in disbelief.

"All this time so close" she whispered to herself.

"Pardon?"

"I suppose your father sent you. Is that it? To get a bit of money out of me?"

"My father's dead."

"Dead?"

"Yes, bless him. I don't know what you meant by 'getting money from you', but I didn't come here to ask for anything other than advice. You see, he gave me the key and ring on his deathbed. Forced them on me, you might say. They meant a lot to him, but I don't know why. That's why I'm here. To find out."

"Then you don't want anything from me?"

"No, well, yes information, but that costs nothing."

"These might mean nothing at all," offered Charlotte.

"That's entirely possible."

"I would say, likely."

"Yes, I suppose so."

"Then, there's an end to the affair. I'm a stranger to you in person and name, aren't I?"

"Of course. How could it be otherwise?"

"Just so. Tell me, dear, is it true? Is your father really dead or did you make it up as a way of seeing me?"

"It's not something I'd joke about."

"No, of course not. Forgive me, but how can that be? You're so young, so your father must have been only middle-aged. He can't be dead. Not he. Yet I can see on your face that he is."

Christabel was too preoccupied to notice the obvious intimacy in her tone.

Now that Charlotte's options grew wider, she felt stronger.

"The key," probed Charlotte, "it really means nothing to you? Tell me whatever you know so that I might be able to fill the gaps in your knowledge."

"No, you're wrong. It means *everything* to me, but only as a keepsake. I connected it with Westkings by chance. Elvington. I have to find someone who knows that name."

"And when you do?"

"It's a long story. I'm hoping someone will tell me why the key meant so much to my father, but I can see that my calling has been a waste of time."

"Just so." She smiled to put the girl at ease in order to extract more. "Still, it can't hurt to hear your story. From the start, mind. Tell me everything. Don't leave out any detail or secret. Only then may I be of some service – perhaps."

CHAPTER XIX

The choice

Charlotte grew steadily more serious as Christabel told her story, scarcely able to bear the tale of hardship that was so very different from her own life. There could be no further question as to her authenticity, and no greater reason to give nothing away in return. Until a few minutes before, this girl had been a total stranger whose misfortune would have meant little to the older woman. Now, she had listened to a story so sad in its reflections that it touched her heart, the more so since the natural feelings of a mother began to reawaken.

After all had been told, Christabel was no wiser in her quest or upon any other matter. Charlotte, on the other hand, now possessed all the pieces of the puzzle that, when merged into one, pictured a potential disaster of cataclysmic proportions. Since James had purged himself by fire, life at 'Samain' had, on balance, improved. True he still walked a tightrope between madness and sensibility, but he no longer looked on his wife and the estate as evils; if anything his feelings for Charlotte had begun to stir. What was she to do now?

"I don't want to let go of his memory. I don't want to believe that he died." Tears filled Christabel's eyes. "Somehow I can't help feeling that by following his wishes, with the key I mean, he'll be waiting for me at the end. Oh, I know that's nonsense, but I miss him so very much. I think of him, at night in my bed, wondering if I could have done more to ease his burden. I've found that I blame myself for a good many things; the times when I was too stubborn or lazy to help in the fields and when I left him a cold supper so that I could go out with a friend. He was father and mother to me and in return I sometimes let him work alone outside until it was so dark that he couldn't see his feet on the soil." She wiped her cheeks. "He said I was a good girl, but then I expect all fathers do. I suppose I shouldn't blame myself for our ills, or because we were poor, but he was too young to die. Don't you see that? Why did it have to be him?"

Charlotte too was close to tears, but was determined to remain strong, even distant. She arose in silence, wanting a moment to reflect before committing her emotions. She dreamily adjusted the clock already standing precisely at the centre of the mantel. Her face was strangely withered, her hands shaky. Her mind replayed passages from the girl's story, word for sad word. Throughout, Christabel sat quietly, having no further cause for agitation.

When Charlotte turned, it was in a manner of self-preservation. She had hit upon the memory of when James had given her a new puppy. That first night it had cried plaintively while shut alone in the kitchen, but while her heart had been wrenched to hear it, James' insistence that it should be left there had been right, and in a few days the whining stopped and it had grown into a fine animal. This thought would now give her strength. She saw the girl, her lost child, yet she pushed back any emotion that could overcome her greater sense of the present. Her life was bound to 'Samain', the people and the land. Christabel was her daughter, but her childhood was lost to the past. It was her body that had given the girl life, yet her maternal instincts were stronger for Edmond, to whom there was no blood tie, yet sixteen years of complete memories.

There was a choice to make – to divulge motherhood or stay aloof. What were the consequences of each? She thought on, leaving the girl to wonder at the woman's behaviour. If motherhood was chosen, then what would be the effect on James? To remain silent would affect nobody, but would condemn her natural child to an unknown future. Should she, anyway, be responsible for Christabel's plight after so many years of separation? She looked well dressed, a bit thin perhaps, but nourished. What good would it do to stir up a hornet's nest just when life was beginning to improve?

That was it, the path that maintained the status quo. Charlotte braced herself, ready to send Christabel away, but, as she drew breath and turned towards the girl, Christabel's gentle smile and open eyes made the words stick in her throat.

"Damn and blast," she muttered.

"Pardon?"

She tried a second time, willing the words out of a body strangely fighting back.

"I can't care," she shouted, meaning nobody to hear.

"Then that's the end of it," returned Christabel stiffly. "I'll take my things and go."

"I won't stop you, you selfish child. Can't you imagine the effect you being here has on me?"

"On you? I don't understand."

"Yes, you do, and even if you don't, you ought to."

"How can that be? I don't understand anything you say."

"Every word from your mouth pierces me. You poor, simple chump. Can't you see that I've lived in luxury while you've known nothing but poverty. It's a hard burden to bear now that I know you."

"Tough times I can't deny, but no more so than for thousands of others, and probably less than some. I'm absolutely amazed that you worry about strangers."

Suddenly Charlotte knew that she had been too open.

"You parade your most intimate details and question the reactions they cause. I'm not made of wood. Here beats a heart."

"I'm sorry. I didn't mean —"

"Stop!" She wiped her nose. "Let's not get carried away. It's nothing personal. A sad story gets a sad response, nothing more."

"I understand."

At last Charlotte knew that she had regained the high ground. She would now be more guarded, more in control.

"You see, my dear, while I appreciate your difficulties, I fail to see how I can be of any help. I have excessive regard for your fortitude, but the only comfort I can offer lies in my duty as hostess. But I'll say this. You have no reason to censure yourself for coming. Indeed, it might be helpful to you to know that you were successful in your quest, for I am an Elvington."

Christabel was shocked.

"Your name is Elvington?"

"Read nothing into that. I confirm it, but not to give you any false hopes, rather, as a means to end your searches. We're an old and large family. I'm afraid it changes nothing, although it might help you decide to return to Cerne with peace of mind."

Christabel's thoughts raced.

"So, despite finding the Elvington family and Westkings, the key and ring remain complete mysteries."

"As they always will."

Christabel looked up at the big window.

"But that crest looks a lot like the one on the key. Doesn't that mean anything?"

"No child, it's quite different. Small variations in heraldry are of vital importance. See the snowflake in the glass? Not on your key, you will agree. Your key must have been modelled for a long-dead branch of our family, whose trinkets are scattered far and wide."

Christabel nodded.

"What does the motto mean?"

"*Ad huc hic hesterna*. I'm no scholar of Latin, but in rough terms I think it means, *the things of yesteryear are still with us*." She felt a chill. "What will you do now?"

"I don't know."

"Then again I suggest you go home."

"But I have no home."

"Come now. You must have come from somewhere. You don't look like you've been living rough and, anyway, you mentioned Cerne."

"These clothes?" She picked at her sleeve. "I was given these by the person for whom I worked. I have no others like them. My usual style is plain and strong."

"Then you must go back."

"No. I have no claim on her. I must find my own place in the world."

"I really don't think you're in any position to be choosy."

"It's not a question of choice. Poor people don't have that luxury. Kindness brought me to Cerne and my father's old friend, but she doesn't live alone. She has a son. John's his name. He made my stay . . . Well, how can I put it? Difficult at times. Really he's a very fine man, but he doesn't know it himself."

"Sounds a fool."

"No, not a fool. It's just that he lets his head rule his –"

"Trousers?"

"I was going to say, heart. He made me feel like a woman, some-one who could be cared for rather than just looked after."

"And being a woman he wanted adult things from you in return?"

"Not in return. He's not like that. He would've liked a relation-ship, though."

"He's ugly?"

"Hardly."

"A drunkard, a womaniser?"

"No!"

"So this handsome paragon of virtue wants to court you. Is that so awful? I'll tell you straight, you won't get many such chances. Or is there more you're not telling? You're hiding something?"

"More? No, there's no more. I know I could grow to want him if I returned, but would I be his mistress or wife?"

"You mean he wouldn't marry you?"

"No. I mean yes. I mean, he would marry me. Only, it's me I'm not sure of. I like him, but I can't see my life spent with him as my husband. I'm troubled constantly by his manner. He courts vanity, and listens well to others with perfect indifference. Yet he's kind and gentle too. Could such a fellow remain faithful? Would he fall as quickly out of passion as into it?"

"Then, dear, forget him."

Christabel squeezed her purse.

"I'll never do that. My life wasn't worth a farthing until I went to live with the Maddens. They gave me a reason to go on when so much seemed to be at an end. More so John really. He showed me a new life and helped me to find my way here because I alone wanted it, even though it was against his interests." Her tone lowered. "I'm an impostor in these clothes. I'd be best going back to the ways of my class. A village girl I was born and I shall never try to be anything else."

Charlotte had listened to enough sad talk for one day.

"No, wait. Please tell me with certainty where you will go."

"I have some money. I can make out until I find work. I'm a fighter. I'll survive."

A horrible sense of dread overcame Charlotte, having offered no more help this time than the first. She looked admiringly at the beautiful girl and imagined her back to rags, sweating under the whip in one of the fearful farm gangs where decent women became immoral by the need to live. She became anxious.

"How much money do you have?"

Christabel opened the clasp.

"A few pounds, as you see. In my world I'm rich! It'll last if I'm careful."

"And after it's gone?"

"I'll be all right. Someone will employ me."

The purse was pressed shut and with the quietness of her nature, she stood to leave. Although the first traces of evening narrowed the possibilities of a bed for the night, she felt unable to ask for help. It wouldn't be the first time she had slept under the hedgerow if needs be.

"Look here, my dear. Let me speak with you a little longer. *Please*. I'll tell you what. Take tea with me."

She nodded, for she was hungry.

"Excellent. Make yourself at home for a few minutes."

"At home!" Christabel laughed. "It could never be that. You should see my home as it was in Shalhurn. Not a place you'd care to enter, although I loved it dearly. Only twice did gentlefolk come inside, the last time just before my father died."

She sat back against the cushion. Something dug into her back.

"What is it?"

She lifted the cushion.

"It's an empty whisky bottle."

"That husband of mine!"

Charlotte took it away.

"I don't suppose you need a maid to tidy up, or someone for the scullery? I can work very long hours. I'm accustomed to it. My keep alone will do."

If Christabel had been any other girl, Charlotte would have welcomed another servant, but not her.

"Your undoubted salvation will be marriage. Pick a good man with plenty of interests. I know of few women who have derived much pleasure from a man's base instincts, so you would do well to find a man with lots to occupy his time. You've done well to stay clear of them so far. Choose carefully when the time comes."

Christabel smiled, breaking into a laugh. Charlotte giggled at the girl's reaction.

"I mean it!"

So the talk continued, about this and that, but nothing in particular and certainly not the trinkets. During this time a fire was laid. The crackle of burning wood was welcoming. Christabel almost washed in its glow, rubbing her fingers over her cheeks and around her neck.

"Look, I can offer you somewhere to stay for the night if it helps."

"Could you? What here?"

"Not here. No, most certainly not suitable. I was thinking of a house across the way owned by an acquaintance. She once worked for me many years ago. She likes to rent out a room now and again when the opportunity comes along, and there'll be no question of you paying. She'll do it as a favour to me."

Christabel nodded vigorously.

"Well, then, that's settled." She wrote a quick note and rang for a maid to accompany Christabel.

"Give her this letter of explanation. Her name is Meg Turner. You'll like her."

"You've been very kind. How can I ever thank you?"

"We all like to help when we can. Oh dear, I forgot our tea."

"It doesn't matter."

Charlotte held out her cheek, inviting a kiss. As she reached the door, Christabel suddenly stopped and turned.

"I nearly forgot. Please may I have my key and ring?"

Charlotte hurried to the mantel, but popped the key up her sleeve.

"Best leave it with me, for safe keeping. You can have it back when you leave Westkings. Anyway, I'll show it around to see if anyone else can shed some light. Have the ring though, it's far more precious."

With some reservations Christabel slipped only the ring back onto the ribbon. She shut the door, leaving Charlotte to feel the empty space where her daughter had stood. Pleased by the thought that she had helped without the slightest risk of public knowledge, Charlotte went to the window to watch the two walk away.

"Why do all the ghosts of the past now appear in my life?" she whispered. "Please, Christabel, look back and see me with affection."

Christabel kept walking, innocent of her crime.

That same evening Charlotte wrote a second letter, confidential to Augustus Fly. It had to be redirected. She wanted to be reassured that all documents relating to Christabel had been destroyed after the burglary, but the communication had a quite different effect. Since his covert work for Charlotte had lost him his junior partnership with the company, on evidence no more substantial than Sir Arthur Schofield's intuitive feeling, he felt that Charlotte owed him more, much more. How to exact his pound of flesh had defeated him, until now. He was now glad that he had stuffed the papers under his bed, especially since a period of gay revelry on the once seemingly inexhaustible funds of one hundred pounds had left him broke, jobless and in danger of prosecution.

CHAPTER XX

Old powers

*T*he evening was young, and with her immediate need for shelter organised, Christabel's spirits grew irresistibly. The countryside here was more open and flat than she had been used to, but with pockets of forestation. Each breeze gathered wild scents as it swept across the large fields and orchards.

The tranquillity was contagious, the atmosphere sultry. Bumblebees were still on the wing where honeybees had given up their search for nectar, and neuroptera danced in the air at the water's edge of a small pond formed by a rusted sluice gate.

Christabel had come to Westkings with an open mind, harbouring no fixed idea that she would find some glorious goal. She had merely hoped that her journey might be the beginning of a new direction to her adult life. She hadn't reckoned on the journey's end merely heralding yet another starting point, an episode to be played out and forgotten.

'Samain', so dominant over its surroundings, felt like an impassioned structure, the very place where hopes could be transformed into reality. Now, as she trod the path towards a life of further manual labour, it became evident that nothing had changed materially since the time she had spent in the Shalhurn valley. Yet, at least for the moment, the security of a roof was enough to make her feel wonderfully, and perhaps strangely, at ease. The manor, its grounds and outbuildings, could be seen as a pleasant sojourn while new plans were considered.

It was surprising to Christabel how important the family of Elvingtons had become to her, although she had knowingly met only one member. Finding the people and a place that had some small, but yet unkown, connection with her father gave her a curious feeling of fellowship, in a spiritual sense if no other. There was not a field of this land she wanted for herself, only the feeling of belonging. Theirs was the abundance, but she could enjoy the fresh clear air and fine surroundings as much as they. The lichen and ivy that blanketed sections of stone wall radiated constancy to all, not only the privileged few. Whatever mood nature cast upon the land, it was for all to feel.

The maid took Christabel to the entrance of the lodgings and handed her the letter written by Charlotte. She was in a hurry to go. The bag was dumped on the step.

"Are you sure you want to stay here, Miss? There's another place further along."

"No, I'm quite happy, thank you."

"It's awfully creepy and I've heard some funny tales about certain goings-on."

Christabel glanced over it.

"Looks pretty ordinary to me."

"Well, if you're sure . . . Goodbye."

The maid hitched up her skirt and hurried away.

After a moment's hesitation, Christabel knocked. The letter was handed over and read on the step. Charlotte had been careful not to mention the girl's surname and asked Meg not to enquire for personal reasons. With a grunt of approval she was invited in.

The door led to a narrow staircase at the far end of the hallway, lit by a single gas lamp. They climbed the stairs and entered the first room off the landing, the lock needing a strong twist to open. A musty odour enveloped the walls. A window was opened.

"This is the best I can offer. My other room is taken by a paying guest."

"Who's this?" enquired Christabel, stroking the feathers of a parrot that was chained by a leg to a pole.

"Humphrey! I'll move him?"

"No, don't do that. I'd like him in here if you don't mind. He's lovely."

"As you wish. Everything else okay?"

"It'll do very well," she replied, throwing her bag on the bed.

"I'm afraid we've already had supper. If I'd known you were coming I could've saved you some."

"Don't worry. I have all I need."

The woman took the jug from where it stood inside the washing bowl, folded back the bed covers and left. A sheet of paper lay on the marble top to the washstand and it caught her attention. She opened it, running her finger along the crease. It was the rules of the house. She put it back.

Christabel carefully folded her travelling clothes and placed them in a drawer, setting out the coarser, grey drab attire for the morning. The aroma of a supper consumed hung in the air, reminding her that she hadn't eaten since taking a few bites in Glastonbury. Removing what little remained in the hamper, she ate the lot.

The bed was comfortable and quickly her muscles relaxed into the soft padding. Voices below in the dining room were like a caressing wave wafting through the air – solace to a lonely person. She quickly fell asleep.

The hours passed and the house fell into a deep silence, although night animals foraged the woods. Then, soon after midnight, the outside became strangely still. Humphrey cocked his head, his eyes staring into the darkest corners of the room. He began pacing the pole, pulling hard against the chain. Christabel rolled onto her back.

A night owl swept past the window, beating a retreat into the heart of the woods beyond. Humphrey gave off a wild shrill, waking Christabel. There was crying from downstairs. She struggled to focus her eyes, her mind spellbound by her dreamy state.

A scraping noise came from nearby. Her eyes flew open, wide and startled. Just as suddenly it stopped. Heavy footsteps moved along the landing and a door was pulled shut. She strained to hear any other sound, any sound at all. Humphrey rattled his chain.

For minutes Christabel propped herself against the headboard, shivering. All had gone quiet again. The dark furniture took on sinister shapes. Deciding to get a grip on the situation, she threw open the curtains, letting a little moonlight into the room. All about seemed ordinary now. Humphrey flared his wings and settled. Slowly she relaxed back onto the pillow, her eyes heavy.

At just past 2 a.m. she was startled again by a sound like furniture shifting across the floorboards. The room was pitch black, the curtains mysteriously closed. She breathed hard, her arms shaking. It could be rats, she thought, but not the curtains. Suddenly the door handle rattled. Her heart missed a beat as the faint glow from a candle emerged through the crack. Christabel peered from behind a raised pillow to recognise the bearer, human or otherwise.

"Hells bells, Meg! You frightened me to death."

"The noise woke you then?"

"Yes."

"I thought it might. I heard it too. Thought I'd better come, in case you were upset by it."

"What in heaven's name was it?"

"Squirrels under the thatch."

"Squirrels? I don't think so."

No sooner had the words passed her lips than the chair in the corner turned. The parrot squawked. Meg dropped the candle, plunging the room into darkness. In the confusion, Humphrey panicked and tried to fly off the perch, falling and snapping its neck. It dangled, hanging by the chain.

"Oh God, no!" pleaded Meg, her shaky hand fumbling for a match. "Tell me you're still here with me?"

"Of course I am."

The glow reappeared. Meg's face was pale.

"Hold my hand, please!"

Their eyes turned to the corner. Christabel let out a cry.

"Heaven's preserve us!"

"What do you want?" cried Christabel, frozen with fear.

"Can you see him too?"

"Yes."

"Thank God. I thought I was going mad."

The candle flickered and went out again, casting the room back into shadowy shapes. Christabel screamed and fell, striking her face against the edge of the cupboard.

"Are you all right?" shouted Meg.

"I will be in a moment. For pity's sake light another match."

"I'd find it easier if you would stop screaming all the time."

Sulphur filled the air as the light returned. This time Meg lit the gas lamp. The room was empty of the 'unexpected', although the chair was some distance away from the wall.

"What did you see?" asked Meg as she handed over a damp cloth to bathe Christabel's wound.

"A man in that chair."

"Then you really did see him?"

"Oh God, it can't be true. Yet, it was, wasn't it? I've seen a ghost, a real ghost."

"He's come before and I absolutely hate it. I always hope it'll be for the last time. Scares me rigid. I know when he's coming, for the animals go quiet. That's why I put Humphrey in here."

"Was it you I heard crying?"

"Probably."

"Have you told anyone else?"

"You must be joking! I mostly keep it to myself. I'm not a witch or nothing. I don't know why he comes to haunt me."

"It's the most incredible thing. You won't believe this, but I'm not so afraid now, and do you want to know why?"

"Tell me."

"Because I've also seen him before!"

"You, Miss?"

"When I left Shalhurn. At least I think he's the same, only he was real that first time, or at least he seemed real then. I've since learned not to believe my eyes. I'll explain it sometime. The important thing is that I would recognise that face and red beard anywhere."

"What are you saying, that you see ghosts regularly?"

"God, no! Yet, maybe I do, at least the same one in different places. I tried telling a friend, but he didn't believe me. Made me think I concocted the whole thing."

"I first saw it – the man, the phantom if you like – at the manor ages ago. He was standing like a shadow behind Charlotte Elvington when the master was in one of his moods. At first I thought I'd had a brainstorm, 'cos I was in a flap at the time and all was confusion, and I used to drink pretty heavily to drown the sorrows of my work. But he kept coming back, each time a bit more real, a bit less misty. That's one reason why I left their employment, to get away from anything unholy and put pay to the bottle. He seems to have followed me here. What worries me is what will happen to me when he takes his final form. What does he want of me?"

"I honestly don't think you've anything to be frightened of."

"Aren't you scared by him, a bit?"

"That's the odd thing, I am and yet I'm not. The thought of him doesn't frighten me now because he's not harmed me on either occasion. Yet no rational person can admit to seeing ghosts, and fear should come with the territory."

"When I know he's coming I become very afraid. I can't help it. I suppose I think one day he might try to drag me to hell. I must have a power."

"Power?"

"The power to communicate with the dead. I once put a charm under a cot and something awful happened to that baby. I think that's why this 'thing' has picked on me. I must have tampered with the unnatural. I can't think of any other explanation. If you saw him, you must have powers too."

"I suppose I might."

"Do you think together we could learn how to communicate with him, or get rid of him if you think that's a wiser course. The phantom might not want to hurt us, but I don't like it all the same. Come to think of it, this is the first time I've seen him in months. I can't call him, you see. He just appears out of the blue. Maybe together we're an irresistible magnet. There must be something that connects us both to him. Should we try to communicate? Are you game to try?"

"No thanks!"

"He won't come back tonight, of that I'm certain. So, if you're okay, I'll pop off to bed, if I can sleep at all! We'll talk in the morning. Maybe then you'll chance whatever fate has put our way."

"Hang on! I'm not being left alone in here? No way!"

"You'd better sleep in my room, then, besides, I can't leave Humphrey like that. Poor thing."

For the second time the possibility of ghosts took a conscious level in Christabel's thoughts. The next morning, however, after several hours of disturbed sleep, it had passed like a bad dream. She remembered the occurrence in a confused way, but the proof had gone, her face showing no bruising, and the wet cloth was now dry and folded on the edge of the bowl. Meg kept glancing towards her at breakfast, but said nothing about it. To Christabel, the experience was dismissed as never having happened.

It was the start of a funny, balmy kind of day, yet a small event of seemingly little significance would soon launch Christabel into a new friendship and future dangers.

Christabel stood casually at the front door, throwing crumbs to early birds. She felt unusually lost, without jobs to do or a home to clean, but Westkings on market day would become a fantastic open party, where nobody could feel the slightest loneliness. Being unaware of the occasion only served to heighten the excitement as the scene grew.

A train of ducks appeared from a gate, comically waddling ahead of a woman with a thin stick. The prime position was hers and she paid a small levy for the space. The ducks entered a temporary enclosure of wooden boxes where, once trapped, they quacked at deafening pitch, frantically flapping clipped wings in a bid to escape the dinner table. Soon, great mounds of food of all descriptions arrived on handcarts and wagons. Dogs began prowling the pitches, fighting for scraps.

It was an hour or so before the first visitors strolled in from outlying villages, the children playing in bare feet as parents began the day's bargaining. A few youngsters gathered around the ducks as the first was bought, cheering as its neck snapped to hang long and lifeless over the edge of a basket. Cloth, leather, pottery, rough furniture, fowl, pigs, baiting dogs, snaring traps and much else were set out, the lane becoming one amazing bazaar where almost anything was available at a price.

"Pay up or clear off," said the levy collector to a man stringing iron pots between poles.

"How can I pay before I sell anything?"

"Look stranger, I've a living to make too." He pointed to a group of pale children climbing over a casket. "And there's another on the way."

The man put his hand in his pocket, grumbling.

"It isn't us you should charge, but them who come just to look."

"Come, come. That wouldn't be right."

"You should charge them who looks, them who buys and them who stays away."

* * *

Christabel took a keen interest in everything for sale. A second-hand pair of working boots caught her eye and she rushed back to her room to fetch her purse. With the change from a shilling she paid a penny for a pie, but on turning suddenly stopped as a little person bound in skintight rags leapt off a cart in front of her, his face emaciated and dirty. His eyes stared into hers, then at the pie and back again.

Smiling, she held out the pie for the urchin to take. He didn't move. Again she beckoned him to take it and slowly his hand crept forward, his eyes remaining firmly on hers. Then, like a snake at the bite, he grabbed it and flew, only to run full flight into an oncoming girl. The pie leapt from his fingers and fell. He watched helplessly as it was trampled underfoot. He almost cried. The girl shook him severely.

"I've told you before about stealing, Fritz. You'll be hanged and go to hell! Where have you been hiding?"

Now he cried. She sniffed him. He carried a hint of cheap perfume.

"So that's where you've been."

Christabel marched over.

"He didn't take it. I offered it."

She looked across with unchanging expression.

"Maybe you did, but I know this little runt. For two days we've been looking for him. He won't half cop it this time! Running away from the master again."

"Didn't steal nothing," protested the boy.

"Nobody said you did," put in Christabel with a soft tone, bending down to his level. "Why do you run away?"

"I want to be with me aunts."

"You little liar. You haven't got any aunts," put in the girl.

"I have so!"

"Who are these aunts of yours?" asked Christabel.

He looked at her with open mouth, then, with one sudden move he fled, weaving between the crowds. Christabel shouted after him, but he couldn't hear.

"What's he done?"

"Done? Nothing. He just don't like work, the little bugger. It's not the first time he's run away, but I reckon it'll be the last. Master Elvington won't put up with his antics anymore."

"Where are his parents?"

"Ain't got none. His mother died of the pox in Portsmouth. He was brought here by Madam Charlotte after she took pity on the lad."

"Smallpox?"

"Bless you, no. The clap!"

"Oh! And his father?"

"The whole of the British Navy I shouldn't wonder!"

"What about these aunts of his?"

"Take no mind. He came here alone. The poor little beggar has been brought up with the smell of the whorehouse in his nose. There's a couple of women on the game who live nearby. He calls them his aunts because to him it's like home from home. He sneaks out to visit them."

"Can't someone stop him?"

"You've seen what he's like! Between us two, those women aren't all bad. They keep themselves to themselves and are kind to him. German sisters I hear tell, that's why we call him Fritz."

"So Charlotte really is interested in prostitution," mused Christabel.

"What? Charlotte Elvington on the game? Don't be daft."

"No, I didn't mean that. I only meant . . . Oh, nothing. Will Fritz run back to them now?"

"Not on market day. They'll be busy doing their bit to keep the husbands amused while their wives shop! If he's upset enough he might start walking back to the coast to find his mother. We've all told him she's dead, but he won't listen. Just wanders around Portsmouth asking for her."

"Can't someone show him her grave?"

"A Christian grave? She had no chance."

"Poor boy. He's too young to understand."

"He ought to know by now. Last time the master found him, he'd walked for three days without a bite to eat. His feet had to be seen to be believed. Huge, burst red-raw blisters, and still he'd carried on with rags torn from his shirt tied around. There was no skin left on his soles and blood had dried between his toes. Really awful it was!"

"We must find him."

"We can't help."

"But we must try!"

"A waste of time. Believe me."

"I wish he'd eaten that pie."

"Don't worry. He'll steal another."

The girl was tiny, clearly a year or two Christabel's junior, with attractive features that were slightly marred by a protruding chin. Emmeline Sturry, or Emmie as she introduced herself, was a lively little fieldhand who made the most of life and possessed a natural self-assurance that guaranteed her welcome in company. Together, the two walked through the market and on towards 'Samain'. As they passed the pieman, Christabel gave him a penny in case the boy returned hungry.

Emmie showed her new friend where she lived on the estate. They climbed the stairs to a long and narrow space above the kitchen. It offered no privacy, the bed-cots tight between timber roof rafters.

"It's not that bad," said Emmie in answer to Christabel's look. "Only in spring and summer are all the beds taken. The rest of the time there isn't enough work for so many people. Right now we've more women working here than there are beds for them, so the lucky married ones get a chance to go home of an evening."

"It's so airless."

"It's the kitchen that makes it so hot. Those of us who stay all year around don't mind, cos when winter comes we're glad of the extra warmth. Anyway, we sometimes sneak down to see if any food has been left out."

"Where are the others?"

"Mostly in the fields. Later they'll go to the inn. That's where they meet up with their boyfriends after supper and shift a few pints. Shame you can't live here, it'd be fun. Have you got a fella?"

"Not really. I have a man friend, but it's not the same thing. He always called me Chrissie."

"And now you're by yourself."

"I don't mind. I'm used to being alone."

"I'd hate that. Anyway, I'd better get on. Don't be a stranger, will you?"

"I won't. I'm living at Meg Turner's."

"Blimey. Rather you than me. I tell you what, come and have a meal with us. I'll square it."

"I'd like that, but won't anyone mind?"

"People come and go all the time. Another face won't be noticed. I'll introduce you to my best friends. Mary Marwell is my closest mate. She's nice, except that she spends all her spare time with her boyfriend. Oh, and there's Louise Stovermoor. She's a bit scraggy, doesn't care much how she looks. No wonder madam insists on taking charge of her own butter making. Says she can't trust hired folk to see to cleanliness. Fancy that. Still, if it gets me out of a job I reckon she can think what she likes . . . How about breakfast tomorrow?"

By evening the market had disappeared and the lane was empty of all reminders except for a few feathers where the ducks had been. Christabel plucked one from the mud and ran it through her fingers. Although the hour was still young, the village had gone to sleep, the little cottages cocooned in isolation. Only the inn on the outskirts remained bright and cheery.

The next morning the women at 'Samain' rose at the usual early hour. One by one they strolled down the steps to the kitchen, where Christabel was already sitting quietly at a table talking to the cook. Her husband, the gamekeeper, had already checked the bird pens and was washing for breakfast.

Joined by the single men from the neighbouring dormitory, they tucked into bread and dripping as Mrs Redmarsh scooped out large quantities of fries from a huge blackened pan. The scene was happily chaotic. The grease that seemed to rise with the smoke from the encrusted hot-pan cast out the normal smells of the farm, while bubbling from the pot on the stove drowned the songbirds that perched on flowered bushes and laden trees. For as long as there were mouths to feed and bellies to fill, boiling and frying reigned supreme.

"You know, deary," said gamekeeper Redmarsh, aiming his chat at the newcomer, "my father and his father afore worked here. As for me, I'm the rebel of the family, exchanging the timber saw for the gun. Couldn't stand working down the sawpit, with wood-dust falling into my eyes. Why, I've been here forty years man and boy and not regretted a day." He turned to his wife with a wry grin. "Seen some things, haven't we dear?"

A young man several seats away listened earnestly, supposing Redmarsh to be too much in the master's pay.

"I'll not be here any longer than needs be."

"Still going on about the army, lad?" returned Redmarsh with a wink.

"Too right. That's for me. See something of the world. Make something of myself."

The others laughed.

"You'll see. I won't be here this time next year." He turned to Christabel. "You'll know why I'm not stopping when you see the master, the great James Elvington esquire. He's a head case if there's ever been one." He looked for support among the others. "Anyway, if things carry on as they are, there won't be jobs for any of you."

"Now, lad, mind your tongue. Gossip like that in the army and you'll feel the lash more than once." His scowl ended the young man's interest in talking. "Don't listen to the boy, maidy. The master isn't a heap to look at, that's true, but there's more to a man than appearances. I remember him as he was and I know he won't let the estate fall into ruin, because I've been here a deal longer than the rest. Now, let's change the subject afore I get my temper up."

"Did I hear my name?" came a shout from outside as the door was flung open.

James Elvington walked in unannounced. His right sleeve hung limp below the elbow. Those with mouths full of food stopped chewing, wondering what he had heard. False chattering slowly broke out to hide their fear. With the offer of a mug of tea, he removed his jacket and took Redmarsh's seat at the head of the table.

A ghastly stump of mutilated flesh protruded from the folded sleeve of his shirt. Christabel turned away, but James had already noticed the unfamiliar face.

"And who's this little beauty?"

"Chrissie, Sir," intervened Emmie.

Christabel nodded, unaware of the consequences had her full name been given. Her glance up was brief and he sensed her discomfort and sniggered.

"Well, Chrissie, maybe you think I'm a pitiable figure?"

"Oh, no, Sir."

He laughed with the others.

"Good, because it's well to see the nine-tenths of me that's whole."

She said no more. There was an air of expectancy.

"Silence, ah! Then I judge you to be a pessimist after all, seeing only the bit that's bad." He rounded on the others. "Damned if I'm not an iceberg to her. She only sees the most obvious bit above the waterline. Aye? Aye?"

She was trapped. But she couldn't be seen to be sickened by his affliction, propriety wouldn't permit that, yet she could hardly make herself look at him and that dreadful arm. After a moment's thought, she gently placed her knife and fork on the plate and looked up, staring squarely at his face to avoid taking in the wider aspect.

"Are you afraid, for you now stare at me hard?" he asked.

"No, Sir."

"But you tremble?"

"I'm not aware that I do."

"Good. Then come here, next to me."

With all eyes on her, she arose from the bench and made her way along the line of backs.

"Come nearer, girl."

She took another step. He offered up his stump, waving it close to her face.

"Here, try touching it."

She didn't want to.

"Come, you said you weren't afraid. Can it be that you are? Do you want to hurt my feelings?"

Slowly she lifted her hand, allowing her fingertips to touch the end. Without warning, he grabbed her arm and pressed it hard against the stump. She struggled to break free, rushing back to her place, embarrassed and confused. James laughed heartily. The rest remained mute.

"There, you all saw it. The little mouse *was* afraid after all."

Christabel lifted her head from cupped hands.

"I'm not. I'm not."

He looked among the faces for support, but found only pity.

"It was only meant as a bit of fun, my dear. Don't you like fun, or is it that you're now afraid I might sack you?"

"She doesn't work here," offered Mrs Redmarsh in an appeasing voice. "She's our guest."

"Is that right?"

Christabel nodded.

"Oh dear! Then I've acted very improperly. I apologise."

She shook her head in defiance.

"Do you have a job?"

Emmie answered for her.

"What can you do?"

The agonised girl wiped her eyes.

"Most things suited to my gender," she said in a voice that was very moving for its simplicity.

"Then good Mrs Redmarsh will find you something. Normal kitchen pay, mind."

She half-smiled.

"You're a funny little thing," he added to show that he really could be kind. "It's no use being sensitive around here, Chrissie. Live your life with a joke and a smile. It's much better. I can't help the wretchedness everywhere else, but at least at 'Samain' we have something to be happy about."

She thought of her father falling asleep in his chair, too tired to eat after a fourteen-hour day in the fields. What did he ever have to smile about? What right had they to be happy when he couldn't be? She dismissed his conciliatory words. Without thinking of the consequences, she spoke out:

"Life, Sir! What is life to any of us – frugal if we're lucky, hard, unhealthy and overcrowded if we're not. You can make mockery of my feelings because you feel superior, and in atonement you casually wave a magic wand and a job is mine. You know I need it, so I'll take it, and to you that's the end of the matter, but still I'm expected to take your humiliation and suffer it, just as I have done. Giving a job is simple to you, yet it's life and death to us. Before you believe I should joke and smile my way through life, have you ever thought what it must be like to have nothing, own nothing, be nothing? What have I to laugh about, or any of us here apart from you? I fear I'll not have work and shelter during the winter months. I fear I may starve without anyone caring. I fear illness and old age. Most of all I fear I'll see out my life existing and not living at all. But what I *don't* fear is you."

The eloquence of her speech took everyone by surprise. Unquestionably, here was a mind too bright, too delicate, too passionate for the rough-folk trick played on her. The dignity of this strange girl and the emotion in her voice affected all, so much so that nobody present went to bed that night without reliving the moment. After James had left, Mrs Redmarsh walked to where Christabel sat and put her arms around her shoulders, a little gesture of gentle-hearted support approved by her husband.

"You talk well," said James, leaning on the wall outside, having waited for Christabel to leave. "I'm at a loss how to apologise further. You were right, of course. I have no idea what it must be like to be poor. I've never given it much thought to be honest. Things aren't all rosy at the manor either, you should know. We richer folk have our share of problems too, but I confess they are of a different nature to yours."

"Do I still have a job?"

"That's one concern you can leave behind. I offered you employment and by God you've earned it."

She smiled in acceptance.

"Made me look rather foolish, didn't you? But then, maybe that's done me no harm. I sense there's something rather noble about you, Chrissie. I feel you wouldn't let your husband down, if you had one. A man would be safe with you."

"I would like to think so."

"Anyway, water under the bridge and all that. I'm glad to say the work for women on the estate isn't too arduous, especially during hay and corn harvests when I can promise with confidence that a festive air takes over the place. Of course the beasts take no account of their keeper's convenience, so hours can't always be regular, but no doubt you'll be used to that. Apart from that, maybe you could help with the hives, the flower and fruit growing and so on. You tend my wife's market garden well and you'll get on splendidly. Funny thing, but earlier today she mentioned you in passing. I was on my way to Turner's when I heard you lot talking at breakfast, and there you were, just sitting there. I'll tell her that I've found you work. Goodbye for now."

Mr Redmarsh accompanied James across to the manor, where they stood talking.

"Ha! I like her forwardness. What did you say her name was? I must keep a weather eye on that one."

"Chrissie as I understand it, Sir."

"Yes, but Chrissie who?"

"To be frank, I don't rightly know."

A tatterdemalion youth strolled from the conservatory, hands in pockets.

"Sam, lad, come here."

He swaggered across.

"That new girl, Chrissie. The one over there." He pointed. "What's her name?"

"Chrissie!"

"We know that, you idiot. Her other name, boy?" said James.

He shrugged.

"Never spoke to her." He spat on the ground.

Here we go again, thought James, staring at his appearance and annoyed by his attitude.

"Lad. How old are you?"

"Twelve."

"Twelve . . . Well?" his temper getting the better of him.

"Yeah, I be fine," answered the boy, kicking a stone across the yard.

"Twelve, what, I mean?" he returned harshly.

The boy looked up in bewilderment. "Green bottles?".

"No! Twelve? Damn it!"

The boy shrugged.

"Twelve, honest."

James grabbed him by the collar.

"Then, boy, if you're old enough to be hanged, you're certainly old enough to learn some manners. Remember this." He let go and caught the youth across the ear with the back of his one good hand. "And if I have the misfortune ever to talk to you again, you will address me as, *Sir*. I wanted to hear you say *twelve, Sir*. Next time you will address me properly or get more of the same." With that he walked away.

Once out of sight, Redmarsh comforted the lad.

"Never mind, Sam. Go and ask Mrs Redmarsh to bathe that ear. Tell her to give you a bun to cheer you up."

"Silly sod," muttered the boy, hands back in his pockets.

*　*　*

Christabel was sitting on the doorstep when she was joined by Emmie and her friends, who were now ready for work.

"Ever see'd the likes of him?" asked Louise, imitating James by pulling one arm out of her jumper and letting the empty sleeve swing. "Fair gives me the shudders to think of him as a husband."

"Shush," begged Mary. But, Louise wouldn't be put off.

"I know how it happened. I was told by someone who heard it from a friend of the sister of one of the indoor maids. It's a laughing matter."

"How's that?" asked Christabel innocently.

"It was years before I came here. The master was a great one for reading late into the night by the light of a candle, as is the way of many men of culture after a long day."

"How would *you* know what men do?" enquired Emmie mischievously.

"I was told, that's how! Are you going to listen or not?"

They nodded.

"According to what I heard, the mistress didn't like it, hating the noise he made as he scraped the pages over with his finger nails, but he wouldn't stop reading, nor turn the pages over in the normal way. So, she told him that if he carried on she would take his books upstairs and throw them out of the window."

"And?"

"Being his own master, he carried on. Then, one morning before he got up she sneaked downstairs, grabbed the book he had been reading and several others from the library, tore the pages out and pitched them from the window, shouting with joy as the bits fluttered down. The noise was intended to wake him and it did. He jumped out of bed and, seeing what had happened, looked for a way to get even. Within seconds he had bundled her dress out through the mullions."

The picture brought on a smile.

"Anyhow, to his surprise she didn't seem dismayed at all. You see, she had anticipated his reaction and had put out an old dress in place of the one she had been wearing. Only, seeing she didn't seem to mind, he went to her cupboard and took out another dress and threw that from the window too. This time it was her favourite. She was so overcome by its loss that he broke down with regret and offered to buy her a new dress at some considerable expense, which seemed to console her. Later, going outside to inspect the mess, she discovered that there was no damage at all to her first best dress. Not a mark. When his back was turned she sneaked it into her wardrobe, tearing the other to ribbons so that nobody could tell if it was one dress or two."

The laughter was vigorous.

"But that wasn't the end. Having paid up he felt easy about reading again, both downstairs and now also in the bedroom, and the scraping by candlelight restarted. Then one evening he fell asleep. Inevitably the candle was knocked over, which set the bed alight. Luckily they awoke in time to get out, but aiming to save the new dress that had cost him so much, he braved the flames to get it and was burned for his pains."

Although Louise grinned, the rest saw little amusement and the group separated. Mary walked with Christabel out into the yard and the aromatic air.

"Men are such fools at times. The more important they are the sillier they become. Still, I suppose they're only what we allow them to be. My Robert will find that out one of these days, and Emmie too if she gets her way with the master's son, although I don't fancy her chances with him once the family find out what they've been up to."

"What's he like?"

"Who?"

"James Elvington's son."

"He's very handsome." She pointed towards the manor. "See for yourself. There he is now."

In the distance Christabel could just make out a figure hazed by sunlight. She held up her hand to shade the brightness from her eyes.

"But I know him!" she said with surprise.

CHAPTER XXI

Young hearts

*A*mong the lush prosperity of the Elvington land, at a time when all around ran and jumped the miracle of newborn life and germination was in the air and on the ground, it was little wonder that the minds of the fresh-faced girls wandered to matters of a passionate nature.

Every new task was greeted with a spring in their step, the monotony of estate life lightened by a tingle of young love in their bosoms. Whispered and giggled talk was of the same kind, with plenty of time for conversation as they slowly made their way to work.

Learning the new daily routine had been a simple task for Christabel and, although James' intervention had gone against Charlotte's own wishes, it meant that she was back in an environment she understood and enjoyed. Her cheerful willingness to tackle the unpleasant with the same enthusiasm as the easy, rubbed off on even the older hardened workers whose inflamed joints pained them mercilessly after a youth spent dripping wet in some field or other. Life for Christabel was happy, physically undemanding and mentally without challenge. She kept close company with Emmie, Mary and Louise by day, but in the evenings sat alone to read in her room at the boarding house or walked the estate and nearby passages. The whereabouts of her father's key was never far from her thoughts; that mysterious object that appeared to have no use but had been instrumental in changing her life.

It was the evenings she particularly relished, when her mind could take flight with the freedom of the blessed, when time was at a standstill and her eyes could look up to the heavens and scan eternity itself. It wasn't that she always wanted to be alone, but that the almost inevitable pairing of men and women from the estate and farms after several jugs of ale at the inn did not appeal. She had joined them once, the third day after arriving, and true to form she had attracted the unwelcome attentions of several men, urged on by the women. Declining in a pleasant way had been a test of her character.

Christabel could not explain to Emmie her outright reluctance to any and all advances, although on reflection she put it down to her time with John, still burning in her heart. Hers had not been a marriage to him or even an engagement, yet nonetheless she felt bound to his memory, pondering on the words of the scripture she liked so much: 'He that is faithful in that which is least is faithful also in much'.

One particular evening Christabel, restless to be out, and with the others gone to the inn, struck out for nearby Kingsden woods. The morning had seen heavy rain, but this had eased during the afternoon, leaving the air clear and fresh.

As a precaution she had left on her working boots, knowing the meadows thereabouts to be particularly slow draining and likely to be soft underfoot. In other respects she had dressed herself prettily as if meeting friends, relying only on a thin shawl for protection against an unexpected drop in temperature.

The early part of her walk took her along level ground past Muncome Hill and Cople wood. She skirted both. Having past an old windmill, the way was hindered by the meandering River Geri, which had burst its low banks to spill onto the meads on either side. Kingsden woods now being close, she decided to press on regardless, although the usually dry stepping stones were themselves marooned some inches below water level.

Her skirt raised, she picked her way through the water that quickly reached ankle depth, searching out each submerged stone before attempting the stride. At the edge of the first coppice, where a slight incline had produced drier ground, it began to rain once more. Within moments the drizzle turned to a deluge driven by a chilling wind. Pulling the shawl up and over her head, she became rather worried, undecided whether to make for the sparse protection of the trees or brave the consequences of a dash home.

The wet soon penetrated the shawl, the first trickle pervading her buttoned collar. She squeezed the neckband tight, yet still the rain ran down her back in veined streams.

The sky turned a thick grey. Instinctively she ran for cover, any cover, pressing deeper into the woods where the greater density offered some protection. Even here, where the evening surrendered to patches of dark and light, many droplets fell from soaked branches, making this refuge only a little more bearable. From the damp earth came a miasmic vapour. Her petticoat steamed, wet up to the knees. She wished she had pinned it up when the weather had turned.

Shivering and a little frightened, she stayed hidden among the great trees of the coppice. An hour passed and the light faded, but not the rain. Then, out of the gloom a glow came her way, hovering at shoulder height. She strained to see who or what accompanied it, the impression of a figure moving vaguely across the wet trenches of mud almost invisible behind the glowing haze.

Still the light came, taking a crooked path and always nearer. She stared hard at the shadowy form, her eyes wide. In a wild moment of panic she fancied it was something scary, remembering the ghostly man in her room. She let out an involuntary scream. The light was stopped by the noise, the lantern pulled in towards a face made heinous by silhouette. Her eyes were transfixed. She felt behind for the tree trunk, side stepping around it and behind.

"Damn to hell this bloody rain," came a voice, the man losing his footing on a sodden root. He stood again, taking hold of the coat he held above the head of a smaller person by his side. "Which way did that scream come from?"

Christabel listened, breathing hard. After a few moments she nervously called back. Under cover of the trees where she stood, the coat was shaken from their heads.

"Emmie!"

"Good Lord, it's you, Chrissie. What on earth are you doing here?"

"You scared me to death."

The man held the lantern close to her.

"Don't I know you?"

She nodded, recognising Edmond. She was surprised that he remembered.

"We met once. Far from here."

"We did?"

"Shalhurn."

"Of course. Now I know. You were the pretty cottage wench."

Emmie looked at one and then the other, breaking their stare.

"Don't tell me you two have already met."

"That we have," replied Edmond civilly, "but that's a story for a dry day." He turned back to Christabel. "So, you were caught out too?"

She smiled, holding out her arms to show quite how wet she was.

"Right. What's important now is proper shelter. It's no use trying to get back until the rain has eased off. There's a derelict windmill not far from here I used to play in as a child. We'll go there. Now, where's that old man?"

"What man?" enquired Christabel.

"The old chap we met by the stream. He led us this way."

"He was here a minute ago," added Emmie.

"Well, he's gone now. I hate to say it but we can't worry about him. He had a warm coat and a scarf. He'll be alright. Let's get on by ourselves."

"I can't go another step," complained Emmie. "I'm soaked through."

Edmond rounded on her impatiently.

"You're going to have to. It's a run for the windmill or stay here by yourself. I mean it."

The lantern blew out and suddenly the evening seemed dark and hostile.

"I'm coming, I'm coming," shouted Emmie, grabbing his arm.

"We won't worry about a light. I know my way without it." He tossed the lantern aside. "Come on, Emmie. Get under properly."

She got under the coat. Edmond turned to Christabel.

"I'm sorry, I don't remember your name."

"Christabel."

"We call her Chrissie," sniffed Emmie.

"Well, Chrissie, don't just drip there. Take my place under here!"

They huddled and crouched their way from the woods to the meadows, Edmond walking ahead of the girls. He could feel his trousers becoming damp where they had been dry before, but said nothing. The three burst into the sheltered darkness of the windmill.

"I'm completely drenched," said Emmie for the second time, her hair a tangled mass of dripping curls.

"How are you, Chrissie?" asked Edmond.

"Fine now, thank you."

She went over to the grate.

"No, leave that to me," insisted Edmond. "I'll soon have a fire going."

She moved back, watching as Edmond foraged for straw, sacking and anything suitable to use as kindling. Soon small flames began to leap between the sticks. Christabel helped to gather more wood while Emmie stood by shivering, placing any damp bits by the grate to dry out. He caught Christabel's beautiful smile as she handed him a bundle of sticks from a chair she had pulled apart. The light from the fire was as cheering as the warmth it provided. The girls sat together on the floor and Emmie leaned over to whisper secretly to her friend.

"It would have to rain tonight. I'd hoped to be alone with him, this of all nights."

"I'm sorry," replied Christabel genuinely, feeling that she had unintentionally intruded on their privacy.

"It's not your fault. It's just my bad luck."

A sudden gust brought rain hurtling through the window where several panes had fallen out, the fire fanned into fierce activity. Edmond rushed over to plug the hole with his coat, but needed help to secure it, turning his face away from the biting cold. Christabel soon had it under control. When she turned back to the fire Emmie was crying, sniffing heavily and drying her cheeks on the back of her sleeve, smudging mud across her face. Christabel gently wiped it off with her handkerchief.

Under the tears Emmie wore a curiously fragile look, which Christabel understood at a glance. She became aware that Edmond was watching them. Emmie looked up and smiled, hoping to see love in his eyes. Christabel was moved by the soft and simple feelings that flowed from the girl, although she wondered how dim were her prospects when Edmond's face held only contempt. It was, therefore, with surprise that Emmie whispered:

"I don't know if I weep for joy or sadness. The fact is, he proposed to me this evening."

Christabel was stunned.

"It was a moment of my life that I shall never forget. He held me close and said the words I've been longing to hear. I looked up into his eyes and I could see that he was mine." The brightness of the memory suddenly fell away. "He gave me a ring, the most beautiful thing I'd ever seen, with gold and stones beyond counting. He explained that it was once his grandmother's, and hers before that. He slipped it over my finger but it was far too big. He said he would have it made smaller, but I wanted to keep it on. So I closed my fingers around it like this." She showed how. "Then the blasted rain started and we had to end our love talk. We started running for cover, but I slipped and the ring fell off. We searched and searched for it without success. When the light went we went back to the gig for a lantern. We carried on looking, but it was hopeless. I couldn't even be sure that we were looking in the same place. Then this old man turned up and he helped us, but I think he led us the wrong way, and now this." She glanced back at Edmond. "I wish I'd helped you two to make up the fire. I think he sees me as useless."

"You poor darling. What a state you're in."

She pulled Emmie close to comfort her.

"I can't go on. He won't love me anymore after this."

"What nonsense. It's often circumstances, not people, that cause sadness. He probably feels badly about the ring. That's all. If he loves you as you say he does, then what matter is it beyond its value in gold and stones. If I judge the man, it's a trinket buried out there, not his feelings."

"Chrissie, I wish I had the courage to run away. Yes, I would truly rather never see him again than hear from his lips that he didn't love me anymore."

"Shush!"

"Will you tell him I didn't mean to lose it? Will you, please?"

She squeezed her reassuredly.

"You'd do better speaking for yourself. I'm a stranger to him."

"I can't. I really can't."

"Yes you can! Remember, you've said you'll be his wife. How can you do that if you cannot face him now over this?"

With Christabel's help she stood up and brushed herself down. She turned to face him, but he was preoccupied looking out of the window.

"It's stopped. I can't believe our luck. Grab everything quickly. Now's our chance."

Without reply the girls did as he asked. The three dashed for the gig and its miserable horse. They all felt better at the prospect of a warm bed, and the talk became jolly.

They pulled into the drive at just before midnight. All about was quiet. Emmie crept to her bed. Mary awoke as a floorboard creaked.

"What are you doing?"

Emmie raised a ladle from a half-full bucket.

"I'm thirsty."

"What!" she exclaimed, looking at her clothes. "Haven't you had enough water for one day?"

They giggled merrily.

Christabel made for the boarding house and quietly climbed the stairs, keeping to the edge to prevent creaking. She changed out of her wet clothes, leaving them in a pile on the floor, and wrapped a towel around her hair. There was a knock at the door.

"Heard you come in. Thought you might like a hot drink."

Meg passed the cup with a shaking hand.

"Thank you. You're up very late?"

"I had to stay up to see you. It's so exciting. He, the 'thing', came back."

"How do you mean?"

"I was going to bed. It was about ten. I'd been waiting up for you so that I could lock the front door. Then I heard noises from your room and obviously I thought you had crept in without me noticing, so I knocked and entered. For just for a split second I saw him, dripping wet. Then he vanished. I'm so thrilled."

The smell of alcohol on her breath was strong.

"Sure it wasn't the gin?"

She pulled back.

"Quite sure," she replied with a hint of a slur, taking an unsteady course for the door. "Hardly touch the stuff!"

Christabel looked for a wet patch on the rug apart from the one she had just made. There was nothing.

"Good night," she said with determination to be left alone.

"I suppose ghosts can get wet?"
"*Good night.*"

Some days passed, during which neither Emmie nor Christabel caught sight of Edmond. Unknown to them, he had been sent away on family business, but this information had not been relayed to Emmie, who daily expected his presence. As each evening passed she grew a little more melancholy. Christabel wished she could help, but she too began to doubt his sincerity.

An estate neglected can sustain a myriad of changes without attracting much notice, passing from run-down to bankruptcy in an inevitably smooth slide. An estate bent on improvement takes on another complexion entirely, however, when any variation from the normal in work or among the labourers stands to be recognised instantly. For those who worked alongside Emmie and Christabel during this period, it quickly became clear that something private was terribly wrong, although neither girl mentioned the engagement for fear that such talk could now be premature.

The Elvington estate had become a jewel of activity in the English countryside, each day a glint from the early morning sun sending the workers like sparkles to different corners of the fields. The unexpected absence of Edmond had, for one young heart and maybe two, removed a vital colour from the pattern. All the twisting of the jewel could not capture a sparkle lost.

A second blow for Emmie came on the back of the first, when she received a letter from her mother. Unable to read more than the most basic words, she took Christabel into her confidence, already assuming that it would be bad news. In the quiet of the evening, when the others had left for the company of men, Christabel sat on Emmie's bed to read it.

My dearest Emmeline.
*I write in the hope that I find you in good health, as I am
thanks be to God. My girl, it is with mixed pleasure that I write*

to you, on account of your brother's (Robert) decision to leave us for good. Knowing myself to be the kind to tell all that is in my heart, I say that I have great foreboding, but can do nothing to change his mind. It is his choice to emigrate to the other side of the world, to Australia no less. I, of course, worry about the kind of people already there, but he says that since transportation ended, this colony is a place for honest folk wanting to try their luck. I have to add that he could be right, as a million other Englishmen have done the same recently, or so we are told. If I was asked, I would have begged him not to go, but then I wasn't. He is gone on Thursday next, so I suppose this will reach you too late to see him away. On this score, be assured I will give him God Bless from you, as he would return.

Dear Emmeline, do not distress yourself over the matter. Your father and I have come to terms with it. At least he will be safe on the steamer and I have made up a fine big basket that will last him well. It may pass that he becomes a gentlemen in that country. Who can tell? So that is all on this matter at present. Do visit us soon and bring that young man with you whom you told us about. But a word of warning that I say private from your father's ears, but strongly — on no account must you give yourself to him without proper regard for your future well-being under Christian terms. No more shall be said here. Your affectionate mother.

Rachel.

"She writes an educated letter, but signs herself Rachel rather than Mother. What's she like?"

"I'm the dunce of the family, if that's what you mean," replied Emmie in low ebb.

With this news on top of the other, despair filled Emmie's young life for several more days.

On the fortnight anniversary of her betrothal, after taking herbs from the kitchen garden to the house, Emmie came by the screened wall bordering the dormitory and saw Louise, Mary and Christabel talking together merrily, but gave no sign of wanting to join them. An hour later, after Christabel was about to leave them for supper, she came flying around the corner with the broadest smile on her happy face.

"He's back!"

Christabel had to stem her own enthusiasm.

"Have you seen him?"

"Just now, up at the house. He had a bag with him. He must have been away all this time on business. Isn't it perfect?"

"Perfect," agreed Christabel with less brilliance in her voice.

That evening the normal evacuation of the dormitory took place, one girl taking unusual care over her appearance. At Meg Turner's boarding house, one girl took less. Edmond had made immediate contact with Emmie and she intended to make up for lost time. Christabel, on the other hand, was by no means overjoyed at the prospect of their reunion – which she kept to herself – and saw no point in making any effort at all. She set off instead in the direction of the inn where she thought she might break a rule and drown her sorrows in company.

In the solitude of the walk she pondered about how she could find herself capable of emotion for a man she hardly knew. She rebuked her weak character, yet pictured him again the moment her mind changed subject.

The noise from the inn grew louder. She stopped outside, peering through the window. Most of the men were already drunk with the women on their laps, while others danced a jig on a table top for amusement.

"You coming in, maidy?"

A young man in working clothes held the door open. She stood silently, unable to decide. He didn't wait, thinking her dress dirty and smelling of smoke from the hives. From inside came a shout above the rest.

"Sit down, gentlemen, and keep your singing clean. This is a respectable place."

With 'a respectable place' echoing in her head, she went in. Her friends were surprised to see her, but quickly made a space and ordered another round of drinks. Bit by bit she joined in the merriment, or at least the best her quiet nature allowed, using the company to dismiss painful thoughts from her mind.

Several men invited her favours, but were turned away. On one occasion when Christabel's attentions were elsewhere, Louise secretly poured a treble gin into her beer until one pint had the strength of six.

Being summer, when mouths were at their driest, the inn kept what the locals called 'biddable hours', allowing a degree of flexibility. It was late, therefore, when the revellers were finally thrown out by a landlord concerned for his licence.

"I'm going home," said Christabel. "I'm mortally exhausted and my head aches."

"Bless me eyes," put in a young man, "she's got a wobble to her step."

"She can barely stand," offered Louise's companion, "but I still reckon she's the prettiest here, if only she'd allow me a kiss."

"I've got an idea," slurred Louise, wishing to regain his attention. He took no notice, so she poked him. "Don't you hear me? I've got an idea."

"Is there money in it?"

"No, but there's fun."

A broad smile came over his face.

"That'll teach her, the stuck up bitch."

While Christabel reeled at the mix of alcohol and fresh air, two men ran off, returning with a wheelbarrow.

"Your carriage, Ma'am," they offered with little perspicuity, and bowed low on shaky legs.

Christabel protested, but was overpowered.

"Get along," cried out Louise.

The vehicle began snaking its way with Christabel's legs dangling from the front. All the men took turns to push, laughing at the frolics.

"This is the right place," sneered Louise, putting her foot on the wheel. "Now, quick, get her out and let's go before we're seen."

They tipped Christabel onto the step under the porticoed entrance to 'Samain'. A string of onions was hung around her head as a last-minute necklace.

"Mustn't lose your jewels, your highness. Now you stuck-up bitch, you've had your carriage ride and we being gentlefolk have brought you home. Sleep well."

They ran off laughing. Through foggy eyes Christabel could make out the doors. She recognised them, but her dulled brain could offer no reason not to enter. Propping against the wall, she raised her arm and pulled the bell handle.

"Glory be," shouted the maid. "Shoo! Get away from here."

Christabel looked on in blind defiance, not frightened at efforts to drive her away.

"What is it?" called out Edmond.

"It's nothing, Sir." She turned to Christabel. "For pity's sake girl, go away before you get yourself into trouble."

It was too late. Edmond peered over the maid's shoulder and burst into uncontrollable laughter.

"Nothing, eh! I tend to agree with you."

Christabel stared back through half-closed eyelids and returned a smile.

"Leave her to me."

"Sir, she's one of the labourers! I'll get Dudds to carry her back. The mistress will have to be told."

While the point was argued, Christabel slid down the wall and into a heap on the step. Grinning, Edmond carried her into the drawing room, laying her on the couch. She fell asleep at once. He threw the onions into a basket.

All night he sat with her, rising only to put the blanket back when it slipped off. At six o'clock she stirred, sitting up slowly, aware that every muscle ached. Slowly she noticed her surroundings. Edmond coughed. She looked around with wide but painful eyes.

"Welcome, Chrissie."

Startled, she grabbed the blanket and pulled it up high to cover herself. Edmond tugged at the bell rope.

"A cup of tea, perhaps?"

She nodded, pushing her long hair away from her face.

"Tell me what happened . . . In your own time."

She searched her thoughts, but it was all a blur.

"Has the cat got your tongue?" he asked, coming forward to take the blanket. She refused to let go.

"I can't remember. How did I get here?"

"I carried you."

"You?"

"How else do you suppose you got in?"

"Did we . . . have we . . .?"

He smiled.

"No, to both."

She looked beneath the blanket and was pleased to see that she still had her working dress on. She let go of the blanket and he folded it. A tray was brought in. He whispered to the maid and she left. Christabel poured two cups and sipped, jerking back at the heat.

"Well?" he urged, throwing the blanket into the corner.

"I'm not sure. Was I with you?"

He shook his head.

"You were drunk."

"Me?"

"Yes, you."

"I suppose I must have been, but how?"

"That's a foolish question."

"But I don't drink!"

"I think you do."

She tried to recall the evening.

"I can remember going to the inn, but after that . . ."

"I happened, after you landed bottom first on my doorstep."

"Did I?"

"Slid down the wall, no less. Funniest thing I've seen in ages. Still, I have a passion for silly things, and foolish things come all the better." He walked over to the basket. "These smelly things were hanging around your neck. I must say, Chrissie, I don't think much of your taste in jewellery."

"Is there anything else I should know?"

"Isn't that enough?"

"I suppose it is." Her head dropped. "I'm so terribly sorry. I can't explain any of it, but you must believe me when I say that I don't normally get drunk."

"I know."

"How?"

"If you were a drinker, you wouldn't be so ill now."

"I'd better go."

"Sit!" he commanded. "Have some breakfast with me before my parents come down."

"No, it wouldn't be right. Anyway, I don't think I could face food."

"Too late to argue. I've already ordered it. Surely you wouldn't want me to eat alone after I've sat up with you all night?"

"Kindly Sir, I really can't."

"What new nonsense is this?"

"I think you know well enough."

"No I don't. Explain yourself."

"Emmeline!"

"Emmie and myself? What of it?"

"I know you've asked her to be your wife."

"And now you think it would be improper for you and I to eat breakfast together, although we are both already dressed?"

"Not improper, no, not that, but what would she say if she knew? Especially after I've been here all night."

"If you think she won't know you were here, you're tragically wrong!"

She looked hard at him.

"You threaten to tell her if I don't stay?"

"Of course not. I meant your friends who left you here won't keep it to themselves. It'll be all around the village by now."

"I can't remember if Emmie was with us last night. If she was, I suppose she'd understand."

"No comfort there, I'm afraid. She was with me most of the evening."

"Oh heavens, what a mess."

"More of a mess than you realise. Me and Emmie —"

"Yes," she interrupted.

"I'm young like you, Chrissie, and not beyond making mistakes. In the matter of marriage, I think I may have acted hastily."

"Oh, God, she'll be devastated. Did you tell her that last night?"

"I meant to, but she was so pleased to see me that it was impossible to tell her anything. I suppose it can wait a day or two. Of course, knowing how a certain other lady felt towards me could help me to make up my mind to get it done —"

She cut him short, although her heart lifted.

"I don't think I want to hear this!"

"Hear me out," he begged.

"I can't." She turned away, hiding her expression. "Is that why you stayed away so long?"

"You couldn't know that! Yes, a few extra days were added to my journey. Thinking time, you might say."

"Don't tell me anymore. It's between you and Emmie. I'm not involved."

"Aren't you?"

"No. At least, not at present."

"Then there's no harm done. Here, I open the door for you."

She swept out. He called after her.

"Chrissie, best say nothing to Emmeline!"

It had been Christabel's turn to be among the early milkers that morning, and around Mrs Redmarsh's breakfast table the workers made much of her non-appearance. Only Emmie was none the wiser and worried about her friend. When she did arrive, after a change of clothes and a wash, Emmie took her to one side.

"I've got to speak to you, Chrissie."

She guessed the topic, but hoped to be capable of feigning enough surprise.

"It's Edmond." She looked about to see that nobody else could overhear. "I think he's gone off me."

"How so?"

"Oh, it's nothing he said. It's more what he hasn't. Last night we went out strolling and I stuck to his arm like a limpet. We spoke of marriage, but I did all the talking. I enjoyed the clear night and the romantic moon, but he put his collar up. I wanted to sit by the stream and kiss, yet he thought it was getting late and took me home. I was in bed asleep a good hour before the other girls got in. What does it all mean?"

Christabel put her finger to Emmie's lips as Louise joined them. It was perhaps providential that she knew something of the shock that was coming, although her support would only be valued if nobody knew of her own growing attachment to Edmond. The three sat at the table. Christabel felt all eyes were on her.

"You were missed from milking," said Mary as she passed slices of thick cut bread, still hot from the oven. "Sleep in, did you?"

Giggles rippled around the room.

"We could've used an extra pair of hands," added Mr Redmarsh, drying his arms. "It's been years since I was called on to do women's work, and a proper bog I made of it."

"It's your fingers, Mr Redmarsh," scolded Mrs Redmarsh as she snatched away her tea towel. "They're too blasted fat."

"You might be right, my dear," he laughed. "Petal wouldn't give me all she had."

"Petal likes the gentle touch," added old Ruby, wiping her plate clean with a wedge of bread held between arthritic fingers, "and that scratty Bluebell needs a constant eye to stop her going off."

"Well, I won't have it! No beast gets the upper hand of me. I may be no good, but I'm damned if I'm not going to try again. Have you milked for us yet Chrissie?"

She answered that she hadn't.

"Then now isn't the time to start. If that Petal plays up anymore, I'll leave her udders to bloat. She'll soon see reason."

"Stick to your gamekeeping, dear," suggested his wife. "Leave milking to those who know how."

"Hum! Right as ever," he conceded.

"Could tie rowen twigs to the bucket, Mr Redmarsh. I hear that does the trick."

"No, Ben, that's to stop the milk going sour."

Emmie couldn't wait to talk to Christabel about the subject nearest to her heart, but became conscious of Louise's continued attention. The clatter of knives and forks became almost rhythmical. Louise reminded Mary of her promise to help to muck out the pig pens. Mary in turn put her arm around Christabel, unsure of her lasting friendship.

"I'm so very sorry about last night. I didn't know what to do to stop it, so I did nothing. Forgive me?"

"I suppose so. What I'm really cross about is that I didn't think of asking for my key back. Goodness knows when I'll get a better chance."

"Were you at the manor, then?" asked Emmie innocently.

"I'll tell you about it later."

"It's only an old bit of junk," offered Louise. "Doesn't open anything, you said."

"Perhaps not, but it's mine and I want it."

"*Was* yours, you mean. I think you've seen the last of it."

"I'll get it back, one way or the other."

"Maybe and maybe not."

"Which reminds me," shouted Ben, "did you know we've got them blessed swallows back in the barn, Mr Redmarsh?"

"If we have, you leave 'em be. Don't go messing."

"Why not?" enquired Mary.

Ben and Redmarsh exchanged glances of exasperation.

"Because, my girl, it don't go well to those who mess with swallows. I knew a man over Midford way who destroyed a nest and for his effort his cows gave blood with their milk – and that's not the only such case I know."

"Such tales," put in Mrs Redmarsh, slapping her husband's shoulder.

"No m'dear, it's common knowledge. Some say it's the revenge of nature upon those who disturb the natural order of things, although it is true, I must admit, that others say it's the flies that swallows feed on that gives the milkers the disease. Either way, I think it best to leave well alone. We don't want to invite trouble."

"Talking of which," added Ben for a second time, "that lad Fritz has been caught."

Emmie smiled at last.

"Thank God for that."

"The poor blighter was huddled in a ditch over Chiggerfield way. Some old boy found him clutching a half-eaten pie."

"Dead?" asked Emmie, cowering from the likely answer.

"Fevered, but still alive. He'd been with those so-called aunts of his when the police broke in and took them away for medical examination. The lad escaped through a window, but they have him now."

"How do you know this?" enquired Redmarsh with more than passing interest.

"Because I took charge of Master Edmond's horse when he came back yesterday, and I heard him saying to Madam Charlotte that he couldn't persuade the old bill to release Fritz into his care. The boy's done for this time."

In the drawing room of the manor a lonely figure sat over his breakfast, pushing it around the plate with a silver fork, but unable to eat anything. For the first time in his young life he found himself besotted by a woman, and not the one he had promised to marry. Christabel alone was in his thoughts.

He had astonished himself by showing no timidity in telling Christabel of his mistake over Emmie, although she had shown no interest in hearing. What curious attraction did she hold that could so free his tongue? He remembered the best he could their first unappreciated meeting in Shalhurn. The few months that intervened had not altered her, or himself, so what had been the agent of change? Still, no matter. The effect was that above all the ladies of his acquaintance, it was her who most fulfilled his concupiscence for womanhood and nothing, nothing, could be allowed to stand in his way, least of all Emmie.

CHAPTER XXII

The Lieutenant

When Edmond took Emmie to a quiet corner of a field to say that he intended to break their engagement, she broke out in a mindless frenzy. Her reply was so full of jealousy that it sent the other fieldworkers scurrying in all directions. He stormed away, leaving Emmie with nothing to show for their betrothal, but a broken heart. Even the ring was lost.

Christabel tried to comfort her, but found it impossible. Then, as if to mock her further, in the next field a marriage party trudged across the grass on its way to church, although on this gilded of all occasions there was little sign of celebration. The procession was scattered along several hundred yards, with the old and frail at the rear, the day being devoid of any real charm because the bride was already with child. At least the reception was likely to become merry, when thirsts would be saturated until it seemed possible that ale would seep through their very skins.

Edmond hadn't expected Emmie's venomous outpouring and was embarrassed by the whole affair. Most of all, he worried that it was likely to colour Christabel's view of him. He flew into the manor, dashed up to his room and started kicking the furniture and anything else in his path, until the floor lay strewn with clothes, books and broken china. It was, though, behaviour of the most affected kind, wild, but sufficiently considered to avoid damaging any treasured possessions.

With so much wrong in her life, Emmie's thoughts turned towards home. She made up her mind to leave as soon as she got her parents' consent. This prospect calmed her, for in truth she was too immature to commit her feelings and energies to anything lasting.

Christabel on the other hand, being older, wore guilt like a hair shirt and remained unsparing in her self-denial of Edmond's company.

"I can hardly believe our paths haven't crossed for so long," said Edmond a week later, catching Christabel scrubbing the kitchen table.

Her reply was to splash more soapy water over the worktop. He smiled politely at Emmie who washed the floor on hands and knees.

"I rode to the barn yesterday, but you weren't there. I missed a caller as the result and he was none well pleased."

She dropped the stiff brush into the bucket, causing water to splash into Edmond's face.

"Then may I suggest that you pay more attention to your society and less to us."

He shuffled uncomfortably, dabbing a handkerchief over his cheeks.

"Fortunately, he returned in the evening and is at this very moment staying at the manor, so no lasting harm was done. You might see him around."

She nodded. He turned to Emmie.

"You know, Emmeline, Lieutenant Charles is quite taken by you. I do believe you have an admirer."

The younger girl was pleased with the prospect, but Christabel saw more in his words. When Edmond left she bent down to Emmie, having left the brush to weep soapy water back onto the table.

"A chance meeting?"

"What do you mean?"

"You with this military gentleman?"

"Oh, him," pretending to be disinterested. "Yes, it was. Why, are you interested in him? I can't see why you should be, seeing's how you stay alone most evenings."

"Oh Emmie, it's only . . ."

"It's only that you can't understand why any man would want *me*. Or is it that you think I still burn with a passion for Edmond?"

"I'm curious to know if you still like him."

"I said nothing before as I wasn't sure of my feelings. It's the strangest thing, Chrissie. When he jilted me I felt angry because I thought he'd found another woman. When I realised he hadn't, somehow I didn't mind being dropped and it stopped hurting."

"Jealousy!"

"No, not entirely, but who likes being second best."

"And now?" she asked, her cheeks burning for the right answer.

"Now I've met the lieutenant I can't see what I ever saw in Edmond. Too much of a boy. When I see Edmond, I find myself finding fault with him, so I guess I'm over him."

Christabel turned to see Edmond discussing shotguns with Mr Redmarsh.

The next day Edmond again came looking for Christabel, this time to relay his mother's instructions that she should tend the kitchen garden at the back of the manor. Released from the guilt of his approaches, she agreed happily.

"I must be honest, Chrissie, I had some small part in suggesting the idea. Do you mind?"

"Today, no."

He didn't quite understand, but her face showed elation. Indeed, her self-denial had now served to make the friendship all the more pleasurable, and, although she felt he'd been mostly to blame for Emmie's unhappiness, the very fact that others, or one at least, had lost their heart to him made the prize even better to win. In this way, many happy days passed in cheerful company, until, on Mary's innocent disclosure to Emmie one night that Edmond had been seen spending a great deal of time with Christabel, the younger girl's emotions were again thrown into conflict.

"I guessed all along that someone had tried to take him from me. How could it be you?"

Christabel's honest nature fought against a harsh reply.

"Emmie, please don't talk like that. You know I never stood in your way. Only the other day you said that it was over between you."

She stamped her feet on the bed.

"How could you! I loved him first. Yes, now I think on it, it was you coming here that spoiled my chances. You made a play for him knowing that we were engaged. You're not a friend. I hate you."

"Emmie, please don't say such things. It's not true. Please listen to my side of the story!"

Emmie turned her back.

"Then, if it means so much, I'll give him up!" said Christabel in a soft tone, holding back the tears.

"You'd do that? Why?" asked Mary, placing her arm around Christabel's shoulders. "Don't give in to such childish behaviour."

"Go on, tell us. I want to know too," added Louise, enjoying the moment.

Christabel got up and took a few steps, resting her head against a roof timber. Her voice was low and quivering.

"It would be misfortune indeed to love a man that girlish friendship alone forced me to give up, but if such an evil was wished on me, I would resolve to forget him."

"Damned if *I* would," shouted Mary. "Especially not to feed the jealousy of that little twerp."

Christabel shushed Mary down.

"I can't believe he's the marrying kind anyway, as poor Emmie has discovered, so little is my loss."

"And what if he asked you?" murmured Mary.

"I don't think he would."

"Maybe, but what if he did?"

"Then I would have to say . . . no."

"For Emmie's sake or your own?"

"Not for mine."

"You know, if you make up your mind not to bend, come what may, it's best that your opinion is the correct one in the first place. I for one can't believe that you've thought it through."

"It's done," she said.

Emmie walked out, alone. A heaviness filled the air. Christabel also left, strolling quietly across the lane to her room.

In the dormitory the girls talked as they undressed. Louise flung back the bed covers and climbed in.

"It's easy for her *to say*, but come the occasion . . ."

"She'll not change her mind," said Emmie, catching the comment as she re-entered the room.

"I think you're right," rebuked Mary, "and I hope you're proud of yourself."

Emmie got undressed in silence, pulled the covers up and closed her eyes.

"Edmond would have kissed her today in the garden if she'd given him the slightest encouragement."

There was no reaction. Mary tugged at Emmie's sheet.

"You hear me?"

"I heard."

"Listen, you selfish cow. Edmond isn't ever going to want you back even if you spoil Chrissie's chances. Are you listening?"

Emmie threw back the top of her sheet, her face now red and tearful.

"Stop picking on me. She's settled to her fate."

In the quietness of a Westking's night Emmie tossed and turned, while across the way Christabel cried into her pillow. Never before had she so wanted a man, paling into insignificance those feelings she had for John, but would have accepted as love at that earlier time. Now she was robbed of the chance to exploit it. She tried convincing herself that Edmond really wasn't the marrying kind, and that in the long term she would have suffered as Emmie had. She even began to believe it. The magnanimity of the true reason made her the martyr to a doubtful cause, for, in truth, he really did return a passionate love. Now, because of Emmie, she had to forbid herself any close relationship beyond that of normal contact between an employer and his servant.

The strain and complications of the previous few days had so distressed Christabel that she fell ill, taking to her bed for the remainder of the week. Meanwhile, having seen early progress in the clearance of the kitchen garden, Charlotte had taken it upon herself to assign Emmie to completing the task. This gave the younger girl further opportunities to see Longborne, that is Lieutenant Longborne Charles of the Surrey Dragoons, who had now been joined at the manor by his twin sister, Catherine.

Catherine Charles, who swept along in a way that made doves look clumsy, and wore nothing that wasn't of the latest fashion or of the greatest expense, possessed every attribute of a débutante excepting one; the grace to know when her frequent views were not wanted.

"Your pardon, Edmond," said Catherine, calling across, "but what is my brother about with that little common girl?"

"Oh, it's nothing more than a trifling matter to amuse himself."

"I suppose you know best. Please excuse my interference." She looked at him dubiously. "And what is this I hear of your attachment to a similar one? Surely it isn't so. I know my brother has his assignations, it has cost our parents a pretty penny to cover his trail of babies and distressed mothers, but you aren't like his usual friends." She smiled sweetly. "If it's female company you desire, for there can't be much to your taste around these parts, I might see that you meet someone of your own type."

She arose and took his arm, but he broke free politely. She became momentarily fierce at the snub.

"Don't implicate yourself with these low folk, Edmond. They only embrace such advances as a means to a comfortable living. They hate us in reality. Personally I don't give a damn about them, but then I see only ignorance and poverty in their faces."

"A low breed?"

"Yes, just that."

"Then perhaps you should look a bit harder."

The swish of crinoline stiffeners voiced her departure. She turned at the stairs.

"I think . . . I will not!"

That evening the light exuding from the drawing room windows was dim and flickering.

"How clever of you to hire this, Edmond," offered Catherine as if his happiness rested on her approval. "I fully declare for all to hear that I'm totally mystified by the workings of the magic lantern. The science is over my scatty female head."

"Your brain is like the horse you ride, sister."

"How so, brother?" she replied, trying not to look embarrassed, but aware of his humour.

"It's a small animal I believe!"

Edmond quickly changed the slide, plunging the room into temporary darkness. There was a thump.

"Oh, hell. What's that for?" enquired Longborne, nursing his arm.

"You want a toffee, brother?" she returned, as if pertinent to his question.

An image of an Egyptian pyramid formed on the screen. Edmond explained how the effect was produced, to which she sighed, giggled and made simple her reasoning on the matter; a fashionable response which Edmond found extremely annoying, as did Charlotte. James didn't, having slept through the first box of slides and having only just awakened. Again the room fell into darkness. Catherine let out a sharp yelp. The light returned as Longborne jumped back into his chair, his sister nursing her foot.

"These are very good," smiled Longborne.

"I think we'll call it a day," warned Edmond as a rebuke.

"Good idea," said Charlotte, taking him too literally and breaking up the party.

Edmond packed away the lantern, taken aback by the lack of enthusiasm.

"And what progress with this young maid, Edmond?" enquired Catherine glibly as she gathered her possessions. "Is her heart broken yet?"

"What's this?" called Charlotte, less amused than Catherine.

Edmond casually dismissed the subject with a wave of the hand.

"I do believe I say the most awful things without thinking," added Catherine as a perfect performer, knowing just how to rekindle a spark without seeming too obvious. "It probably wasn't you at all I saw hanging around the herb patch the other morning."

"Be quiet, Catherine," rebuked Longborne.

She went red-faced.

"I was only asking . . ."

"Shut up!"

"But . . ."

"*No!*"

She reached into her purse for a handkerchief, squeezing a tear from her eye by discreetly pinching the tip of her nose. Charlotte reached for a bottle of smelling salts. She sniffed the noxious fumes and spluttered.

"Take her up, Longborne."

Catherine allowed him to escort her only as far as the door. Ruefully, as an encore, she turned.

"I'm sorry if I upset you, Edmond. It wasn't on purpose. Perhaps if we pleasantly engage ourselves tomorrow, you may not think of that third person."

She swept out, her silk dress flowing in a ruffled train. The door closed and all fell quiet.

"You know she must go!" said Longborne.

They all agreed, with the stipulation that it should be sooner rather than later.

"I'll tell her," he offered.

As the Charles twins lived up to and beyond their income, with nothing set aside that could otherwise be invested on improving their lifestyle, it was incumbent upon Edmond to provide a carriage for her departure and a small purse in the guise of a parting gift. Longborne offered to give it to her, first taking out several coins for himself while alone in his room. She accepted the purse with just the right measure of reluctance.

With the abandonment of a millionaire, Catherine prepared to make a grand departure by redistributing a number of the small coins among the servants.

"God bless you, Ma'am," said the cook, as one silver threepenny bit changed hands.

"And don't forget what I said," added Catherine. "You must let that Sturry girl know that Edmond has been seeing Miss Chrissie. Do you understand?"

Another coin followed the first.

The departure itself was as stage managed as her grief, avowing sorrow at having to leave them before she wished, but that it was a consequence of her full social diary. In such pretence all gathered played out their roles. She kissed Edmond fondly and her brother, and embraced Charlotte tenderly, on her oath promising to love her always. Then, just as every play has its curtain, so amid much waving the carriage pulled away. Christabel, who had only that day ventured out of her room and still felt poorly, caught Catherine's eye. Quickly Catherine called out one last goodbye to Edmond, blowing a fond and obvious kiss.

James, the only one affected by the artificial behaviour, stood longer in the drive than the rest, waiting until the carriage had completely vanished from view before returning indoors.

"I shall miss her, Longborne," he said. "How thankful I am that I thought of slipping her twenty pounds for the journey."

Longborne raced to the window in the hope of catching a glimpse of his sister, his hand fondling a mere handful of coins in an otherwise empty pocket.

CHAPTER XXIII

The return

People who enjoy the country for its earthy beauty discover little out of the way places where they feel almost mystically content, at one with familiar surroundings that always seem fresh no matter how often visited. For Christabel it was Muncome Hill, where the grass always smelled succulent after a light rain. Yet, on the next two occasions when she walked its meandering paths Edmond appeared unexpectedly, riding from the opposite direction. The full folly of these mischances, as she believed them to be, did not dawn on her until Emmie made a passing remark that she had broken her vow not to see him. The cook had earned her bribe.

Anxious that she should not meet Edmond again, the following evening Christabel made for the more open spaces of Butley St David, where the views were less agreeable, but there would be little chance of his presence. Yet, on her return he once again came into view, his horse panting heavily from much hard riding.

He dismounted. With Emmie on her mind, she made no effort to talk, hoping that he would become bored with her company. This ploy passed him by, as he was happy just to walk silently in her companionship. He only became unsettled as they reached the gates to 'Samain', where they went their different ways.

If ever there was a time when Christabel needed the wise coun-selling of parents, it was now, when her young heart fought against nature in the pursuit of nobleness. Feelings between Christabel and Edmond, which had started by accident, now raged, the one party, the more guilty, venting free expression and the other, the innocent, subduing all signs of returned affection in consideration of the ungrateful feelings of a third person. As daily encounters would only deepen the malady of love, she decided to avoid his company by all means within her power. Flesh and blood could not withstand their meetings, so distance had to be the chosen tool of intervention. On reflection, she knew she had given him few signs of endearment and so, as yet, little harm was done. She clung on to this thought.

So decided, during the daylight hours she surrounded herself with friends, making it impossible for Edmond to pass anything, but the most general remarks. In the evenings, when she longed to be out, she remained alone in her room, holding herself aloof to his chance meetings. Once or twice she caught sight of him galloping from the manor gates towards the hill, ducking under the windowsill as he returned later, a broken man. As he trotted along the drive, she could only press her face to the glass.

July turned to August, dog days of hot and dry weather that made every task a chore even to willing hands. Then one evening, when summer sunbeams no longer imbued every creature on the land and its ripening warmth faded from the fields of golden corn for another day, Christabel at last decided to seek the advice of the one person nearest to a parent, that being Isobel. Through no inten-tional snub, she had written only once since arriving in Westkings. Isobel, incidentally, had viewed this as a sign of Christabel's con-tentment, believing that she had settled in well and would write again sooner or later, or make a courtesy visit. As John too flour-ished, Isobel decided to let matters take the quiet course.

To the young hearts of Westkings – the hopeful and the disillu-sioned – the hamlet was the centre of the universe, the focal point of love's comedy of errors, but events had moved just as swiftly in the Cerne Valley as elsewhere, the humbug of romances not distracting fate from its duty to all.

Isobel, long tired of soliloquy, had made it her purpose to lift the poor from perdition brought about by ignorance. She considered it her duty to bring to the attention of the women of the poor classes, who were unlikely ever to attend one of her rallies, the dangers of appearing abandoned when the dreadful Contagious Diseases Act of parliament threatened their very liberty. She also believed more strongly than ever that a Christian country could no longer tolerate the inevitability of perpetual ill health among the least fortunate, those accustomed to grave sanitary conditions and inseparable from poverty.

In consequence, during many such mercy visits she had spent long evenings in damp and draughty cottages, sitting by the merest embers of a fire between a mud floor and a thatched roof ensconced with ranky moss and soaked through. On other occasions she had knocked on ill-fitting doors, but had been left out in the cold and rain:

"Please, I've come to talk with you. To help you."

"What do you want with us?" came from within.

"Your salvation, if only you will hear me out."

"We don't need no help. We're in our bed to keep warm. You should've called earlier."

"I did."

"Didn't you see the door was open?"

"Yes."

"Well then. If it was open it showed we'd be back soon. Lor, if we were going out for long we'd have shut it fast. It's too late now. Get off with you and leave honest folk to their sleep."

Isobel's errands, only sometimes received with kindness, had brought her to the very causes of illness. Unaccustomed to it, she fell to its dangers and died among the splendours of her own bedroom the week before Christabel's letter arrived.

John, who took delivery of the letter, intended to travel to

Westkings with the news of his dear mother's death and to bring Christabel back for the memorial service. In the event, fate again interfered in their lives, and the very day John saddled up to leave he received a stunning communication from the family solicitor giving the shocking news that Isobel's last will had been contrived to allow him an income of only two thousand pounds per annum for the next five years, when the bulk on the inheritance would at last become his. Handsome although such a sum was, it was not the five thousand pounds a year he expected from the farm and investments. Such a blow quelled any thoughts of Westkings. Instead, he alleviated his grief in the woeful company of local society, which, having even less than John, attached itself to his disappointment and purse. Isobel had also intended to make modest provision for Christabel, but her time had been so occupied of late that she had overlooked signing and returning the necessary papers, which still lay folded in her bureau drawer.

With no reply after three weeks, Christabel became concerned, but with harvest underway she could do nothing. For the past two days grey clouds had threatened to soak the crop, and now everyone was called out to the fields to help gather in. Miraculously, after just one more grey morning the summer sun broke through once again and all seemed safe. A new field was being opened, with a swathe cut by hand sickle as a path for the mechanical sail reaper to follow. The men, working piece rates as a bonus to beat the rain, remained on their feet from dawn to dark; the women with bronzed bare arms and necks, and grasping at the straw to form it into neat sheaves with a gather and twist, laboured only until mid-afternoon. Then Christabel made for the hives and later gathered the herbs needed for the evening meal at the manor.

The next day began as a soft dawn, the midsummer air heavy with the chorus of flitting insects humming over the heads of drowsy beasts in the meadows. Men started to group by an eastern hedgerow that kept their legs in shadow and their backs and heads in the sun that grew hotter by the minute. Then, together, they wandered into the cornfield where the sail reaper was being harnessed to two strong horses. Here, away from cover, the sun scorched down. Even the breeze was driven away by the corn standing nearly as high as the reaper's wheels.

To 'clat-clat' the machine moved off, its five tined sails revolving vertically and then horizontally through bevel gearing to comb the stems onto a semi-circular wooden tray that held the cutting edge. Slowly the tray filled with stems, sufficient for a single sheaf. In no time the operation was moving efficiently, the men with their shirt sleeves up working furiously as bundles were dropped behind.

Much is spoken of the glorious English harvest landscape, where summer's sun and nature's bounty meet for the happy benefit of the harvester and his smiling family. Resting by a hedgerow during a casual walk, such a scene indeed would give a city dweller an impression of beauty and grace, of man and nature in harmony; England's green and pleasant land. Such perceptions were not shared by the workers in the field, however, their hands cut from grasping the straw and their arms wounded as if by lashes. That they seemed happy at the start of the day was undeniable, especially after the women arrived to help, when fun and friendly vulgarity broke out, but it didn't last.

Not a million miles away John, after weathering the initial shock of his disappointment, began to take control of his life. He quickly established himself to live within the income carefully contrived by his far-sighted mother. He found two thousand pounds used wisely could not only sustain him adequately, and even provide for extravagances, but was sufficient to fund the improvements around the farm needed to update working practices and boost profit. To those friends who had offered him sympathy by helping him to spend his money, he chose a new policy of financial concealment and actually enjoyed new responsibilities. In money matters he had matured quickly.

It was an awful time for Isobel to die, just when she might have lifted Christabel from a life of servitude. John now wished that he had set out for Westkings those weeks before, to pay honour to a woman whose friendship he and his dear late mother had so missed of late. Although belatedly, he believed that he had a duty to go, to take by word of mouth the overdue reply to her letter. He also knew that he was determined to try once more to win her affection. This time there would be no awkwardness or blundering. He was now a man of authority and would exude just this. If she felt anything for him, he had become a worthy suitor.

Poor John. The truth was that Christabel had given him little thought since Edmond's arrival on the scene, although so far the younger man had made no difference to her own situation as a common workhand now turned part-time harvester. She was happy, undeniably happy, cheerful to be among friends and finding her broken heart mending day by day.

As coincidence would have it, it was the day John finally set out for Westkings that Christabel was asked to help with the corn for the last time. Already a light shower had spoiled what had otherwise been a dry gathering and work was apace. With Louise as a partner, she once more took her place alongside the other women in the golden reaches, following the path of the reaper around the final standing square, bundling the wet stems and forming them into stitches of ten or more sheaves leaning upright, one against the another.

A full six hours of back-breaking toil had passed when a lone rider trotted into Westkings, reading the address from Christabel's letter. John's spirits were high as he passed through the hamlet, but the boarding house was an anticlimax. Meg pointed him towards 'Samain', where he would find her. He turned with awe, suddenly feeling inextricably apprehensive. What were her circumstances, he wondered? She had said nothing in her letter. Was she enjoying the comfort of this marvellous place? Oh God, if that was the case she was probably lost to him. Yes, it all made sense. Surely she would have returned to the Cerne Valley had she not found good fortune here?

He dismounted and approached the porticoed doors, longing to know what lay behind. There were other considerations too, and he held back from pulling at the bell. What of this man she talked about in her letter? Her comments on him were veiled. Did he live here? Suddenly there was so much to think about. The thought flashed through his mind to go home, but not to ring after such a journey would be foolish when so much could be gained. As a failed suitor it took courage to proceed, but there really was no other sensible option. He stepped up to the door.

Charlotte considered herself one of the great gentlewomen of Wessex, especially now that the estate was saved from ruin. While the harshness injected into her character over many troubled years had greatly changed her, and with it the prestige of the Elvingtons, she hung on to the belief that 'Samain' itself was edifying to callers.

Everything she now did was calculated to raise esteem, to bring renewed respectability to the family she had once disgraced. Her dislike for certain members of Wessex society, especially those who had delighted in blackening the Elvington name during the lowest ebb of the past vexation, was not allowed to stand in the way of her using them as tools of influence. Carefully she drew society back, using the manor as the web to inveigle the socialite flies. She grew skilled at sorting the true wealth from the impostors, keeping a diary on those who deceived the world of their true fortune when only by contrivance could they pass themselves off as seriously rich. Those who passed the test were ensnared, unsuspectingly used to attract even greater persons to the manor. Such was her success that the hypocrisy of the dealings became praiseworthy in itself.

It was in this manner that Charlotte gladly received the seemingly well-healed John into the lustreless elegance of the drawing room. By her side sat the lieutenant, the biggest impostor to have entered 'Samain' and the only one Charlotte had failed to recognise. Such was the confidence of his personality that she found it impossible to question anything he said or did, instead doubting her own judgement when in disagreement. His presence was, however, brief. On seeing John's horse being led away, and not wishing to prolong the visitor's stay, he leapt up and threw back the window.

"You! Leave that damned horse out front. Who told you to move it?"

The stable hand stood pale and silent. Nobody in the room thought to question Longborne's right to interrogate.

"Tie it back, damn you fellow, and get about your business."

He watched as the lad led the horse in a large circle and back to the rail. The window was shut.

"Excuse me, Charlotte. I think I ought to have a word with him. Can't let this sort of thing go unpunished. Not good for the servants to think for themselves, you know."

He pulled a leather crop from the stand, smacking it twice against his boot.

"Must you, Longborne? I'm sure it was an innocent mistake."

"Well, Charlotte, if you ask me not to, I will of course obey. I'm your guest, and if you think I'm interfering . . ."

"Oh, no! No! Not at all. If you think it's necessary, you must do what's fitting. Only, if you mean to beat him, remember he's only a boy."

John needed to speak to Charlotte alone and saw an opportunity. Anyway, if this was the man in Christabel's thoughts, he had a real rival. What better start, then, than to humiliate him.

"Actually, I asked the boy to unsaddle the mare. He was only following my instructions. Anyone can see that the animal is fatigued."

Charlotte smiled before turning to Longborne, unsure of how to defuse the situation. John's intention had been to unsettle Longborne and it did. His features became hollow. Clicking his heels, he strode from the room with the forced step of a military man, replacing the crop as he left as a sign of acquiescence.

With Longborne gone, John explained that he had expected to find Christabel living here, his matter-of-fact tone hiding his grave disappointment that she wasn't.

"And so you think she should've stayed in Cerne?", enquired Charlotte, remembering her conversation with Christabel when she had first come to Westkings.

"That, I can't judge until I know her present circumstances. I know I wanted her to."

"Then maybe you should take her back now."

"I would like that, but only if she wants to. Did she speak of it?"

"Honesty compels me to say, no. She spoke of many things, including you, but not of returning. She had this silly notion that a key in her possession somehow linked her father with the manor."

"Oh yes, I know all about that. Did it?"

"Alas it was time ill-spent. No pot of gold, I'm afraid!"

"Is that what she wanted? If it was I've misjudged her. Nothing her father said could've given that impression. I thought she only wanted to know why it meant so much to him. She always gave the impression that she didn't care for unearned wealth, unless of course she's changed since leaving Cerne."

"You know her well?"

"I like to think so. By the way, you haven't said where she is. I really want to see her."

John didn't stay more than another ten minutes, held tight-lipped at the prospect that Christabel had chosen fieldwork here rather than a more comfortable life with him. Before he left a maid had brought in two glasses of wine and Charlotte had risen to toast the girl, lost in silent pride for her daughter.

"Not before this time and probably never again will I drink to the well-being of a worker. God bless Christabel, that lowly girl fortune may still honour."

She sipped. John followed irresolutely.

"I see that you don't have my conviction."

"I can't understand the purpose for such a toast. What's she to you? I wouldn't be pleased if you mock her."

She took his hand.

"Come," she insisted, "I'm genuine in my regard."

John looked deeply into her eyes and smiled.

"Then, Madam, I beg your forgiveness and drink heartily to her. To Christabel, an English rose."

"What's going on?" shouted Longborne, slamming the door behind him. "Who's Rose?"

"I'll bid you good-day," said John to Charlotte, nodding courteously to Longborne as he passed.

"What's he so smug about?" asked Longborne with a bewildered look once the door was shut. "Have I met this girl, Rose?"

"Oh, nothing," she replied, feeling superior.

Outside, John squared his hat as he climbed the mounting block. Charlotte hurried through the hall to catch him. He was adjusting the saddle when she arrived by his side.

"Your groom needs a good talking to," commented John. "The girth's so lose I could've fallen off."

"I'll get Longborne to . . . No, I'll do it myself." She unfastened the other stirrup, giving the strap a hard tug. "You still hold her dear, don't you?"

"Nothing's changed for me. Poor she might be, but there's something precious about her."

"Then don't be unhappy. See her with a good heart."

"I always do! I'm not unhappy at all. Quite the opposite, in fact. I can see there's no new barrier between us. She'll always be my Christabel."

"Then, go and tell her that. Take her in your arms and return to Cerne. God bless you, my boy. You'll find her in the fields towards the church."

John trotted off, waving as he went. She called after him.

"And mind you're respectful of her. Humble she might be . . .", she waited until he had passed into the lane and then added in soft tone, ". . . but as proud as any Elvington."

Charlotte was happy. Her expectations for Christabel's future had soared. And, having by such good fortune seen John to be of considerable standing, as she noted in her diary, she assumed that he might one day make up for the love she had not shown her daughter. It seemed that Christabel's adult life was bound inextricably with the plans and intentions of this young man. If all went well and she was asked to the wedding, she would allow herself to show affection publicly.

Fine china and savoury fancies brought the family and Longborne together for high tea. The formality of this light meal, its usual dull and contrived conversations in polite company, had been lifted of late by Longborne's eloquence. The hostess gladly allowed him to steer the talk in any direction he wished, knowing that there would be a good story at its conclusion. If Longborne told a witticism, he was the first to laugh heartily, so sure of its merit. A sad tale was greeted with genuine tears, and on all other matters his judgement was rarely questioned. "Pass the salt", accompanied by the wink of his eye, was enough to bring the room to laughter, so primed were the listeners for his merriment.

"You're unusually thoughtful, Longborne dear," commented Charlotte as they ate in silence.

It was true. Not an hour previously he had intercepted a lonely man walking towards the manor. From a stoop, the man had given his name as Augustus Fly. The conversation that followed had armed Longborne with particulars he had no right knowing, and yet he couldn't see how best to use this new knowledge to his advantage. Nevertheless, there would be profit in it somehow and Fly had left with a valuable jewelled snuff box in his pocket, unaware that the letters JBE were engraved beneath the lid. Longborne had taken the files to his room, where he had read the contents with relish.

"Your pardon. I was only thinking, you can lose anything except things already lost."

"What the devil are you talking about, Longborne?" asked Edmond between bites.

He turned casually, as if to undermine the question, preening his moustache with a napkin.

"I'm talking, young friend, about this chap who called earlier. John something or other was his name. A friend of that Chrissie girl."

Edmond sat up.

"Her friend? Who was he? What did he want, Mother?"

Charlotte shook her head.

"Anyhow," continued Longborne, "it seems that he's come to take her away."

"How would you know that?" enquired Charlotte briskly. "Unless of course you listened in on our private conversation?"

"Mother!"

"Well, Longborne? Explain yourself."

He was not alarmed by her tone.

"I could read the look in his eye."

She was unconvinced.

"Apart from that, Madam, I saw him outside."

"And he told you?"

"Yes."

It was possible, although unlikely, but Charlotte dropped the subject.

"Anyway, Longborne," said Edmond with obvious irritation, "what's the meaning of your stupid riddle?"

"Riddle? Oh, apparently this chap has fancied her for ages, but has got nowhere for his pains. So you see, he has nothing more to lose, as he can't lose again what has already been lost! Love is a game and not all are good players. I consider myself a captain."

Edmond suddenly realised who the man could be. Christabel had spoken of John Madden occasionally, and if it was, for him to have come all this way to see her without prior arrangement indicated serious intentions. Out of nowhere had appeared a rival and the thought shook him. Suddenly angered, he lashed out at the bearer of the bad news.

"Oh be quiet, Longborne. I'm beginning to resent your bloody childish ways." Suddenly the afternoon turned sinister. "Has he left, Mother?"

"Here? Yes. I sent him to the fields."

"How long ago?"

"Not long, but I don't understand your interest."

"Can't you tell?" added Longborne with a grin.

Charlotte turned back to her son with a look of stone.

"Edmond!"

"It isn't anyone's business, but mine."

"And your business is the estate," put in Longborne, trying to win back Charlotte's approval. She nodded.

"Must everyone have an opinion on my life?"

"What is it, son?"

"Nothing. Just leave it be."

"Tell me. I insist."

"You can't make me say what everyone in this room already suspects."

"Ah! Men with secrets are men with guilt."

"For God's sake, Longborne, shut up or get out."

"Edmond!" shouted Charlotte.

"That's a bit strong, friend. There's other society beyond these walls. Insult me and I might feel constrained to leave."

"I wish you bloody well would!"

"Edmond!" cried Charlotte for the second time.

"No, it's time someone put a stop to this buffoon."

"Buffoon, be damned," burst out Longborne, rising majestically after throwing his napkin onto the table. "See what you've done. You've gone too far this time. I *shall* go."

Charlotte stretched out her hand to him, but Edmond caught it and pulled it away.

"Let him go!"

She gave way.

"I'm sorry, lad."

Longborne's face grew long. He had overplayed his hand. He waited for any excuse to return to the table and his comfortable living, but after a minute it dawned on him that he would not be rescued.

"Damn you, Edmond!"

He stormed out.

"Edmond, don't you think you've been –"

"Take your blinkers off, Mother. I'll no longer ally myself with a man who might be fierce in battle, but is no gentleman in peace."

Leaning on the upper bar of the gate, John looked across at the fieldworkers gathering the crop. He felt no superiority over them, and on seeing Christabel tried to draw her attention.

He asked a passer-by whether he could enter the field and help, but was advised not to.

"This is no place for a gentleman, Sir. The master wouldn't be happy to see you among them. Kindly, I must ask you to remain on the wrong side of the fence until they stop!"

Another strip was cut and gathered before the workers put down their tools and huddled in groups to eat. A cider barrel rested on a wheelbarrow wedged by straw, a wooden cup dangling from the tap by a chain.

Now that work had stopped, John cheerfully left his horse by the gate and made for the crowd. He offered no apologies as he strode past the first group to another and then a third. Through slit eyes shaded from the lowering sun, Christabel looked up at the towering figure.

"John?"

"Yes, it's me."

She jumped up.

"Oh, my God. John, John, John!"

She hugged him dearly.

"Steady. They'll think you're glad to see me."

"I am. I really am." She hugged him again. "When did you arrive? Why are you here? How are you?"

"Now, now. One thing at a time."

He invited her to sit and sat beside her on the ground. He took out her letter from his pocket, which she recognised at once.

"So she did get it. I began to wonder. How is she?"

He took her hands in his.

"It's a thousand pities that I've come with joy in my heart, but bad news on my lips."

"Bad news?"

He nodded.

"My sainted mother died a short time back. That's why you haven't had an answer."

"Died?"

A strange emptiness dropped to the pit of her stomach.

"It was all rather sudden and unexpected, but there was no pain, thank heaven."

"Died," she repeated quietly, taking in the word. "I just can't believe it. She was so fit and strong when I last saw her, and little time has passed."

"Little time when you're young with so much ahead, but seemingly longer when you're old, I fancy."

"Why is it that everyone I love and loves me has to die?"

"Not everyone, Chrissie. Let's walk over there, where we can talk alone."

They arose and strolled from the others, Christabel moving like clockwork while absently picking the ears from a stem of corn. The conversation languished until they drew near the lane.

"I came with more than just the purpose of telling you of my mother."

The words floated into obscurity. Christabel became vacant, her deep eyes showing neither blue nor brown, grey nor green, but a kaleidoscope of fragments without beginning or end. He could see nothing, but emptiness. He looked away to ease the moment.

"It's going to be a wonderful sunset," he said softly.

"I should have been there, at her side. Why did I come here?"

"Chrissie, Chrissie. Take a grip on yourself. You know why. Besides, there was absolutely nothing you could have done."

"I should have stayed. Showed her that I cared. I let her down, after all she did for me. God, I'm selfish."

"Stop it! Don't talk that way." He took her gently in his arms. "For heaven's sake, this melancholy doesn't fit you well. Why should you feel the slightest guilt? She was old and her own ambitions to be philanthropic brought her downfall, but she wasn't alone. I was there."

"I'm sorry, John. I didn't mean to suggest that she would want me more than you."

She began to cry.

"God, you're a worrier! Let's get a few things straight. I didn't think you meant that, and my mother didn't feel abandoned."

"Strangely," she said, wiping her eyes, "I feel abandoned by her! Isn't that ridiculous?"

"Ridiculous. Look, you're young and loved. What more could you want? As for your situation, well, it's of your own choosing if you won't listen to what I've come to say."

She stared passively, almost mournfully. John kissed her cheek and ran a finger down her soft marble skin in the trace of a tear.

"A person cannot control the time of birth or the time to be gathered. Wasn't it Shakespeare who wrote 'Had I but died an hour before this chance, I had lived a blessed time; for, from this instant' . . ."

". . . 'there's nothing serious in mortality'."

"Yes, that's right. You know it?"

"Do you know what he meant by it?"

"I think so."

"I wonder."

They strolled into the small copse of trees that edged the lane. At length she sat on a fallen trunk, gathering the sights and sounds of the country. He sat by her, leaving a small distance between them. She turned, resting her hand on his.

"Dear, John. You're so good, so kind, but, yes, Shakespeare was right, for I feel I have nothing to go on for. Mortality is my burden."

John admired her for understanding more than he, but his words had brought the wrong reaction.

"For God's sake, Chrissie, there's nothing dark about my mother's death. She wouldn't have wished you to take on so and neither do I. She lived a long life, even useful at its end, and now it's our turn to live."

"You've had time to reconcile yourself, John. You must allow me the same patience."

"Tolerance, calmness, perseverance and, ah, endurance. Yes, these sound like my qualities."

A smile curled her lips.

"That's better."

In the background the rustle of harnesses became audible.

"I must go back."

"Can't we talk a little longer?" pleaded John.

"I can't keep the others waiting."

He walked beside her, but not with her, for, out of the shade, she again became lost in memories. Just short of the others they stopped. He felt hurried as they watched the man climb on board the sail reaper.

"Look, Chrissie. Now that we have met again I feel a lot easier. I didn't know whether you would even speak to me. I'm really pleased we're still friends." He laughed at the thought. "You wouldn't think it, but I felt embarrassed to face you. I should have known how welcome you would make me feel."

Again she glanced sideways as the reaper moved off. His speech became urgent.

"What of your life here? You haven't told me any of that."

"There isn't time now, or very much to say for that matter."

John looked hurt.

"All right. It isn't Cerne, but I like it well enough. Nothing came of the key, you know!"

"So I understand. Still, it was worth a shot, if only to get it out of your system, but not if you now intend to make this place your home. Why not come back with me? I can afford to look after you, and you know I'd like to."

She shook her head.

"My mother would've wanted it too," he added.

"That's not fair! That's emotional blackmail."

His stare dropped.

"Sorry. You're right. I was wrong to say that, only, I would do anything to take you back with me."

A distant shout called Christabel back to work.

"I really must go, John."

"Can't you just say, yes? It takes but a breath."

She backed away.

"I'll talk to you later. Where are you staying?"

"Confound where I'm staying. Won't you come with me now?

"My heart's too heavy to think. It's too important to decide on the spot, without reflection. Anyway, I've work to complete and I can't let the others down. Give me time to consider everything."

"But you must already know the answer. Why delay and make me pine away the hours? Were you happy before I came?"

"I suppose I was."

"Really happy, I mean. As much as in Cerne?"

"I can't say one is better or worse. I've been happy and sad in both. Cerne *was* my home. This *is* where I live now."

"Is that your answer?"

She raised her shoulders.

"I don't know."

She suddenly turned, picked up her skirt and ran to the reaper. He shouted after her.

"Shall I leave or stay?"

"That's up to you. I won't leave here, not yet anyway."

Outside the field a stray dog barked around the hindquarters of John's horse. He strode over and beat it away with a stick, stroking the horse's nose until it calmed. With a heavy heart, Christabel watched him ride away. He didn't look back. To her surprise, the thought that he might not return hurt her.

Try as she might to concentrate on her work, her mind kept returning to Isobel, and thereby, John. For his part, he had never been so unsure of what to do in his adult life. He was bitterly disappointed, almost hardened to Christabel to the point of anger. Yet, and here was the irony, he could understand her viewpoint and so felt he was wrong for wanting too many answers too quickly. He remembered as a child that he had once dressed for a party, but his mother had insisted he should groom his pony before going. Although a small task, he had argued with her and dug his heels in, and as the time passed for the party to begin he had been torn between really wanting to go and not giving way. Strangely, he felt the same now.

Less than an hour passed before he trotted back, but she was too far away to notice. It wasn't until another break was called that she saw his horse tied to the fence and John sitting cross-legged on the grass beside it. She called out and they met halfway.

"Hello again. Look, I'm sorry about earlier. I suppose . . ."

She put a finger to his lips to silence him. He took the hint.

"I've brought some meat and cake. You can share it with your friends if you like, or have it with me. I don't mind which."

She took it from his outstretched hand.

"I'm so pleased you came back, and the food looks great."

She spread the fare on the grass and took a chicken breast.

"I've decided that I'm not staying," he said in a low tone. "There's no point."

She stopped eating.

"When did you come to that conclusion?"

"Just now. I've been watching you. You were completely wrapped up in your own little world. The truth is, you don't need me. Probably haven't given me a single thought since leaving Cerne."

"If that's what you think!"

She put the chicken back in the bag.

"I have no reason to believe otherwise."

"Do you remember, John, when I first arrived in Cerne and that night you tried to kiss me?"

"Yes. I'm embarrassed that you recall it."

"And I asked if you always offered your affection so quickly?"

"I know."

"Well, that's your problem. You're the most impetuous man I've ever met. Lovely, but impetuous. Everything has to be instant. Do you like me, yes or no, *now*! Are you coming here or going there, *now*! Do this or do that, but tell me *now*! Other people can't decide quickly like that. They need time. I fall into the latter category."

"You're right, of course. I know I'm impatient. I suppose I'm used to getting my way, but, then, when it comes to matters of the heart, surely an answer must be instant to be true. To love someone is to feel a constant inner burning. A wish to be with them all the time, to hold them and see their returned love through every action they make. If it has to be thought over, it's not deeply felt."

"You're too much a knight errant tilting at windmills, John. Too much a romantic."

"Is that how you see me? Am I really that foolish?"

"Not foolish. Over protective maybe."

"Protect isn't the word I would use. What's a better one?"

"Smother!"

"Oh, that's worse. I'm crushed if that's what you think. Is it?"

"No. Sorry, that was hurtful."

"No matter. I get the general picture. I can't understand it, but I get it all the same. With one breath you say you're alone and unloved, with everyone dying who loves you, yet with the next breath you say to show you affection is to smother you. I can only conclude that I'm either dead or the wrong man. As I feel pretty alive, I can work out the rest!"

"I didn't say that I was unloved."

He reached into his pocket.

"Is this the reason for staying?"

"My letter?"

"Don't be obtuse. The man you mention?"

"You've read my personal correspondence to Isobel?"

"Calm yourself. I wasn't prying. I had to sort out my mother's effects and in doing so came by it. She intended to give you something special, you know, but that's another matter for another time. What of this fellow you write about?"

"He's not a fellow, as you put it, but a gentleman like yourself."

"Do you stay here for him?"

"I suppose I do in a way, but not as you're thinking."

"God, that's the answer I feared."

"Hear my qualification. You misunderstand."

"I understand all right." He stood. "Goodbye, Chrissie."

"Wait! Don't walk away. You don't give me a chance to explain." She ran after him, grabbing his arm. "You silly beggar. He's not a lover, just an acquaintance of sorts."

He listened with more hope than belief.

"I just thought . . . Well . . . You might have dismissed my memory in favour of him."

"How could I ever forget you, John. I could no more forget my own past, for you're part of it."

"But as a brother, not a lover!"

She shrugged her shoulders.

"You know I'm a much changed man of late."

"I can see that. I suppose you're very rich."

"In ways more important than money, you silly girl. In a real sense my life is only now beginning. Yet, without someone to share it, everything remains pointless."

"Poor thing. You're not used to being alone."

"Surely if anyone knows what that's like, that person must be you. So why must we both feel this way, separately. You can't like this work. Just look at your hands. Are those the hands that left my house? I think not. Look Chrissie, I came here with the intention of approaching you calmly, but my blood now pumps at a high rate again. You're tired and dirty, but I don't give a damn. Don't you see, it's true, honest, deep and faithful love that blinds me to it. I can offer you so much if you will choose to share it. Away with drudgery. Doesn't that sound good?" He stepped close to her. "Say one word in my favour and I will take you home. Our home in the valley!"

Christabel, heightened in colour and strangely inarticulate, jerked away, but only to relieve the pressure of his will, to offer space to think. Her head was exploding, thoughts racing every which way. In the confusion a voice called out for her to return to work. A second command followed quickly upon the first, now harsh in tone.

"There's not enough time to think," she cried.

John grabbed her arm.

"Take no notice of him."

"Chrissie, get here *now*," thundered the man.

She shook loose.

"I really have to go."

"No you don't."

"Stop it, John. Stop pressuring me. Understand, I am home. I *am* home!"

He jumped in front of her, denying her space to pass. He spoke quickly.

"How can you say that, unless your heart keeps you here? Be honest with me. You owe me that."

"Oh, God. He'll kill me for keeping him waiting. Okay, you're right," she shouted. "There is someone, but, John, friends don't tell each other everything, so don't ask more than I will willingly part with."

"Who is he? It's that arrogant popinjay in uniform, isn't it"

"I'll not tell you his name."

"Cannot or will not?"

"Whichever you want to believe, but let me go!"

The damage was done. He took the reply squarely, as a man, hurting only inside. She was lost to him, so further pressure would be useless.

"Okay, Chrissie, you win. Off you go to the corn if that makes you happy."

"Please John, don't let us part like this. It always seems to happen when we meet."

"You mean a brother and sister shouldn't fight?"

"I can't think what I mean. I suppose it's best to face the truth. We must always be friends, good friends, but I love another."

"Love! Suddenly you leap to love when only a few minutes ago you denied it! You once said I was attracted to you because you were a new face. Why isn't the same true of you and this man?"

"A woman knows."

"More than a man?"

"Possibly."

"Then I'll not return. My feelings are a barrier beyond which simple friendship cannot endure."

"That's all there ever has been between us. Admit it, John, please, for both our sakes."

"I can't, and I'm surprised you say it."

"I say it because it's true. Isn't it?" She squeezed him. "Isn't it?"

He shrugged.

"There, and the better for bringing it out into the open. Why can't our friendship remain strong no matter who else we love? I don't get upset at the thought of you meeting other women. Listen to me. I'll never let anyone stand between us. Trust me to know myself."

"You've had your last warning, my girl," came a voice so close that heavy steps could be heard approaching.

She quickly kissed John and ran.

The man stopped short at seeing John.

"Oh! Begging your pardon, Sir. I didn't realise the maid was engaged with a gentleman." He raised his cap. "I'll give her one more minute, Sir, but we have work in progress."

The reaper was now on its return leg, heading straight for them. They descended a slight camber in the field to clear a path.

"I wonder what your friends are saying?"

"That I have a very handsome caller, I shouldn't wonder," she replied with a smile.

"Anything else?"

"That she must settle her affairs quickly."

They came to the southern fence and stopped. John lifted himself onto the top rail. He looked around and saw the completeness of the country scene, understanding in the calmness of the moment that what was unfamiliar to him was everyday to the others.

"Perhaps my coming wasn't such a good idea after all. You have your life here. I see that now. Stupid of me to think that the old days matter to you . . . Chrissie, if I'm honest, how can we be friends when with every meeting I want to hold you in my arms as a lover?"

She snuggled to his leg, but he gently resisted.

"And what of this man, this unknown authorship of affection who has you spellbound? If you marry him, am I to cheer at your wedding? Will I look at your children and not wish them mine? Please don't spare me the crumbs. I know it's my failing that I can't endure it. In all faith I have to be honest to myself and say *goodbye*, and mean it this time."

She said nothing, her eyes staring into the distance. With no other reaction to his pleading, he jumped down and with one huge effort vaulted the fence to the next field.

"Don't throw me away," she said in a gentle voice from her side of the fence.

He turned to face her.

"I was sure there was more between us, something you don't say has died with separation as you deny it ever existed. Well then, go, make this your home. Throw yourself at the feet of this nameless man, but hear this. Neither you nor all the time until eternity will convince me that once we didn't share something rare and wonderful. Don't deny it to me of all people. Poor thing, this man, for not knowing your first love."

"How can you say such things?" she cried, despair sounding in each syllable. "You talk as if you're telling me something I've forgotten. You forget, I was there. How can I not know the truth?" She slumped, leaning against a post. "I used to think growing-up would be the most wonderful thing in the world. To be taken seriously in your own right and not to have to listen to others. Now I see that age doesn't come into it. I'm as helpless to your logic as ever I was as a child."

He was moved by her broken spirit.

"Does that outburst mean that I am damaging to you?"

"It's the choice you force me to make. You say I can't have your friendship without a price, and it's a price I fear I cannot afford."

"Oh, but you can afford choice, because you have one. Only I have no choice. I don't have two women hanging onto my coat-tails. I suppose this other man doesn't even know I exist?"

"I have spoken of you, but please don't assume by that –"

"Don't say it," he cut in with hand raised. "If you don't want me freely, then what good would it be winning you at all? How much longer will you work in the mud?"

"The others do it without complaint."

"Look at them, Chrissie. Are they happy? What a gloom-stricken bunch they are. Don't you hear the cry of their abandoned babies?"

"What will you do?"

"As you reject me? I suppose I'll make new plans on my own. Go away from here, that's for certain. Chrissie, don't you ever question why this man hasn't helped you? Does he get pleasure from seeing you like this?"

"Christabel!" shouted the man with the reaper.

"Bye, John." She took to her heels but stopped midway. "You're wrong, you know, but then you don't know him as I do. I don't suppose you'll ever understand. I give you no hope of marriage, but I will always be your best friend, like it or not. I love you in a special way, the way I loved your mother!"

Hurting and red with self-pity, he jumped back onto the fence and pointed angrily.

"Then I blight and damn you. The children I will never father curse you too."

She ran as fast as she could, covering her ears.

"I didn't mean that," he said in low voice, knowing that she wouldn't hear.

There was no defence for John against the changes time had brought to Christabel, and at last he understood that her youth and new experiences had guaranteed a greater alteration in her character than life now offered him. He lived well, but she was living. Fate was saying to her 'go, taste independence', just as it had once to him in years past. There was a timewarp of sorts. Although their weeks together in the valley had been happy, much had now happened in separation, and her ways as a confused child had disappeared in a flourish of womanhood, with old associations giving room for new. He could do nothing but accept it.

He strode away, glancing sideways a dozen times in the slightest hope of her return. He reached his horse and led it along the wild paths that paralleled the lane, where the little brook wove its way over and around glinting stones on its rush to nowhere. A bird sang. He stopped, releasing the reins as he peered narrowly into the depths of the trees. The horse wandered free, its head low.

John sat on the bank, unsure of what to do next. It would be necessary to visit Charlotte before leaving the district, but that needed courage under the circumstances. His mind wandered back with warmth and regret to his first meeting with Christabel and that near accident with the milk cart. He could still feel her warm hand in his as they danced over the Cerne Giant and laughed at the girl's reluctance to be drawn onto its exaggerated form. How simple life had been and how stupidly he had let it slip through his fingers. What a curse that in his eagerness to show his feelings he had driven her away. He gritted his teeth at the lost opportunities.

"Hell and blast!"

"You, Sir," came a voice from the path.

He turned and saw that the caller was scarcely a boy turned man. In no mood to trifle, he turned back.

The youth approached.

"Do I address John Madden?"

Although surprised at hearing his name from the lips of a stranger, he merely nodded, his thoughts deeply elsewhere.

"I am Edmond. Edmond Elvington."

"Oh yes?" returned John.

"Confound you, Sir. Do me the courtesy of facing me when taking pleasure on my land."

John arose.

"You mind people walking here?"

"Not normally."

"Then, with that established, I wish to be left alone."

"No, Sir. I have come specifically to talk to *you*. I think you know what about."

"I do? I think not, as I don't know you," replied John with honest ignorance.

"I believe you do. As I know your name you must assume that I've been speaking to Christabel. She says you've been bothering her."

Christabel's name was enough to interest John. Suddenly all was clear, but surely this youth couldn't be his rival? He looked him up and down and was almost heartened by the experience. The only thing this man had that he hadn't was youth itself, about eleven years he estimated. Was this his attraction? Still in his twenties, he had never considered himself over the hill, but perhaps to Christabel he was. Age suddenly worried him, for it was the one thing he could do nothing about. Yet, he didn't feel anything but young himself. He composed himself.

"Did she say I had bothered her?"

"Perhaps she didn't use those exact words, but that's what she meant. What's your purpose with her?"

He smiled.

"I thought not. You must be Charlotte's son?"

Edmond nodded.

"My purpose, you ask. The same as yours I shouldn't wonder."

"I think not. Didn't Christabel tell you about me, about us?"

"No, not a dicky-bird! Your name never passed her lips, yet, interestingly you wouldn't be here unless she had told you about *me*."

Edmond was surprised to be caught in a turnabout situation that put him on the defensive.

"I intend to marry her, you know."

"So do I. At least I don't need to ask my mother first for permission. I suggest you grow up before making such decisions."

"I'm of sufficient age. Anyway, you're too late. No gentleman would come between promises freely given."

"She's accepted your proposal?"

"That's none of your business."

"Then she hasn't?"

"It's understood between us, at least, it was. I intend to ask her formerly very soon. At the moment she keeps avoiding me. Women!" He realised that he had said too much. "You will only complicate her mind. She needs to be mastered."

"I wouldn't try that!"

"You mean you would take her as an equal?"

"I'd have her no other way. Once I thought to change her, but not any more. She is more of a natural lady than anyone else I know."

"She might find that a tempting offer, if it were true."

"Believe me, it is."

John's horse was now drinking from the stream. He took hold of the reins.

"We remain rivals, then, or should I say let the best *man* win."

"I have already won."

"Perhaps. We'll see."

"I don't care for you or your manner, Sir."

John smiled.

"I had another acquaintance once who didn't like me, so we worked really hard at it. Now he hates me!"

He laughed loudly as he mounted and rode away, leaving Edmond by the stream.

To think I was ready to give up, he thought to himself. I'm not that bloody old either!

John had made no plans to stay overnight in Westkings and, in truth, would have returned to the Cerne Valley that evening had

Edmond not given him reason for slight hope. Those few words, "she keeps avoiding me", rang in his ears. He enquired for a room at the ale house, but was diverted to the vicarage as the only place likely to have a spare bed.

The vicar being away, it was his mangy housekeeper and her squalid odd-job husband who bade him enter into a house that he had been warned was not known for its cleanliness. Gloom was all about, the little light that penetrated the grey stained windows falling on books that stood in irregular piles from floor to waist height. Every chair was similarly covered, while the table too was cluttered except for one tiny corner where a knife, fork and plate encrusted with the slops from an abandoned meal had been left since the vicar's departure.

Pushing past the obstacles, John was shown into the best parlour, which, although it had not been touched in months, at least offered the comfort of an empty chair. A fire was lit to give both light and warmth, and a small supper prepared. While he ate from his lap, the housekeeper began cleaning vigorously, throwing up clouds of dust until he was forced to leave for an evening walk in the fresh air. The large lantern was wiped inside and out, and boxes emptied of wind-fall apples that had been left to rot. Around and around she went, continuing long after her husband fell asleep against the wall with a pint pot held firmly in his grasp. An hour or more later she stopped and the house fell strangely silent.

John returned and was amazed at the difference, although sickened by a fuggy atmosphere choked with dust and sweet polish. He slipped a sovereign into her pocket, away from her husband's eyes. She crossed to the mirror and smiled, playing with her hair until it was loosely gathered on top and pinned. Turning down the lantern, she gently nudged her husband. He looked up in horror.

"Gor, you'll do us a mischief if the master gets a fancy to have the whole house like this."

The business of cleaning and polishing and the myriad of other small jobs that crop up unexpectedly once hard work gets underway had been aching labour, but then it had been profitable too. Maybe, she thought, she would keep it clean for other visitors. She turned for bed, leaving the duster hanging off the mirror.

The next morning began with some confusion at 'Samain'. News quickly spread among the household of Longborne's secret overnight departure, together with several valuable pieces of silver. Having resolved to go before he was kicked out, Longborne had also felt no diffidence at taking a dairymaid with him to feather his nest.

Across the lawns in the dormitory, the women gathered around a letter left on Emmie's bed. Still to be discovered was a bundle of letters tied with string to Mr Redmarsh's front door, addressed to Christabel in Longborne's handwriting.

CHAPTER XXIV

Yesterday's girl

Charlotte was impatient to discover what had taken place between John and Christabel, so much so that she appeared unexpectedly indifferent to Longborne's sudden departure. In this she was alone. To the rest of the household, and the indoor servants in particular who were responsible for the silver and its safe keeping, their thoughts were single-minded.

The house was thrown into disorder while an inventory was begun, leaving James and Edmond to worry about the best course of action given that Longborne had been a guest and close friend. Anyway, guilt could not be laid squarely at his door without positive proof, however convincing the evidence against him. To involve the police might be premature and very embarrassing.

With so much happening, it was astonishing to Charlotte that Edmond of all people already knew much about events that had taken place between John and Christabel.

"Yes, Mother, I spoke to the girl yesterday, and to him after that. That cock of the north might have been sure of her favours when he left you, but events proved him wrong."

"I'm sorry indeed to hear that," replied Charlotte, "but why on earth would she refuse him? That puzzles me greatly."

"You shall never know."

He turned away to hide a look of complicity.

"I can't think when I was greater shocked than today. First Longborne and now this. It's all too much of a turnaround. I think I shall sit awhile. To think, Christabel had the chance to make something of herself with a most personable young man. Then there's Longborne, with all the aspect of goodness, but the soul of a devil."

"We can't be absolutely sure he stole anything. It could be coincidence that we were robbed on the night he left."

"A charitable thought, and one that does you credit, Edmond. However, why would he skulk away like a thief in the night if not guilty of some crime? Why not leave in the ordinary way, by the light of day? No, we must face the truth. That man has wronged us . . . By and by, Edmond, explain to me how you knew about a meeting between John and Christabel. You show keen interest."

"By and by, Mother, why are you so interested in the girl at all? I have wondered that ever since she came. I know you have been asking after her daily."

"I hardly think so, Edmond."

"I know so, Mother!"

There was a sudden upsurge of noise from the servants' hall, followed by shouts and quick footsteps. The door burst open.

"My pardon, Ma'am. Redmarsh is here and he's terrible fussed. Red as a beetroot. Ran all the way to give you this."

Charlotte took the letter.

"Give him a stiff brandy and tell him to wait."

She unfolded the single sheet of paper. It was signed Emmeline Sturry, but this shaky and unskilled signature did not match the refined writing that preceded it. She read the letter:

Dear, kind Mr Redmarsh.

I have gone from here. Forgive this ingratitude, but it is as unexpected to me as you will find it. To my surprise and

*everlasting joy the fine and handsome Lieutenant Charles has
asked me to go with him. Knowing him to be of good character
and only wishing me his lifelong love and affection, I agreed.
Imagine me as the wife of an officer in the Surrey Dragoons.
How my parents will wish me well once they are told, only
please say nothing until the arrangements are made. In return I
can offer him only the few tokens of my stay at Westkings to
which I have helped myself.*

*To Edmond, I give back his ring, which I lost that time ago,
but has now been found. Anger, not honesty, compels me to,
although I had intended to keep it. In this I go against
Longborne's wishes, who sees me wronged. If Edmond wonders
how I have it, tell him Christabel found it on one of her walks
and gave it to me to avoid meeting him herself. I think she must
have been searching for it to find such a small thing among the
undergrowth. I should thank her for that, but I can't. By this
letter I have the chance of giving her back some of what she
has heaped on to me. I talk, of course, about misery. Knowing
it will find its way into Madam's hands, I offer up the image of
Edmond's callous affection for Christabel after he had made
love to me. Make of that as you will.*

Emmeline Sturry.

"Oh, James, *James*," shouted Charlotte, running through the hallway, waving the letter above her head.

"Good heavens, dear. What is it?"

She thrust it into his hand.

"The rascal. Now we know a bit more. He can't have gone far
with her in tow and with just one horse between them. Come,
Edmond, there isn't a moment to lose. She has my silver!"

Edmond hesitated, scanning the letter. He peered furtively at his
mother after reading the final sentence, who returned a reproving
glare.

"Nothing will be gained by rushing headlong, and you can take
that look off your face too, Mother! This isn't the time to go into

matters past. Anyway, for goodness sake look, Mother, you have missed the most important point, something not in the words."

"Which is?" growled Charlotte.

"That the girl couldn't have written this. She has no skill with the pen and certainly couldn't manage such a fine document. I tell you, this is not her doing."

"You mean Longborne contrived it?"

"Just so. My guess is that he's tried to lay blame on her for the missing silver, cunningly wrapping it up among some words Emmie might have dictated. She would never know."

James agreed.

"That poor child. What has she got herself into?"

"He obviously doesn't know the extent of her literacy, or lack of it. Was the ring inside?"

"No!"

"I thought as much. She probably gave it to him, but he's slipped it into his pocket after all."

"Then why would he write about it in the first place? Why not say nothing, as it was supposedly lost?" asked Charlotte.

Edmond pondered the question.

"Maybe as a further ploy to make us believe that she really did compose it. After all, it nearly worked judging by your last comment."

"Well done, my boy," smiled James, placing his one good hand on his shoulder. "You have saved us from haranguing the wrong person."

The gesture brought a strange sense of companionship between James and Edmond, a tingling of affection. It had been so long since father and son had felt anything sincere, so long since they had made genuine contact. The hand on the shoulder was savoured. It was a moment, fleeting yet sanguine, that Edmond never forgot. In years to come, even as an elderly man looking back on his youth, it was this reflection of his father he most treasured. That moment Edmond knew that his efforts to save the estate had been worthwhile. For once, Charlotte felt on the outside.

"Do we now have to go to the authorities?" enquired Charlotte testily. "It would mean making this letter public. We must consider Edmond's reputation."

"What about my silver?" protested James.

"Perhaps under the circumstances, it takes second place."

Bloody cheek, thought James, pondering how Longborne might have performed the perfect crime.

She kissed him.

"You'll agree with me once you've calmed down and considered the facts. Now, be off and have a word with Redmarsh. See if he can shed any light on where they might have gone. You had also better give him the day off." James still looked upset. "I didn't mean we shouldn't find them, James, I only meant we can't involve the police. You still have your bull whip, don't you?"

James visibly cheered at the prospect. Edmond arose to follow his father out.

"Edmond, sit down a minute. I want to speak to you now that your father's gone, and it won't wait."

"I know, Mother. I was expecting it."

Edmond slumped back casually into the chair, quiet and detached, while Charlotte's knees trembled at the answer he might give.

"I'm sorry," he offered.

"Well, that's a start."

"I should never have invited Longborne here. I've always known him to be an old fraud, but you must admit that he's quite likeable. Somehow he seems to get away with things by the strength of his personality, but I never thought he would go this far. I can only believe —"

"Stop it! I don't care a fig about him, nor that silly girl he has taken up with, or for that matter the silver, precious though it is to your father. For pity's sake, Edmond, I want to know how far things have gone between you and Christabel."

He laughed, in the way people do when hoping to avoid looming trouble. It cut no ice and he stopped.

"You absolutely amaze me. You don't ask how this Emmie came to have Grandma's ring, but you ask about Christabel. Where's your sense of priority?"

There was a tap on the outside of the window. James gestured that he was going to walk to Redmarsh's cottage. Charlotte waved back. He left and she turned back to Edmond.

"I'm waiting, young man."

"Very well, seeing how you insist. I like her. She's a good sort. Is that what you want to hear? Yes? No? Perhaps you would like a few lurid details. Well, sorry to disappoint, but there are none to tell. She's honourable beyond her years." He smirked, enjoying the rebellion. "Now, do you also want to know about Emmie and me? That is a story worthy of the telling."

"I don't give two hoots about that stupid child. If you want to be ridiculous, you'll only hurt yourself."

"But grandma's ring? It's lost."

"I know. Damn you for that."

"But a relationship with Christabel is different? Why?"

"Because . . ." She hesitated. "Because . . . Well . . . The truth is that I knew her father and I made certain promises to him –"

"That no son of yours would go near this waif's daughter? Pull the other one."

"Stop interrupting. The fact is that Jack was an old man with old-fashioned ways."

"Not that old. Probably little older than you, I shouldn't wonder."

"No, you're right, he wasn't. He became old by the hardness of his life."

"Yes, yes! Once upon a time . . ."

A second tap on the window indicated that James had forgotten his hat and was only now leaving. Charlotte nodded impatiently.

"When I consider the high hopes I had for you, and how you earned my respect by your work around the estate. Now you talk and behave like your drunken friends."

"No, really, that's too much. If you think that, all I can say is I'm sorry for giving that impression. It's so far from the truth."

"Oh, don't bother to apologise. I see it clearly. Now I think upon it, perhaps it's the right time for you to visit our properties in Surrey, assess their rents and land values and make yourself known to the tenants. The time away will help you to cool off. Clear your mind. You will return in a few months with proper respect."

"I can't go now!"

"There's no better time. Your father can sort out this mess with Longborne in his own way. Plenty of strong help around here should he want it. He can be a tiger, even one-handed."

"You want rid of me for other reasons, don't you?"

"Nonsense."

"Then I plead to stay."

"No, you may not, and if you disobey my wishes, I'll see to it that you too will be disinherited. What good will all your hard work have been then?"

"You too! What do you mean?"

"Did I say that? Just a slip of the tongue."

Edmond stormed from the room. After sitting alone for some time, Charlotte opened a drawer and extracted the iron key, the one she had given Jack a lifetime ago. Suddenly she heard James enter the hall and quickly tried to push the drawer shut, but there wasn't time. He caught her furtive look. With her heart pounding, she asked if he recognised it.

He rolled it between his fingers.

"This?"

"For God's sake, James, can't you remember? Doesn't it mean anything to you?"

He shook his head.

"Have you not noticed anything strange about Chrissie either?"

Again his face looked blank.

"How hard can you make this for me! Look, I can't permit Edmond to court her, to make love to her because she is . . . Oh dear! She is . . . I mean . . . Oh, for heaven's sake, they're related."

"What in heaven's name are you talking about, woman?"

"Must I spell it out? Whatever the consequences to us, you must be told." She closed her eyes. "She is *my* daughter and he's *your* son!"

"Your daughter?" His expression suddenly hardened. "No, you're not trying to tell me this Chrissie girl working for us, the one *I* hired, is baby Christabel?"

She nodded.

"No baby anymore. Time has passed by. It's seventeen years since I gave Mere my baby and that key. Only a greater crisis now could have made me admit it."

She allowed James time to recover from the shock, watching his reaction in suspense. She whispered his name and stroked his cheek with the back of her fingers, but it passed him by. His air was deep and serious, so sullen that she sank. She began to cry, so certain that she had been mistaken as before in telling all.

"Chrissie is Christabel? I should have realised. I've heard others call her name, but stupidly never made the connection. It's an uncommon name, but not unique. God, I must be thick! I need to think."

He left the room. Once clear of prying eyes, he took out of his pocket the bundle of letters addressed to Christabel, but handed to him moments before by Redmarsh. On opening the first, he immediately recognised them as documents that should have been in the safe of Schofield and Fly. He quickly put them back into his deep pocket and made for his bedroom. At the top of the stairs he stopped, opening the window to bawl at a dairymaid who chased a runaway cow across the formal lawn. She slipped and the beast jogged onto the drive and through the gates. James leaned out.

"You all right, girl?"

A dirty smile came back. Within moments the beast returned, chased by two men with ropes. She curtsied and ran to head it off. Cornered, the cow stopped and was taken prisoner. James found himself laughing at the antics and his mood mellowed. It seemed that life for ordinary folk was so uncomplicated. An unfamiliar man with long red whiskers stood at the gates, watching events from a distance. They exchanged glances and waves before he walked away.

The swing between personal crisis and outside reality in a matter of moments awakened James to his own good fortune. He leapt down the stairs faster than he had climbed and burst through the doorway, planting a kiss on Charlotte's receptive cheek. She was stunned.

"You've been wanting proof that I can be like other husbands." She shook her head.

"I think you have! My arm shows the mad dog I've been. Not recently, I grant, but bad memories never really go away. What you've told me may be that proof. Besides, too much time has gone by for old grievances to cast new shadows over us."

"Oh, James."

Her face showed real tenderness.

"Dry your eyes, my dear. I want no more tears in this house. You know, it's strange, but somehow in the bad old times I felt that we were living a sort of trial life, as if a future time would give us back our youth and a second chance to heal the pain we inflict or suffer. Such foolishness."

"That's the best —"

"No, Char, let me finish. It occurs to me that whatever has gone between us, we have gained little and lost much. Now we have the chance of not one child but *two*. Yes, I will acknowledge Christabel's right to be called *our* child, if you can forgive me enough to allow me to adopt her as my own. Go, get her and bring her home, and send for that son of mine whom you have taken as yours too. Whatever else, we must put pay to their unnatural relationship."

Charlotte was weak with astonishment. She fell upon James and embraced him warmly before scampering along the hallway to give a maid the order to fetch both Edmond and Christabel.

"The children will be with us soon."

The words sounded peculiar, thin and light-headed, but strangely calming.

James and Charlotte abstractedly filled the moments looking at things about them of no particular importance, adjusting the position of this or straightening that, but wishing to say or do nothing that might change of mood until the maid returned. A spider dangled from a lamp. James blew it gently, spinning it like an acrobat and causing the creature to curl its legs into a ball. He stopped blowing and it unfolded. He blew again and the spider dropped to the ground at the end of its gossamer line, lost among the colours of the rug. Charlotte tip-toed upstairs and returned with a sewing ring. She had barely added a new row on the printed cloth when, breathless, the servant came running back.

"He's gone."

"Who's gone?"

"Young master Edmond. I've checked his room and his bags aren't there. Grey Boy was saddled up. This letter was on his pillow. It's to you, Sir."

Charlotte seized it and tore open the flap. Quickly, her eyes scanned the lines.

"It's all right, we can be calm. He says he was too embarrassed to say his farewells personally, but he's gone to Surrey as I told him. He goes on that he knows what to do and will take the opportunity of selling off those empty cottages that Blundle reported have been falling into disrepair. Oh, and he will forward his whereabouts in a day or two."

After offering the letter to James, she placed it in her purse.

"Well, that's all right then."

"Two birds with one stone. Good show. Now, that only leaves Christabel and catching that rotten bugger Longborne. I feel in the mood to teach him a real lesson. First things first, so send the maid for Christabel."

She returned in an even greater fluster.

"Sorry, Madam, but Chrissie isn't about either, and *her* bag has gone."

"Oh, my goodness, they've fled together," cried Charlotte. "That must be it. What have I started? I've been a fool letting her stay here. What if they . . . Oh God."

It was easy to believe that two runaway couples were loose, the bands of assumed affection having already been confirmed in Charlotte's mind by circumstantial evidence. While Longborne and Emmie had indeed flown expeditiously and secretly, making for a destination known only to the lieutenant, the assertion that Edmond and Christabel were also together was, however, wrong.

Christabel, having been privy to the contents of Emmie's letter, as related by Redmarsh in casual conversation, had felt great self-reproach for any role she might have unwittingly played in their elopement. She had, therefore, been in low spirits when Edmond had called by to say that he too was leaving. The conversation between them, although surprisingly hurried, had covered many subjects, including all that had happened at the manor. During these brief moments together Christabel had noticed the Elvington crest embossed on Edmond's saddle and had remarked on the fine workmanship as she ran her finger over the outline in the hope of having her hand held.

"No, Chrissie. That 'snowflake', as you put it, is of no significance at all. It merely denotes that my father was the youngest son. It's the main features of the crest that form the family link. Instead of a 'snowflake', my uncles have a crescent, molet, fleur-de-lis and other symbols. None of these little differences are of any importance whatsoever beyond marks of ascendancy. Who told you that they mattered?"

Charlotte's face was conjured up in Christabel's mind, her injurious words recalled in silence.

"Oh, nobody in particular. I can't remember now."

He remounted.

"Well, goodbye Chrissie."

He held out a hand, which she gladly took, his slight squeeze returned fourfold. Their pulses quickened by the touch.

"I was hoping to make you happy. At least we part as friends."

With Emmie gone of her own choosing, there really was no further reason for the two young folk to stay apart, that is except for Christabel's shyness to make the first move after her earlier false indifference. All she had to do was to pull down the barrier she had so deliberately and successfully built to keep them apart. She waited anxiously for him to sweep her into his arms and declare his love once more, so that she could unexpectedly throw herself upon him. Couldn't he see that having begun to love him she was now powerless to stop?

She prayed silently that he might chance fortune once more, but as the seconds passed terror struck her that he wouldn't. She tried to encourage him, although the dryness of her voice failed to convey the tender meaning of her words. Anyway, being so used to her contempt, he could no longer recognise change.

"Am I to believe that you could leave me?" she asked through a forced smile.

He winced, thinking it to be another friendly put-down. He let go and their fingers slipped apart. With a quick squeeze of his heels under the beast's belly he was off, a hand lifted as the final gesture of farewell. She staggered back, face pale, watching him leave, hoping upon hope that he might still turn back. That he didn't was entirely due to his own feelings, which could not withstand another gaze on a creature so perfectly meeting his desires. Why hadn't she given him an indication of love, so that he could have declared himself this last time? he thought.

There she stood, ill-used, guilty only of morality and nobleness. She felt like crying, but couldn't, the degree of her grief too violent to manifest itself openly.

With the thought that a great deal of her present troubles were punishment for being responsible, even in small part, for the break-up of an engaged couple and the introduction of Longborne into her friend's affections, Christabel had resolved to repent her sins by journeying to Emmie's parents. In this manner she hoped to soften the blow that would undoubtedly befall them once they found out that Emmie had run off with a man of dubious character. James was bound to write, which would also mean the matter of the stolen silver. She might, if she was quick in her travels, advance Emmie's case for elopement and comfort the Sturrys who were devout Methodists, or so she believed.

After walking no more than half a mile from her lodgings, Christabel stopped to look back for the last time on the great house and other buildings that made up Westkings. She somehow knew she would never return. She rested her bag on a wall. Her eyes scanned the views, each feature bringing back memories of the happy months now ended. She doubted whether she would ever be so happy again, although the pain of Edmond's leaving made her own going almost sweet.

Due to the turmoil caused by the morning's revelations, most of the Elvington fields were as yet empty of labourers. Yet in the far distance she could just make out the full figure of Louise sitting on a stool beside a dairy cow that had waited longer than usual for milking. Away from the mead, on a rough path adjoining the lane, an old man staggered to load churns onto a wagon that would be taken to the milkhouse after all had been filled from buckets.

James and Charlotte were already standing impatiently on the steps to the manor when the carriage was brought around, pulled by two ponies. Nothing was more important now than to prevent Edmond and Christabel from spending a night together, and in this their plan was to trace Edmond's route to the Surrey estates. If it meant driving all day, they would persevere.

The warmth of the sun rapidly heated the inside of the carriage and soon James was asleep on the back seat, his head bouncing on Charlotte's shoulder. In stark contrast she was alert and looked diligently from the window.

Once the carriage pulled away from the hamlet, it struck Charlotte how few people were to be seen. It was as if the whole order of the countryside had been thrown into disarray. An iron-monger making door-to-door calls passed by, his gig laden with boxed vegetable boilers, brass trivets, goffering irons, beetle traps and a fine line in jelly bag stands, among other goods. The man raised his cap as they sped past.

Charlotte sat back in despair. Other vehicles were infrequently seen, including a few traps of the type hired when a horseman had a passenger in tow. Presently, though, as the carriage continued its winding path she caught sight of another figure in the distance, about to turn off onto a track that cut through the river valley. The peasant girl had a bag. As they drew closer the figure was unmistakable.

"Stop!"

The vehicle came to a dusty halt. She flung open the door and jumped out. The girl dropped her bag and stood open-mouthed.

"Ma'am?"

"So here you are. I'm surprised you're alone and on foot."

Christabel was still in shock from being followed.

"You left without giving notice. Whatever takes you away must be very urgent?"

"Important, rather than urgent, Ma'am," came the reply.

"It wasn't something you could discuss with me?"

"With respect, it's a private matter."

"It doesn't involve me at all?"

"Only indirectly, I suppose," she replied with honesty. "Why does my going bother you?"

"Because your haste means you're hiding something from me, something I should be told. Something that greatly affects my family, I shouldn't wonder. So, I want to hear it from your own lips."

"I really don't know what you mean." She thought for a moment. "You don't suspect me of taking the silver?"

Charlotte looked askance.

"Pish to the silver. You're no thief, I know that. Now listen here, Christabel, you're an intelligent girl, too clever by half to love someone for no better reason than you were told not to or for social climbing. So, if I hear from a third party that you have affection for someone you shouldn't, I'm compelled to take it seriously. *Now* do you understand?"

"No, not a word. My thoughts and feelings have remained entirely private."

"What are you running away from then?"

"I'm not running away, as you put it. I merely can't stay, that's all, but, equally, I can't discuss my reasons for leaving Westkings. I owe you much and I wouldn't hurt you."

"Not deliberately, maybe, but in other ways you might and probably already have. Let's face facts, your going has something to do with Edmond, hasn't it?"

"In a manner of speaking, I suppose so."

"I thought as much. Where are you meeting?"

"Pardon?" was her only reply.

"Now, look here, Edmond is a most delightful young man, made better by his coming fortune. You, on the other hand, have nothing beyond good looks that time will fade into memory. You mustn't let your inclinations blur these realisms. I depend on your common sense. You'll not disappoint me, I'm sure."

Christabel assured her that she always tried to think clearly.

"Don't play games with me. I'll tell you this, Edmond has had several unimportant romances with local girls. You must know that much yourself. Fortunately, he has always had the good sense not to let them go too far. I wouldn't like to think that now you'd been the cause of my greatest displeasure. Am I making myself clear?"

"I understand," said Christabel in a monotone, wondering how unlucky she was if even her failed romance could lead to trouble.

"James' opinion of you of late has been a revelation, and I'm inclined to believe that he would be partial to your remaining with us. I, on the other hand, now think that it is best if you don't, so long as you go alone. Are you alone?"

A small smile grew on Christabel's face as she mockingly looked about for an ethereal presence.

"Insolent child. How do I know you don't plan to meet someone? I'll come straight to the point, then. What arrangements have you made to meet Edmond? Be warned in your reply as I know much of what's going on."

The suggestion startled Christabel.

"Meet Edmond, Ma'am? Why, none."

"Don't come the surprise with me. You have plans for him. So, I've got news for you that'll put pay to any little scheme."

Blushing at having her name linked with Edmond, Christabel could stand no more. Without another word she picked up her bag and turned to walk off.

"Stay!"

"Why should I? You've already made up your mind. Nothing I can say will change what you think is the truth."

"Hear me out. I demand it! Please?"

Already downtrodden, Christabel prepared herself for further bad news. A face of cold resignation peered from the shawl.

"I've something to tell you of such magnitude that I think it would be best if you heard it while sitting in the carriage."

Charlotte opened the door and invited her in once James had been bundled out. They sat on opposite sides.

"Do you remember this?" She pulled the key from her purse and placed it in Christabel's palm. "Well, I lied to you."

"Lied?"

"Yes, and I feel no remorse. Listen, Christabel, if I say there are times when people are forced to do things, bad things, that in other circumstances they wouldn't dream of, often in such cases against their wishes and better nature, could you understand and forgive?"

"I might, depending on the circumstances. I suppose it depends on the seriousness of the lie too."

"Let me put it another way. There are deceitful lies and white lies, but either once said may have to be covered by more lies to keep a truth secret. This is what has happened between us. The deceit, *my* deceit, began when you brought me that blessed key, but the falsehood it concealed started way before that."

Charlotte paused at the innocence of Christabel's expression. She looked away, regaining courage by watching James struggle to light a cigar.

"If it pains you to tell me whatever it is, then don't," said Christabel in a soft tone. "You obviously don't like me and, anyway, I'm leaving this place, so what's to be gained? Just give me back my key and I'll go."

"Don't patronise me. It's not a question of like or dislike. I doubt you'll be half as gracious once I'm finished. Please don't interrupt again. It's hard enough to confront you as it is. The fact is, that thing you hold *is* an Elvington key."

"Yes, I know. I've found that out myself from talking to Edmond. If that's all you lied about, I couldn't care less."

"I told you to remain silent. However, now that you bring up Edmond again, answer me this, honestly. Have you ever been lovers in a physical sense?"

"What! How can you think that?"

"Good, then I take that as an emphatic 'no'. We are spared that at least."

"I know I could never be what you want for him, but —"

"*Stop*! Don't go on. Did I say you're not good enough? There is another, greater reason for my question. Be prepared for a terrible shock." She drew breath. The words, when released, came out in a single, unstoppable eruption. "I have to say that you are none other than my own daughter. You're not a Mere at all, but an Elvington. It follows, therefore, that you are half-sister to Edmond! Now do you see my concerns?"

"What?" Christabel was left breathless. "Don't talk such rubbish. Me and you? Edmond and myself? What new game is this?"

"It's true, hard to believe as it is. The fact remains that I gave you away as a baby to your natural father. Nonetheless, you *are* mine."

Christabel stared at the cold composure of the woman. Her forehead became lined with thought.

"Come, Christabel," added Charlotte, "haven't you wondered at our likeness?"

Christabel looked at Charlotte, her eyes travelling over her face.

"That's right. Take a good look at me. Can you not see it?"

Christabel shook her head.

"We're not at all alike. It can't be so."

"Look again. When I see you I'm looking at myself in my youth. Picture me as a younger woman, not as I am now. My eyes, my lips, my nose. See mine – see yours."

She stole a second quick glance before turning away.

"What I say is true and you must believe me. You are the child of my flesh, much good will it do you now that you conspire to shame me. Disinherited once and so shall it remain, unless, maybe, you can convince me that you understand the position we all face. Then there is a chance that I may yet have you back. What do you say?"

"I knew my father."

"So did I, that's the trouble. I knew him too well. Think, child, he has always been your father. It is your mother who changes."

Christabel sat blankly.

"For goodness sake, Christabel, do I have to spell it out? I gave you to Jack Mere and Verity soon after you were born a bastard at the manor. See, I know both their names. Jack worked for me as a young man and was your father right enough, but I was, and remain, your birth mother."

Charlotte's tone was scolding. Christabel thought of Verity's gravestone in the churchyard that bore the inscription 'MOTHER'.

"No! I won't believe any of it. Why do you want to tell me such horrible things? You're making up more lies."

Charlotte went to touch her.

"Get away from me, you witch." She grasped the door handle.

Charlotte seized her arm.

"Then how did your father come by the key, the very key that opens my jewel case from which I gave him a ring too? I gave them to him the very moment he took you from my arms."

Christabel's hand pressed against the outline of the ring hanging out of sight around her neck.

"You and my father? Never. Not in a million years. Tell me he stole them, anything, but not that. Please!"

"I can't. It wouldn't be true. I gave them to him and that's that. It was all I could do at the time. We conceived you amongst the shrubs at the back of the manor. Believe me, I paid for it too; I have my own scars."

"I don't believe any of it. Not a word."

"You want the details?"

"Why you disgusting . . ."

She slapped Charlotte across the face with sufficient force to knock her backwards against the padding.

"Go on, do it again," taunted the older woman. "It won't alter a single thing. I was wrong about you. You're just a common urchin after all who wishes my son had taken her to the shrubbery too. Only that would be incestuous. Your father was a real man with sweat on his muscles."

"And what did you have to offer him to take you there?" returned Christabel in pure venom.

"Offer!" she cried. "You must me joking."

"Get away from me. You're wicked. Evil! Here, this is what I think of the Elvingtons." She threw the key from the window. "It brought me to you and now I'm free again. I've had everything taken away from me except for my memories and name. Now you try to rob me of even these. And why? What can you be up to? I was never anything to you, but plain Christabel Mere the worker, and by God I will never again be under your influence. A mother doesn't give away her baby, for *any* reason. You must really hate me to say such dreadful things."

"No, Christabel, not hate. Never hate!"

"Well, let me tell you this. Edmond doesn't want me. Did you take that in? Watch my lips. *He doesn't want me*, although I worship him. There was a time when he loved me back, but I allowed friendship for others to get in the way. It is all past now. I hope God can forgive you for mocking my dead family, for I never will. Nothing's new. I'm life's rubbish to you, and I hate you!"

"Good!"

"Yes, good!"

Charlotte jumped out and ran to James in floods of tears. When she returned Christabel had gone. She climbed back into the carriage without looking towards the figure running through the fern. James sat besides Charlotte.

"She took the news badly?"

"Oh, shut up!" she sobbed.

"Pardon!"

"Sorry! The truth is she didn't believe a word I said. Oh, what have I done?"

"What *have* you done? What did you tell her?"

She wouldn't answer.

"It's not too late to go after her. Make it up while there's time. I can still see her over there." He pointed. "If I shout, she will hear me."

"No, don't! It wouldn't do any good, besides, I don't think I want to try again. It's safer like this. She has a past in which I've had no hand. When the crunch came, I sided with Edmond out of instinct bred from years of caring for him, and spared no feelings for Christabel whatsoever. That can't be right, can it? Only she is *my* real child."

James shook his head.

"And, do you know, I don't think at this moment I care. She said something that was so true. She said I had no right to take away her childhood. Verity was her mother in any real sense, not I. I can't take that from her. Only, why was I so aggressive?"

"You were hard with the innocent child? Why, in God's name?"

"I really don't know. There seemed no easy way of telling her, or perhaps it was that she could have taken Edmond's affection from me. After all, they might be half-brother and half-sister, but they're not blood related at all. We could've left them alone."

"Good grief, you're right. How stupid I've been in thinking it mattered. But if you had already realised this, why didn't you say so?"

"Because it still seemed wrong."

"What a fool I've been. Still, you've been the bigger fool. There's a world of difference between the love someone has for a parent and the love for a husband or wife. One doesn't diminish the other. They're not rivals. You idiot, Char. You'll never know what you've thrown away today, not as long as you live. I only hope you don't come to regret your actions. She hasn't done a thing to hurt us — I doubt if she's ever done anything to hurt anyone. Still, what's done is done. Come on, let's drive on to Surrey."

"Is there any point now?"

"The change of air will do you good. However, consider this. Should we tell Edmond about Christabel? At best he would condemn us, at worst he might question his own antecedence or even go after her to reunite with a sister he never thought he had. He's not the sort to let her live poor. What do you say?"

"All right" she whispered. "You know best. Let sleeping dogs . . ."

"But, before you agree to say nothing to him, are you sure you've fully considered what I've said? Then there is Christabel. By letting her go like this she'll never want to see you again and will probably be poor for the rest of her life. Are you certain you can live with it?"

"I think so."

"Thinking's no good. Are you *sure*?"

"Yes" she added positively.

The carriage pulled away and quickly passed along a ridge before descending from the area through which Christabel made slow progress on foot.

So much had happened that morning to change many lives that it was impossible to believe anything more lay in store. Yet, just as Christabel was about to step from the track to pass through woodland, a rider came furiously towards her, calling out her name. She rushed up to embrace John, to tell him of her experience with Charlotte, but, once dismounted, he held her at arm's length with unexpected formality. Standing erect, he enquired politely why she had gone so suddenly. Prepossessed by his unexpected tone, she answered equally as formerly, holding back much of her news.

"Why did you stay overnight in Westkings, John? You said you were going home."

"Actually, Christabel, it's fortunate that we meet. I'm sorry about yesterday. I've been riding hard to give you this. I had almost given up hope of finding you."

He handed her a letter that he had worked on for most of the night. She began to unfold it.

"No! Please don't read it now. Not while I'm standing by you. You might read it after I've left."

After a courteous bow, he remounted and rode away. Anxious as to its content, Christabel took up her bag and walked to where the verdure of a flowering hedgerow hid her presence from the view of others.

The letter was a full two pages long, small-written on both sides, in a hand so perfect and accurate that it was surely the result of many failed attempts that lay screwed up in a waste paper basket.

My dearest Christabel,

Don't be put upon by receiving this letter, or by the apprehension that I have tried here to repeat yesterday's sentiments. It is not my intention to do so, so you may read on without dread. I ask only that you spare the time to hear me out, to offer justice to my case. I refer, of course, this one and only time, to misplaced affection. If in doing so I offend you further, then you must forgive the awkwardness of my situation and a lack of skill in putting my thoughts in any other way.

Yesterday, when you accused me of not knowing and thereby not understanding the motives of Edmond Elvington – as I have since found him to be – you were entirely correct to believe just this. Through no wish to make furtive searches on matters private to yourself, but to satisfy my own honour, I spoke to a number of persons in the village who know him well. I have become disturbed by their evidence. Your superior knowledge of him as a friend – nay, I fear more than that – may give you course to question my findings, but I beg your forgiveness and pray for an open mind.

From the moment you mentioned him, not by name you may recall, I thought his motives were open to scrutiny. Why, I asked myself, had he not taken you into the bosom of his family, as any other man would be proud to do; that I surmised from talking earlier with his mother (although at the time I didn't know she held this position). You may also recall that, in contrast, I told my mother of my feelings for you. Indeed, I also thought nothing of linking my name with yours to a stranger of the eminence of Charlotte Elvington. Many people censured me for wanting you for my wife, for, like it or not, people are generally intolerant of such things. I knew that while your family had nothing compared to mine, a shortage of capital never led you to lack propriety, which so often betrays those less fortunate than myself. In short, no man could want for a better partner, putting aside your beauty, which is for all to admire. Please see that this is offered only as a judgement, and endeavour to forget my personal feelings.

To be specific, I would have little difficulty finding one, two or more witnesses to verify that this young Elvington spreads his affections too thinly to be a gentleman. I can almost hear you deny it, but hear me out. It appears that he was earlier engaged to another girl of similar standing to yourself, which was also kept dark. This may be news to you, but I have it on good authority. It seems that the girl secretly asked the vicar whether she could be married in his church, being a Methodist, but that

her entreaty was premature. I will say no more on that, being a
personal grievance of that poor soul. All I have heard on this
subject has come from the vicar's own housekeeper, who keeps
an ear to the ground and most probably also in the crack of the
door. I do not condone her behaviour, but to my discredit I make
use of what she tells me. You may find this repugnant, perhaps
even unbelievable, but the young girl was not the first to carry
his favour, and he being so young himself. I have come across
his sort before; men who can fall passionately for one woman,
truly believing her to be God's greatest creation and show the
highest veneration, only to fall as quickly out of love when
another pair of pretty legs waggle his way.

For the accuracy of everything here told I stand assured.
You may match it more particularly with your own experiences.
If you find my words prejudiced, you may by reason of
conscience approach the good lady with the big ears at the
vicarage. Fear not, an approach will not injure myself, for I am
leaving for Cerne the very moment this reaches your hand. I do
remain your friend. Bless you.

John Madden

If Christabel had expected a new plea from John on opening the letter, she had misjudged him gravely. This time he did not break down or, against his own advice, offer affection once more. The lines contained nothing of his feelings and, by this, his motive in telling her of his findings had to be considered selfless.

The words in the letter stirred further emotions in her, but such as they were appeared difficult to clarify. Was she willing to believe any of what he said about Edmond's character, and, even if she did, was it to change her opinions? Much of what she had read she already knew to be true, making the other assertions more credible. But, did any of it actually matter any longer, since Edmond too had ridden out of her life?

Christabel's look became worn. Wasn't it just another of life's little ironies that she was expected to bear, an open sore to fester, but never heal. It was all becoming too much of a burden to suffer alone – and she was alone. Her parents and Isobel were dead, Edmond had gone and Emmie had forsaken her. Only John vowed to remain a friend, but jealousy had made him rigid to her and, anyway, how could she forgive his meddling? She screwed up the letter and threw it away. Grasping the handles of her bag, she strode into the woods and out of John's influence.

CHAPTER XXV

Mortal girl to immortal woman

Among the cottages and small farm buildings in far-flung English villages may be discovered many good sources from which to study rural life. A neat row of terraces might hide such a diverse grouping of dwellers as could be accounted for anywhere.

In one such house might be the jack of all trades, a much valued employee of an absent landlord capable of turning a willing hand to any job with acceptable skill. He could be found reconstructing a drystone wall, reforging a bent plough coulter or arranging bulbs for the coming season's garden. Next door could be the drunkard, in a room so wretched with neglect that he presents the health hazard of the little community. Past the old couple who sit outside their front door every fine day then may reside the tattler, content to while away the morning at her gate while her eldest daughter hangs over the suds in the Monday washtub.

Then there is the joker, a pleasant character with whom everyone laughs to avoid being the next butt of his humour. Often he may double as the village musician, scraping away at a battered fiddle with injurious tone, but to uproarious jollity. Last may be the quiet availing man, put upon because of his obliging nature. To his home of an evening come upwards of a dozen persons, seated around the walls of his tiny room waiting to consume his home-made ale.

Christabel's goal of Stirminster Oak, where Emmie's parents lived, was one such village that lay on the southern edge of Dartmoor, midway between Plymouth and the beautiful Forest of Bligh, still a good sixty miles from Westkings. The few stone-built cottages standing in neat rows of four-house terraces, the little whitewashed shops and the bricked roads gave it an air of prosperity, presided over by a mansion high on the hillside with its own ascending drive, the lord having grown rich on royalties from land leasing and mining rights.

The village had grown after copper was discovered in the sur-rounding hills, the convenient riverway enabling a double-berth quay to be constructed for small twin-masted ships that could sail laden out of Plymouth Sound for the continent. When the copper had been exhausted arsenic was discovered, safe to be mined until baked into a toxic poison. Thus, the village had become an efficient working machine, the chandler taking care of the sailors' needs while the minerals were quickly loaded on ships using tipping bogies that ran on rails. Tiles over the quay ensured that all spillages could be swept up for collection. Prosperity, though, was above ground.

Christabel's journey was going to be long and hard. She had not had time to prepare for it but, nevertheless, her mind was resolute. Above all, she knew that she had to be quick if she was to arrive before James' letter.

After the first day Christabel emerged from Salbutt, only a valley's walk from Westkings, facing the endless green-grey miles of coun-tryside stretching out before her. Another three days and forty miles on she awoke from a leafy bed in the early dawn of an ashy September morning, roused by the crack of a mighty oak branch ripping away from its disabled trunk. Once again she gathered up her few belongings, took some bread and water, and set off into the subdued scene ahead.

For the last two days a chill had filled the air, the up-knoll and down-valley passage past Taunton and Exeter leading her into the Wittcombe Vale, wending through exposed farmland of small fields that afforded little protection. The pale paths then cut straight swathes into the upper reaches of the hills, unprotected from the elements except for ragged lines of post and wire fences that kept her from using the lower slopes on which patches of dark green firs grew and where, in early morning, wispy mist bathed their pinnacled tips.

Every once in a while a rider galloped past, a sound so carved into her heart that she stopped and turned on each occasion, staring into the distance as if expecting the familiar faces of Edmond or John. Throughout this period she found no difficulty walking alone, her rather reduced appearance concealing the features that had attracted two known suitors and others that had remained silent. Indeed, she enjoyed the monotony of her own steps, but this was almost bound to end and for the first time during her journey, while she stopped to pick wild fruit, a one-horse-fly came slowly by and halted. Deliberately paying no attention, she continued picking, but nevertheless, listened attentively for the slightest sound behind her back.

"I say good-day to 'e, little missy."

Her face, framed by a black shawl, turned and forced a smile.

"Good-day, Sir," she replied civilly.

"Why, you're a young wench under all those wrappings. What are 'e doing here all by yourself?"

"I'm making for Stirminster Oak, Sir."

"Oh, well now, that place is just down-a-ways, a mile or two hence. I might as well take 'e there meself for company."

He climbed down, but she politely declined his offer.

"Come now. You're fair worn to a frazzle. I won't hurt you, although I'll amit readily enough that I'm partial to a bit of young flesh when I've got the cash. Is it money you want to give me the company I crave?"

An outstretched hand beckoned. A dog that had lain supine in the fly between baskets of eggs lifted its head at the familiar voice, barking as it climbed onto the driver's seat ready to jump down.

"Be still there, or I'll break 'e neck!"

He brandished a whip at the animal. Whimpering, it turned back to the baskets. On legs made rickety by drink, with a bias of direction, he stepped back to Christabel.

"Now, what's the answer, maidy?"

Alarmed, she looked for help, but the road was empty of traffic. She could try running, but it would mean leaving her cumbersome bag behind. Anyway, he might set the dog on her.

"So be it. Walk if 'e must."

Grunting, he turned away, then, just as Christabel's guard was lowered, he swung around and rushed headlong at her, using his full body weight to knock her down. Although not fit or young, his burden of fat and flab was beyond the girl's resistance. She couldn't move, although she struggled with all her strength.

He became brutal, overcome by the first sight of forbidden flesh as he ripped open her dress. With eyes popping, she dug her nails deep into his cheeks, drawing lines of blood to the surface. It was too little. Having felt his wounds, his hand crashed down across her face with tremendous force. She swirled in semi-consciousness and the sickening movement of the sky above. With arms outstretched, she clutched at the long grass.

When the foul deed was over he ran his hand coarsely through the grass to wipe away the scent of her ravaged body, then left laughing. She lay stunned for minutes by the roadside as the vehicle pulled way, the dog barking.

"Slut!" he shouted from the distance.

Hardly breathing, she let go of the grass that had stained her palms green and tried to move her legs. She felt spears of pain.

Blinding tears fell in cascades as she pulled her clothes over her body.

"Oh, no. Please, not this as well."

No person heard her plea.

CHAPTER XXVI

Dorchester days

The remainder of the walk to Stirminster Oak was, indeed, only a short distance and all downhill, but for Christabel, now bruised and in shock, the steps were exceedingly painful. She went no farther than the crossroads at the head of the village, diverting right for the cover of a ruined cottage and away from people sitting at the foot of a small stone bridge that spanned a cascading stream. Here, within its broken walls, she stripped off the shawl and the torn dress beneath, placing them inside her bag after first removing her one best outfit.

With hair now curled up under a trim bonnet, she stepped out a changed woman. After a furtive glance sideways, she dipped a hand into the icy water of a horse trough and splashed her face, wiping away the tear stains, but not the memory. Now she was as ready as she could be.

Houses of a similar type may look the same after a superficial glance, but each bears the character of the occupier. Christabel, through Emmie's descriptions, knew the nature of her friend's parents and was not in the least surprised to come across a mid-terrace of stern and uncompromising appearance. The gate hung level, the paintwork was a sombre brown and in good order, and the little garden was formed in neat if uninspired patterns with clipped edges and well-tended shrubs. She walked to the front door, careful first to pull the gate shut.

As she stood on the step ready to ring the bell, she at once felt inextricably vague, unsure of whether she had been right to come at all. What could she say to them? It was all very well setting out with good intentions, but what if James' letter had got there first and they already knew of Emmie's elopement? What if they had banished her name from the house for ever? What good then was her gesture? From what she knew, Emmie's father was the antithesis of all men she had known.

These eleventh-hour reflections, so simple, had not struck her during the miles of walking, when her mind had been preoccupied with selfish thoughts. Now they loomed large. Yet, in honesty, there was another urgent need to see the Sturrys. She had not completed the final half mile of her journey easily and could now feel real pain when breathing deeply, not the kind she was used to from working but an inner sort, racking and burning that she didn't understand and it frightened her. Again she breathed hard and the sensation grew worse. Dizzy, she pulled at the bell chain, one hand resting on the architrave for support. Wind rustled leaves that pulled on their stems and sent dust swirling down the lane.

The door opened and Christabel fell into Mrs Sturry's arms.

"Joseph, Joseph! Come quickly and bring a blanket."

Christabel sipped water from a glass held by the woman.

"You poor dear. What on earth has brought you to this state?"

Christabel politely refused more water. Mr Sturry, now sitting, lifted the Bible from its resting place on the mantel. He opened it at the bookmark.

"For I am persuaded that neither death, nor life, nor angels, nor principalities, nor powers, nor things present, nor things to come, nor height, not depth, nor any other creature, shall be able to separate us from the love of God, which is Christ Jesus our Lord. Amen to that."

"Amen," repeated his wife.

They stared at Christabel.

"Amen," she added hesitantly.

He closed the book.

"Well, child, perhaps now you're recovered you might tell us what afflicts you. We are all under the everlasting mercy of Christ and our house is yours for as long as you may need help. Come, let's start with your name."

"My name is Christabel Mere."

"Mere? That rings a bell. Where from, I wonder?"

"I am, or rather have been, a friend of Emmeline's."

"Of course, you're the one from Westkings. She mentioned you."

Christabel nodded.

"And that's why I'm here in a manner of speaking."

Mrs Sturry looked apprehensive.

"Heaven's preserve us. What excellent timing. Perhaps you can tell us the truth of this, if you will."

She took a letter from the bureau and handed it across. It bore the Elvington seal. Christabel scanned the lines, then folded it back into the envelope.

"Could you read it?" enquired Mr Sturry.

"Yes."

"Then from what you know can you confirm or deny the contents? Please tell us. We've been in agony since it arrived yesterday."

Hearing the right answer meant a lot to them, but it had to be the truth. Shyly, she peered from one anxious face to the other.

"Sincerely I'm sorry, but it's all true."

"All of it? Even the bit about this man stealing silver to pay for their elopement?"

She nodded.

"Then Emmeline is a lost daughter. From today I only have a son."

"No, Joseph, don't say that. You can't mean it."

She took a photograph from the mantel. He immediately snatched it.

"Don't disobey me, Rachel. She has always been rebellious, but this time it's gone too far. Think back to her school days. We couldn't make her learn. Give her treats, beat her, it made not a jot of difference. She always went her own way in the end. I tell you, Rachel, I knew it would come to this. Well, I forbid her name in my house. She's a common little tramp plus a thief by consent."

Rachel gestured helplessly to Christabel.

"I know Joseph is right, but then Emmeline is still my little baby. Whatever she's done, whatever trouble she's in, I can't help but love her. What on earth made her do it?"

Before Christabel could answer, Joseph knelt to pray.

"She isn't bad, Mrs Sturry," whispered Christabel after Joseph closed his eyes. "She's just headstrong. She doesn't think of the consequences before she does things, that's all. She's been swept off her feet by a more experienced man, a man in uniform. Nobody knew her better than me."

Christabel watched Mr Sturry get up to leave.

"Good Sir, I know how it seems and I understand if you feel ashamed. Believe me, Emmie will come to her senses. Of that I'm completely sure. I doubt she knew that he had stolen anything before she left with him. He pretends to be well off to everyone and would appear capable of looking after her."

The puritan could not be reached.

"Rachel, we have spared the rod with that child and now we are punished. My mind remains made up. You, my dear young friend, can stay with my blessing. Pity Emmeline didn't model herself on your behaviour."

It was pointless to argue further. Quietly Mrs Sturry took the photograph from the table and placed it back onto the mantel. She turned to Christabel.

"And what of you, dear? You have problems of your own. I can see that."

Christabel's head dropped to her lap, cupped in long fingers. She had held back her own emotions long enough.

"I, I . . . I've . . ."

No words could pass her shivering lips. Instead, she burst into hysterics, crying and flinging her arms about the older woman.

"What on earth's going on?" demanded Mr Sturry as he re-entered the room.

Mrs Sturry shook her head to keep him away.

"Now, now. Nothing can be that bad."

"Yes it can," stammered Christabel between gulps. "I'll fight him. I'll fight him." She beat hard against Rachel's shoulder.

"Flight who, child?"

With a spasm of pain she jerked back, her eyes hypnotised.

"Don't let him touch me!" she shouted.

Mrs Sturry pulled her close, grasping Christabel's head in her hand.

"The man was so strong."

"The man?" enquired Mr Sturry. "What man?"

"The man who . . ."

She pointed to her bag and he lifted out the contents, holding up the ripped and bloodstained dress.

"Someone did this to you?"

She nodded.

"My God, there's an animal loose in the countryside. Did he do anything else?"

Again she nodded.

"He took . . . He might have killed me. I'm not bad. I couldn't . . ."

Rachel squeezed her tightly, barely able to control the girl's sobbing. Catching Joseph's eye, she mouthed that he should say something appropriate.

"Let us pray together that you do not carry his child."

Rachel glared at him in anger. He shrugged innocently.

"I would like to pray," said Christabel in a thin tone.

Many miles south of this scene, where the River Frome skirts Dorchester, Longborne and Emmie were locked inside a room in a small guest house within eyeshot of the prison and its ugly tall hanging tower that dominated the skyline. They had quickly spent or gambled away most of the cash raised from selling the silver, the only purchases to fall back on being a cheap engagement ring and a small volume of poetry in which Emmie had pressed leaves gathered during their lovers' walks.

On the table were placed a few coins still warm from Longborne's pocket, the total sum of his affluence and alone insufficient to pay for their lodgings.

"We could, perhaps, visit my uncle in Winchester, although how we get there I don't know. Haven't you got anything left in your purse, Emmie? Look again."

"What's the use. I've turned it out twice already and you haven't left me a farthing piece. I was never so poor as I am now. And what about your promise to marry me? Day after day you put it off and put it off. I need a wedding ring!"

"It's no use talking of marriage, you silly cow, when we can't even pay to get to Winchester."

The wretched state of her situation, in the dismal company of a man who had never entertained a true passion for marriage and now nightly returned to this meagre room at late hour with the smell of solicited gin on his breath, forced Emmie to take rational stock of her undoing. Only poverty now kept him in her company, there being no better option than to assume the pretence of propriety to keep creditors from the door.

It should not be supposed that anything, but the dire dread of the consequences of sedentariness, would have led Emmie to seek the urgent help of those she had earlier abandoned, but such was her misfortune that humiliation was a welcome partner if it led to her getting away. She had always believed her affection for Longborne to be sufficient to overcome any difficulties. How painful it was to discover otherwise.

It was, therefore, upon this subject that she wrote in desperation to the one person she could still face, her scorned friend Christabel, stealing the cost of postage from Longborne's nearly empty pocket. The letter was of lamentable spelling, the contents alarming.

* * *

"Lor, who do you think is writing to the maid, Chrissie, me dear?" enquired Redmarsh, hovering around his fat wife as she bent over a flying pan at breakfast, the very smell of which was plump and wholesome. She offered a reply.

"Try again, Mrs Redmarsh. Think of someone less likely."

She had no ideas.

"No? Well, all right, I'll tell you to relieve the misery. It's that scram giggle-brain Emmie Sturry. Here, it's in black and white, although the spelling's so poor that I can barely make it out."

His wife rubbed her hands on her apron.

"Did you open it, husband?"

"Of course I did. How else would I know what it says?"

"But it's private, Mr Redmarsh."

"How can it be, me-dear. I can't see it gets to its destination without looking inside. See, the envelope only reads: 'The cow Dery, Saman, Westcings'. Wonder it got here at all."

"And what of her? Has she married him b'now?"

"That's the disgrace, me-dear. It seems she hasn't. What's more she thinks he's going to leave her in the strange place she finds herself without means of support. The blighter might do that, right enough."

"What are you going to do about it, husband?"

"As to that, I don't rightly know. 'Tis no real concern of mine. Chrissie told me she was going to see Emmie's parents. I suppose I could send it there. I have the address somewhere, but it will take a confounded long time."

"That's right, do that and be shot of it. Shouldn't get too involved, 'specially as it's a police matter. Anyway, I can't worry for those who bring bad luck on themselves."

"Come to think on it, maybe there *is* a way of getting it to Chrissie quicker. You remember that young fella that hung around the estate just before she went away? The same one you saw coming from the big house t'other week."

"John, by name."

"Aye, that's the one. I hear he's come back to Westkings on

some unfinished business. Maybe I should see what he thinks I should do with it. Could save a deal of trouble, not that I mind the effort you understand."

All changed on the release of the letter into John's hand.

"Good heavens! And I was to leave for home today. This changes my plans."

"Then you will take over the matter from me, Sir?"

"Gladly. Leave it with me. Your duty is done well, friend. I'll need the Sturry's address though, if that's where she's gone, but first I must go quickly to Dorchester and do what I can for the wench. That's the more urgent."

"You're a good friend to those who don't deserve it, Sir. I wish-e-well."

"We all need someone, sometime, and, considering her plight, your thanks might be premature. I must ride hard and fast."

"I don't know what I could have done if you weren't here to take it. If . . ."

"Best let tomorrow look after itself. It's today that matters. If you'll excuse me, Redmarsh, I'll go in haste."

"Afore then, Sir, can I ask if you know anything as to why the master and mistress left so sudden like and where they can be contacted? Only, I don't rightly know what I ought to do about taking on extra hands for the milkers, we being two maids short-handed."

"I really can't say as I'm not in their confidence. I too came back to speak to them and found them gone. My advice to you is that you should do whatever you think needs to be done. They can't ask more."

Redmarsh thanked him and left.

True to his word, John rode quickly to Dorchester where, in late afternoon, he burst in on the wretched scene. Plagued by debt and unable to leave their room during daylight, the two runaways sat apart among the debris of several parsimonious cold meals. Emmie recognised the caller at once, but only as Chrissie's rejected friend. Her surprise at his arrival was matched only by Longborne's fury as she took refuge behind him.

"Get out of our room, damn you!"

"Most willingly. Collect your things, Emmeline."

"Don't you dare touch anything!"

John stood firm between them. Although shorter than Longborne, he was solid and strong and more than a match.

"You must decide now, for yourself and in his presence. Do you want to stay or go with me?"

"Go with you."

A hurt expression instantly appeared on Longborne's face, turned on with extraordinary skill. He melted, wounded onto a chair. She watched him beg her with his eyes to stay, so sincere in their aspect that she thought him misjudged.

To John's amazement she added: "Only, perhaps I should stay."

Letting go of John, she walked over to Longborne and sat on his lap, running her hand over his head and down his wavy hair.

"You see, he does love me. Why else would he beg me to stay? I was wrong. He was right, as usual. If he'll still have me, I'll stay after all."

"Good God, Emmie, don't be such a fool. What about your letter?"

"How did *you* come by it?"

"It's a long story. Christabel has left Westkings, you know. I'm told she's with your parents."

"With *my* parents!"

"It's possibly my fault. The point is, she thought that she was helping you by speaking to them. You've no idea the trouble you two have caused."

Longborne saw weakness and looked up at Emmie to intervene.

"Please go now," she said to John.

"Very well, but I think you're mistaken."

"He loves me."

"We'll see," was his terse reply.

He turned for the door. Longborne kissed Emmie and followed him out.

"We had an unhappy moment, that's all. She's right. We do love each other and we will be married as soon as I can find the money to settle our debts here and pay our passage. I want to marry her, but I can't afford to."

"You honestly intend to do that?"

"Certainly. You have my word as an officer."

"Very well, then." John reached for his coat. "Will ten pounds see you right?"

"Twenty would."

John peeled off two extra notes.

"Take the twenty, but mind you use it wisely."

"I'm in your debt, Sir. Be assured, I'll threat this as nothing more than a temporary loan. When I return to my regiment –"

"Married?"

"Of course. I've said so."

"Then take it as my wedding present. You must honour the girl."

That evening Longborne did not return from his drinking, the twenty pounds remaining intact in his pocket except for two shillings spent on gin and five more on a hired horse.

John, having dealt with the plea to his satisfaction, saw no further reason to pass the letter personally to Christabel. Instead, he went home to the Cerne Valley by the direct route after adding his own brief note to the letter, which he posted to Stirminster Oak.

CHAPTER XXVII

The Sturry's mission

"Yes," said Christabel in a whisper, "but I hardly know how to tell you what it says."

Mr Sturry sighed deeply, hopelessly wanting to know what was in the newly arrived letter, but equally determined to remain true to his beliefs.

"Is she well?"

"I think she is healthy, but . . ."

"Then, that's the end of my interest."

The table was set for breakfast and he sat at his usual chair. Christabel joined him, leaving the letter open and by his fork. After a little time he pushed it back to Christabel, unread.

"Is she married?"

"No," she murmured. "She says not, but then a note has been added that indicates that her prospects were much improved since writing. To be honest I'm not sure what to make of it, since I don't know who added the postscript. I'm still quite —"

"Stop! I forbid you to go on."

"Hear Christabel out, my dear," entreated Rachel. "What harm can it do?"

His napkin crashed onto the plate.

"What harm? What harm? My good woman, do I still not know

you or you me?" He turned to Christabel. "Did anyone ever love you?"

"I think someone did, once."

"Long ago?"

"No, not long."

He now faced his wife as to emphasise the expected reply.

"And did you run off with him?"

"Of course not." She knew that she had trapped her friend and looked sad. "Nothing happened at all."

Mr Sturry's face showed triumph.

Christabel stopped eating, placing her knife and fork neatly in the centre of the plate.

"You may see me as better than Emmie in this, but you would be wrong. I was never asked. How can I know what I would've done in similar circumstances?"

"I know," replied Mr Sturry with confidence. "Over the past days I've seen a rare and marvellous maturity in everything you do. There is nothing wilful in your character. Truly, you have been misused by that rogue who attacked you. Oh, on that matter I admit I might have thought once that perhaps you should've fought back harder, even if it cost you grave and fatal injury. However, now I know you, I can accept your submission. There hangs the difference. My daughter's evils are self-imposed."

Clutching the letter to her breast, Christabel left the room. The door closed and slowly he turned to his wife, his eyes moist.

"When I came down this morning I saw the shadow of a young girl cast on the wall by the fire. I thought for an instant that it was our little girl."

"Oh, my darling!"

Over the passing days of this twilight month it had become clear that winter would be early. The countryside kept up its manifestation of summer, but away from the eye subtle changes were taking place in advance of the deep cold.

Christabel was a good judge of such things and soon returned to the table where Rachel was wrapping pasties. She had put on several extra layers of clothes, ready for the outside cold. Rachel glanced at the bag resting at her feet.

"You're not leaving, surely?"

Christabel nodded, crossing to offer a gentle hug. She could see Mr Sturry through the bay window clipping the garden shrubs in a downcast manner, dressed too stiffly for such work.

"You don't have to go. There's absolutely no hurry whatsoever. We like having you here. Please don't let that little tiff at breakfast worry you."

The girl heightened in colour, taking a last look around the room. "You know where I'm going, don't you?"

It seemed to Rachel that she did.

"It's my little girl, isn't it? She needs your help?"

"Perhaps, but I'm not entirely sure. She certainly did once, but now?"

"The letter?"

She nodded.

"Then I should go with you."

"I think you should."

Rachel was momentarily excited at the prospect and arose from the table, until she caught sight of Joseph, when she sat again.

"He would never let me." She took Christabel's hands, shaking but firm in grip. "No, I can't go. It wouldn't be fair. Joseph needs me too. He might not show it as I do, but he's very worried. Only, for him morality is a crusade. You'll have to go alone, but, please, keep in touch."

"Do you want to read it, the letter I mean? I think you should."

Christabel took the letter from her bag and gave it to Mrs Sturry. Dropping onto a chair, she scanned the lines of broken sentences, stopping every so often to consider the sentiments behind the jumble of words. Presently her hand lowered to her lap.

"Goodness, she tells a squalid story. She speaks of this man in so many contrasting ways. She begins by hating him, but later tells of her experiences with a candour that makes me think that she enjoys remembering. Then she finishes by asking for urgent help, but that extra paragraph by her friend indicates that she doesn't want it now after all and has money. Frankly, I don't know what to believe."

Rachel cautioned Christabel not to look on Emmeline with benevolence. It was plain that her daughter regretted the outcome of her passion more than the act itself. Christabel took up her bag. Once again she was to leave the security of a good home for an unknown future, although this time without the motivation of hope in her heart.

The Sturry's home had reminded her of the safe times she had spent in the Cerne Valley. True, the houses were not a match in status, but in each lived good people with whom she was made comfortable after tragic experiences. In a way she longed not to go, needing the faithfulness of love, that unshakeable constancy of spiritual beings around her. Every friend she ever had seemed a million miles away and, through the circumstances of their part-ings, she could not be sure whether they even thought about her in return. She could be alone except for the Sturrys, cut off from the care of others while *she* remained faithful to *their* needs.

Together the two women walked out into the open. Christabel smiled sweetly at Mr Sturry as he joined them. He embraced her, kissing her cheek. His lack of usual caution shocked Rachel.

"So you leave us? I thought you would after that damnable letter came. Here, I have this for you." The handkerchief held a few coins among its folds. "And before you say anything, I want you to put it away. It's little enough, but we aren't rich folk. It should keep you fed during your journey, with a bit to spare." He smiled at her pensive look, knowing that she had little money of her own. "Let us know where you get to. There's always a bed here for you."

Rachel's pasties were given to Joseph in a basket. The smell of fresh crusty pastry wafted through the cloth.

"Come, Christabel," he said, "we'll walk together as far as the crossroads."

She asked where he was going with the food.

"To the mines. It's our little bit of charity work. Would you like to come with me? It's only a half-mile or so and quite interesting."

She wanted to get on her way, but said that she would like to.

Together, they strolled through the village and down past the chandlers, where suddenly the bustle of business opened before them. Both quays had a ship at rest. Inside their hulls men worked furiously spreading untreated arsenic from bow to stern. It was ordered confusion, with bogies scuttling along the rails in fast succession carrying fresh supplies. They walked through, heading up a hill towards the mine where the throb of a large steam engine drowned the shouts of men.

"That's the old mine entrance," said Mr Sturry, pointing towards a sloping path that ran into the hillside. "The copper was exhausted years ago and so it's now abandoned. You see that hole over there with the tripod above, that's where people were lowered by rope into a deeper mine."

They took a narrow cutting through trees that led to a much newer entrance.

"This is where we part company, I'm afraid."

"Where are you going?"

"Haven't I told you? These pasties are for some of the wretched men who work down that hole, the ones who live so far away that they sometimes sleep underground just to grab a few hours rest between shifts."

"Aren't they poisoned by the dust?"

"I should think so, over a lifetime. Rachel makes sure that the pasties have good, thick pastry seams that can be held like handles and then thrown away to prevent contamination of the food."

"It must be terrible down there. Can I go down and look?"

"I don't advise it. It's not at all pleasant."

"No, truly, I'd like to see for myself."

Mr Sturry led the way into the dark tunnel by the light of a single candle. They fought to adjust their eyes to the semi-darkness. After some minutes several new stars could be seen in the distance hovering in the gloom, slowly turning into brighter lamps where the men worked.

"Good-day to you, Bill," he shouted. "I'm surprised to see you again. This must be the third day you've left the missis to fend for herself."

"Fourth as it happens, Sir, and I'm staying down here until pay day. Them eight children of mine can help out at home, the blighted good-for-nothings. Anyway, t'will stop me having a ninth!"

"Perhaps if you went home more often Betsy wouldn't be so glad to see you!" He turned to Christabel. "Begging your pardon for the joke."

"It's all of us having to share two beds that's the best stopper. No, in truth I like it here. I've cut myself a nice little square hole in the wall, all snug with a bit of straw I lifted from the stables. I've no complaints, especially with your good lady providing tasty meals. Shall I take the basket for the men, Sir?"

Away from the mine Christabel and Mr Sturry strolled back to the terraces, where she alone continued along the wind-blown lane to the stone bridge. She turned to wave, but he had already gone indoors. She stopped for one last look. Stirminster Oak had been home for days that had merged unnoticed into weeks. She pulled the shawl over her head and tucked the points into her belt, but paused as her hand felt tightly squeezed between the leather and her stomach. Looking up from the foot of the village onto a bleak scene ahead, she faced her own fear – she was pregnant.

Although tempted to cover much of the journey on foot to save the few precious coins, the urgency of Emmie's original entreaty ruled this as impracticable and instead she took a coach from the nearest town. As she skirted Shalhurn and the Cerne Valley, she felt pleased to be in familiar surroundings, where the poor natural drainage caused flooding in the fields that attracted herons. She soon found herself humming songs remembered from childhood, when only little unimportant things scared her. The thought of Dorchester was not so appealing, but then, adults often have fewer choices in such matters than children.

Dorchester was as bad as she had imagined, an endless sea of faces in a maze of brick and stone. Despite the fine architecture and exclusive shops, to Christabel it was confusion.

Having been directed to the guest house, Christabel was horrified to learn that Emmie had been thrown out some time before for debt, her few possessions confiscated. She had been sent, penniless, to the workhouse.

With new urgency in her step, Christabel hurried to that place on the edge of the city, its huge flat facade broken only by rows of identical windows on four floors. It was a building of function, where stark realities were played out in the atmosphere of an open prison and only the poorest submitted to its endless cycle of work and sleep.

Christabel was almost pleased when she searched through all four floors without finding her friend.

"If she's not here," the old caretaker offered, "you might try the charity hospital down the road about half a mile. That's where many end up."

The hospital offered little more comfort than the workhouse, having been founded in the premises of a weaving mill abandoned more than a quarter of a century before. It survived by public donation and was a place where only the most wretched were sent, the more unfortunate of these moving progressively from floor to floor as their health deteriorated until, on the uppermost level, their meagre lives slipped away and they headed for a pauper's grave. Much of the machinery that had powered the looms remained in place at ceiling height, the cogs, wheels and belts now silent and decaying. The looms themselves had been sold, and patients' beds now stood over holes in the floor where buried bolts had been hacked free. But, despite the gloom, it was as clean as hard scrubbing by zealous staff could permit, and nurses and doctors worked with skill and dedication.

Christabel was shown around by one of the main benefactors, an industrialist turned politician who spent much time there for self-publicity. Hollowed faces stared back from the top of the sheets, ghostly white and with every feature of their skulls depicted under the thinnest covering of skin. Where a faint smile was offered, sunken gums left the few remaining teeth exposed at the root.

"Why's this bed empty?" demanded a nurse.

"The patient died this morning."

"Wasn't he in surgery only yesterday?"

"Yes, Ma'am."

"Ingrate!" shouted the benefactor.

Christabel hated the place and was much relieved to go.

"Did you ask to see the workhouse records? She might have been there and left. Some do leave, you know, other than feet first!"

A quick revisit to the workhouse revealed all. Christabel looked at a scrap of paper on which was written Emmie's new whereabouts – Messrs F & W Franks. It seemed that Emmie had bartered her engagement ring against the debts, a poor exchange which the authorities had accepted.

The red brick factory was easy to find and she entered under the wrought iron sign:

MAKERS OF TORTOISESHELL HAIR ORNAMENTS

"Yes Miss, the new girl," came the welcome reply to her enquiries. "She's here all right. Good little worker too, so she is. You're fortunate, they're having a break just now so you can pop up for a few minutes. Mind, don't let Mr Frank catch you after the bell goes. He's a right hard stickler for time and will dock her half a day's pay if she misses the start. Just follow the stairs to the left, and be careful of the loose handrail."

As Christabel climbed the open treads, a great din could be heard coming from the lower room. There, women pushed and shoved as they vied for bottles of ale passing among them, laughing and swearing and crawling among the fallen shell dust. Above, the atmosphere was calmer. She entered. This room was also full of women, but the atmosphere was more subdued and pleasant. One girl sat apart, taking warmth from a blazing fire. Christabel recognised her instinctively.

"Emmie!"

The girl turned at her name, her eyes shining out from an otherwise completely white face.

"Chrissie! Oh, my God, Chrissie, you came. I knew you would."

"How are you, Emmie? You look awful."

"I've missed you too," she smiled back.

What is this place?"

"It's home," she replied in a downcast way. "God, so much has happened since I last saw you. I don't know where to begin."

"I suppose the Lieutenant left you?"

She nodded.

"Things couldn't be much worse. I don't like it here."

"I suppose it's better than that other place."

"You've seen the workhouse? That's the only thing I can be grateful to Longborne for. He wanted my ring back, but I told him it was stuck fast and he believed me. Without it, I would still be there."

"What's happened to your face?"

Emmie wiped her sleeve across, leaving it no better.

"Blasted dust gets everywhere, up your nose and down your knickers, and look at that." She held out her tattered skirt. "I did it this morning. That's my machine." She pointed. "I was leaning across to adjust the blade when it got caught in the belt wheel. See, no guard. I suppose it was built for taller men in trousers. Anyhow, it pulled the front clean off."

"At least you weren't hurt."

"Only last week the same thing happened to Hilda Walker. She was only twenty-two."

"Was?"

"She got her dress caught and was dragged in. It virtually took her leg off and the surgeon did the rest. They buried her yesterday. Her machine was closed down, but only to have the cloth untangled and a new cutter fitted." She began to cry but tried to cover her tears. "I really don't like it here. The worse is I haven't even got a change of dress. When I couldn't pay for our lodgings they took everything I had. They poked in all the cupboards and what they didn't want they burned. I sleep in here under the machines. What have I done to deserve this, Chrissie?"

"It's all right, Emmie, I'm here to take you away, but first, put on my spare clothes. They're a bit patched, but at least they've been washed recently, and you do smell something rotten."

For the first time in a long while Emmie had hope.

"This is a horrible place for those used to the open country-side."

"Amen to that. Still, from what I've seen, it's worse down-stairs."

"Mr Frank tries to separate the women into 'devils' and 'angels', as he puts it. We're the 'angels' up here. Most of them below are daughters of seamen and some of the things they say would turn your hair white. Mr Franks says he won't allow anyone back who has an illegitimate child, but he always does."

"Why so?"

"Because they make the best workers. He, Mr William Franks that is, can't do without them. But those women have been kind to me in their own way, so I'll not say anything against them. On the other hand, Mr Frank Franks is a high-collared church-goer who will give a good collection on a Sunday, but beat his children for the other six days and keep the housekeeping small. He and William don't get on and argue constantly in front of us as if we don't exist. They inherited the business from their father. It's a bit run down now."

The air in the factory was choking for those not used to it, but Christabel sat patiently as Emmie received a long lecture on gratitude while collecting her small earnings. Having said her farewells, they walked away from Emmie's past mistakes. For Christabel too there was a sense of occasion, for at a stroke she had been lifted from excessive loneliness.

"I suppose my father has cut me off?"

"Silly goose. He loves you, but you *have* disappointed him. Give him time and he'll come around. Tell you what, I'll write to him and build you up. The letter will get there before we do and will smooth the way. Now, what do you want to do, head for home or what?"

"I don't think I'm ready to face him quite yet. Perhaps when I'm back on my feet a bit. But I will, one day. I know that."

"Then I shall write and tell him that you're well and with me. That will do for the moment."

"Give both of them my love."

The girls left Dorchester in the distance and made for open country, having first purchased some second-hand clothes for Emmie.

"We must find work. It won't be easy this time of year and it's right stubborn soil around these parts. Still, we can't be choosy."

Emmie grabbed Christabel's shoulder.

"Before we go on, I have to clear the air. You do forgive me for what was said about you and Edmond in that letter?"

"I'm here, aren't I? That's best forgotten. However, as you brought it up I must ask. You didn't write it, did you?"

"No, not a word. I'm ashamed to say I asked Longborne to put that bit in. I'm so sorry."

Christabel smiled her reply.

"You needn't have worried about Edmond and me. There really never was anything much between us. He went off just before I left."

"I thought you'd get married."

"Marry me? Whatever gave you such an idea?"

"He wanted to, but I couldn't bear the thought. I didn't give you two a chance, did I? Your unhappiness is my doing and yet you still come to my rescue."

"Who said I'm unhappy? Anyway, I told you, he's gone and I'm here. I'm plain Miss Mere. Nothing more and probably never will be. Come on, the world owes us a living."

CHAPTER XXVIII

Heron lands

October turned to November and still the girls had found no permanent employment. Their happiness at emerging from Dorchester had long been left in the mud of the turnip and swede fields where they had hacked the sodden earth in temporary work. Even chances of this disagreeable labour were dwindling rapidly as the landscape began to change in harmony with the coming winter.

The dairy farms too had no use for extra maids. It was the time for shedding labour and wintering animals. Like decaying lilies in a pond, it was from the remaining nucleus that survived the radical changes that the following year's growth would flourish.

The month grew ever more gloomy as the chill tightened its hold on the land, the bounty of the earlier harvest in full retreat. The little money they earned was hardly enough to sustain them through their treks from one farm to another. Their lives were indeed wretched.

By the third week Emmie had had enough. She pulled off the bandages that wrapped her legs and flopped to the ground.

"I can't stand anymore of this. Not when I've got a home to go to. I'm leaving right now. You coming?"

Christabel straightened her arched back, pushing the short-handled hacker into the ground with a mud-caked boot. She had been expecting Emmie's resolve to break.

"They're your parents, not mine. You go if you like, I don't blame you for that, but I'll chance my luck a while longer."

"Don't be daft. Come with me. They made you welcome, didn't they?"

"Very."

"Well then, you've no reason to be coy. I don't mind telling you, you're far too tolerant for your own good. I can hardly stand your endless piety. How we ever became friends in the first place I'll never know."

The fortitude Emmie referred to, Christabel herself remembered seeing in the look of old farm labourers who could not get work during the winter. Such people were familiar to the countryside and yet they always seemed to survive to fight another year, but their lives gave grave warning to the folly of growing old in poverty. Her own sorrows were trifling compared to the problems facing these for whom youth was only a memory and who were now reduced to relying on the goodwill of the parish for their existence.

"I *shall* stay," whispered Christabel. "You know we haven't any money left? How will you get there?"

"I don't know and frankly I couldn't care, so long as I start off now. I can't stand another hour of this. I'm due for yesterday's pay, so that'll have to do." She untied her rag apron.

Christabel looked very sad.

"Oh, for goodness sake, change you mind and come. You really are your own worst enemy."

Christabel reached for her neckband and tore it free.

"Here, take this. You may need it."

She slid the ring given by her father off the band and placed it in Emmie's outstretched hand.

"I can't take that, it's gold!" She tried to give it back, but Christabel walked away.

"I'll stay for a few more days and that way I'll have some money before I move on. You must sell the ring if needs be. Anyway, I don't need it to remind me of my dear father. He's always with me. I feel it constantly."

"But you'll want this and much more when the baby comes."

Christabel was stunned. She had said nothing about a baby, and as yet she showed very little.

"How did you know?"

"Put it down to a woman's intuition, but you might have told me yourself."

Christabel untied her grey serge bonnet and sat bewildered on a small pile of turnips, searching for something to say. She just couldn't tell of the circumstances. There was no generosity in her heart over that matter, only hatred. She had decided never to mention it or even think of it, in case it affected her feelings for the baby when it arrived. Better that she let people believe it was a love child. Christabel bore the tide of distress as Emmie pressed the subject, but she was not going to let her friend rake up a past that was best forgotten.

Getting no answers, Emmie slowly worked herself up into an angry frenzy, as false images were conjured up in her mind. Still Christabel remained detached, even when it was suggested that the baby's father was none other than Edmond.

"That's it, isn't it? Why didn't I realise before? You wouldn't allow anyone else near you. It all makes perfect sense now I think on it. No wonder you couldn't tell me. Thought you'd be mistress of 'Samain' one day, instead of me?"

Still Christabel said nothing. Instead she buried her face in her hands as she relived that dreadful moment. Accepting silence as confirmation, Emmie turned and stormed away, throwing her gloves into the mud. She was soon a distant figure on the dimming landscape.

Christabel watched her go, tears running down her cold cheeks.

"If we can only meet as enemies, I hope we never meet again," she whispered, winding the torn ribbon around her finger.

* * *

During the coming days Christabel worked in solitude, saddled by the thought of life's injustices. She had became almost unaware of the other women trudging along the columns of vegetables. While Emmie had been around, she had talked emotionally about their time at 'Samain' and of their lives before the lieutenant had ruined everything, but now she was alone the same memories were no longer sustaining.

The next day mist was everywhere. Although there was work to be finished, Christabel too had a mind to leave. She knew the farms to the east of Dorchester were of the kind she preferred and decided to chance luck in finding new employment that was less arduous. Once decided she left immediately, using the banks of the River Frome as a guide to an area of Puddleton Forest known thereabouts as the Vale of Herons.

The high ground of Puddleton Forest was reached by long paths that cut the coniferous forest into parcel lots, affording poor views until the end was reached and the valley below opened out before her. She descended quickly, although an almost miraculous swelling of her stomach over the past days made caution necessary. Here, a few fat animals grazed the land.

To Christabel the land felt right. This was dairy country, generally flat low-lying land with only the occasional tumuli or ancient barrow offering height to three sides. The farms themselves were small, with the houses of several separate farmers nestling close together as if the hub of a giant wheel, and the hedgerows radiating outwards as the spokes. Looking hard, she could make out the unmistakable shape of herons circling over the fields, while others rested on sluice gates that were rusted open with age.

Christabel was confident that her experience of general farm work would be enough to attract employment, but as she passed from one farm to another in despair she offered herself for harder tasks as hopelessness grew. Presently only the smallest farm remained. The farmhouse itself was more a random collection of smaller buildings and lean-tos than a single construction, although all now merged under a common roof. The name 'Drake Dairy

Farm' was crudely painted on a sign that swung above the main entrance.

Repeated knocking at the main door brought no answer. Drawn by the smell of cheese and the sound of dripping whey, she walked to the lean-to. This too was unattended. Exhausted and hungry, she dropped her bag in dismay and reached up to unhook a hanging cloth. The cheese inside was not ready for eating, but times were desperate and Christabel scooped out a soggy lump. It tasted good in small quantity. After rehooking the cloth and crouching in the corner among discarded sacks, she fell asleep.

"Who the hell are you?" screamed a large woman of hard features.

Christabel awoke with a fright. It is a fact of nature that good-looking people can get away with indiscretions by nothing more than their appearance, making confrontation less likely once a soft smile on a gentle face is offered. Christabel had remained beautiful beneath her wrappings, so much so that she still looked incapable of doing wrong. She jumped up.

"Don't panic, I'm not going to hurt you."

Christabel didn't move. "Come, come, tell me what you're up to. That's all I ask."

Weary, cold and hungry, Christabel told of her journey and need for work.

"Impossible. There'll be no extra hands needed around here 'till spring. As much as I would like to help, I've absolutely nothing to offer. The truth is, there's hardly enough on my farm to keep myself in body and soul. The best I can do for you is to give you a good hot supper."

Christabel confessed to having helped herself to some cheese.

"That's okay, if you can stomach it. You may even take a wedge with you when you leave, but a slice of mature I think, not that rancid stuff."

Throughout the meal of hot meat soup and bread they talked of hard times in the country. Quickly the farmer realised that

Christabel knew as much as she, and offered her a job for the following April. It was also agreed that she should stay the night.

"I seem to have ruined my life for the sake of others. I can see that now. What will become of me? Are you sure you have nothing? I'll work for no more than a roof over my head, the warmth of a fire and some hot food."

"I only wish I could say yes, but you would be taking the food from my mouth."

"Then I've no choice, but to offer myself at the Mop Fair. It's my last hope."

"Obviously I can't tell you what to do, but my advice is that you should think twice about that. I was desperate once and offered myself at a Mop Fair. 'Twas a horrible experience for rough folk, but for you it would be mortifying. After that, I made up my mind to marry the first man with land who asked me. My dear Albert was no great catch, twice my age and with a head as free from hair as a boiled egg, with an ugly moustache fit for a walrus that hung to his bottom lip. But he left me this place in return for the love I showed him, and for all his faults he was a kind and honest man."

"What about the fair?"

"Let me tell you, we were gathered on Old Lady Day, men and women, young and old alike, all to be stared at and looked over in the market place like so many cattle. The farmers or their gaffers didn't seem in the least interested in experience or good character, choosing first all the strong men and these others well known to be inclined to agree to low wages if ale was thrown in or a flitch of bacon. Later the farmers came to the women, to be poked and prodded, those not chosen by the end of the day falling victim to the gangmasters. These are the worse employers of all. I tell you straight, if you ended up in an agricultural gang you'd rue the day you left home. You see, a gangmaster fixes a price with a farmer to clear this or that field or lift his crop. It is then up to him how he goes about the task. It is said he'll drive hired folk on throughout the day and into the evening to get his return quickly, taking a stick to anyone who slackens the pace. Sometimes they don't even let the women leave the field for a pee, making them squat in the open. No, take my advice, stay well away from Mop Fairs."

"That's all very well, but what else can I do? I can't do nothing and I have to eat."

"Give me until morning to think over the problem."

The next morning the farmer came downstairs yawning, having overslept. She had worried about the girl well into the early hours and had slept only after coming to the decision to share the little she had if Christabel agreed not only to help around the farm, but also allow herself to be hired out to other farmers if any small jobs came up. This might sustain them both until spring. To her surprise, however, Christabel had already left, leaving a note resting against a jug on the table.

> *I'm sorry for putting you in an embarrassing and impossible position. I'm sure I can find work and I will always be in your debt for the food. I have taken a small piece of cheese, as you offered, in return for which I have milked your two cows. The bucket is on the step, cleaned for next time. I'll come back in April.*
>
> *Love Christabel*

She rushed out of the house and into the lane, but Christabel was not to be seen in either direction. If she had looked up and ahead she might have seen a figure disappearing over the ridge into Puddleton Forest, wrapped once more in dry working clothes.

Every age of man has its idiosyncrasies, its own moralities that, in normal times, can best be measured by the standing of the middle classes. The Victorian age was no different, although because of the endeavours of some to make morality and pride in the nation the uppermost qualities by which all should be judged, it only served to highlight the worst in those that could not, or would not, attain them.

Few people under the protection of the great British Empire were poorer than Christabel who, now a month later, was reduced to taking any odd job in exchange for a single meal. Although hunger often bit hard, it was the effect that this had on the unborn child rather than her own well-being that concerned her most. Yet, through all deprivation, she remained a worthy soul, but even the high-minded have a limit to their endurance and Christabel had reached hers.

Although the very morality of the age would condemn her for bearing a child when unmarried, instead of lying dead under the boot of her aggressor, she decided for the sake of the baby to throw herself on the mercy of the church. Weak and staggering, she made for the nearest town, her head spinning and stomach empty. Looking down from a hill over the Forest of Bligh, she at last saw lights. Gripping a tree to stop herself from collapsing, she took deep breaths before attempting the steep descent, but the heavy intake of air overwhelmed her senses and she instead fell to the ground, rolling unconscious down the slope.

She might have let go of life then and there, for her body had nothing left, but in the depth of her soul she felt a strange power urging her to hold on, a voice of calm softly bathing her in whispers carried low on the breeze. It told her to resist, to pull on the last ounce of strength to keep alive the flicker that danced in her heart. It told her she was blessed now and for always. Without the strength to stand, she stared into nothingness as the light faded into evening.

Night fell and only a furtive figure in a tattered coat and battered cap was about, setting snares of looped wire and moving expertly from one hole to another. By chance, Christabel had come to rest on one of his favourite rabbiting grounds and in the darkness he stumbled on her. His lantern cast a mysterious light, but there was no doubting the form of a woman. He prodded her with a ferret spade, fearful of being accused of her murder. He could feel the hangman's noose around his neck. Unsure of what to do, to his relief he heard a slight sound, although the body remained still.

That strange mixture of Victorian virtues had reached even a lowly poacher, and in no time he had looked to his conscience and hoisted Christabel onto his horse. Holding her tightly, he trotted away into the bleakness of the forest night along secret tracks that he needed no light to follow. The humanity of his act filled him with an undeniable triumph that was new and warming. With the greatest care, he carried her into his hut in the depths of the wood, well hidden from view and covered outside on all four walls by gibbeted crows and other vermin rotting macabrely where they hung. There she was made comfortable in his bed and a warming fire was lit that sent a luminous fog into the still air.

Virtuosity, though, had its price, and his was an empty bag where normally several rabbits would have been. It was this rather than having a strange women in his bed that put him on the defensive when his wife burst in clutching a pheasant trap of hazel rods and two fine birds for the pot. He begged her understanding. Honed with the senses of the animals she lived to trap, she instantly knew something greater was amiss with the girl. Standing between the bed and her husband, she lifted the corner of the blanket.

"As I thought. She's lost a baby."

The life yet to begin outside the womb had been taken, the bearer scarcely aware of its going. Such was the loathsome burden of respectability.

CHAPTER XXIX

Be faithful to beautiful things

The inspiriting idea of welcoming Edmond home from Surrey with the first grand ball hosted at 'Samain' for many years filled Charlotte with a pleasure that went beyond pride in its success. The boy had left with a heavy heart, but a man had returned to his father's house with apparently no care for a certain lady's existence. Indeed, it was more than that, for he had found much satisfaction playing with the girlish sensibilities of the attending débutantes.

Meanwhile, in the Cerne Valley, John had been restless for assurance of Christabel's well-being. He too had been asked to the ball, but having received no news to his enquiries as to Christabel's whereabouts, he had declined. For, despite his many rejections at her hand, he still hoped that one day she would come walking down the drive dressed in that silly working bonnet. His new responsibilities to the farm, its workers and the village as a whole had truly, this time, changed him. Even his face had given up its clear handsome look for the more interesting features of a worldly man.

One morning, on a day that was quite bright and warm for the season, John went out walking and ended up at his mother's grave. The headstone was grey and cold, too harsh in its aspect for his liking, yet he always felt a subtle diffusing atmosphere that was hard to explain. That day a new grave had been dug close by and somehow the sight of the deep rectangular hole gave such an overwhelming sense of the finality of death that the aura disappeared. On the new headstone that lay at an angle against the heaped soil was inscribed 'BE FAITHFUL NOW FOR DEATH DEVOURS ALL BEAUTIFUL THINGS'. That instant he made up his mind to forward a letter to Christabel's last known address, that being the least presumptuous contact.

Consequently, when John heard back from Mr Sturry details of all that had befallen the two girls, as recently explained by Emmie on her homecoming, he became much moved and greatly troubled. There could be no doubting that Christabel needed help. In telling the story to her father, Emmie had put much of the blame for their sad circumstances on her friend, although the suggestion that Christabel's child had been sired by Edmond Elvington was enthusiastically squashed by her father. This revealed, Emmie became ashamed and sorely regretted having been so horrible to her.

The forest retreat covered in dead animals was upsetting to Christabel when she had recovered sufficient strength to walk outside, and so she chose to stay indoors most of the time. Only later did she wander out in the afternoons when the sunset cast wonderful images among the tall branches. While she could not approve of poaching, she owed much to the trappers and found herself remaining silent on the matter rather than condemning them. Yet, like all things that are temporary, the day came to move on and uppermost in her mind was something the wife had said to her, so profound that it struck her deeply.

"I know we're wrong folk, but you mustn't let that alter your own good character. You have lived with us and learned to think like the animals because that's our way. Now you must go out and show the animals how to live!"

Before leaving the forest forever, Christabel planted wild flowers at the rear of the hut in memory of her baby. The trappers stood by arm in arm as she kissed the soil.

"Don't be afraid. We'll take care of everything. That we promise."

After Christabel had gone, the little underdeveloped body that had been placed in a wooden box was taken to the churchyard, where it was left with a small coin on the lid. In the morning it would be hidden by the grave-digger at the foot of a coffin during a regular burial.

While John searched feverishly for Christabel among the many small villages around the Vale of Herons, she had already made her way in another direction several miles to the north. She had decided to return to her childhood village of Shalhurn where she hoped a welcome would await her from old friends. There she could rest, take stock of her life and begin afresh in the new year. There was also another reason for going. The loss of her baby had made her homesick for her father and now she wanted to visit his grave too and that of her mother, Verity.

The first night was spent at Pennystone, just four miles from the forest edge, but sufficient for her first real exertion since losing the baby. She found an inexpensive guest house and bargained strongly to exchange a brace of the poachers' pheasants for a room and breakfast. She still had another brace in hand. By mid-morning of the third day she had come so close to Stirminster Oak that she could see the stone bridge. Believing Emmie would not welcome a visit, she skirted around without stopping to see the Sturrys.

Caudle Brook led her through the Wiltcombe Vale to where the River Cam took over, whereupon she went slightly out of her way to rest for the night at an inn in Middleton, where the remaining pheasants paid the bill. As she brushed her long hair before retiring, she thought how the next day would see her back where she really belonged. The thought brought a smile to her face.

The final day started brightly. Even the last few diehard birds circled in the winter sky before heading away from English shores for warmer climates.

Christabel arose early and became invigorated by the crisp air that poured through the window of her room. It was a day for doing great things. Her journey lay in the general direction of High Hill, a ridge that circled Minterne Magna that would bring her to the last big climb before home, known locally as Nine Mile Ride. In spring such a walk would burst with the rich colour of apple orchards, but not now.

John, who had been up and ready to leave by dawn, had also decided to work his way towards Shalhurn and, if she wasn't there, to head eastwards over Minterne Hill. However, soon after starting his horse threw a shoe and he was forced to return and hire a one-horse gig.

The fallen leaves over High Hill and beyond unfolded a brittle carpet of nature's brown, the bare trees twisting upwards demanding their importance to be recognised. As Christabel approached each, the solid trucks and huge branches revealed a web of finer twigs converging into a tangle.

Now well on her way, Christabel became aware of the rumbling of wheels and singing. She pulled over to one side, waiting to be passed. The path being crooked, it took some time before the vehicle came into view and then, owing to a strong wind that blew into her face, the driver had to draw close before either could recognise the other.

"Good-day, my pretty."

She shuddered as a deep chill pierced her spine.

"Hold fast. I remember you . . ."

The dog that lay between the baskets began to bark.

"Be still there or I'll take my whip to ya hide."

She looked deeply into his face and those of his two companions. Anguish struck cold as she recognised her earlier attacker. She turned to run.

"Quick Jack, don't let her get away."

In blind panic she darted around the corner without a single glance backwards, but ahead lay open fields. A thicket of gorse ran in a line to her left. Ignoring the prickles, she found a gap and

ripped it open with her bare hands until sufficiently large for her
body to scrape through. With blood oozing onto her palms, she
pulled the stems back over the hole. The covering was sparse and
she could easily see out. Soon two men ran past. They quickly
realised that she could not have run farther without being seen and
turned back to thrash amongst the undergrowth.

For minutes that seemed like hours she remained crouched and
motionless, hardly daring to breathe, but her heart pounding in
her ears. Suddenly a rustle came from behind and she turned to see
Jack pulling at the gorse with his stick. He had circled around. She
was trapped if he saw her. Quickly she tore open the entrance and
leapt out, but only into the arms of another.

"I've got her," he shouted as he tightened his grip.

To capitulate a second time was not on her mind. Like a person
possessed she pulled and kicked, grabbing at his hair as he tried to
hold her at arm's length.

"Quick Jack, quick. I can't hold her much longer. She's making
me bald."

Jack came running from the thicket, brandishing his heavy stick.
He meant to strike her, but couldn't for fear of hitting his friend.
Throwing it down, he grabbed for her legs, moving in sideways to
cushion her kicks. As he bent she caught him under the chin with
her boot and knocked him backwards with a sickening crack of
bone. Her captor let go, holding his head in pain where Christabel
had torn out a clump of hair by the roots.

The third man, who had wanted no part of the attack, now leapt
from the vehicle in defence of his friends. All three re-formed
around her, cursing and angry. She grabbed Jack's heavy stick from
the ground, waving it wildly at anyone who came close. Still they
circled, taunting and lunging to wear her down.

"Please, I beg you, leave me alone. I've done you no harm. Dear
God, help me."

"Nobody here called by that name, missy," Jack hissed, "and
nobody for miles to help you either. Shout all you like, it'll make no
difference."

"I haven't got anything you can want. Take my bag. I don't care."

"We don't want pretty knickers and such things. It's *you* we want. You were woman enough for me last time, now it's time to show t'others what you're made of."

"Not again. Never again!" she screamed.

With a mighty swing she thrust out at her tormentor, striking him squarely across the skull. With eyes peering disbelievingly upwards, he sank to his knees, blood flowing down his forehead and out of his nose and ears. He dropped on his face.

"The bitch has killed him dead. Come on, get her!"

Stunned by the deed, Christabel dropped the stick. She felt nothing as they tied her hands to the rail of the cart and heaped Jack's limp body into the back. As the vehicle moved off towards Evenbury, in the opposite direction to Shalhurn, which lay in the far valley, only slowly did she emerge from her hypnotic state, amazed that she could have done such an thing and still feel no remorse for her violence.

CHAPTER XXX

So proud

The following morning began with a wet dawn. It looked likely to pour until at least midday. Once again John was up and out to continue his search for Christabel, although his spirits were as low as his clothes were damp. Ignoring the first few riders encountered unexpectedly in the half-light, his curiosity was raised when the trickle became a steady stream of wet men clutching lanterns, a chilled strain showing on their faces. Something unusual was afoot, so he stopped to ask.

"It's a bad business, Sir. Last evening a small transport was spotted passing through the high street under the cover of darkness, with what can only be described as a mortally wounded body on board. Once seen, the two drivers shot off in the opposite direction on foot. We've been out looking for them. There's armed police everywhere."

"No luck so far, I fear from your expression?"

"None whatsoever, Sir. This blasted rain has washed away any tracks."

John bade his farewell and moved on.

The hours crept by, but anxious riding achieved nothing. Occasionally he saw a figure on foot in the distance and his vigour returned momentarily, only to be dashed by the smile or frown from a stranger. No wagon or gig passed without scrutiny, and so it went on, mile after mile, hill after vale.

Frozen to the bone, John finally had to rest and get warm. He found a small isolated house and called up to an open window, asking whether he could buy a hot breakfast and food for his animal. The welcome was sincere and both were provided in abundance.

John sat and dried by the fire, eating off a tray. When the clock struck 10:30 a.m. and the moment arrived to leave, only the great purpose ahead made him put back on the wet overcoat and hat and step out once more into the endless rain.

On the advice of his host, John headed towards the lofty path that skirted High Hill, mindful of the hazardous drops in such weather. The climb was steady and he let his horse take its time dragging the gig to the peak. Then, at the top it stopped raining.

It was now that true love played a hand in a manner that only those capable of the deepest emotion could understand. The view that greeted John was breathtaking and he paused. It also allowed time for the animal to regain strength, but at once he felt a strange and possessive meeting of souls, just as he had felt at his mother's grave, a closeness that drew him instinctively to the edge of the road. He peered over and there, many tens of feet below, lying awkwardly among the shrubs that had prevented her falling further, was Christabel.

The sight was like an explosion within his body. The earlier slowness of his movements, brought about by the damp and his exhausted state, gave way to a wildly pumping heart. Like a fox escaping the hunt, he quickly picked his way down the steep bank. There was little to grab and danger was all about, but foot by foot he descended towards the outcrop. He slipped the last few feet uncontrollably, ending just below where Christabel lay. Quickly, he scrambled back up using roots as anchor points, all the time calling to her.

He could hardly believe his eyes. Christabel lay motionless, hollow cheeked and ivory white, and dead to all appearances. He ripped his coat off and placed it over her sodden body. Her hair fell long, soaked in the mud. If she was breathing, it was too shallow to detect. He went to find her pulse, but to his horror discovered that her hands were tied behind her back. Swearing revenge on whoever had done it, he cut them free. At his touch she gave a slight quiver and her eyes half opened.

"Oh God, Chrissie, my dearest love, I thought you were dead. Now I've found you I'll never leave you again."

It took a moment for Christabel to register John's voice, but a weak and joyous curl to her lips brought life back to her face.

He kissed her forehead over and over.

"Don't worry, I'll soon have you out," he promised, looking up at the steep climb with anguish.

He took her icy hands, rubbing warmth into her fingers.

"I'm blind," she whispered.

He looked disbelievingly at her unseeing eyes, moist and clear, but without direction.

"You'll see again. It's probably just shock."

"Even you can't help me this time," she said weakly.

His eyes filled with tears.

"I don't care if you are. I have you back and that's all that matters. I'll be your eyes forever."

Having made the promise, he looked up to see how he alone could get her up the slope. All possible routes were extremely steep or had obstacles blocking the way, but he had to try if she was to survive, even if it cost him his life. Thinking of the consequences of failure, he mustered unnatural strength, crouching to take her full weight.

The first slight lift brought severe pain to her face. He stopped immediately and gently lowered her down again. He took a different hold, one that cradled her spine, unsure that his footings could take the combined weight. He lifted, but slipped after the first step, cushioning her fall with his body. Now holding her tightly with one arm, he desperately clung to the hill while he dug his heels into the soft earth for grip. Once more the rain began to fall. With water dripping from his nose and chin, he made a new attempt to climb, but slipped again.

"I'm done for," whispered Christabel, as John held her close to shield her from the rain.

He was torn by silent panic.

"Someone will come along soon. We'll have to wait for help. I'll do my best to keep you warm." He brought his face close to hers and two souls soared as one.

How long it would take for anyone to pass by John could only guess, but at least the rain tailed off again and quickly the air warmed as the sun tried to break through gaps in the cloud, producing a soft, candlelight hue that bathed the land.

"Tell me what happened," he entreated as he ran his hand gently across her face to brush aside tangled hair.

Christabel shook her head and he didn't ask again. John talked of other things to keep Christabel conscious, his private thoughts wild and worried yet his conversation gentle and cheery. When after a few minutes he looked down at her, she had slipped back into sleep, so he let her be. If she had to die, why wake her to the moment.

John too felt tired from his efforts and had to fight to remain alert. He shivered from the cold, his lips blue. Now and then he heard noises from above, only to see a hare or other animal scamper through the undergrowth, scared by his shouts.

When the sky darkened once more, and the first trickles of new rain fell and all seemed completely hopeless, a fall of loose stones showered past him. He slowly looked up. There, at the top, he could just make out the legs of a horse kicking at the edge of the path – his horse and gig he had abandoned hours before. Someone was trying to capture it.

"Steady boy, steady," came a voice.

John cried out.

"Is there someone down there?"

"Help!" shouted John, waving his arm.

With police still out in force after the morning's search, it took little time for more faces to appear.

"I need a stretcher down here," called John.

"How many casualties?"

"One. She's in a very bad way."

"I'll lower a rope."

The officer turned to a colleague.

"Did you hear that. He said *she*."

"A rope is no good. She needs a stretcher," shouted John.

"We'll get you up first, Sir. Is she secure without you?"

"I want to stay down here with her," shouted John.

"Now, Sir, be a good gentleman. I can see there's no room for both of you and my sergeant. Just put the lady down careful like and leave the rest to us."

John knelt beside Christabel, patting her cheek until her unseeing eyes flickered open.

"Everything's going to be okay," he whispered. "Help has arrived. I'm going up now because there's not enough room for me and the rescuers. But don't worry, I'll only be up there. Chrissie, I love you so much." He kissed her gently before tying the rope around his waist.

The moment John reached the top the sergeant roped up and was lowered with a stretcher and blanket. Wrapped in a blanket, John was given a shot of whisky.

"Now, Sir, what's this all about?"

John could only recount the few facts he knew. When he finished, he was told why the police were out in such force.

"And you got them?"

"Bless you, yes, Sir. We picked up a couple of live-uns but an hour ago. One of them sang like a songbird. If it hadn't been for that, we wouldn't have walked back to the station along this path. No saying how long it would have been before someone else came by."

"I'm sorry, I don't understand."

"No, of course you don't. Let me explain. It seems that there was a struggle up here yesterday involving those blackguards and probably your young lady, if I may call her that without offence.

Attempted rape, I shouldn't wonder. Only it appears she clobbered one of them good and proper, which stopped their pretty game. I expect she was bound and tied to the cart. I suppose – and herein I'm guessing at this stage of the enquiries – fearing what they might still do to her, she probably managed to break free from the cart, but fell over the side of the hill. They must have left her for dead."

"The bastards. You say you got them?"

"Banged to rights, Sir."

"I'll kill them when I get the chance."

"Now, now. That sort of talk does nobody any good."

The sergeant climbed back up. He whispered to the officer.

"I see." He turned to John. "There's no good way of putting this, Sir, so I'll come out with it straight. I'm so sorry, but I'm afraid the young lady is very seriously injured indeed. The fact is the sergeant, who is trained to know such things, doesn't hold out any hope of moving her alive. She may not have a broken back, but she has serious internal injuries and possibly a fractured skull. I'm afraid you'll have to be strong, Sir. She hasn't long to go." He patted John's shoulder. "Best get down there again, I'm thinking. I'll lower you myself."

John took the news badly, while in truth he had expected it. Although he meant to be brave, he couldn't hold back his desperation at losing her again.

"Don't weep for me," whispered Christabel. "I'm not afraid of what's coming, my dearest faithful, John." She held up a hand, which he took and pressed to his face. She smiled at the touch. "I'll not be gone from you as long as the trees live and the grass grows around Nine Mile Rise. You must live for us both. I think I was spared for this moment."

"What do you mean?" he asked gently.

"You'll not understand. It was the wish of an angel."

Her steady hand took his that shook. She was breaking his heart more fully than she ever had before.

"Don't cry for me. I could never love a man more than I feel for you now. If only it had come to me before. I think I've always loved you, but my vision was blinded by the attraction of new experiences that excited me. Now *I am* blind, but I see it all so clearly." She felt a tear fall from John's face onto her cheek. "You know, worse than death would be to spend a life without you, and I'm afraid I've done something that would take me away." She convulsed. John strengthened his hold. "God knows I'm glad you found me. I couldn't bear to die alone. Dear John, you needn't worry. I welcome release from this life in the sure knowledge that I'll be reunited with my beloved father and mother, and that in heaven one day you'll come looking for me. I'm truly ready to die. Don't deny me your blessing. Remember me as a flame in your heart, my dearest darling. I fly with the herons."

With these words parted from her mellowed lips she squeezed his hand and life passed away silently and unknown to all, but one. She had made him proud and strong, so strong that he concealed his heavy sobbing from all, but the creatures of the earth.

CHAPTER XXXI

A case to be answered

$\mathcal{A}$ new year had begun and already the blackthorn had burst once more upon the Wessex countryside. Emerging butterflies stretched their coloured wings over the awakening land and birds began ritual courtships of song and dance. The wind, low and strong, breathed through the heaths and hedgerow. It was England as it had always been.

In Westkings, farmer Redmarsh sat at the table to be served by his fat wife, and elsewhere folk went about their tasks in the time-honoured way. Nothing much had altered from the previous year.

Insignificant to all the comings and goings in the shire was the fate of two rough and embittered men, grim faced and shackled. Joseph Sturry crept quietly into the oppressively dark-panelled courtroom, the trial nearing its conclusion. He looked across at the pair, but his eyes fell singularly on the one pleading his final cause.

"We didn't mean her any real harm. It was all Cockle's doing and she killed him dead. We was bringing her in to face the crime when she jumped off the cart and flung herself over the edge. I don't know how she got loose, as she still had her hands tied when she went. Maybe the rail broke." He drew a hand over his dry mouth, assembling his thoughts. He grabbed the bar to stop his hands shaking. "As she stood on the edge before jumping she stopped and looked back at me. I thought at first that she was only going to threaten to jump. I couldn't believe she would actually do it. I was paralysed with shock. Horrible it was. I'll never forget that face. Not as long as I live. It'll haunt me forever, as God is my witness. Then she sort of looked straight through me, as if I was glass and someone else was standing behind. I turned, but nobody was there. Then she spoke gibberish. She said, 'I now understand what you are. You've always been there for me. Now I know I'm right. God forgive me this day for what I do'. With that she turned, looked down and went over. They were her exact same words, I swear."

"You say she jumped, not fell?"

"I know she did."

"And what of this other person to whom she spoke? You say there wasn't anyone there?"

"Not a living soul. Nobody, as God is my witness. The three of us were alone."

"Then was she mad in your opinion? Is that your defence? Is that why you say she jumped?"

"Not at all. No, not mad. She was clear minded, although in saying this I might put the rope around my neck. I can't explain her behaviour." He shook his head in disbelief. "The truth is, I think she jumped only because of what she thought we would do to her."

"She had obviously suffered greatly the first time at Cockle's hands and wouldn't go through it again. Do you agree with my submission?"

"I guess so," he replied with head bowed.

"Then you admit freely and in the presence of all those here that you men gave her reason to believe that she would suffer more pain?"

"I think she thought it likely, yes. But it was Cockle who wanted to hurt her, not me. I stayed on the cart until she went wild."

"Shut up you fool. You'll hang us both," exclaimed his friend.

"Constable, take that man to the cell. Now, Trotter, continue with your evidence."

Although his freedom, maybe even his life, lay in the balance of his words, Trotter could only think of Christabel.

"Like I said, she wasn't going to have us touch her. Honest, *I* wouldn't have. It was all Cockle from the start. He's the one who couldn't keep his hands off young girls. He was a right bad lot." He looked pleadingly at the judge. "If I could have my time again, I wouldn't taunt her. For pity's sake, believe me. It was the others. I alone tried to stop her jumping."

"Let me understand you. You were party to catching Miss Mere, even though you could see she was terrified?"

"Not at first, but I joined in later . . . Yes."

"But you expect us to believe you didn't mean her harm? After all, if she was caught, Cockle would hurt her, wouldn't he? You knew that."

"Yes," was the weak reply.

"And after she jumped you looked to see whether she was dead or dying?"

"No. We got out quick."

"Then there's little to tell you apart from Cockle. I'm sure the court can imagine her fright. If any of you had shown an ounce of mercy to that poor creature she would be alive today. Remember that, Trotter, for what remains of your life." His piercing stare lasted several moments. "Have you got anything more to add?"

The room fell into expectancy. Trotter's mind was exhausted with guilt by association. He had plundered his memories, unfaded by the lapse of time. Her face was before him, real and anguished and he wanted to stretch out his hand and wipe the tears from her face. He wanted to; he couldn't. But to part with a bit of what he felt was to vivify the dead. Thus, he was stirred into making Christabel's own plea, to become an earthbound mouthpiece to an angel.

"Please, I *do* want to say one thing more. Since it happened I haven't had a single easy night's sleep. Oh, not because of what might happen to me, but because of her. You see, she pleaded to be left alone and we wouldn't listen. Having begun the deed it seemed impossible to stop. Fool's honour, I suppose. Call it what you like. Once we got her into the cart by dead Cockle's body she kept calling out, 'John, John'. It was pitiful to hear. We tried to shut her up, but she just kept on calling his name."

"Did you manage to silence her? Admit to striking her if you did."

"No, not that. We tried to shut her up with threats, but in the end we left her to it. Of course, Cockle would have, but he was dead."

"Anything else?" enquired the judge.

"I can hardly say," he added pitifully.

"Do it man! Purge yourself of all the crime. You're already condemned."

"She said something like . . . She couldn't spend her life locked up in goal. She had to have space to soar with the herons. I didn't understand what she meant!"

"You have a good memory. Pity you didn't put your mind to better use."

He didn't reply.

The judge turned away from the defendant, needing a few moments to himself. Even in death Christabel had touched the heart of a stranger.

When word of Christabel's death reached outlying districts, many people searched into their souls for comfort, remembering the harshness of their treatment of her. Others were deeply saddened and a few dispassionate, but such feelings were, by necessity, confined to those who had not acted badly.

Emmie belonged to the first set, having seen nothing of Christabel since the swede and turnip hacking. On a warm sunlit morning she joined John as he sat on the head of the Cerne Giant remembering past times with a stricken heart. He had been writing in his diary.

"Oh, Emmie, how could she choose to die? Would it have been so awful to submit once more and live?"

"You don't really need me to answer that. She wasn't prepared to be defiled again and yet she thought she would be condemned for defending herself. You must always think well of her."

"Can I believe she loved me in the end? I want to, but can I be absolutely sure?"

"Be sure, John. The liberty she chose was death. In heaven she waits for you. Don't let her dying be in vain."

"She put so much faith in me and I failed her in every way. My love for Christabel destroyed her."

"That isn't so. Her fate wasn't in your hands or anyone else's she loved. If anyone was to blame, it was me, but even I know she wouldn't have felt malice for the way things turned out. Remember the look in her eyes, John, and tell me I'm wrong."

"But I ache for her."

"I know. I know. She once told me after an evening walk under the stars that her life was like a celestial see-saw; full of joy one moment and acute misery the next. I think she always believed her life might come to an untimely end. All her family died before their time." She put her arm around him. "Can't you believe in her? She chose to wait for you in a place where no person can part you, where nothing bad can ever befall her again. Give her that peace, I beg you."

"The parish wouldn't even let me buy her a proper plot in the churchyard. They said they understood the reasons for her violence, but manslaughter and attempted suicide were still sins. Little do they realise how she prized life, the trees and flowers, animals and birds, the seas and stars. All creation was a great wonder and joy to her. I wish I had said to Christabel when she lay there dying, 'take my hand and I'll lead you there'. My life is so empty without her."

"It's all so unfair."

"I'll never be able to speak to her again. What will I do in a month, a year, ten years?"

"You talk, John. She'll listen."

For the first time John felt strong faith. He knew that what Emmie said was true. He would be reunited with his first and only love, the woman who had held his life, his very existence in her smile since that day she had ridden in his reckless cart to Nether Bow.

CHAPTER XXXII

All seasons pass

Some years later, under the watchful presence of a church tower with one crooked and three straight pinnacles, a small group of fresh-faced children passed up the muddy lane to make fun of the lonely spinster lady who daily tended three graves.

After they passed by, the woman stood to wipe her brow with the sleeve of her dress, a gold ring once given in friendship hanging from her neck by a ribbon.

It had been John's final mission of love to have Christabel buried in Shalhurn close to her parents, although the newest grave was separated from the others by the thin boundary wall of the churchyard, resting alone outside the consecrated ground in a field that grew little. Yet, God's soil knew no such barrier, and where the wall had fallen, a line of forget-me-nots had taken root between the close graves. Christabel was happy once more.

"God bless thee this day and for always," came the voice of Jacob Stone that was carried low by the wind, heard only by Emmie as she continued to clear weeds from around the graves.

* * *

"I'm so proud of you, Pete, and what you've achieved."

Helen watched as Pete was given the honour of making the first chisel cut in a new stone monument to be erected where the Shalhurn church had once stood. The pencil outline read:

THE MERE FAMILY – REUNITED IN A VILLAGE UNDERGOING
RESTORATION AND CONSERVATION – 2004